When the Music's Over

Also by Peter Robinson

Caedmon's Song
No Cure for Love
Before the Poison

INSPECTOR BANKS NOVELS
Gallows View
A Dedicated Man
A Necessary End
The Hanging Valley
Past Reason Hated
Wednesday's Child
Dry Bones that Dream
Innocent Graves
Dead Right
In a Dry Season
Cold is the Grave
Aftermath
The Summer that Never Was
Playing with Fire
Strange Affair
Piece of My Heart
Friend of the Devil
All the Colours of Darkness
Bad Boy
Watching the Dark
Children of the Revolution
Abattoir Blues

SHORT STORIES
Not Safe After Dark
The Price of Love

When the Music's Over

Peter Robinson

HODDER &
STOUGHTON

First published in Great Britain in 2016 by Hodder & Stoughton
An Hachette UK company

1

Copyright © Eastvale Enterprises Inc. 2016

The right of Peter Robinson to be identified as the Author of the Work has been
asserted by him in accordance with the Copyright, Designs and Patents Act 1988.

A CIP catalogue record for this title is available from the British Library

Hardback ISBN 978 1 444 78671 2
Trade Paperback ISBN 978 1 444 78672 9
Ebook ISBN 978 1 444 78673 6

Typeset in Plantin Light by Hewer Text UK Ltd, Edinburgh
Printed and bound by CPI Group (UK) Ltd, Croydon, CR0 4YY

Hodder & Stoughton policy is to use papers that are natural, renewable
and recyclable products and made from wood grown in sustainable
forests. The logging and manufacturing processes are expected to
conform to the environmental regulations of the country of origin.

Hodder & Stoughton Ltd
Carmelite House
50 Victoria Embankment
London EC4Y 0DZ

www.hodder.co.uk

For Sheila

A sudden blow: the great wings beating still
Above the staggering girl, her thighs caressed
By the dark webs, her nape caught in its bill,
He holds her helpless breast upon his breast.

WB Yeats, 'Leda and the Swan'

'Twas brillig, and the slithy toves
Did gyre and gimble in the wabe:
All mimsy were the borogoves,
And the mome raths outgrabe.

Lewis Carroll, *Through the Looking Glass, and What Alice Found There*

PROLOGUE

They threw the naked girl out of the van on the darkest stretch of road. First she felt the wind whip as one of them slid open the door, then she was in free fall, tumbling through space. Her hip bounced on the hard road surface and she felt something crack. Then she hit damp grass and rolled into a ditch full of stagnant water. She could hear their laughter and whooping over the loud music, but soon even the music had faded into the distance and there was nothing left but silence.

She lay in the ditch winded, her hip hurting, head spinning, and tried to take stock of her situation. She had no idea where she was. Somewhere in the countryside, obviously, miles from civilisation. She struggled to push herself up out of the foul, muddy water. As soon as she moved, she gasped at the pain, which shot first through her hip, then seemed to diffuse through every atom of her body, as if someone were pushing red-hot needles into her flesh. The stuff they'd given her back in the van was wearing off, the last couple of hours fading like a dream as she awoke into pain, but even as it faded it rushed through her when she least expected it, distorting her senses. There was a whooshing sound in her ears, like big waves crashing, and her vision was blurry.

She had also cut her shoulder on something, a broken bottle in the ditch, perhaps, and she became aware of other cuts and bruises as the pain started to focus on more specific parts of her body. She tried to clean the mud and blood off her skin as best she could with water from the ditch, but it was too dirty, and she only succeeded in spreading the filth all over her body. She felt that she resembled some primeval creature crawling out of the slime.

She limped into the darkness and stumbled in the direction from which the van had travelled. There was nothing she could do about her nakedness except hope someone decent came along, someone who would wrap her in a blanket and take her to hospital. Being naked and muddy were the least of her problems. Her brain wasn't working properly, for a start. The road surface seemed to be undulating beneath her, and the overhanging trees were assuming threatening shapes. She shook her head to try to make it all go away but that only made things worse. She felt dizzy and had to support herself against a tree trunk for a moment. The bark was pulsing under her fingers like the dry scaly skin of a reptile. Her hip hurt so much that she was certain it was broken. And she felt terribly torn up inside. She was certain she was bleeding internally. She needed a doctor. He would give her painkillers, maybe even morphine. Then her pain would disappear and she would drift on warm soft pillows without a care in the world. But they would want to take swabs and samples. They'd call the police and then she would really be in trouble. The police wouldn't believe her. They never believed people like her. Besides, in her experience, such kindness was unlikely. No Good Samaritan would come along and give a lift to a naked girl covered in mud. That wasn't what the sort of people she knew did with naked girls. It wasn't the kind of thing that happened in her life.

It was late July, but a long week of rain had just ended. The night was muggy, and a gauzy mist hung over the dark landscape. No street lamps, only the hazy light of a haloed half-moon. Somewhere in the field beyond the drystone wall a sheep bleated, and she thought she could see a lone light shining in a farmhouse upper window. Should she head for that?

Would they help her? There was the ditch and a stone wall topped with barbed wire in her way, but there might be an entrance further ahead. If she found a gate, she decided, or a gap in the wall, that's what she would do. Head over the field towards the light.

How late was it? Or how early? She had no phone or watch. She couldn't remember how long she had been in the van. Surely dawn couldn't be far off. The sun rose early these days. But everything was still dark, and the trees and walls were silhouettes of scarecrows and demons closing in on her. The road was narrow, and there was no pavement, so she walked on the hard surface. Stones dug into the soles of her feet with almost every step. If a car came she would have plenty of warning. She would hear it and see its headlights from far away. If a car came . . .

She hadn't been walking for more than ten or fifteen minutes when she thought she heard the distant drone of an engine and saw lights playing between the shadows and trees ahead, refracted in the mist down the winding road. A car! It was travelling in the opposite direction she was walking, the same direction the van had been heading, but that didn't matter. As the car came closer, she at least had enough sense to stand back, near the edge of the ditch, so it wouldn't hit her by accident. She threw away her dignity and waved her arms in the air. The headlights dazzled her, and the small van shot straight past. She watched it in despair, then she saw it stop with a screeching of rubber about a hundred yards ahead. She couldn't make out what sort of van it was. The engine purred and the red brake lights glowed like a demon's eyes in the mist. Shaking off the feeling of apprehension that came over her, she started hobbling towards the van as quickly as she could.

I

Detective Superintendent Alan Banks stood in front of the mirror in the gents and studied his reflection. Not bad, he thought, tightening his mauve-and-gold striped tie so that it didn't look as if the top button of his shirt was undone, which it always was. He couldn't stand that claustrophobic feeling he got when both button and tie pressed on his Adam's apple. There was no dandruff on the collar or shoulders of his suit jacket, and his dark hair was neatly cropped, showing a hint of grey, like a scattering of ash, around the temples. He had no shaving cuts, no shred of tissue hanging off his chin, and he wore just a faint hint of classic Old Spice aftershave. He straightened his shoulders and spine, noting that there were no bulges in his jacket pockets to spoil the line of his new suit. His wallet and warrant card were all he carried, and both were slim. He fastened the middle button, so the jacket hung just right, and decided he was ready to face the world.

He glanced at his watch. The meeting was due to begin at nine sharp, and it was about three minutes to. He left the gents and took the stairs two at a time up to the conference room on the top floor of the old mock-Tudor building. Timing was an issue. Banks didn't want to be the first to arrive, but he didn't want to be the last, either. As it happened, he ended up somewhere in the middle. Detective Chief Superintendent Gervaise and Assistant Chief Constable McLaughlin stood outside the room chatting as they waited outside. Banks could see through the open door that some people were already seated.

'Alan,' said McLaughlin. 'New duties not proving too much of a burden, I hope?'

Banks's promotion to detective superintendent had come through a short while ago – a bloody miracle in this day and age, or so he had been told – and he had spent the last few weeks learning the ropes. 'Not at all, sir,' he said. 'I had no idea how much I was getting away with before.'

Gervaise and McLaughlin laughed. 'Welcome to the real world,' said the latter. 'Shall we go in?'

McLaughlin went ahead. Banks turned to Gervaise and whispered, 'Any idea what this is about?'

She gave a quick shake of her head. 'Very hush-hush,' she said. 'Rumour has it that the chief constable himself is going to be here.'

'Not crime stats or more budget cuts, then?'

Gervaise smiled. 'Somehow, I doubt it.'

The conference room was sparsely furnished, nothing but an oval table, tubular chairs and institutional cream walls. They took their seats around the table, and a few minutes later Chief Constable Frank Sampson – soon, it was whispered, to be *Sir* Frank Sampson – did indeed arrive. When he was followed shortly by the new police and crime commissioner, Margaret Bingham, Banks knew that something important must be brewing.

But the last person to arrive, a minute or so after everyone else, was the biggest surprise of all.

Dirty Dick Burgess was now some sort of deputy director or special agent at the National Crime Agency. More commonly known as the British FBI, the NCA dealt mostly with organised crime and border security, but it also worked against cyber crime and the sexual exploitation and abuse of children and young people. Burgess flipped Banks a wink before sitting down. Even he was wearing a suit and a crisp white shirt instead of his trademark scuffed leather jacket, though he could have done with a shave and a haircut, and he had foregone the tie completely. Clearly the British FBI didn't bother dressing up for a visit to the provinces.

There were eight people seated around the table when the chief constable opened proceedings by introducing them all to one another. One of the people Banks didn't know, by either name or sight, was the lawyer from the Crown Prosecution Service. Her name was Janine Francis, and she was not one of the CPS lawyers that he usually dealt with. The eighth person, still only vaguely familiar to Banks, was the county force's new media liaison officer, Adrian Moss, an ex-advertising agency up-and-comer and political spin doctor with a flowered tie, fresh-scrubbed youthful appearance and a breezy, confident manner. A motley crew, indeed, Banks thought, as he tried to imagine why they might all have been brought together under one roof. It had to be something big.

'I know some of you must be wondering what all this is about,' said the chief constable, 'so I'll make it simple and get straight to the point. I assume you're all familiar with Operation Yewtree and its investigations into sexual abuse, predominantly against children and primarily by media personalities? In the wake of the Jimmy Savile business and the successful convictions of Rolf Harris, Gary Glitter, Dave Lee Travis and Max Clifford, among others, I'm sure you can imagine that a lot of past victims have been encouraged to come into the open over the matter of historical sexual abuse.'

Historical abuse. The words brought about an immediate sinking feeling in Banks's gut. A function of the political correctness of the times, historical abuse investigations were intended to right the wrongs of the past and to send the message that no matter how many years had gone by, if enough people cried foul, someone would be sent off. They were also a way of appeasing the victims of such crimes, of giving them a voice some of them had been seeking for years, and perhaps even 'closure', that much overused word, both things of which Banks approved in principle. In practice, however, it often turned out to be a different matter, a witch hunt where victims were often disappointed, and the reputations of innocent people sometimes went down in tatters. No detective in his right mind wanted to be part of a historical abuse investigation. Banks checked the faces of the others. Their expressions gave away nothing. Was he the only one who thought this way? Did it show?

'I'd like to think we've all learned a thing or two from the way these incidents have been handled over the past couple of years,' the CC went on, 'and one of the things we should have learned by now is to keep things close to our chests. I ask you all not to speak of what's said in here to anyone outside this office. Not even to your colleagues. Adrian.'

Moss glanced from face to face. 'Yes,' he said. 'No doubt you all know there's no way we can keep this from the media for ever. They'll get hold of it eventually, if they haven't already. It's my job to make sure that nothing gets said to them by anyone involved unless it goes through me first. Am I clear?'

He was obviously enjoying his temporary power over such an eminent gathering, Banks could tell from the triumphant expression on his face and the undertones of evangelistic delivery in his speech. And Banks didn't even know what 'this' was yet.

'Mistakes have been made in the past,' Moss went on. 'That business with the BBC cameras in position to film the raid on Cliff Richard's home before Sir Cliff knew about the search himself, for example – and we don't want any of that sort of behaviour dogging our footsteps. As you know, the investigation into Sir Cliff was dropped, and Paul Gambaccini had some harsh words to say about the way he was treated by the police. We've ended up with egg on our faces often enough, and we have to make sure that doesn't happen this time. When the media do come knocking, as they will, we want everything calm and by the book. Nothing they can get between their teeth and run with. Naturally, celebrities are of interest to them, and celebrity misdeeds are manna for them. We not only have to prosecute this, we need to be seen to prosecute it. It won't take them long to gets their nibs sharpened. I can tell you now, there's a media shit storm due in the near future. My job, ladies and gentlemen, is to manage the flow of information, and to do that I will need the cooperation of all of you. Everything goes through the press office. Is that clear?' He had a sheen of sweat on his forehead as he scanned the room. Most of those present beamed back at him. Moss was one of the chief constable's and the police commissioner's golden boys. Now that the brass seemed far more concerned with publicity and image, people like him were more important to them than detectives, Banks thought. Burgess was the only one to appear unimpressed, the beginnings of that characteristic cynical, seen-it-all smile appearing in the twist of his lips.

'Thank you, Adrian,' said the chief constable. 'Now we all know where we stand, let's get down to brass tacks. You are all here because from now on you're going to be working together in one capacity or another on the same case. Assistant Chief Constable McLaughlin will enlighten you.'

Red Ron cleared his throat and shuffled his papers. 'You're here because we're going to be conducting an investigation into Danny Caxton,' he said, pausing for a moment to let the name sink in.

Danny Caxton, thought Banks. *Shit.* Celebrity, personality, presenter before presenters had even been invented. Household name. *The Man with the Big Smile.* Caxton had started his career in the late fifties with a few pop hits. He wasn't a rock and roller, more of a crooner, a part of the Jim Reeves, Val Doonican and Matt Monroe crowd. Perhaps the girls didn't scream at him the same way they did for Elvis or the Beatles, but plenty drooled over him as their parents had drooled over Johnnie Ray or Frank Sinatra. From what Banks could remember, Caxton obviously had good business sense and he must have realised early on that a career in pop balladry doesn't last for ever. In the early sixties, he started to diversify. He had always had good comic timing and a knack for impersonating famous people, in addition to having the personality of an affable host. He compered variety shows, both live around the country and on television, cut the tapes at supermarket openings, judged beauty contests and quickly became the regular host of a popular talent-spotting programme called *Do Your Own Thing!* which lasted well into the late eighties. That was his catchphrase, too: 'Do your own thing.' Spoken with a tongue-in-cheek knowingness that tipped a wink towards its hippie origins. Even during the sixties and seventies he had the occasional novelty hit record, and he made a couple of dreadful swinging sixties films when he was already too old and square for such roles. He would have known Jimmy Savile, Banks realised. They were of the same generation. Caxton went from strength to strength: summer seasons, Christmas pantomimes, a successful West End musical comedy. He had married a pop singer at some point, Banks remembered, and there had been an acrimonious and public divorce not long after. His career had slowed down in the early nineties, but he still appeared occasionally as a guest on chat shows and had even hosted the odd Christmas variety special in the noughties.

'I'm surprised to hear he's still alive,' said Banks.

'Very much so,' said McLaughlin. 'At eighty-five years of age.'

'And what does the CPS think?' Banks asked, glancing at the lawyer. He knew there had been some confusion in the Savile business as to whether the CPS hadn't gone ahead with a prosecution because he was too old and infirm, or because they thought the police had insufficient evidence. Banks knew the CPS had already been criticised for not acting sooner over Sir Cyril Smith, the Rochdale MP, who had been abusing young boys for years until his death in 2010. Now, no doubt, they were eager to show the public they were taking the lead on child sexual abuse and exploitation.

'He's fair game as far as we're concerned,' Janine Francis answered.

'And when did the offence take place, sir?' Banks asked Red Ron.

'Summer 1967.'

Danny Caxton was almost at the height of his success by 1967, Banks remembered. Everyone knew who he was. He was still a handsome devil, too, or so hundreds of mums thought. Christ, even Banks's own mother had sat fixated in front of the screen drooling over him while his father snorted and Banks disappeared upstairs to listen to his Rolling Stones and Who records.

'I'll give you a brief outline,' McLaughlin went on. 'There's a useful bio and a summary of events so far in the folder before you. Take it away and study it later. He certainly had an eventful sort of early life. Overcame a lot of adversity. He was born in Warsaw in 1930. His parents saw the writing on the wall and got Danny and his brothers and sisters out in 1933. They got split up, and he grew up with distant relatives in Heckmondwike.'

'That could have a serious effect on a person's mental health,' said Banks. 'I mean, just trying to pronounce it.'

There was a brief ripple of laughter, then DCS Gervaise said, 'Be careful, Alan. My dad came from Heckmondwike. Anyway, it wouldn't be too hard. Just omit the vowels and it'd be perfect in Polish.'

McLaughlin waited for the laughter to die down, then went on. 'For the moment, I want you to consider the following. The complainant in this case is a woman called Linda Palmer. She was fourteen years old at the time of the alleged assault.'

Banks had heard of Linda Palmer. She was a poet, lived locally, had been written up in the paper once or twice. Been on BBC2 and Radio 4. Won awards. 'The poet?' he said.

'One and the same. She first called Childline, and they told her to get in touch with us.'

'And why do we believe her?' asked Gervaise.

'Same reason we believe any claim of historical abuse,' said McLaughlin. 'Her story's convincing, and we hope it will be even more so after you have all finished your tasks.' He glanced towards Janine Francis. 'The CPS has given a green light to continue with this, even on what little we have so far. That's why what Mr Moss said about managing the media is so important. We don't want to draw flak the way some other county forces have done. On the other hand, we don't want to appear to be operating in secret. And we know how difficult it is to keep a low profile in a case of this magnitude. You'll just have to do your best for as long as you can.'

'What are the facts?' Banks asked. 'Briefly.'

'That's what we want you to find out, Alan. You'll be conducting the initial interview with Linda Palmer. You'll also be interviewing Danny Caxton. Mr Burgess here will be monitoring the case nationwide.'

'Surely it would be protocol to send a female officer to interview Linda Palmer?' said Banks.

'Not necessarily,' said McLaughlin. 'The detective she talked to when she first called in is a female, a DI MacDonald, and she asked the same question, but Ms Palmer said she didn't care as long as it was someone who would believe her. She doesn't want any special treatment. That having been said, you have three extremely competent female officers on your team.'

'What did Linda Palmer accuse Caxton of doing, exactly?' Banks asked.

'According to Ms Palmer, Danny Caxton raped her.'

'And she's just come out with this story?'

McLaughlin sighed and glanced at the police and crime commissioner.

'That's irrelevant,' Margaret Bingham said. 'The reasons women have for coming forward so many years after a traumatic event are complex. It's not, at the moment, your job to question these motives, merely to ascertain their veracity.'

'And how do we do that?' Banks asked.

'The way you usually do it,' McLaughlin answered. 'Use your detective skills. We also have trained child protection officers who specialise in knowing the sort of details true victims are likely to remember, and whether they are telling the truth. If you have any doubts after you've talked to her, you're welcome to go over her statement with one of them, if you wish. And if it makes you feel any better, Ms Palmer *did* report the incident shortly after it occurred in 1967.'

'And what happened to that investigation?' Banks asked.

'That will be another aspect of the case for you to determine,' said McLaughlin. 'Clearly it was derailed at some point, for some reason, as Mr Caxton wasn't brought to justice at the time, and he's never been charged with raping Linda Palmer or anything else since.'

'Don't you think that might be because he never did anything?' said Banks. 'I mean . . . nearly fifty years ago . . . It's about as cold a case as you can get.'

'I know,' said McLaughlin, 'and I sympathise, Alan. But some of Jimmy Savile's crimes went back further than that. We've got historical abuse going back to the early sixties and before.'

'I get that you don't like it,' Margaret Bingham interrupted. 'But you'd better get used to it. All of you. We might have dropped the ball in the past, but not again. Not on my watch. There's going to be more and more cases of historical abuse coming up over the next few years. People who think they've got away with something for ever. *Men* who think they've got away with something for ever because of their fame or their wealth or their power. Or just because they're men. This was the brutal rape of an underage girl by a man of thirty-seven, and I expect you to go about it investigating it as you would if it had happened yesterday.'

'That's not possible,' said Banks.

'Oh? And why not, *Superintendent* Banks?'

'No physical evidence. Dodgy memories. Missing statements. With all due respect, ma'am,' Banks went on, 'you're a civilian. So is Mr Moss. Most of the people you're talking to here are veterans of many investigations, and the fact of the matter is that you simply can't investigate a crime that happened almost fifty years ago in the same manner as you can investigate one that happened yesterday. All you have to go on is the accuser's statement. I understand all about cold cases solved by new DNA evidence. They're the ones that make the news, and I've seen *New Tricks*, but those are the exceptions. Do we even have any DNA in this case, for example?'

'I have no idea,' said Margaret Bingham, clearly irritated by Banks's objections. 'That's for you to determine. And I may be a civilian, as you say, but I am the police and crime commissioner, and I have every right to ask my officers for their best efforts. That's what I'm asking. You put as much time, effort, intelligence and investigative skills into this as you would into a sexual assault that happened yesterday. Believe me, you'll have all the resources you need at your disposal.'

That was a good opening move on his part, Banks thought. Piss off the bosses and the crime commissioner at the first big meeting of the new job. But he'd never had much time for

Margaret Bingham and her agendas. She and Adrian Moss would make a fine team. 'Yes, ma'am,' he muttered.

McLaughlin cleared his throat again. 'Though the Met is technically in charge of Operation Yewtree, Mr Burgess here from the NCA will be bringing his expertise of the Child Exploitation and Online Protection command to bear on the case.'

Burgess tipped his hand in a mock salute. 'At your service,' he said.

'What will your role be?' Banks asked.

'Co-coordinating between you and the Met, mostly,' said Burgess. 'I'll be trying to make sure that the left hand knows what the right hand is doing. The case is unwieldy enough already. Linda Palmer was living with her parents in Leeds in 1967, but the assault took place in Blackpool. She now lives near Eastvale, a village called Minton-on-Swain, and Danny Caxton lives out on the coast, as you probably know already, though he lived in West Yorkshire for some years. In Otley. If we involved all the local forces – not to mention the rest that will soon come into play as the complaints add up – you can imagine what a mess we'd have on our hands. That's why we decided on one SIO for Linda Palmer, one team manager, and that's you. It's your job to keep a firm hand on the rudder. I'm available to provide updates and background intelligence from other sources wherever possible. Believe me, in this investigation, the different county forces involved *will* be talk-ing to one another, and complete records will be kept of every interview, every allegation, every scrap of evidence. We have several complaints about Caxton from around the country already. The one thing you can be certain of is that there will be more complainants coming forward once the news gets out, and there's strength in numbers as far as we're concerned. How many depends very much on the access and opportun-ity Caxton had to satisfy his needs. It's my feeling, given his long and wide-ranging career, that he had plenty. They'll all have to be traced and investigated. Possible witnesses tracked down. Locations probed. I'll be searching for similarities in the complainant accounts.'

'Just how wide is this investigation?' asked Gervaise.

Burgess looked at Chief Constable Sampson, who put on a suitably grim expression and said, 'So far, according to the NCA, we have seven independent complaints about Danny Caxton spanning the years between 1961 and 1989. All from females between the ages of fourteen and sixteen at the time. The county forces involved have done as much background checking and taken as many preliminary statements as necessary so far, but we, and the CPS, feel it's time to move quickly now. The CPS also happen to feel that ours is one of the crucial cases, that it has a good chance of netting a positive result.'

'Why is that?' asked Banks. 'As far as I've heard so far it's no different from any other such case. One person's word against another's. What gives us a better chance of making a charge that sticks?'

'Simply this,' said Chief Constable Sampson. 'Linda Palmer has informed us that, in her case, there was someone else present. There was a witness.'

When DI Annie Cabbot and DC Geraldine Masterson arrived on the scene around half past nine that Wednesday morning, the whole eight miles of Bradham Lane were already sealed off from where it began at a T-junction two miles west of Eastvale to where it ended beside a bridge over the River Ure.

'It would be in the middle of bloody nowhere,' said Annie. 'We'll have to get a mobile unit out here and find the bodies to man it. And we'll have to run the Major Incident Room from HQ. There's not enough facilities out here.'

The uniformed constable standing by the police tape bent to talk to them. 'There's an officer and a patrol car down by the bridge at the far end, and two officers at the scene,' she said, then pointed. 'The crime scene is three miles down there.'

'Thanks,' said Annie. 'As long as we don't have to walk.'

'It's a hard road surface, ma'am,' said the officer. 'And a rough one at that. Not much chance of tyre tracks, but you never know what the CSIs might find. I'd go carefully.'

'We will. I know those CSIs.'

The patrol officer untied the tape at one end, and Gerry drove slowly along the narrow road.

Annie was intrigued by the shapes of the trees. Some seemed dead and stunted, standing there like men doing handstands, or the twisted and darkened shapes of burned bodies in a pugilistic stance. Others made a dazzling symphony of green in the breeze after last week's rains, leaves glistening and dancing in the morning sun. The road meandered, and on a couple of occasions, there were narrow unsurfaced lanes leading off, signposted to villages or farms Annie had never heard of. It would be easy to get lost here if you took a wrong turn, she thought. Here and there were passing places in case you met someone coming the other way.

The first sign that they were close to their destination was a patrol car blocking the road ahead and a cyclist in bright purple Lycra leaning against the bonnet, head in his hands. A female PC stood next to him, notebook in her hand. A male officer, also making notes, sat in the car. The sleek bicycle leaned against the drystone wall. Annie bet it weighed about two ounces, cost a fortune and went like the clappers. So many cyclists had been inspired by the Tour de France's Grand Départ in Yorkshire that you could hardly move for them on the roads these days. Some of them looked quite fit in their Lycra, too, Annie thought, though not this one. He needed a few more thousand miles on his speedometer to get up to snuff.

'This is Mr Roger Stanford,' said the PC. Then she gestured towards the misshapen bundle lying in a cordoned-off area several yards further along the road. 'He found the . . . er . . . her.'

'Thanks,' said Annie. 'And you are?'

'PC Mellors, ma'am. Stephanie Mellors. Most people just call me Steph.'

Annie gestured for PC Mellors to follow her a short distance from Roger Stanford. 'Tell me, Steph,' she said, 'what do you think? First impressions?'

'You mean did he do it?'

'Well, if that's where you want to start.'

Steph shook her head. 'He's gutted, ma'am. A blubbering wreck. You can tell. I don't think he's faking it.'

'You look a bit peaky, yourself.'

'You haven't seen her yet, ma'am. It's never easy, something like this.'

'Too true. What do you think happened?'

'From my limited experience, I'd say she was either hit by a car or beaten to death.'

'Have you any idea who she is?'

'No. There's no ID, and as far as I can tell from . . . you know . . . I've never seen her before in my life. It's such a strange thing. She's not wearing a stitch of clothing.'

'OK. Let's have a word with Mr Stanford.'

Roger Stanford was still leaning on the bonnet of the patrol car with his head in his hands. He wasn't crying, Annie noticed, just propping his head up as if it were too heavy with images of violent death to hold itself up. He would need to be investigated, being the person who had found the body, but he didn't need to be treated like a suspect. 'Mr Stanford,' she said, touching his arm. He raised his head, a blank expression on his face, as if he had been startled out of a deep sleep. Annie introduced herself. Gerry stood beside her, notebook at the ready. 'What time did you find the body?' Annie asked.

'It would have been about a quarter to nine.'

'Is this journey part of a routine, or are you on holiday?'

'Daily routine. I live in Bradham and I work in Eastvale. Clinton Estate Agents. I usually pass here about a quarter to nine. That's how I know. I keep track of my times.'

'There are quicker ways.'

'No nicer ones, though. I always make sure I have plenty of time.'

Annie looked him up and down. 'You go to work dressed like that?'

'Oh, no.' He pointed to the little bundle strapped to the back of his saddle. 'I change at the office. We have a shower there, too.'

'Very civilised.' Annie made a mental note to take in the bundle of work clothes for forensic analysis. Maybe he didn't do it, but she couldn't go around letting things like that slip by. 'So you make this same journey every morning?'

'And evening. More or less. Every weekday.'

'Do you ever notice anyone else using the road?'

'No. I mean, once or twice I've seen a tractor out early, pulling a few bales of hay or something from one field to another, and once there was a farmer shifting some cows over the road, blocking the way. Maybe the occasional car, but they're few and far between, thank the Lord. Cars are . . . well let's just say they're not always sympathetic towards cyclists. Usually the lane is deserted. That's why I like it. Nice and quiet.'

Yeah, thought Annie, and cyclists are a pain in the arse as far as motorists and pedestrians are concerned. They don't stop at red lights, they go the wrong way up one-way streets, they ride on the pavements when it suits them, and the list went on. But she said nothing. 'Let's go back to this morning. Anything unusual at all?'

'No,' said Stanford. 'I set off the same time I always do, around a quarter past eight, and I got here as I said, about a quarter to nine. It's only about six miles, but there's a tough uphill stretch, and I wasn't really pushing my speed.'

'Did any cars pass you?'

'No.'

'See anyone on foot?'

'No one. It was a perfectly ordinary morning – until I got here.' He put his head in his hands again. 'The first thing I saw was the crows. That poor, poor girl . . .'

'I'm sorry I have to ask these questions Mr Stanford, but the sooner I'm done, the sooner you can go home.'

'Home? But I haven't . . . I have to . . .'

'I'd go home if I were you, Mr Stanford. Phone your work. They'll understand. Delayed shock and all that. We'll have someone come around and take a statement from you this afternoon. Who knows, you may have remembered something else by then.'

'He's already given his address,' said Steph.

Annie nodded. 'You're free to go, Mr Stanford. If I have any more questions, I'll be in touch. But I'd like to take the clothes you're carrying to our lab. We'll let you have them back good as new. Is that a problem?'

'My clothes? But . . .? Oh, I see. But surely you can't think I did it?'

'Just for purposes of elimination, Mr Stanford.'

'Of course.' Stanford walked over to his bike, still stunned, unbuckled the bag and handed it over. Then he got on the bike and rode back, rather wobbly, down the lane.

'Where are the nearest houses?' Annie asked PC Mellors.

She pointed. 'Nearest farmhouse is over there, at the other side of that field.'

Annie could see the house in the distance. 'Unlikely they'll have witnessed anything,' she said, 'though it's not so far away.

Someone might have heard a car, for example, especially as the lane is little used by traffic.' No houses lined its sides, she noticed, only trees and fields of grazing sheep beyond the ditch and the drystone walls. That said, it was certainly a scenic route if you weren't in a hurry. But it's hard to see pretty landscapes at night. On the other hand, she realised, if you wanted to avoid the Automated Number Plate Recognition cameras, the speed cameras and all the rest of the Big Brother paraphernalia that makes any road trip practically a public event these days, then Bradham Lane was your route of choice.

Annie glanced over at the body by the roadside and took a deep breath. No sense putting it off any longer. 'Come on, Gerry,' she said. 'Let's go have a butcher's at what we've got.'

The girl lay curled up in the foetal position, half in the long grass that edged a ditch, hands covering her face, as if to protect it. She was naked, and her body was streaked with mud, dirty water and blood. The soles of her feet were crusted with dried blood, and small stones from the road were embedded in the skin. There were no obvious bullet holes or stab wounds, and her throat seemed unscathed. Not so the rest of her. She could have been hit by a car, Annie supposed, but it would be up to the medical professionals to determine that. It was hard to see her features because of the position of her hands, but Annie noticed between the fingers that one eye was swollen shut, her lips were split and bloody, with a tooth protruding through the lower one, and her nose was crooked. Squatting to examine the rest of the body again, Annie noticed signs of bruising around the ribs, stomach and right hip. There were also signs of a scuffle in the earth around the body and, not so far away, the only obvious skid marks on the road surface, far too faint and blurred to give a decent tyre impression. In the absence of a medical and CSI opinion, Annie was convinced that this girl had been beaten to death, kicked, perhaps even jumped on. And girl she was. Despite the injuries, Annie could see that the victim was hardly any older than fifteen or sixteen. She sensed Gerry's presence beside her and stood up.

'My God,' said Gerry, hand to her mouth.

Annie put a friendly hand on her shoulder. 'I don't think God had much to do with it, do you? And I'd like to say you get used to it, but you don't.' Not so used to it, Annie thought, that you become indifferent to it, that you don't feel that tightening in your gut and that surge of anger that someone had done this to a fellow human being, or don't feel you're going to put your all into catching the bastard who did it.

'But she's so young. She's just a girl.'

'I know.' Gently directing a pale and trembling Gerry away with an arm around her shoulder, Annie headed back towards the uniformed officers. 'Come on,' she said. 'It's time to call in the heavy brigade.'

'Well, Banksy, what a turn-up for the books. You and me working together again. Just like old times. Congratulations, by the way. The promotion. Long overdue.'

They were basking in the sunshine at one of the tables outside at the Queen's Arms, eating lunch: monster fish and chips and mushy peas, with a pint of Timothy Taylor's for Banks and a cheap lager for Burgess. Cyril, the landlord, had taken on a new barmaid to deal with the summer rush, an attractive blond Australian called Pat, to whom Burgess had already taken a shine. Luckily, Cyril wasn't around, as he and Burgess had history.

'So what's your official title these days?' Banks asked. 'What do I call you?'

'I always fancied "Special Agent". It has a ring to it. But in actual fact I'm a non-executive director. Sounds like a dull second-rate businessman. Mostly I go by plain "Mr Burgess" these days.'

'Like a surgeon.'

'Exactly. It's got class, don't you think?'

The cobbled market square was buzzing with shoppers and tourists, and clogged with parked cars. Young girls in vests and tight denim cut-offs over black tights hung out around Greggs eating pasties, then disappeared into the amusement arcade next door. A gaggle of serious ramblers, with walking-sticks like ski poles, expensive boots, baggy shorts and maps in plastic bags around their necks gathered by the market cross. A few people sat on the plinth around the market cross waiting for a local bus. Not far from Banks and Burgess sat a group of bloke-ish tourists in garish shorts and even more garish shirts, their faces flushed and eyes glazed from sunburn and beer. They were talking and laughing loudly enough that nothing Banks and Burgess spoke of could be overheard.

'Have you done this sort of thing before?' Banks asked.

'Once or twice.' Burgess sat back and sipped his drink, studying Banks over the rim of his glass. 'I was peripherally involved in Operation Yewtree when I was back at the Yard, so I know the way things go. Look, Banksy, you probably thought the same as I did when all this stuff started coming out. You thought it was some sort of witch hunt, wondering who'd be the next celebrity to be accused of groping a young publicist fifty years ago. Different times, you'd say, and you'd be right.' He leaned forward and tapped Banks on the chest. 'You probably even thought, what's so wrong with pinching the office girl's bum, maybe suggesting a hotel room after work for a bit of hanky-panky? Right? I might even have a go with young Pat here, given half the chance. After all, I'm only human, and if you don't ask . . . But that's not what this is about. We're not talking about a bit of how's your father in a dark corner at the office Christmas party. A hand casually resting on a knee in a restaurant. A surreptitious brushing up against a nice pair of tits. We've all done that, all had a kiss and cuddle in the broom cupboard and a bit of slap and tickle under the stairwell with that secretary we fancied all year.'

'Speak for yourself,' said Banks. But he remembered. It was just such an indulgence in a dark corner under the mistletoe at an office Christmas party that had led to the only affair of his married life. He didn't much care to be reminded of it now, though at the time it had seemed exciting and dangerous; it had made him feel alive at a time when he had felt the world and his marriage were falling apart around him. Looking back, it just made him feel guilty. Maybe it was some kind of poetic justice that his ex-wife Sandra had finally left him for another man.

'But this is something else,' Burgess went on. 'It's not even a matter of someone sticking his tongue down a girl's throat or squeezing a breast. Believe me, I've had enough access to statements that I can say what we're talking about here is the deliberate, arrogant and systematic abuse of innocent young girls – underage girls – by people who believe they're above the law. People so blessed and so famous that in the general run of things they probably get more free pussy than they can shake a stick at. And what do they do? They pick on vulnerable thirteen-, fourteen-, fifteen-year-olds, and they assault them and rape them, force them to do vile stuff, and then tell them they ought to be jolly grateful for getting raped by Danny Caxton or whoever. These girls end up so terrified, so fucked up, that often the rest of their lives are blighted. They see themselves as natural victims and that's what they become. All their lives, people abuse them just the way Caxton or whoever did all those years ago, and they can't stop it. They can't even figure out why. But even that's not the point. The point is that these bastards, and I mean bastards like Danny Caxton, have been getting away with it for years and making us look like the fucking Keystone Cops. They've abused these girls and boys, just like those Pakistani grooming gangs in

Rochdale and Rotherham, and nobody did a fucking thing about it. Not the parents. Not the social workers. Not us. Well, times have changed, mate, because here comes the cavalry, with a vengeance.'

'I never did think that,' said Banks.

'Think what?'

'That this business is insignificant, that what we've been asked to do doesn't matter. And I'd certainly agree that some very influential people have got away with a lot of serious crimes over the years. Nothing new about that. It's just so bloody difficult to put a good case together after so long, like I said at the meeting. That's all. Memories change; evidence gets lost. People become convinced that something happened when it didn't, or that things happened differently. It's damn near impossible to sort out who's right in most cases. All you end up with is a shifting sandstorm of accusations, lies, half-truths, minor transgressions and full-blown felonies. Nobody knows what the truth is, in the end.'

Burgess ran his hand over his unruly hair. 'Too true. Too true. But we're getting better. The CPS are building stronger cases, they're more willing to prosecute, getting more convictions.'

'So we ride their wave of success?'

'Why not? Isn't it better than riding a wave of failure? Besides, since when have you not risen to a challenge? This time they think we're in with a chance. They rate this Linda Palmer as a credible complainant. According to them, she's definitely not some fucked-up alcoholic with a chip on her shoulder.'

'That's good to know,' said Banks. 'Does Caxton know we're on to him?'

'Probably. He shouldn't, but I wouldn't be surprised. He's still got friends in high places. I want you to go and talk to him tomorrow. After that, we'll get a team in to search his premises before he gets a chance to destroy any evidence there might be in his papers and on his computer. You can talk to Linda Palmer today. I trust your instinct enough to know that you won't need a child protection expert to figure out whether she's telling the truth. I know you, Banksy. I think once you get the bit between your teeth, you'll take to it like a duck to water, if you'll forgive the mixed metaphor, and you'll be only too glad to bring down the wrath of God on arrogant bastards like Danny Caxton.'

'I will?'

'I think so.' Burgess finished his pint. 'Another? I wouldn't mind having another word with that buxom Australian barmaid. I like the way she pulls a pint.'

'You need real cask ale to get a full show of flexed muscle, not that piss you drink. All she has to do is flick the lever.'

'She can flick my lever any time. Why do you think I'm offering to buy you another one? Out of the goodness of my heart?'

Banks rolled his eyes. 'I'd better not,' he said. 'Not if I've got to get this crusade off the ground and talk to Linda Palmer this afternoon. Can you tell me anything about her, other than that she's a poet and claims to be a victim of Caxton's?'

'I've never met her,' said Burgess, 'but from what I understand, she's got her head screwed on right. I've talked to plenty of others who've been in her position. Memories are unreliable, you're right about that, very vague sometimes. Like chasing shadows of shadows. You just have to keep at it. Gently, mind. They're sensitive souls, these victims of historical abuse. Especially poets. Some of the girls buried it right away. Really deep. They were just kids, after all. Some went through years of analysis and therapy without really knowing why – why they couldn't hold down a job, why they couldn't handle a relationship, why they couldn't bring up their kids properly. Some of them just turned to drugs and booze to help them forget. Some even committed suicide. But Linda Palmer isn't like that, from what I understand. She's different. She's got her shit together.'

Banks finished his drink and stood up. 'OK,' he said. 'Thanks for the pep talk.'

Burgess gave a mock salute. 'My pleasure.'

As Banks walked away, he turned and saw Burgess disappear inside the pub with his empty glass and a spring in his step.

2

The CSI van arrived about an hour after Roger Stanford had cycled off into the distance. Annie and Gerry remained by their car, under the shade of the trees, as the various specialists got to work. The uniformed officers donned latex gloves and overshoes to join in the roadside search. It was going on for half past eleven, and by all the signs, Annie thought, the day was going to be a scorcher. The morning mist had already burned off. She wished she were at home in the garden on a sunlounger working on her tan, with a thick Ken Follett lying open on her stomach and a long cool drink within reach.

'What do you think?' Gerry asked.

'Hard to say yet,' answered Annie. 'Give the boffins an hour or so and they might come up with some ideas. We don't even know who she is or how she got here. Nobody local's been reported missing.'

'Early days yet,' said Gerry. 'She can hardly have walked here.'

'True enough. Let's go talk to Doc Burns. He's been with the body long enough. He should have something to say by now.'

They walked a few yards along the road, noting the officers and CSIs probing the ditch and long grass for any clues as to what might have happened. There was a chance that the girl's clothes and bag were nearby. A purse or mobile could help them with the identification. Others had climbed over the drystone wall and were searching for anything that might have been thrown over there. Peter Darby, the police photographer, was busy with his trusty Pentax, which he wouldn't give up despite offers of a state-of-the-art digital SLR. He took digital photographs, too, of course, with a pocket Cybershot, as did many of the CSIs and investigating officers these days, but the Pentax shots were the 'official' ones, the pictures that got tacked to the whiteboard during briefing sessions and progress meetings.

Dr Burns was scribbling in his notebook when Annie and Gerry arrived by the corpse. 'You two,' he said.

Annie smiled. 'DCI – I mean Detective *Superintendent* Banks is on another case. High profile, probably. He's too good for the likes of us any more.'

Dr Burns smiled back. 'I doubt that very much,' he said.

Annie was joking. The few times she had met with Banks since his promotion, usually for a drink after work, he had seemed much as normal, complaining about the paperwork and boring meetings, but around the station he had been far more remote and preoccupied. Hardly surprising, she thought, given his added responsibilities. His new office also put him further away from the squad room, so they didn't bump into one another as often during the day. Annie had put in an application for promotion to DCI, but budget cuts were back with a vengeance since Banks had scraped through. They were already reducing the senior ranks, and there were plenty of constables and sergeants out there who had passed their OSPRE exams and were still without positions to take up. The truth was, she'd have to take a few more courses and kiss a lot more arse before she got a promotion. Gerry, too, however well she did in her sergeant's exams.

'So what have we got?' she asked Dr Burns.

'Just what it looks like, at least until Dr Glendenning gets her on the slab. He might well discover some poison hitherto unknown to man, or signs of a blade so thin and needle sharp it leaves no trace to the naked eye. But until then, my opinion is that the poor girl was beaten to death.'

'No chance it was a hit and run?'

'I'd say that's very unlikely, judging by the injuries and the position of the body. I wouldn't rule it out a hundred per cent – hit and runs can cause any number of injuries similar to the ones this girl has – but I doubt it.' Dr Burns paused. 'Besides,' he added, 'you might ask yourselves what a naked girl was doing walking down this lane in the middle of the night.'

'Oh, we'll be doing that all right,' said Annie. 'Can you tell if she was beaten by a blunt object or anything? Is there a particular weapon we should be searching for?'

'From what I can see, I'd say fists and kicking. Mostly the latter, while she was lying on the ground trying to protect her face and head, knees up to try to cover her stomach.'

Annie stared at the stained and bruised body, stiffened in the foetal position. She had curled herself up in a ball like that to protect herself from a rain of blows, but she had died anyway.

'Any idea how many attackers?'

'Could be just one,' Dr Burns said. 'But again, you'll have to wait for the post-mortem for a definitive answer.'

'What about her clothes? Any idea when or why they were removed?'

'None,' said Dr Burns. 'As far as I know, nobody's found any trace of them yet, and they certainly weren't removed *after* the beating.'

'Any signs of sexual assault?'

Dr Burns gestured towards the body. 'As you can see, there's evidence of bruising and bleeding around the anus and vagina.'

'Any idea what killed her?'

'Could have been the blows to the head.' Dr Burns pointed to areas where the blond hair was dark and matted with blood on the skull, the broken cheekbone, the mess of the mouth and ear. 'It could also be internal injuries,' he went on. 'It looks as if someone stamped on her. A beating like this is likely to rupture the spleen and God knows what else. I think her hip is probably broken, too.'

'Any ideas on time of death?'

Burns sighed. Annie knew it was the question all crime-scene doctors and pathologists hated because it was so difficult to answer accurately, but she had to ask. 'Based on body temperature readings and the fact that rigor is advanced, I'd say it happened sometime between one and three in the morning. It was a warm night.'

'Thanks,' said Annie. 'Are you finished with her?'

Dr Burns glanced at the body again. 'God, yes,' he said. 'But I don't think you are. Not by a long shot.' And he walked off to his car.

Annie asked Peter Darby and one of the CSIs if they had also finished with the body, and they said they had. She had a raincoat in the back of the car – always a sensible precaution in Yorkshire – and while they waited for the coroner's van, she took it out and spread it gently over the girl's body. For some reason she didn't want the girl's nakedness on display, even though everyone at the scene was a professional. Gerry still seemed especially pale and shaken by the sight.

'Excuse me for asking,' said Annie. 'I realise I should know, but I can't remember. Is this your first murder victim?'

Gerry offered a weak smile. 'You usually keep me in the squad room chained to the computer.'

'If you want to talk, or anything . . . As long as there's a large glass of wine in it for me.'

'Thanks, guv.' Gerry straightened her back and stuck her long pre-Raphaelite locks behind her ears. 'What next?'

'We wait. Stefan's gang are good, but they take their time. I think whatever happens, high-profile case or not, Alan's going to find himself senior investigating officer on this one, so we'll report to him when we get back to the station. First priority is to find out who she is. We'll need to start checking on missing persons as soon as possible, and see how soon we can draft in a forensic odontologist to get working on dental records. We also need an artist's impression. From what I could tell, her face is too badly disfigured for a useful photo ID. We'll check with local schools, even though they're on holiday. Social services. What's your gut feeling on this?'

'I think we need to know whether she was dumped or killed here, for a start.'

'It seems a good out-of-the-way place to dump a body,' Annie said. 'Or even to kill someone. We should talk to whoever lives in that farmhouse over there.'

'Ladies!'

Annie turned around to the source of the voice. It was Stefan Nowak about a couple of hundred yards up the road. 'If you'd care to come here,' he said, 'I think we might have something interesting for you.'

'I still find it hard to understand how a fourteen-year-old girl could be sexually assaulted in front of a witness and nothing was done,' said DS Winsome Jackman, as she parked the police Skoda in the tiny, charming village of Minton-on-Swain. 'She did report it at the time, you say?'

'She says she did,' said Banks. 'Different times. Didn't you follow the Jimmy Savile and Rolf Harris cases?'

'Not really. They don't mean anything to me. I mean, I know who they are, and it's terrible what they got away with, but they had nothing to do with my life. They weren't part of my childhood. I'm paying more attention to that Bill Cosby thing in the States.'

'They were part of my childhood,' said Banks. 'Not a big part, maybe, except when Savile was a DJ on Radio Luxembourg, and I used to listen under the bedclothes, but a part, nonetheless. The *Teen and Twenty Disc Club*.'

'The what?'

'It's what his radio programme was called. You could even write in to become a member, get a card with a number and a charm bracelet with a disc on it. I wish I still had mine. They're probably worth a fortune now on the creepy souvenirs market. I've still got my *Radio Luxembourg Books of Record Stars*. You know, it's funny the little things you remember, but it made you feel special that Elvis was a member, too. I even remember his number: one one three two one.'

'Elvis Costello?'

Banks laughed. 'Elvis Presley. Believe it or not, Winsome, I was an Elvis fan back then. Still am.'

'But isn't that when he was making those terrible films? We used to get them on television when I was little.'

'Just between you and me, I used to enjoy those terrible films. I still listen to the soundtracks now and then. *Girl Happy*, *Fun in Acapulco*, *Viva Las Vegas*. Mostly pretty bad songs, but a few gems, and say what you like about Elvis, he had a great voice.'

'We had a pastor who did terrible things to young girls the next village over,' said Winsome. 'Not to me, but girls my age.'

'What happened to him?'

'The fathers ganged up and ... well, it wasn't very nice. They used a machete. He was lucky to be alive, or maybe not, but he wasn't able to harm any more girls after that. My father was livid. There was nothing he could do to stop it, but he could hardly arrest them all, either.'

'It was a bit like that when I was a kid,' said Banks, standing for a moment to breathe in the fragrant summer air. It was late July, and the village gardens were in bloom. Banks could see why Minton had recently won a best-kept Dales village award. The inhabitants clearly took great pride in their gardens. 'Maybe without the machete. But it was like everyone knew who you should stay away from. Word gets around not to go near that Mr So-and-so at number eight, and we wouldn't. Nobody ever said why.'

'But people in the community knew who the perverts were?'

'Yes,' said Banks. 'Without anyone telling them who was on a sex offenders list, if we even had such things then. And as often as not, the community dealt with it. I think they stopped short of murder and castration where I grew up, but one or two local pervs upped sticks for no apparent reason. Warned off, I should think.'

'But they'd only go somewhere else.'

'That's the problem. If what we're hearing is true, people like Danny Caxton didn't even get warned off, so they just carried on as they liked, year after year.'

'And nobody stopped them. *We* didn't stop them.'

'No, we didn't. Here it is.'

The three small cottages stood on the opposite side of the road from the main village, and Linda Palmer lived in the one with the green Mini parked outside. Banks and Winsome opened the gate, walked down the narrow hedge-lined path and flight of stone stairs, then Banks knocked on the sturdy red door. It was a warm afternoon, and even though he had slung his jacket over his shoulder, he could already feel the sweat sticking his shirt to his skin, trickling and tickling down the groove of his spine. The heat didn't seem to bother Winsome. She was as cool as ever in her tailored navy jacket and skirt.

When the door finally opened, he found himself face to face with a tall, slender woman with short ash-blond hair cut in a jagged fringe. Her hand gripped his and then Winsome's in a firm handshake.

'Come on in, both of you,' she said. 'I'm sorry I took so long to answer the door, but I was out in the garden. It's such a beautiful day, it seemed a shame to waste it. Will you join me? Or do we have to sit on uncomfortable seats in the dark to do this?'

'We'd be happy to join you,' Banks said.

She moved ahead of them gracefully, looking good in close-fitting jeans and a loose white cotton tunic. The interior of the house seemed dark after the bright sun, but before their eyes had time to adjust they went through the open French windows and found themselves outside again. This time, they were in a different world. The river wasn't very wide at this point, and it ran swift and deep at the bottom of the sloping lawn, the sun flashing like diamonds on its shifting, coiling surface, its sound constant but ever-changing. The opposite riverbank was overgrown with trees, some of them willows weeping down into the water, others leaning at precarious angles, as if they were about to topple in at any moment. Above the trees, it was possible to make out the pattern of drystone walls on the higher slopes of the opposite daleside, Tetchley Fell reaching high above Helmthorpe, close to where Banks lived, and much greener this summer after the rains.

But it was the river that drew one's attention with its magnetic power, its voice and its shifting, scintillating movement. The garden was just a swatch of lawn that needed mowing, edged with a few beds of colourful flowers: poppies, foxgloves, roses. Fuchsia and a bay tree hung over the drystone wall from next door. At the bottom was a low iron railing decorated with curlicues, and beyond that the riverbank itself. A white table and four matching chairs awaited them in the shade of an old beech tree, along with a jug full of ice cubes and orange juice. The French windows remained open and Banks could hear music playing quietly inside. He recognised the opening movement of Beethoven's Pastoral Symphony.

'I thought cold drinks might be nicer than tea,' Linda Palmer said, 'but it's up to you.'

'Cold is fine,' said Banks, hanging his jacket over the back of the chair. His tie had disappeared soon after the morning meeting.

'Good, then. Let's sit down, shall we?'

They sat. Banks noticed an open book face down on the table beside an ashtray. It was called *Dart* by Alice Oswald, and looked slim enough to be a volume of poetry. Beside it sat a black Moleskine notebook with a Mont Blanc rollerball lying across its cover, which seemed a bit upmarket for a poet. Perhaps they got paid more than he thought. Linda Palmer poured the drinks, which turned out to be freshly squeezed, judging by the pulp and tang. It was good to be in the shade in the warm summer weather. A light, cool breeze made the garden even more comfortable. A black cat came out from the bushes, gazed at them with a distinct lack of interest and stretched out in the sun.

'Don't mind her,' said Linda. 'That's Persephone. Persy, for short, though that makes her sound male, doesn't it?'

'It's beautiful here,' Banks said.

'Thank you. I just adore it. We get a kingfisher sometimes, sitting on that branch over the water, scanning for fish. I could watch him for hours. Plenty of other birds, too, of course. The feeder attracts finches, wagtails, tits of all kinds. We get swifts and swallows in the evening, an owl at night. And the bats, of course. It can be really magical when the moon is full. Sometimes I don't think I would be at all surprised to see fairies at the bottom of this garden.'

'Do you live here alone?'

'I do now. Not always.' A faraway look came into her eyes. 'Two children, both grown up and flown the coop. One husband, deceased.'

'I'm sorry to hear that.'

She inclined her head. 'It was two years ago. Heart attack. Charles was a good man. He was an English prof at Durham.'

'Did you ever tell him and the children about what happened?'

Linda gave a slight shake of her head, and Banks knew not to pursue the matter. Not yet, at any rate. Now that he could examine her more closely, he noticed that she had a few crow's feet around her eyes and crinkles at the edges of her mouth, but that only accentuated her beauty rather than detracting from it in any way. Her pale complexion was smooth, lightly freckled, the lips still full, a generous mouth. She wore no make-up, but with her skin, she didn't need it. The features of her heart-shaped face were strong, but not too sharp or angular, the Nordic cheekbones well defined, nose in proportion with everything else. But it was her dark blue eyes that really tantalised. Banks could sense warmth, humour, tenderness and curiosity under a guarded surface, and a hint of sadness, loss and pain beneath all that. They didn't flit around in search of an object to settle on, but remained fixed on whomever she was talking to. Her hands, usually a giveaway sign of age, seemed even younger than the rest of her, long tapered fingers and soft skin. No rings or jewellery of any kind. There were certain women, Banks thought, such as Cherie Lunghi and Francesca Annis, who seemed to become more attractive with age, and Linda Palmer was one of them.

'As I understand it,' he began, 'you rang county HQ two days ago after being advised to do so by Childline, and you talked to a Detective Inspector Joanna MacDonald. Is that right?'

'Yes.'

'Why did you call?'

'I didn't know who else to talk to. Was I wrong?'

'No, I mean, why now? After so long. What was special about the day before yesterday?'

'Nothing.'

'So why?'

'I can't explain it that easily.'

'Was it anything to do with other recent events?'

'Of course it was. It's a need that's been slowly building up in me. I've been plucking up the courage. You might not believe it, but I'm nervous as hell about this meeting. Would I have come forward if all those women hadn't complained about Jimmy Savile? I don't know. I like to think so, but probably not. I don't think they would have all come forward, either, if they hadn't known there were others with the same story to tell.'

It was true, Banks knew. At one point in the Savile investigation, the police had their knuckles rapped for not letting the accusers know they weren't alone. In some ways, though, it was hardly their fault; they were only thinking of what possible repercussions such collusion might have if the case went to trial. 'So it wasn't that you forgot about it and just suddenly remembered?'

'No. I never forgot it. And before you ask, I'm interested in neither money nor notoriety. In fact, I would prefer it if you kept my name out of the papers.'

'Anonymity is guaranteed in cases like this,' said Banks.

'Even if I had to . . . you know . . . testify in court?'

'Even then. There are special protocols in place to deal with this matter in the courts and so on. And you can't be cross-examined by your alleged attacker in person.'

'Thank you.' She paused a moment. 'May I ask you if any others have come forward?'

'It's early days yet,' Banks said, 'but yes, there are others. Believe me, you're not alone.'

A blackbird sang in the garden next door and bees hummed and crawled inside the foxgloves and fuchsias, legs fat with pollen. The sound of the river was a constant background, threaded with the Beethoven Pastoral.

'It's something I never thought about back then, when it happened,' Linda said. 'That there would be others, that he would have done the same thing to someone else.'

'You were fourteen,' Banks said. 'Hard to be anything other than the centre of the universe at that age.'

Linda managed a sad smile. 'I did report it to the police at the time, you know.'

'Do you remember who you spoke to?'

'I can't remember his name,' said Linda. 'I wasn't going to tell anyone, not even my mum. I was frightened, and I was ashamed. But I'd been unable to sleep, I was off my food, just not myself at all, not functioning well, and Mother was desperate with worry. She even took me to the doctor's. She kept on pushing me, and finally I told her what happened.'

'But not your father?'

She hesitated. 'No. He . . . he wouldn't have handled it well. I know it would have come out eventually if . . . well . . . but at the time, no.'

'Did the doctor examine you?'

'No. He just said I was run-down and needed a tonic.'

'How was the policeman? I mean, how did he treat you?'

'Sympathetic, nice enough, but I'm not sure he believed me.'

'Oh?'

'Just his tone. It was difficult, him being a man, like it would have been for my father. Hard to talk about what happened. He seemed more embarrassed than anything else. And that office. It was like the headmaster's study where you went for the cane.'

Banks smiled. He could imagine it had been difficult. These days, if something like that had just happened to her, she would have been talking to a sympathetic woman in a special room with muzak and subdued lighting. Candles, probably. Maybe even the Pastoral Symphony. 'I doubt you were down for the cane all that often.'

She arched an eyebrow. 'You'd be surprised.'

'If you'd be more comfortable talking to a female investigator,' said Banks, 'that can be easily arranged. I know you told DI MacDonald you weren't bothered, but DS Jackman here can take over.'

Linda Palmer smiled at Winsome. 'It's all right. No offence, but I'm OK. Really.' Then she turned to Banks again. 'You're the one they sent. It's your case, isn't it?'

'Something like that. But, as I say, that can be changed. We can accommodate whatever you want. Both DS Jackman here and DI MacDonald are excellent officers.'

'I assume you were chosen because you're good at your job. Are you good?'

Winsome glanced at Banks as he shuffled uncomfortably in his chair. He could see the faint outline of a grin on her face. Enjoying his discomfort. 'I'm not one to blow my own trumpet,' he said. 'But I've had my fair share of success.'

'You'll do, then.'

'Thanks very much.'

Linda glanced at Winsome again, and they both laughed. 'I'm sorry,' said Linda. 'It wasn't meant to sound like that. The thing is, I really don't care who I speak to. It was a long time ago, and I'm a big girl now. It was different then, when I was only fourteen, but a lot of water's gone down the river since. Even my gynaecologist is a man these days.'

'OK,' Banks said. Burgess was right; this was no damaged witness. Linda Palmer could function better than most. Might that make her story seem less credible to a judge and jury? Banks wondered. Would people demand more wailing and gnashing of teeth, a history of drug and alcohol abuse? 'I just wanted to make sure. I understand you heard nothing more of this original complaint?'

'That's right. Nothing except excuses, at any rate.'

'Did you make inquiries?'

'My mother did.'

'And what happened?'

'At first she was told that the investigation was ongoing and that it might take a long time. In the end they told her that the matter had been dropped due to lack of evidence.'

'So it was your word against his, and they believed him?'

'I doubt that they even talked to him. He was too high and mighty. But, yes, basically. That's what I took it to mean. A fourteen-year-old girl. Everyone knows the kinds of hysterical fantasies we have with the onset of puberty.'

'How did you feel about it?'

'How do you think I felt?'

'I can't imagine. Disappointed?'

'Not disappointed. You'd have to have expected something to feel that, and I suppose, deep down, I didn't. Expect anything, I mean. And the whole thing was frightening for a young girl, talking to the police and all that. I couldn't imagine being in a courtroom in front of all those serious old people in their wigs and gowns answering questions about what happened to me. I was shy. I had an overactive imagination, even then. But the main feeling was as if I didn't count. As if what had happened to me didn't matter. I was a nobody. You have to remember, I was just a kid from a working-class background, and we never expected much from the ruling classes. I mean, I couldn't have articulated it that way back then, but that's what it amounted to. Money and privilege ruled. Still do, for that matter, no matter what the clever southerners try to tell you. I'm sorry, there's me on one of my hobby horses again.'

'It's all right,' said Banks. 'Did anyone ever pursue the matter beyond that point?'

'Not that I know of. There seemed no point. We'd had our shot, and we missed. What were we to do? Start a campaign? My parents . . . you have to understand, something like that, it wasn't something they could talk about. They'd both had strict upbringings. Sex wasn't something we talked about in our house. My father in particular. Which was why we never told him. If he ever thought anything was wrong, he probably just wrote it off as some sort of "female" problem. Time of the month. If he noticed at all. I suppose he would have found out if anything had come of it, but it didn't. And he died two months ago. Maybe that's another reason I feel I can talk now. *Need* to talk now. He can never know.'

'What about your mother?'

'My mother was ashamed. She tried not to show it, but I could tell. I'm not saying she blamed me, but when she looked at me, I could tell she wished I'd never brought such unpleasantness into our house. She wanted rid of it, so we swept it under the carpet.' Linda seemed uncertain whether to go on, then she said, 'I'm not even sure she believed me. I think she realised there was *something* wrong with me, but the visit to the police was more like a visit to the doctor's with a troublesome pain or an unexplained lump. When the investigation went nowhere, it was rather like getting a clean bill of health. You know, it's not cancer, after all, it's not polio. More relief than anger. Mother died a few years ago, and by the end I think she had even convinced herself to forget it had ever happened. Neither of us mentioned it to anyone else, or even to each other again. We simply got on with our lives.'

'No crime in that.'

'Keep calm and carry on. I know.'

'I mean . . .'

'I know what you mean.' She sat forward suddenly, linking her hands on her lap. 'It's what lots of people did, their generation especially. My father was part of the D-Day landings, but he never spoke about it. I once saw a big puckered scar on his side when we were on a beach somewhere, and I asked him about it. He just brushed it off as nothing, but I recognised it from pictures I'd seen in books. It was a bayonet wound. He'd got close enough to the enemy for hand-to-hand combat in the war, for crying out loud, but he never talked about it. He probably killed the man who wounded him, and that was why he was still alive. I just felt guilt, that's all. I tried. We tried the best we could, the best my mother and I could. We got nowhere. Now I'm different. I don't mind talking about it. I don't even really care if everyone finds out. Maybe I secretly want them to. I want to know why nobody did anything. And I want them to do something now, if they can. Is that so strange?'

'No,' said Banks. 'Not at all. That's what we're here for.' In a way, Banks knew, she was probably right about her mother. In many cases, the parents didn't believe their children's stories, which made it far worse for the children, who felt alone, humiliated and ashamed enough to start with. No wonder so many ended up blaming themselves.

'What do you need to know?' Linda asked. 'Ms MacDonald didn't ask me very much on the phone.'

'She just wanted to get a general outline of the complaint, the basics. I'm afraid I need a lot more.' Banks glanced at Winsome, who had her notebook and mobile out on the table. 'Do you mind if we record this?'

'Not at all,' said Linda. 'As I said, I *want* to talk about it.'

Winsome set the mobile's voice recorder on.

'Where did the assault take place?' said Banks.

'In a suite at the Majestic Hotel in Blackpool, a big old place behind the Pleasure Beach. It's where he – Danny Caxton – and his entourage were staying during the summer season. It's not there any more.'

'Why were you there?'

She cocked her head to one side. 'Looking back, God only knows,' she whispered. 'Remember, I was only fourteen. Danny Caxton was famous. He was handsome like a film star. And he was a nice man. Or so he seemed to his public. He had one of those affable, trustworthy personalities. On the outside. Maybe that was another reason nobody believed me. It was after a matinee, and I was at the stage door on the pier auto-graph hunting. I used to do that back then. My friend Melanie was supposed to be with me but she cried off at the last minute and went to one of the amusement arcades instead. She wasn't really interested in autographs.'

'Did you tell your parents where you were going?'

'I probably said I was going to try and get some autographs, yes. They knew I collected them. They were used to me going off by myself. I was a solitary child. A bit of a loner. Don't get me wrong. I wasn't antisocial, and I was really glad Melanie was with us that week. But I still needed to do some things by myself. I always have.'

'So you were on your own?'

'Well, there were a few others after autographs, but no one was actually with me, no. You might remember he'd recently started hosting that talent show, *Do Your Own Thing!* at the time, and I suppose I thought I had talent. I used to watch it regularly. I had dreams of being an actress or a singer then, the next Julie Christie or Dusty Springfield or something. People told me I had a nice voice, and I'd had some good parts in school plays. I wrote my own songs. I'd even played Juliet at school earlier that year. Most of the celebrities, they just hurried by and scribbled in the book without even looking at you, if they bothered at all. But Danny Caxton was differ-ent. He noticed people. He really seemed to *see* me. He stopped to talk to me. *Me.*'

'What did he say?'

'He asked me my name, what I did.'

'You told him you were at school?'

'Yes.'

'What else?'

'What I was interested in. That's when I told him about . . . you know, singing and wanting to be onstage. As I said, I was usually a shy teenager, but there was something in his manner that could sort of bring people out of themselves. It felt nice to be able to talk about my dreams to someone. Most of the others had gone by then. I was last in line. He had my book in his hand and his pen ready, but I was gushing about my favourite pop singers. He knew them all, of course – I mean really *knew* them – and that was when he said maybe he could help me, and somehow the autograph got lost in the excitement. He never did sign it.'

'What did he mean that he could help you?'

'He said maybe he could arrange for me to come to a filming of his programme in the TV studio, to be a part of the audience, that maybe if I was good enough I could even be on it. It was a friendly invitation, you know, a bit mysterious, a bit promising, the hint that there'll be something good at the end of it, that I might even get to meet Helen Shapiro or Kathy Kirby. They were both in Blackpool at the time, in different shows. Can you imagine? He said I was pretty and I carried myself well, I had elegant posture, and that was always important if you wanted to be successful in show business. He said they were always needing extras and whatever for the TV show, or for a Christmas panto, and maybe he could get me a start.'

'Then what?' Banks asked.

'I fell for it hook, line and sinker, didn't I? He'd finished signing autographs, so he went back to his car. Just before I set off to see if I could track down Melanie in the amusement arcade, someone asked me if I'd care to talk to Mr Caxton now, that he had some free time.'

'Who was this?'

'I don't know. A sort of aide or assistant or something. Famous people like Danny Caxton had other people to do things for them. He was there later, in the hotel.'

'Did you recognise this assistant from anywhere?'

'No. I'd never seen him before. He wasn't someone from television or the live show. I would have recognised him then. We'd been to see the show a few days earlier with our parents, Melanie and me. An evening performance.'

'What did he look like?'

'I don't really remember. Younger than Caxton. He seemed nice enough at first. There was nothing that really stood out about him.'

'Go on.'

'Well, I didn't think twice about it. I went over with him and hopped in the car. It was really plush. A Rolls-Royce or something. Inside it smelled all of soft leather, and when it moved it was like floating on air.'

'That's very brazen,' said Winsome. 'Whisking you off in his car in public like that. Did anyone else witness this?'

'I don't know. Most of the other autograph hunters had drifted away by then, or gone chasing after Jess Conrad. I know I felt special, like a princess, getting in the car.'

'You weren't suspicious?'

'Why would I be? Believe me, I've flagellated myself time after time for not being, but how could I be, really? I was fourteen, my head full of dreams of the stage, and here was this nice, funny man from TV who everybody loved saying he could help me. He was in your living room almost every night. It was broad daylight, Blackpool in high season, there were people all around. Would *you* have been suspicious?'

'Probably not,' Winsome admitted.

Banks could see by Winsome's expression that she wouldn't have been, that she understood exactly where Linda Palmer was coming from. Perhaps the analogy with the pastor in Winsome's neighbouring village, whom everyone had respected, helped make it clear to her. Like the pastor, Danny Caxton was in a position of trust and power.

Beethoven's storm broke, starkly contrasting with the serenity of the garden and the cloudless blue of the sky.

'I mean, back then we didn't worry about perverts all the time,' said Linda, 'and I don't think I'd ever heard of a paedophile. We were all warned not to take sweets from strangers, of course, or get into cars with strange men we didn't know, but Danny Caxton wasn't strange. He was . . . he was like someone we knew, really, a kindly uncle. He wasn't the sort of person our parents meant.'

Annie was sweating by the time they reached the spot where Stefan's officer waited. It was about half a mile south from the girl's body, and despite the light breeze and some shade from the leafy trees, the heat was getting to her. She felt out of shape and realised that, despite the yoga and meditation, she hadn't got back to working out again yet. She made a mental note to rejoin the small fitness centre in Harkside, where she lived, as she was far more likely to use that than go after work – or, God forbid, *before* – to the larger one in Eastvale, despite its advantage in having more fit males around. She glanced at Gerry, who didn't seem to be showing any effects whatsoever from the walk. Well, she was in her twenties, Annie thought, a willowy redheaded thoroughbred, though she herself was only in her early forties, and willowy enough. Plenty of time to shape up. Only Banks seemed never to have to bother with all that. No matter what he ate and drank, he stayed as lean and agile as ever. Still, it would catch up with him eventually, Annie thought, with a grim sort of satisfaction.

Signs of activity was all Stefan had said when Annie had asked him what they'd found. When they finally reached the spot, she saw that another area of the roadside had been cordoned off with police tape, and there were three white-suited CSIs kneeling and swabbing the ground nearby, collecting samples in plastic or paper bags. There was also another faint skid mark on the road, as if a car or van had slowed down quickly, swerved, then speeded up again.

Even before Stefan pointed out the finer details, Annie could see that the long grass edging the ditch had been flattened and was crusted with dried mud. The dirt along the edge of the road surface was similarly disturbed, and a track continued, almost recognisable as muddy footprints, for several feet in the direction where the body lay.

'So she was hurt before she got to the place where we found her, where she was killed?' said Annie.

'Be careful,' Stefan said as Annie squatted and leaned towards the ditch. 'We found barbed wire and a broken bottle in there. Both were submerged, so we don't expect anything in the way of trace evidence, but they've gone for testing. Some of the cuts on the girl's side might have been caused by the wire or broken glass.' He gestured to the fencing above the drystone wall. 'It was obviously discarded when this was added. No doubt one of the farmers had problems with kids getting in scaring his sheep or whatever.'

'What are you saying, Stefan?' Annie asked. 'That she was in the ditch here?' She was glad to see a sheen of sweat on the crime-scene manager's handsome face. At least someone else was human, and that it was the ever-so dreamy, ever-so cool Stefan Nowak was even better.

'If you observe the way the dirt and grass are disturbed here, I'd say it indicates that someone climbed out of this ditch on to the road and started walking north, back towards the Eastvale road. The water's dried up, but you can see the outlines her muddy feet made. No shoes. And it seems as if she was limping. I'm saying there's a strong likelihood it was our girl. If she was naked, she would have been covered in filthy ditchwater and mud, like the girl's body back up the road. And she would also show evidence of barbed wire and broken glass cuts, as the body does. If you move closer, you can also see that a handful of grass been pulled out right there.' He pointed. Annie could see it. 'To my thinking, if someone crawled out of the ditch, they had to get in there in the first place. It's an explanation. She went in here, and for some reason, she tried to get a hold on the grass, perhaps to prevent herself falling in or help haul herself out.'

'So she was moving fast when she went in?'

'Possibly. I'd say so. Rolling too fast to stop herself. And you saw the hip injury. Dr Burns says it's probably broken. A fall could cause an injury like that, if she bumped it on the road surface, for example. You know what I'm getting at, don't you, Annie?'

'Someone chucked her in the ditch, most likely from a moving vehicle. You can see where it skidded on the verge close to where she came out. The grass is flattened in a direction that indicates the vehicle was travelling south. She climbed out again, after getting a mud bath and cutting herself up a bit, then started walking back the way she'd come – hence the muddy footprints – most likely hoping for a lift home. Which means she wasn't actually beaten to death until later, further up. Unless she simply collapsed and died of her injuries.'

'I'd say she was most likely killed by the roadside up there, where the body is, but she was already naked and injured when she got there.'

'Well, the position and attitude of the body certainly bear that out. But the vehicle she was thrown from had already . . . I mean, what happened? Did he turn back for her?'

'There's no evidence of that so far,' Stefan said. 'You can see the sort of swerve those skid marks indicate. Someone stopped or slowed rather quickly and lost control of the steering for a second or two. It happens.'

'Could they have got out and run after her? Or could someone have been with her?'

'I suppose so,' said Stefan, 'but there's no evidence of anyone else in the vicinity, and there's only one set of footprints. We'll check, of course. We're doing a complete workup on what tyre tracks we've got. I wouldn't hold out a lot of hope because they're just faint blurs, and you can't get decent tyre impressions from skids, but there's always a chance we might get enough to check against the manufacturers' databases. For now, I'd say there were two cars.'

'Two cars?'

'Yes. Even from such small samples and skid marks we can see how the tracks differ. There was the van here, the one she was likely dumped from, travelling south. Then there was another van that stopped to give a naked girl a lift quarter of a mile up the road in the middle of the night. It was also travelling south, but it didn't get as far here.'

'Van? You said van.'

'Judging by the track width, both were commercial vehicles of some kind.'

'You say this second van was travelling in the same direction as the one that had dumped her?'

'Yes. Again, if you look closely, you can see the way the grass is flattened a short distance south from where her trail ends.'

'So the van would have been coming towards her, and she'd have had to turn to run back to it when it stopped. That would explain why her tracks continue on north past the spot where she's lying back there. Bloody hell,' said Annie. 'What a mess. She ran back to the van when it stopped, and then the driver killed her. Or could the van have hit her? *Could* this have been a hit and run, despite what Dr Burns said?'

'I really can't speculate on that, but you've seen her body, same as I have. You'll have to talk to Dr Glendenning when he's done the post-mortem. No doubt the good doctor will be checking her skin for any signs of paint or any traces that might have transferred from a van. But you also have to remember that if she was hit by a van, it could have been an accident.'

'She'd have been like a deer in the headlights.'

'Probably.'

'Was the other van following the first one?'

Stefan thought for a moment. 'I'd say not. She had time to walk some distance from where she was dumped from the first vehicle before it came along. That would probably have taken her ten or fifteen minutes, the shape she was in.'

Gerry walked over and stood beside them. 'Did you catch that?' Annie said. 'A naked girl gets tossed in a ditch from a moving vehicle. She gets out, makes her way back up the road, maybe hoping for a Good Samaritan or at least a working telephone box, then someone else comes along and either runs her down or kicks the living daylights out of her.'

'That's about the way I see it,' Stefan said. 'And judging from the skid marks and pattern on the verge up there, I'd say that when he'd finished with her, he turned around and headed back the way he came.'

'You're saying "he", Stefan. Is it just a figure of speech or do you really think it was a man?'

'Sorry,' said Stefan. 'It's mostly just a habit. Easier than saying "he or she". But now that you mention it, I find it harder to see a woman than a man doing what was done to her.'

'And what are the odds of some stranger just happening along this road, seeing a naked woman walking and turning out to be a passing psychopath, deciding to beat her to death?'

'That's just the problem, isn't it?' Stefan said. 'Probably close to zero.'

'Did anything happen in the car?' Banks asked.

'No. Caxton went on being the perfect gentleman, chatting, solicitous of my comfort, anxious to help me with my dreams. Giving advice about how to behave onstage, how to deal with stage fright. Stuff like that. He even gave me a cigarette and a glass of champagne. It was the first time I'd ever tasted it.'

'In the car? Was there a driver?'

'Oh, yes.'

'And was the other man with you?'

'Yes, but he was in the front with the driver. He didn't say anything the whole way.'

'Were either of them ever questioned?'

'I don't know. I don't think anyone was.'

'And the hotel staff saw you when you arrived?'

'No. We went into a sort of underground car park at the back and got straight in a lift. I don't remember going through reception or anything, or seeing anyone else. Not then. I suppose maybe because he was a celebrity he had a discreet way in. To be honest, I didn't really notice. I was on cloud nine. I was with Danny Caxton and he was going to help me get into show business. I could already see my name in lights.'

'Did the driver and the other man go in with you?'

'Not the driver. Just the other man . . . he . . . yes.'

'OK. Then what happened?'

'We went up in a tiny lift to the fourth floor, a big suite of rooms, all wood panelling and old world elegance. Gilt-framed pictures on the walls. Constable prints, Turner, stuff like that. I remember one of a horse standing by a tree. A Stubbs, maybe. It was a sad horse.'

'What happened?'

'We drank more champagne. I had never really drunk alcohol before, except a sip of my dad's beer once when he was out, and it went straight to my head. I suppose I was giggly, a bit silly. I think I even sang him a song or something.'

'What did Caxton do next?'

'He changed. Just like that. I asked him what I should do next, you know, to get started in the business, and he led me towards the bedroom and said something about passing the audition, that people have to pay for what they get, and they should be grateful. I don't remember it all exactly. I was feeling a bit dizzy. He said the first thing was to take some photos.'

'With your clothes off?'

'No. There was still no suggestion of funny business. He said they were to show agents and whatever. A portfolio. Anyway, the other man, the assistant, took some. He had a Polaroid camera and it was the first time I'd seen one. It was like magic the way the photos came out. I think he took some more later, too, you know, while . . . I thought I could hear the sound of the camera.'

'How were you feeling by the time he took the photos?'

'I was feeling nervous. Danny Caxton was scaring me a bit, saying things, and the way he looked at me. I felt my heart beating fast. I didn't know what he meant. And the smile had gone. I suppose I was a bit tipsy, too. Like I said, I wasn't used to drinking. I asked him where Helen Shapiro was, and he laughed and said he didn't know. I think he said something rude about her, but I didn't really understand it. Then he sat on the bed and patted the spot next to him. I sat down. I think I told him I wanted to go home.'

Banks could tell that despite Linda's calm veneer she was getting upset the more she spoke. It was hardly surprising, given what was to come. 'You don't have to tell us all the details right now,' he said, 'but did Danny Caxton rape you?'

Linda looked Banks in the eye first, then Winsome. 'Yes, he did.'

'And did you struggle?'

'As best I could. I didn't know what was happening, what he was doing. It might be hard for people to believe this today, but I was a virgin, and I was ignorant of the realities of sex. Oh, we talked about it at school, but that was all a load of nonsense, like rubbing willies and so on. It wasn't anything like . . . Yes, I struggled because I was scared. But he was far stronger than me. And it hurt.'

'Then what happened?'

'After?'

'Yes.'

Linda averted her eyes, staring down at a robin hopping over the lawn by the fence. 'It gets very hazy, but when Caxton finished, he rolled off me. I tried to stand up. It was hard. I was winded, and he'd made me sore . . . you know. I felt sick from the champagne. But Caxton said I couldn't leave yet, and he pushed me down again, then he told the other man it was his turn, to hurry up.'

'And what happened then?'

'The younger man raped me, too. There was something . . .' She stopped, as if trying to find the right words. 'Something reluctant about him. Like he didn't really want to do it, but he wanted to please Caxton. Maybe he'd been pushed into it, you know, maybe Caxton was challenging him to be a man or something. But what happened had excited him, and he'd passed a point of no return. I don't know. Maybe I'm being fanciful, using hindsight, but I don't think he felt comfortable.'

'But he did it anyway? Did he rape you as well?'

She turned her head away. 'Yes.'

'So this man was both a witness and an assailant. You didn't mention this to DI MacDonald?'

'No. I just told her someone else was there. I never told my mother, either.'

'Or the Leeds police?'

'No. I was too ashamed. Somehow, it seemed . . . being raped twice . . . I just couldn't.'

'Did you tell your friend Melanie?'

'I've never told anyone.'

'Where's Melanie now?'

'She died a few years ago.'

'I'm sorry to hear it,' said Banks.

'We'd lost touch, more or less, over the years.'

'Did they talk to each other, this man and Caxton, use names or anything?'

'Not that I remember, no.'

'I know this is a bit delicate,' said Banks, 'but did either of them use a condom?'

'No. I thought later it was a miracle I didn't get pregnant, but I didn't.'

'What happened next?'

'I was crying and I just wanted to go home. It was like I didn't exist for them any more. I just walked out of the room in a daze.'

'Nobody tried to stop you?'

'No.'

'How did you leave the hotel?' Banks asked.

'Through reception, out the front.'

'Caxton didn't make you go by the back entrance, where you'd come in, have his driver take you?'

'He didn't even give me bus fare.'

'Did anyone see you leaving?'

'I should imagine so. I felt as if everyone could see what I'd just been doing. I was so ashamed. They had to know, just from the way I was walking, though I probably didn't seem odd at all, just a bit dishevelled. I know it's ridiculous, but it just felt that way, like "whore" was emblazoned on my fore-head. I suppose it's because that was how I felt inside. I thought everyone could see it. I can't say I saw them, though. I was in a daze. I didn't really notice anything.'

'What did you do?'

'I don't know. I must have just walked around. I don't know where or for how long. Maybe the Pleasure Beach. The sands. I remember I missed dinner and everyone was angry with me. I just told them I'd been walking around and lost track of the time. I said I didn't feel very well and went to bed early.'

'Now think carefully,' said Banks. 'You say you'd never seen this other man before, but did you ever see him again?'

'That's where it gets unclear,' said Linda, a tone of regret and desperation in her voice. 'I honestly can't remember. I think I did, but I was a zombie for weeks, months after. I put on a good enough show. But inside. I don't have much recall of the aftermath.'

'OK,' said Banks. 'Calm down, Linda. There's no hurry, no pressure.'

'I just have this memory of seeing a picture of him some-time after he raped me, but it's not clear where, or even if I really did. It might have been in a newspaper or something. It might even have been an image in a dream. Or a nightmare. I had plenty of those.'

'A magazine, perhaps? Or a billboard? Was he also famous?'

'No. I'm pretty sure he wasn't. At least, I'd have known if I'd seen him on TV or anything. No, if it really happened, it was just a fleeting glimpse, half-forgotten. Most likely a news-paper. Half created, half perceived, perhaps.'

'Wordsworth,' said Banks.

Linda's eyes widened. 'You know poetry?'

'No, but we did "Tintern Abbey" at school. Even went on a school trip there. It was one of the few I liked, a big favourite of our English teacher's – he was very big on the Romantic imagination – and I've never forgotten those lines, or at least the paraphrase. It's something that comes up a lot in my job.'

'"Of all the mighty world / Of eye and ear, – both what they half create, / And what perceive." Yes, that's what it's like, really, trying to think back to that . . . that day. I don't know how much I perceived or how much I'm making up, filling in, when I try to remember it.'

She had just about put her finger on the whole problem of historical abuse cases, Banks thought – or Wordsworth had. No real evidence, just a mix of fact and fiction. But there had to be a way to crack it, to crack Danny Caxton. Linda wasn't the only victim, and in these cases there was strength in numbers, in independent, believable testimony. When it came right down to it, most people had no reason to lie about some- thing like that; the only problem was getting their memories as clear as possible. Even then, Banks knew, you could ask five people to describe an event they had all witnessed together and you'd get five different accounts.

'You mentioned a newspaper,' Banks said. 'Is that where you might have seen his picture?'

'It's what comes to mind. You know, passing a rack of papers at the newsagent's or a quick glance at someone's paper getting on or off a bus. It feels like it was that sort of flash.'

'How long after the assault?'

'I can't remember exactly. It wasn't all that long, though. After summer but before winter. October, maybe. As I said, I was in bad shape for a few months, maybe a year, though I still managed to function. School, and all that. I was just jumpy, and I got depressed sometimes. I lost interest in things. Reading. Songs. Hockey. Hanging out with my friends. They started to think I was weird and ignore me. My marks went down, of course. My mother took me to a child psychologist, but I don't really think that did any good. The same doctor who'd given me the tonic before gave me some more pills, but

I only pretended to take them after the first few made everything even more fuzzy. I suppose they were all just trying to help. I was probably behaving like a real brat.'

'But you never sought the photograph out later, tried to find it again?'

'No. I just wanted things to get better, to *feel* better, and when they started to, when the anxiety decreased and it felt like a heavy weight was lifting from me, I moved on, tried to forget.'

'Would you recognise the man if you saw the picture again?'

'Perhaps. I couldn't describe him, but I think I might recognise that photo if I saw it again. Memory's a strange thing. But I can't say for sure.'

'So you didn't ever go back and tell the police you'd seen a photo of the man who was with Caxton, a man who had also raped you and perhaps taken photos of you with Caxton?'

'No. They'd dropped the case by then. I don't know that it would have changed anything.'

'You have to let the police decide things like that, Linda,' said Banks. 'People don't always know what matters and what doesn't, what's important and what isn't.'

'But doesn't having every little thing thrown at you clutter up your investigations?'

Banks smiled. 'We've got a special unclutter gadget that separates the wheat from the chaff.' He paused. 'No, seriously, please tell me *everything* that comes to you. Don't self-censor.'

'OK. But I don't think I can remember anything more right now. I'm exhausted.'

Banks handed her his card. 'Ring me anytime if you do. And I mean anytime.'

She took the card and read it, then shifted her eyes back to Banks. They seemed filled with a kind of dreamy wistfulness, or it could have been tears. 'That's very kind of you.'

'Would you be willing to repeat all you've told me in court, if it came to that?'

'Yes, I think so.'

'You'd better be certain. The defence counsel won't make things easy for you.'

'They'd do their job, I suppose. I'd be more comfortable doing it if I wasn't alone. If there were others.'

'I think you can count on that.'

'You know, sometimes I feel a bit like a phoney in all this.'

'Why?'

She gestured around her. 'My life wasn't ruined. I've made a successful life for myself. Oh, I get jumpy sometimes, I have panic attacks, and I still have bad dreams – long winding corridors, something nasty behind the door, rooms beyond rooms, but they're just typical nightmares.'

'Drugs? Drink?'

Her eyes narrowed, with a glint of humour. 'Are you asking me if I'm a junkie or an alcoholic?'

'Not at all.' Banks felt himself blush. 'It's just that sometimes people who've experienced . . . you know, they reach for . . .'

'Oblivion?'

'Something like that.'

'I had my moments. I was seventeen, eighteen in the late sixties, early seventies. People were experimenting. I was deep into that scene, the poetry, the music, the Eastern philosophy, the clothes, and, yes, the drugs. It took a while for the psyche-delic drug culture to work its way up to Leeds, but my friends and I tried pot and acid, mescaline, speed, Mandies. Never the hard stuff, though. No coke or heroin.'

'What happened?'

'I got bored with it all, like watching the same cartoon show over and over again at the News Theatre. So I went to university to study English literature.'

'And drink?'

'At university? Who didn't?'

'In general. Now.'

'The occasional glass of wine. Hell, the occasional bottle of wine. So what?'

Banks smiled. 'So nothing.' Thinking he wouldn't mind sharing a bottle with her as they talked right now, in the summer garden by the riverside with Beethoven's calm after the storm playing. But he pushed such thoughts out of his mind. The garden had cast its own special spell made of bee drone, blackbird song, the scent of roses and the music of the fast-running river. The warm and hazy air could do things to your mind, too, distract you, slow thought down, alter its direction. He was here to help this woman get justice for a terrible thing that had happened to her years ago, not to entertain fantasies about chatting with her about poetry and music and life in general over a glass of wine. He needed to break the spell.

She cocked her head. 'Do you ask all your victims questions like this?'

'Everyone's different. I don't have a set list. I do have a few things I want to know, then I let the conversation flow from the answers. That's often when I find out the most interesting stuff. Besides, it's not often that both suspect and victim are celebrities.'

'I wasn't a celebrity. I was a fourteen-year-old girl with a head full of dreams of a glamorous life, like being a rock star or an actress. And if you think being a poet is a celebrity leading a glamorous life, then you know something I don't. And I don't want to be thought of as a victim, either. If you're wondering if what happened inhibited me, blighted my life, then the answer's no, it didn't. That's why I feel like a phoney. In small ways maybe it did. For a few months, maybe even a year, certainly, I was a mess, like I said, no doubt about that.

But it was a long time ago. Sex, for a while, you know, that was out of the question. It was difficult to relax. I was afraid of the dark. I'd flash on *his* face, on top of me, his smell. *Their* faces. I didn't . . .' She broke the mood with laughter and turned to Winsome. 'I always thought the sexual revolution was invented by men to get their own way.'

'You might not be far wrong about that,' Banks said. 'Winsome here wasn't even born then.'

'Winsome? That's a lovely name.'

'Thank you,' said Winsome.

Linda gazed down her gently sloping garden towards the river. 'Everything came all right eventually, in my twenties. I think I managed to compartmentalise things, draw a veil over the experience. I knew it was there, and it infiltrated my dreams sometimes, but I could control it most of the time, if that makes any sense. As far as missing the sexual revolution was concerned, all I'd really missed was a dose of clap, crabs, premature ejaculations and probably an unwanted pregnancy. I'm sorry. I don't mean to shock you. I shouldn't say things like that, of course, but it seemed that was all so many of my girlfriends had to talk about when we were students. I suppose all I had to do was meet the right man. Charles. We married in my late twenties, had children. I started a career in teaching, always writing in whatever spare time I had. Poetry. Spent a few years teaching at a Canadian university in my forties. Creative writing.' She looked around at the garden. 'We came back and settled here, then Charles became ill. I have to say, though, on the whole, that it's been a happy and productive life so far. Fulfilled in so many ways. I count myself lucky.'

'Except for an encounter with Danny Caxton.'

Her expression darkened for a moment. 'Except for him, yes. And it makes me feel terrible that he did the same thing to others. That he got away with it for so long. But I never thought of it like that until I heard about Jimmy Savile. In an odd way, it was that day in Blackpool that brought me to poetry, though. I mean, I'd been interested at school, but about a year or so later, when I came out of the deep despair, I picked up this book of poems. I don't remember where. I don't even know what made me pick it up. It was by Sylvia Plath. *Ariel.* Do you know it?'

'No,' said Banks. 'I mean, I've heard the name, even seen her grave at Heptonstall, but I haven't read the poems.'

'I won't say I understood them, but they sent my head in a spin. Direct hit. Blew me away. Shivers up the spine, the whole deal. The violent imagery, the anger, the dark fire of her imagination, that fingers-on-the-blackboard feeling. It went right to my soul, if that's not too melodramatic a way of putting it. I went right out and bought everything she'd written. As soon as I read her I knew I wanted to be a poet. Soon I was writing poems, myself. Imitating Sylvia Plath, of course. Then I branched out, read others, the Beats, the Liverpool poets, the Russians, Hughes, Heaney, Harrison, Larkin, Hill. And I'm sure I imitated them all. Except Hill. You can't imitate him.'

'You didn't dismiss Ted Hughes as a misogynistic swine?'

'Because of what happened with Sylvia? You *do* know a bit about poetry, don't you? Or at least about poets. Quite the Adam Dalgliesh.'

'I'm afraid I don't write it.' Banks didn't tell her that he had also read some Tony Harrison after a dying coal miner had mentioned him in conversation a year or two back. Enjoyed the poems, too. Harrison seemed to put his finger on how certain things, especially education, can cut you off from your roots. Banks felt that, especially as his father had never approved of his becoming a policeman, and he was sure that Linda understood it also, coming from a working-class background and ending up being a famous poet. All her old friends would be nervous around her now, thinking she had somehow transformed herself into an exotic and remote creature. Weird, indeed.

'Ah, well. Who needs the competition? No. I think Ted Hughes was a brilliant poet. As far as life skills went, they both sucked.' She put her hand to her mouth. 'Sorry, is that on the recorder?'

Winsome smiled. 'Never mind. I don't think anyone's going to take issue with your opinion about Ted Hughes and Sylvia Plath.'

Linda clapped her hands. 'Well thank heaven for that. More orange juice?'

Banks and Winsome exchanged glances. 'No, I don't think so,' Banks said, standing up. He almost felt like telling her it had been a pleasure talking to her, but he remembered what they were there for. 'I appreciate your cooperation,' he said. 'I'm sure we'll want to talk to you again and ask some more questions, if that's all right?'

'You'll come again?'

'Yes.'

'That's good.'

'And if you remember anything in the meantime, however unimportant it seems, call me. It might be a good idea to . . . never mind.'

'No, go on. What? I'm intrigued.'

'It's a lot to ask,' Banks said, 'but sometimes with such old memories, it helps to work at them a bit, make an effort, perhaps write things down as they come, if they come. I mean, you're a writer after all. But it could be painful.'

'No,' said Linda, giving him a curious, probing look. 'A journal. A memoir. It's a good idea. I'll try. I promise.'

She stood up and saw them out. As they walked back up the garden path, Winsome turned to Banks and said, 'Well, she certainly wasn't what I was expecting. What do you think? I believed her.'

'Me, too,' said Banks. 'I think we're in with a chance on this one. I think we might just nail the bastard, especially if her memory gets jogged a bit by writing about it. We could do with finding out that other man's identity, though. Let's get back to the station and prep a few questions for Mr Caxton tomorrow, then I think we can head out early tonight. We've got a lot of homework to do before our trip to the seaside tomorrow.'

3

When the two detectives had gone, Linda Palmer breathed a deep sigh and refilled her glass with orange juice. It hadn't been as terrible an ordeal as she had worried it would be, but she still felt shaken and wrung out. She had felt again while talking to them how terrified she had been all those years ago when she went to the police station in Leeds with her mother. It had taken a great deal of her inner reserves to appear as calm and relaxed about the whole thing as she had done today, shaking inside the whole time.

She wondered if she had seemed too detached to the detectives, too unemotional. Perhaps they hadn't believed her. Weren't victims supposed to behave differently? Cry, perhaps, or tremble with fear at their recollections? She worried that she may have been too flippant, too devil-may-care, laughed too often. She had wanted them to know that what had happened hadn't ruined her life – that was important to her – though it had caused her a great deal of pain and suffering. She hoped she hadn't gone too far in the direction of nonchalance to make them suspicious of her story. She hadn't told them everything, of course, not all the myriad details that were etched somewhere in her memory and would, she knew, remain there for ever, along with the buried feelings that accompanied them. Though they weren't easily accessible, the memories and feelings were still there, locked in the box she had put them in to retain her sanity in the months after the events of that summer's day in Blackpool.

She drank some juice then felt in her jeans pocket for the packet of Marlboro Lights and disposable lighter. She didn't smoke much, but she needed one now, despite the wonderful sweet-scented summer air. Go on, she told herself, pollute it. Make the birds cough on your second-hand smoke. Give the blue tits cancer.

Well, it was done now, set in motion, and things would be what they would be. Her life would never be the same, whatever the outcome. She wondered about the other women – she couldn't bring herself to think of them as victims, though no doubt they were – and what they had gone through, what they remembered, what they were like now, how their lives had turned out. Perhaps it would have to be enough simply to know that they existed out there somewhere. There would be no collusion, of course. There would be no girly sessions in the pub. So what did he do to you, then, love? Nasty. You know he did exactly the same thing to me, and it hurt like hell. Was it your first time, too? The media would keep identities strictly secret, though how they could do that in these days of phone-hacking and a self-righteously obtrusive press she had no idea.

She didn't even think she would mind all that much if people did know what she had been through, that she was one of the complainants against Danny Caxton. What if they did find out? What was the worst that could happen? The whole country would know that she, Linda Palmer, award-winning poet, was a victim of rape. Maybe it wasn't such a bad idea. At least she had a certain standing in the community, a respected voice, unlike those poor girls who were groomed in the inner-city areas and used as sex objects. Nobody listened to them; they were simply written off as drugged-up slags and sluts who deserved what they got.

Linda closed her eyes, listened to the water and felt the shadows of the leaves dancing on her eyelids. The river was a constant presence in her life, it seemed. She drew in a lung-ful of smoke and leaned back in her chair, which wobbled as she did so, stretching out her legs and opening her eyes again. Persy lay where she had settled, sleeping in the sun. Soon she would have to move, as her patch would fall into shadow. The kingfisher had appeared on his branch, still and watchful. As usual, when she saw him fly in the late sun, she thought of Gerard Manley Hopkins' poem: 'As Kingfishers Catch Fire'.

As Linda exhaled the smoke, she saw it in her mind as if it were the smoke coming from the funnel of a steam train. She could almost hear the rhythm, wheels clacking over the joins in the track, feel the gentle swaying of the carriage and creak-ing of old woodwork, the rattling of the doors. It was the summer of 1967, and they were going on their annual holiday. Two glorious weeks in Blackpool. Linda, her mum and dad, and for the first time her best friend Melanie, along with her mum and dad, too.

But was it a steam train that year? Hadn't they stopped running by then? When did the diesels take over? Memory. Memory. She was sure it was a steam train, and they had a compartment to themselves, all six of them. She could remem-ber seeing the smoke drift by the partially open window, remember its acrid smell. She could see the dark engine ahead when it turned a long curve, chugging and puffing along, carrying them towards . . .

Linda sat up and stubbed out her cigarette, startled by the power of her memory. She hadn't let herself remember that holiday for many years, but talking about it to the detectives today, thinking about it after she had read the news item about the latest celebrity jailed for abusing girls years ago, then thinking about it again after her father's death, had brought it back to the front of her mind from the dark box to which she had consigned it. Whether she wanted it to or not, the box was opening, and perhaps, just perhaps, she was strong enough now to face its contents. She thought about what Banks had said about writing things down. Writing was her business, after all. Perhaps it was time.

She had kept a diary back then, she remembered. Every year her Aunt Barbara bought her a Letts Schoolgirl Diary for Christmas. It had a thin pencil that slipped down the spine, a page for each week and all sorts of information about world capitals, flags, holidays, time zones and units of currency. There wasn't a lot of room for writing, though it more than sufficed for most days, and she had made her carefully concise entries scrupulously every day, no matter whether or not she did anything interesting. The diaries were all gone now, of course, dumped in one of the many clear-outs she had experienced over the years. What would she have written on the nineteenth of August, 1967? she wondered. 'Got raped. Not very nice.' Oh stop being such a wag, Linda, she told herself. Get on with it.

Still she faltered, half unwilling to plunge herself into the darkness that surely awaited her inside the flimsy box she had constructed to hold her memories of those days, but she was already doing that, anyway, by talking to the police, wasn't she? No doubt she would have to testify in court, too. When she thought of the burden of all that, of the jury's eyes on her, the Sphinx-like judge with his hooded eyes – for it would surely be a man – the hawkish defence lawyer, cynical and aggressive in his attack, making it sound as if everything she said was a lie, like they were on television, she felt suffocated, and a sense of panic engulfed her. On the other hand, maybe all this was a way, not so much of exorcising the past, but of somehow domesticating it, transforming it, making it a part of herself rather than something separate, to be shut away in a box in the dark. She knew that despite all the analysis and self-probing she had subjected herself to over the years, she hadn't succeeded in integrating herself with her experience. Whatever else a memoir might turn out to be, it would certainly be a leap into the unknown.

Persy rolled over and found the sun again. Linda picked up her notebook and pen and began to write. Let it be a steam train, then, she thought. The kingfisher sat on its branch across the river and continued searching for fish.

Annie experienced a sense of déjà vu as Gerry drove down the rough track to the farmhouse, though the weather was different from her last visit to a farm, when she was making inquiries about a stolen tractor. Back then, the freezing rain had lashed down on her, the ground had been a mass of churned-up mud and dung. Today the sky was blue, the sun beat down and a sleepy sort of torpor imbued the air. Even the farmyard smells were aromatic. Almost. From where she stood, Annie could see clearly the line of trees along the road from which she had just come.

It was a youngish man who opened the door. Early thirties, Annie guessed, his hairline already receding but otherwise trim and fit, with that weathered skin and healthy sort of glow that came from working outdoors.

'Can I help you?' he asked.

Annie and Gerry flashed their warrant cards, and a frown darkened his forehead. 'But what could you possibly . . .?'

'Mind if we come in for a minute, sir?' Annie asked.

'Oh, no, of course not. Sorry, I'm just . . . er . . . yes, please, come in.'

They followed him into a bright, airy living room. All the windows were open and a gentle cross-breeze helped cool the place. It also carried in the whiff of the farmyard smells. A woman sat on the sofa, and when she stood to greet them, Annie could see that she was very pregnant.

'Sit down, please,' Annie said. 'Sorry to bother you. We won't disturb you for long.'

'But what is it?' the woman asked, slowly subsiding back on to the sofa. 'I'm Mandy, by the way. Mandy Ketteridge. My husband Toby. Please sit down.'

'I'm DI Annie Cabbot, and this is my colleague DC Gerry Masterson. There's nothing to worry about. Just a few routine questions.' They sat in the flower-patterned armchairs opposite the matching sofa.

Toby sat beside his wife and took her hand in his. 'Isn't that what you always say when you mean business?' he said. 'That it's just routine?'

'You've been watching too much TV, sir.'

'Probably.' Toby looked lovingly at his wife. 'As you can see, we don't get out much these days.'

'How long?' Annie asked Mandy.

'Eight and a half months.'

'Is it your first?'

Mandy nodded. 'Have you . . .?'

'No,' said Annie. 'Never met the right fella.'

Toby squeezed his wife's hand. 'Mandy's getting a little nervous, though the doctor assures her that everything is fine.'

I don't bloody blame her, Annie thought. If it were me, I'd be scared stiff. 'I'm sure it is,' she said. She glanced at Gerry, who already had her notebook and pen out, and guessed that motherhood was probably the furthest thing from her mind at this stage of her career. Toby and Mandy were watching them both apprehensively.

'It's nothing to be worried about. Honestly,' said Annie. 'Our visit, I mean.'

'Well, it's not every day we have the police here,' said Toby.

'I should imagine not. You own the field that stretches up to Bradham Lane, don't you?'

'That's right.'

'There's a section of the wall topped with barbed wire. How long has it been like that?'

'About two years.'

'Any reason?'

'To stop people getting in.'

'You were having problems?'

'No,' said Toby. 'Not us, specifically. But Glen on the other side said he'd caught some lads trying to make off with several of his sheep one night. Passing them over the wall where they had a van waiting. We heard so much about rural crime and being vigilant and all, we thought that was the best solution. Why? Is it illegal?'

'No. Nothing like that,' said Annie. 'There were a few strands of barbed wire in the ditch. Know anything about that?'

'If someone got hurt,' said Mandy, 'we're really sorry. The workmen who put the fence up must have left it there. To be honest, neither of us has been out there for ages. And who'd want to go in the ditch?'

Annie glanced at Gerry. 'No one,' she said. 'Not willingly, at any rate.'

Mandy put her hand to her mouth. 'Has something terrible happened? Has someone drowned or something?'

She certainly was jumpy, Annie thought, perhaps afraid she might have the baby right on the spot. Eight and a half months was a bit close for comfort, and she did look fit to burst. 'It's nothing like that,' she said, thinking it was something far, far worse. And Mandy Ketteridge would hear about it soon enough. Perhaps better now she was primed rather than later. 'Someone was found dead there. By the roadside. A girl. We think she was murdered.'

Toby squeezed his wife's hand again. 'Oh, my God,' said Mandy, sounding oddly calmer now that it was out. 'But . . . I mean . . . what has it to do with us?'

Annie gave her best smile. 'Nothing, I hope.'

'I'm afraid we can't tell you anything,' Toby said.

'I'm not really suggesting you had anything to do with what happened,' Annie explained. 'It's just that this is the nearest farmhouse to the scene and we wondered if either of you might have seen or heard anything.'

'A murder? Near our house?' Mandy sounded incredulous.

'Yes. Is there anything you can tell us?'

'When did it happen?' Mandy asked.

'We don't know for certain, but we think during last night, or early morning. Say between one and three. Were you at home then?'

'Yes,' said Mandy. 'Both of us. With me being so close to my time, Toby doesn't like to leave me alone. Especially at night.'

'We're usually in bed before eleven,' said Toby. 'We watch the ten o'clock news then lock up and head for bed. Sometimes Mandy's there already, this past while, reading. Or munching on a tuna and banana sandwich.'

'Liar,' said Mandy, nudging him gently. 'I do not. Well, maybe just the once.'

'And during the night?' Annie went on.

A shadow crossed Mandy's face, the flicker of a memory. 'It was a warm night,' she said. 'Humid. Hardly a breath of air. We don't have a fan, so we leave the bedroom windows open. It helps a bit. And I've not been sleeping very well.' She gave a thin smile and patted her belly. 'As you can imagine.'

'Did you hear something last night?'

'Mmm. It would have been about two o'clock, give or take

a few minutes. I was lying awake. I wanted to go to the toilet, but I was so comfortable and . . . well . . . the baby was quiet. I wasn't in the least bit sleepy, but I was trying to put off getting up, you know how you do.'

'What happened?'

'Well, it was all very sudden, but I thought I heard a car and some loud music. The music got even louder for a few moments, and I heard a car door slamming, then it all faded into the distance.'

'Could you tell what direction it was travelling in?'

She thought for a moment. 'I couldn't swear to it, but I think it was going south, coming from up Eastvale way. At least, I seem to sort of vaguely remember the sound travelling in that direction, if you know what I mean. But I can't be certain. I wasn't really paying attention.'

'Can you describe what you heard in any more detail?'

'As I said, the music was quite loud at first, even when the door wasn't open, like you get in the city sometimes.' She squeezed her husband's hand. 'Toby always says they must have their stereo speakers on the outside.'

'But sound carries well out here?'

'Oh, yes. Especially with the windows open. It's so quiet and flat between here and the road, and that's the direction the bedroom faces.'

'Did the car go by quickly?'

'That's just the thing. I mean, I could hear the engine, you know, first in the distance, then getting closer. Then I could see the light from the headlamps over the field, and I realised it must be going down the lane, which seemed odd, especially at that time of night, some kids playing loud music.'

'You were watching by then?'

'I was sitting on the edge of the bed. It was just the glow from the lights I could see, not the actual headlamps themselves, and – yes, of course. It must have been travelling south. That was the direction the lights were moving. Silly me. I'd forgotten.'

'You thought it was kids?'

'Well . . . that's who does it, isn't it? I don't mean to sound prejudiced or anything, I don't even really mind that much, but it's usually kids who drive around with loud music playing.'

Annie thought of Banks. He liked it loud sometimes. 'You mean like rap music, hip hop?'

'No, no. Nothing like that. That was the strange thing. That's what you'd expect.' She smiled. 'But it wasn't like that at all. It was that song I'd heard on the radio a year or two ago. I remember it because I liked it. It was on all the time. The two Swedish girls.'

'First Aid Kit?' Gerry suggested.

'That's right. "My Silver Lining". It just seemed odd that someone would be playing that song so loud in the middle of the night. I could hear it clearly because when the car slowed down . . .'

'Slowed down?' said Annie.

'Yes. I distinctly heard it slow down. The engine changed sound, and that's when I could hear the music even louder for a while as if . . .'

'As if what?'

'As if someone opened the door or something, just for a moment. Which they must have done because it closed a few seconds later. And I thought I heard laughing and yelling or whooping, but I'm not sure about that.'

'So the car actually stopped for a while?'

'No, I don't think it stopped. At least, the engine never stopped. Just slowed down. It sounded as if it skidded a bit first. I heard the tyres squeal a bit. It must have been going fast. Maybe it idled for a few moments. I don't know. All I know is it shot off again just a few moments later, after the door slammed shut. Burning rubber, as they say. And the music went back to what it was like before.'

'How much later?' Annie asked. 'This could be important, Mandy.'

Mandy bit her lip. 'Not long. I mean, seconds, not minutes. It was very fast.'

'You seem to have a remarkable ear for details,' Annie said. 'Did you hear anything else?'

'Well, I was just lying or sitting there in the dark with the windows open. You tend to notice every little sound, don't you, every creak and animal noise. I didn't hear anything else for a while. I went to the toilet, and when I got back to bed, a short while later I heard another car. No music this time. But it was odd, two cars out there so close together in one night.'

'How much later?'

'I'm not sure. Not long. About ten or fifteen minutes after the first one.'

'Again, this could be important, Mandy. Think carefully. Was it the same car as the one before? Did it sound the same? Could you tell?'

Mandy frowned in concentration. 'I don't think so,' she said finally. 'I think it sounded different. But honestly, I couldn't really tell. I'm not good at mechanical things.'

'What did the second car do?'

'It stopped.'

'Completely?'

'Yes. I couldn't even hear the engine, but I could still see the glow from the headlamps through the trees.'

'And it started up again?'

'A few minutes later.'

Bingo, thought Annie. That *was* long enough to beat the girl to death. The second van, coming from the same direction ten or fifteen minutes later, when she had managed to stagger a quarter of a mile or so back up the road after being thrown naked out of a van.

'Did you hear anything during the time it was stopped?'

'I heard a car door slam, then someone's voice. It might have been a scream and some shouting. I thought it was just someone being noisy. A drunk stopping to be sick or something, and her friend shouting at her. I'm sorry.' She put her fist to her mouth and started sobbing. Toby put his arm around her.

'You weren't to know,' Annie said. 'It's a wonder you could hear anything at all from so far away.'

'My hearing's good, as a rule. And as I said, sounds carry in the country in the dark. Mostly I just heard the car engines and the music in the distance, and the music was so loud and unusual. That's why it seemed odd . . . I . . . I'm sorry. Perhaps if I'd realised what was happening, called the police . . .'

'There was nothing you could have done,' Annie reassured her. There was no way Mandy could have heard a girl being beaten to death almost a mile away, even if she had heard the music, the car engines and the whooping. And perhaps a scream. The victim would have stopped screaming soon after the first blow and the sounds of punching and kicking would have been muffled and wouldn't have carried over the distance.

'You said "her friend" a moment ago, when you mentioned being sick. Did you hear a woman's voice?'

'I must have done, I suppose.'

'And a man's? The friend shouting at her?'

'Yes.'

'Was he angry?'

'I don't know. I could only hear sounds, not words or anything.'

'But he shouted?'

'Loud enough for me to hear. Yes.'

'Is there anything else you can tell us?'

'Well, there is one thing. The second car turned and went back the way it came. The gears made a sort of crunching sound, like when you do a three-point turn in a hurry. And again I could see the direction from the glow of the lights. That seemed odd.'

'It didn't drive on down the lane?'

'No.'

'Did you hear anything, Mr Ketteridge?'

'I was fast asleep,' said Toby. He smiled. 'Getting as much in as I can before the wee one comes along.' He patted his wife's knee and stood up. 'I think my wife should rest now, if you don't mind. You can see she's distraught.'

Annie handed him her card. 'If either of you thinks of anything else, please don't hesitate to phone. And we may need to come back for a statement. We'll be in touch.'

As they walked towards the door, Mandy looked over at them and said, 'We're not in any danger, are we? I mean, a murder so close to our home. There isn't some sort of maniac on the loose, is there? Are you sure my baby's not in any danger?'

'No,' said Annie. 'I can't think of any reason why you would be.' Outside at the car she turned to Gerry. 'I never knew you were a First Aid Kit fan.'

'Hidden depths,' said Gerry, with an enigmatic smile. 'Hidden depths.'

The bottom of the door slid easily over the few scattered bills and junk mail the postman had delivered after Banks left for work that morning. He didn't even bother bending to pick them up. They could wait.

His front door led directly into a small study where he kept his computer, a comfortable armchair, table lamp and couple of bookcases. It used to be his main living room, but that had changed after the fire, when the insurance had allowed him not only to have the gutted cottage restored, but to enlarge the kitchen, add a conservatory at the back and an entertainment room along one side. That was where he usually watched TV or DVDs, kept his audio and video equipment and entertained visitors. He had speakers rigged up all over the house, so he could listen to music in just about every room. And now there was an extra en suite bedroom upstairs for when Brian or Tracy wanted to stay.

The problem was that Banks rarely saw his children these days. Brian was either on the road with his band, the Blue Lamps, or in the recording studio, and Tracy was studying for a master's degree in Newcastle, working part-time as a research assistant to one of the profs. She also had a boyfriend, Geoff, who lived in St Andrews, and she spent most of her spare time up there with him. Still, they both phoned from time to time, and both were happy and doing fine as far as Banks knew. For a while, Banks's last girlfriend Oriana had lived with him on and off, but they had split up, amicably enough, a month ago and all vestiges of her presence were gone. Definitely off. She was a beautiful, intelligent and desirable young woman, and he missed her. But he was used to living alone, and he soon settled back into his old routines.

Banks first went upstairs to his bedroom, took off his suit and shirt and put on jeans and a T-shirt. It was another sultry evening, and back downstairs he opened the windows in the conservatory before pouring himself a large glass of Barossa's best Shiraz and raising a silent toast to Peter Lehmann, his favourite winemaker, who had died not so long ago. He felt like listening to something a bit different from the string quartets and trios he had been playing lately, so he flipped through his CDs in the entertainment room and put on Lana del Rey's *Ultraviolence*. He hadn't expected to like her after all the hype over her first album, but he'd seen a performance clip from Glastonbury and had enjoyed both the sound and the summer dress she was wearing. He took easily to the spaced-out music, the sound-wash of distant, distorted, swirling guitars and haunting background vocals of her second album, and her delivery, attitude and lyrics intrigued him. She seemed curiously disengaged yet full of disturbed and conflicting emotions and imagery, the voice both vulnerable and threatening. It was often uncomfortable listening. Anyone who dared quote the old Crystals song 'He Hit Me (And It Felt Like a Kiss)' in this day and age had a lot of nerve. And if Del Rey's version of Jessie Mae Robinson's 'The Other Woman' wasn't as powerful as Nina Simone's, it was still pretty damn good.

Naturally, the title track 'Ultraviolence' got Banks thinking about the Caxton case, as well as the unidentified victim on Bradham Lane Annie had told him about. As detective superintendent, he was head of the Homicide and Major Crimes Unit, so in addition to the Caxton investigation, he also had to keep on top of any other cases the squad was handling. He knew he could trust Annie to do a thorough job, and he had no intention of dogging her every footstep. Yes, she herself had been raped – he remembered the shock he had felt when she had first recounted the experience to him in a cosy Soho bistro – but she would use her anger to fuel her search for who had beaten the poor girl to death. And if her foot slipped and happened to connect with his wedding tackle when she found him . . . well, these things happen to the best of us. Even in this day and age. Banks would probably be too busy to be of much use to her, but he would keep an eye on the case and try to be there if she needed him.

When Banks thought about his own assignment, he realised

that he felt differently about Danny Caxton since he and Winsome had talked with Linda Palmer. It wasn't simply that he believed her story – though he did – but that he had found her honesty, strength and intelligence in talking about it had inspired him. He wanted to get Caxton, however old and famous he was. Wanted to knock that 'Big Smile' right off his face. As easy as it was to be cynical about historical abuse claims – and Banks was as guilty of that as anyone – he didn't doubt that bad things had happened back then, things that had not been investigated for a variety of reasons.

Banks wanted to find out why there had been no official investigation after Linda Palmer had reported the rape. That must have taken a lot of courage for a fourteen-year-old girl, even if her mother had pushed her into it and accompanied her to the police station. Why had nobody done anything? DCI Ken Blackstone, who worked out of the new Leeds District HQ on Elland Road, might be able to help him answer that question, and it would be good to see his old friend again. But he didn't hold out a great deal of hope. Like memories, old police files become discoloured, crumble to dust and blow away in the wind. Or someone nicks them.

Banks was also interested in the other man Linda had mentioned. If someone else had been present, someone even younger than Caxton, there was always a chance that he was still alive. Tracking him down would not only result in the apprehension of another rapist, it could also help strengthen the case against Caxton, especially if the accomplice could be made to talk. From what Linda Palmer had said, he may have been a reluctant participant, which meant that he may have been plagued with conscience over the years, something that might make him keen to get things off his chest in the hope of making some sort of deal. But how to track him down? Even the scene of the crime no longer existed.

All in all, Banks knew that he had his work cut out. Everything his team came up with would be fed into the Home Office Large Major Enquiry System (HOLMES) along with information from all the other county force investigations into allegations against Danny Caxton. If something was there about the other man, it would turn up. The days when a rapist or killer could commit a crime in one county and no other counties would know about it were all but gone since the problems with the Yorkshire Ripper investigation. It still happened occasionally, mostly due to human error, which no number of computers could ever eliminate, but even before the NCA came along, the Ripper case had taught all the county forces a huge lesson.

Banks refilled his wine glass and replaced Lana del Rey with Mark Knopfler's *Tracker*. There was a pleasant cross-breeze, but he still felt his T-shirt sticking to him. It was that time of day he loved, between sunset and dark – the gloaming, as the Anglo-Saxons called it – when the swifts had returned to their nests and the bats had yet to come out. The light seemed to possess an ethereal, ineffable quality, perhaps intensified by its transience, and Knopfler's smooth vocals and flowing melodic guitar work provided a fitting accompaniment.

It never got truly dark for long in the northern summers, and Banks had found himself adapting his routine to the cycle of the day. It meant he didn't get as much sleep, as he found it difficult to drop off while it was still light outside, so he tended to stop up later. But he rose early, and he usually stayed late at the office most evenings and ate a sandwich while he finished the day's paperwork. Once home, he'd do exactly what he was doing now, if he didn't nip down to the Dog and Gun for a quick pint and a chat with Penny Cartwright, or whoever happened to be there from the folk crowd.

He didn't have much of a back garden, and, though he

sometimes went out front and climbed over the wall to sit on the banks of Gratly Beck by the terraced falls, as often as not he spent his evenings in the conservatory. With the windows open, it was almost like being outside. There had been too few evenings spent this way since his promotion. So often he had been stuck with extra paperwork or away overnight on a course or at a conference. Where he was sitting, he could smell the sweetness of the honeysuckle clinging to its trellis, watch the shadows darken on the slopes of Tetchley Fell and the setting sun paint the sky orange and purple along the valley in the west. Times like this, he wondered how he had managed to live in Eastvale at all, let alone London. He imagined Linda Palmer sitting in her garden by the river composing poems. He wished he had that talent, or any writing ability at all. At least, he thought, he should read some of hers. And maybe also *Ariel* and *Dart*.

He had recently started working his way through an anthology of English verse he had found in the second-hand bookshop off the market square, often out in the garden with a cup of freshly brewed coffee first thing in the morning. Early encounters with Chaucer and Spenser had almost defeated him, but he had skipped them, along with a number of other unintelligible contemporaries, and moved on. The old ballads presented him with no problems. He already knew most of them from recordings by Martin Carthy, June Tabor and others. He also knew some of Thomas Campion's songs from Emma Kirkby and Iestyn Davies recordings. Next he breezed through the selection of Shakespeare's sonnets, then Tichborne's 'Elegy' moved him almost to tears. Now he was feeling a bit bogged down in Pope and Dryden, who probably thought they were wittier than they really were, but he was certain there were more delights to come. Not knowing what was coming next was part of the fun.

It was well after dark and the bats were flitting all over the back garden. Mark Knopfler had finished a while ago. Wearily, Banks put his empty wine glass in the sink and went up to bed. It was no insult to the beauty of the music that he fell asleep with his earbuds in listening to John Tavener's *Lament for Jerusalem*.

4

'Have you ever been to one of these before?' Annie asked Gerry as they clicked along the corridor to the post-mortem suite, footsteps echoing from the high ceiling and green-tiled walls. The antiseptic smell made Annie feel vaguely nauseated.

'No,' said Gerry.

'A lot of firsts these days. Nervous?'

'A bit. I don't want to make a fool of myself.'

Annie flashed on the time, not so long ago, when she got out of a helicopter feeling airsick and went straight to the scene where half a body had burst out of a bin liner. The left half. As if the victim had been neatly sliced in half from top to bottom with a chainsaw. She had been sick. 'You won't,' she said. 'Besides, it's nothing to be ashamed of. Even Alan gets a bit green around the gills when he has to attend one of these. It's like a murder scene. You never get used to it, but you learn to cope. I suppose the advantage with this sort of thing is it's all scientific. Sterile. Clinical. Not like finding a girl's naked body dumped by the roadside.' Or the left half of a body spilling from the plastic bag on the windswept valley bottom. She turned to Gerry, taking something from her briefcase. 'Here, put a dab of this under your nose. It's Vicks. It really does help a bit. The smell in there's the worst.'

'Thanks.' Gerry dabbed the mentholated goo on her upper lip. 'It reminds of me of when I was a child and my mother would rub it on my chest just before bed when I had a cold.'

'Exactly,' said Annie, applying a dab to herself. 'Dr Glendenning will tease you about it if he smells it. He can be a bit of a jerk – he's old school – so just ignore him. OK? Ready?'

Gerry nodded and they opened the swing doors and entered the room where Dr Glendenning and his chief anatomical pathology technologist Karen Galsworthy already had the body waiting on the slab. Dr Glendenning glanced over at them. 'Nice of you to join us, ladies. Why don't you get yourselves kitted up.' Then he sniffed theatrically. 'Someone got a chest cold, have they?'

Annie gave him a dirty look.

They were two minutes early, but Annie was well aware that Dr Glendenning treated everyone who entered his domain as a latecomer. Of course, as he occasionally joked when challenged, most visitors *were* late. They put on their disposable overalls and hairnets, adding plastic goggles and mouth masks. There was always a chance that the body was infected with some communicable disease, or that bits of bone and flesh would spray up when Dr Glendenning or Karen Galsworthy used the electric saw. You didn't want a bone fragment in your eye. She hadn't told Gerry that, of course.

The walls were covered with dazzling white tiles, which made the dirty body on the stainless-steel table seem all the more out of place. Rigor mortis had passed completely now, and the girl lay on her back, arms at her sides. Now that she could see the girl's face Annie noticed that she had been very pretty even with the bruising, as well as young.

A bulky microphone dangled above the table, and cameras fixed on the walls filmed the procedure from a variety of angles. The surface of the body had already been examined microscopically for any trace evidence, samples taken, and Karen Galsworthy was busy washing it down when they went in. She seemed to be working gently, Annie thought, sadly and respectfully, as a funeral home worker might prepare a body for burial.

The odontologist had been and taken dental impressions, which might help them identify the girl. All he had said, according to Dr Glendenning, was that there was nothing unusual about the dental work. It looked very much, the doctor went on, as if the fist blows came first, knocking her to the ground and stunning her, then a flurry of hard kicks to the head, back, buttocks and chest while she was lying curled in the foetal position. And he was adamant that it had not been a hit and run.

The water sluiced off the mud and filthy water that had dried on the victim's skin and sent it running into the gutters on either side of the table, then away down the drain. It couldn't go into the general sewage pipes, Annie knew, in case of blood contaminants and other nasty things, so the resultant mess went into tanks where it had to be specially treated later before it was carefully disposed of.

When Karen had finished, Annie could see that the victim was slim with small, high breasts and long, shapely legs. She was of average height, and everything was in proportion. Her blond hair was parted on the left and fell over her ears and as far as the nape of her neck, showing dark brown roots and two pink streaks.

As always, Dr Glendenning's first task after the body had been undressed – not necessary today – and examined for trace evidence was to carry out a careful examination of the surface. The removal of the dried mud and scum might have revealed identifying marks or injuries that hadn't been noticed before. This case was no exception. Dr Burns had estimated time of death at the scene between one and three in the morning. Dr Glendenning didn't disagree or put forward a shorter time period. He pointed out the dark bruise-like stripe down her left side, interrupted where her hip and shoulder had touched the ground, and the bruising around the broken right hip. 'Post-mortem lividity indicates she died in the position she was found – on her left side, curled up – and that the body wasn't moved,' he said. 'There are signs of a bit of scavenger activity – it was a warm night – but not too much. I've seen the crime-scene photos, and she was still in the foetal position when she was brought in here last night, so in my opinion Dr Burns is right, and she was protecting herself from a rain of blows. Or trying to.' He pointed to cuts on her hips and upper thighs. 'And I've matched these with the samples of barbed wire and broken glass recovered from the scene.'

Despite the extensive recording equipment, Gerry busied herself taking notes. Annie suspected she was doing it partly to take her mind off what was happening, distancing herself, becoming a fly on the wall. It seemed to be working, as she showed no obvious reaction to anything Karen or Dr Glendenning said or did.

'And I'd like to add,' Dr Glendenning went on, 'that I also agree about cause of death. We've sent blood samples to toxicology, of course, and we'll be sending stomach contents and anything else we can find once we've got her opened up. I imagine we'll find a nasty mess inside, but it's my opinion that the blows – kicks, judging by the patterns – were the direct cause of death. The girl was severely beaten. Severely. I've not seen such a vicious attack in a long time. The damage to the head alone could have caused death, but it also appears that several of her ribs were broken, and one of them could easily have pierced her heart or lung.'

'Footwear patterns?' Annie asked. 'From the shoes or boots.'

'A definite possibility,' Dr Glendenning granted. 'But don't hold your breath. Such impressions would be vague and hardly likely to ensure a conviction. Unless there are unique elements, of course.'

'Hate crime?' suggested Annie.

'Someone certainly hated her.'

'Or hated women,' said Karen.

'Whether that was the actual motive,' Dr Glendenning went on, 'I can't honestly say.'

Annie knew that Dr Glendenning wouldn't be drawn on motive. In her experience, the presence of such a high degree of violence was linked to hate crimes or crimes involving partners. 'You always hurt the one you love' was a lot truer than the songwriters could have guessed. Such overkill could also be linked to crimes in which someone had been taught a lesson. Excessive violence served as an example and a warning to others and was common in gang-related crimes. It was unlikely, in Annie's experience, that the girl had been killed by a passing stranger, unless they were dealing with a violent psychopath, and such creatures were thankfully rare. An artist's impression of the girl without facial injuries would be appearing in the newspapers and on TV soon. Once they knew who she was, they could start questioning her family, friends and acquaintances, and Annie was willing to bet it wouldn't take long to find out who had done this. But they had to identify her first.

Dr Glendenning finished examining the girl's fingernails. 'She bit them to the quicks,' he said. 'Not a trace of anything.'

'How old would you say she was?' Annie asked.

'Fifteen or sixteen,' Karen answered. 'We can perform some more scientific checks later – testing the carbon levels in her eyes, for example – but going by height, shape, skin, bone structure and general appearance, I'd be surprised if she were older than sixteen.'

'And Karen is *very* good with ages,' said Dr Glendenning. 'If I believed in it, I'd say she has a sixth sense for such things.' Dr Glendenning went on to examine the surface of the skin, where the girl, it was now clear to see, had several tattoos, including a butterfly on the top of her left breast and a heart above her shaved pubic area. She also had a birthmark on the inside of her right thigh. Gerry made sketches and noted the locations, as they would help in identification. He lifted up her left hand to show them the white criss-cross marks on her wrist.

'Scars,' he said. 'Self-harm, by the looks of it. Perhaps a suicide attempt. More likely a cry for help. She'd never succeed doing it that way. You need to cut along the vein, not across it.'

'Thanks for that advice,' said Annie. 'I'll remember it. Any idea how old?'

'The slash marks?' Dr Glendenning studied them more closely. 'Hard to say. Not recent, though.'

When Dr Glendenning turned the body over to examine the back, they discovered that she also had a tattoo shaped like a whale's tail, the kind one often saw on girls wearing low-rise jeans and midriff-baring tops. Her back was covered in dark bruises and Annie imagined she could even see where ribs had been broken. Without the dirt and dried mud, the parts that weren't bruised looked so pale.

'No needle marks as far I can see,' said Dr Glendenning. 'And I think we would be able to see them now if she had them.'

Gerry wobbled a bit when Dr Glendenning and Karen began their examination of the girl's private parts, but she managed to hold on. Finally Dr Glendenning put down his speculum and moved away. 'There's evidence of serious sexual abuse,' he said. 'Both vaginal and anal. Also of recent sexual activity. It appears the abuser didn't wear a condom. Karen's taking swabs, and we'll get them analysed for traces of DNA as soon as possible. The poor girl wasn't in the water for very long, it seems, which is fortunate for us.'

'We think she was still conscious then,' Annie said. 'She managed to drag herself out as soon as she landed and stagger some distance.'

When they had finished with their examinations of the exterior and private parts, Karen placed the body block, a rubber brick, the kind Annie remembered diving for at the bottom of the pool for her life-saving bronze medal, under the girl's back, to raise the front of her body for internal examination, and Dr Glendenning picked up his scalpel to begin the Y incision.

Annie glanced at Gerry, who had turned a bit pale, but was still holding her own. When the front of the body was open, exposing the glistening inner organs, the smell got worse, despite the Vicks, and Dr Glendenning and Karen exchanged serious expressions before going on. Even at a cursory glance, Annie could tell that things were not right inside. Not right at all.

When Banks and Winsome arrived at the gates of Xanadu, Danny Caxton's palatial spread on a promontory between Whitby and Redcar, it was the early afternoon of another beautiful summer's day. Banks had spent most of the morning setting up the mechanics of the investigation, trying to make sure he overlooked nothing. He had also arranged for checks into Caxton's connection with any hospitals, care homes, schools and charities – anywhere he might have been likely to find vulnerable victims and people with a vested interest in keeping things quiet. The TV companies he had worked with also had to be fully investigated, including everyone who had worked with him on *Do Your Own Thing!* and as many of the young performers and invited audience members as possible. It wasn't exactly *Top of the Pops* but Banks imagined it would have provided plenty of opportunities for indulgence on Caxton's part. Preliminary checks had shown that he had always stayed at the same hotel in London when he was down there for recording. It was an out-of-the-way place, not especially convenient for the TV studios, and not exactly up to the level of luxury one might have expected for a man as wealthy as Caxton. These were all keys to finding more complainants: places, networks, groups, routes, access.

When witnesses or accusers were found, their testimony had to be validated. Dates, times, places and so on all had to be checked, photographic records uncovered if they existed. At the time, Caxton had been 'untouchable' and that feeling could have made him careless, led him to make mistakes. Priorities for Banks after Caxton and his ex-wife were finding the 'witness' and trying to discover what had happened to the original investigation, or lack of one. When he got going on all that, he knew, leads would start popping up all over the place, many of them red herrings, all needing to be thoroughly checked out. He could only interview the major players with Winsome; he would have to leave the rest to the team he had been allotted.

Burgess had phoned to share the news that some of the other cases against Caxton were strong enough, though no one else recollected a witness, or a second participant, the way Linda Palmer had. The earliest complainant to come forward so far was a seventy-year-old woman from 1962, and the most recent in her early forties, from 1988. According to Burgess, their accounts matched that of Linda Palmer in terms of the suddenness and brutality of his attacks, though both were roughly fondled, not actually raped. Like Hobbes's view of life itself, Caxton's attacks on women were nasty, brutish and short. He struck swiftly as a rattlesnake, and swift as a snake's bite, it was over. Though Banks was willing to bet it didn't seem that way to the victims; it certainly hadn't to Linda Palmer.

The drive over the top end of the North York Moors had been spectacular, the roads far busier than usual because of the glorious weather. He had kept the music quiet – playing some acoustic Richard Thompson and a Keith Jarrett &

Charlie Haden CD – and Winsome hadn't complained. After a hurried lunch at a country inn outside Goathland, going over their preparatory notes one last time, they were ready for the interview.

Winsome had been reading up on Caxton's biography during much of the journey, and as they crested the final rise before the imposing wrought-iron gates with a sculpted stone lion on top of each gatepost, she repeated to Banks, 'I still don't see what the point of this is, guv. It's his word against hers. He'll deny everything, if he's got any sense. Stalemate.'

'Maybe he'll slip up,' said Banks. 'Perhaps we'll rattle him. Who knows? Besides, don't you want to get a look at how he lives, the lion in its lair? At least we'll go away with some sense of the measure of the man, maybe even knowledge of a few of his weaknesses.'

'I hope so,' said Winsome. 'But why not take him into custody for questioning? He's got home advantage here. We could put him in an airless interview room, make him wait . . .'

'We don't want to make that move yet,' said Banks. 'Don't forget, there are others. Linda Palmer wasn't the only one. As Burgess said, there'll be county forces queuing up to have a chat with him before long. We're first in line. And when push comes to shove, we'll be the ones to bring him in.'

Banks announced their arrival at the intercom by the gate, and without a word from the other end, the huge heavy gates in the high walls started to rumble open. As Banks drove along the narrow drive, he could see Caxton's mansion ahead. Xanadu. Hardly a gesture towards originality in its name. Built in the style of a Palladian villa, with symmetrical wings on either side of the central portico, itself modelled on the Greek temple, it came complete with Doric columns and pilasters, all of white marble. In the rolling grounds to their right stood a Victorian folly, and a short distance from the north wing was a row of garages, most of them open. Banks could see expensive cars of all colours, makes and periods: an E-type Jag, a red Triumph MG6, an old Bentley and even a huge pink fifties Cadillac convertible with wings big enough for take-off. It was the sort of car that might have belonged to Elvis Presley. Maybe it had. Banks wondered if the Rolls that had picked up Linda Palmer nearly fifty years ago was really a Bentley. Even if it was, there wasn't any chance of trace evidence after all that time. Still, there may have been other girls in the car, more recently, and the collection was worth the thorough search that the team would be carrying out after Banks and Winsome had left. Right now they were waiting just down the road, beyond the rise.

Banks pulled up in front of the portico steps, about as imposing as the ones in *Rocky*, and he and Winsome began to climb, more than half expecting a butler in full livery to answer the door at their ring.

The slight, dapper man with a silk handkerchief protruding from the top pocket of his jacket *could* have been a butler, but Banks doubted it. For a start, his suit cost more than Banks's annual clothes allowance, more than his annual salary, in fact, if you included the gold cufflinks and matching tiepin that held down an old-school tie of some important sort. He had a few strands of wispy grey hair on his head and a thin grey moustache. He didn't smile or reach out his hand to shake, just said, 'Good afternoon. My name is Bernard Feldman. I'm Mr Caxton's solicitor.'

'That was quick,' said Banks.

'Word gets around.'

'So I gather. Can we come in?'

Without replying, Feldman turned and started walking away from them. Banks and Winsome exchanged glances then started to follow him across the parquet floor of a foyer almost as big as a football field. The hall was dotted with

Greek columns here and there, like something from a Cecil B. DeMille film set, and large reproductions of classical scenes in ornate gilded frames hung on the damasked walls. Banks couldn't resist a quick detour to study them. Each had a brass plate under its frame, like in an art gallery, and he saw *Leda and the Swan* and the *Rape of the Daughters of Leucippus* by Rubens, two of Titian's *Danaë* series and Tiepolo's *Apollo and Daphne*. Certainly a theme there, he thought: naked women struggling in the grip of men. Not just tales from Greek mythology.

'Mr Banks?'

Feldman had stopped to call him on. Banks walked over. 'Just looking,' he said.

'They're not the originals, of course.'

'I think some of the world's major art galleries would be rather upset if they were,' Banks replied, not wishing to be thought a philistine. 'Who painted them?'

'A friend of Danny's. I can't remember his name. They're quite valuable, for copies, apparently. I know nothing about art.'

'Whoever it is, he'd make a good living as a forger,' Banks said, gesturing back towards the paintings. In reality, he probably was. But it wasn't forgery as long as you didn't try to pass them off as genuine.

Feldman carried on walking, Banks and Winsome dutifully in tow. About ten minutes later, or so it seemed, they found themselves in an enormous glassed-in conservatory, like a section of a botanical garden or an expensive hotel restaurant. It stood before a full-size croquet lawn, which, in turn, overlooked the North Sea, sparkling today and matching the sky for blue, whitecaps dashing for the shore, which was hidden from their view at the bottom of the cliff. A few sailboats listed further out, catching the sea breeze. In the centre of the croquet lawn was a swimming pool. Tempting today, but not much use most of the time in this part of the world, Banks thought, which was probably why Caxton had an indoor pool, too.

'Impressive,' said Banks.

Feldman led them over to a glass-topped table where a man sat in a white wicker chair, bade Banks and Winsome be seated, and sent another man, who seemed to have appeared from nowhere – the real butler, maybe – off to bring tea and iced water. Only when all that was done did he introduce Banks and Winsome to Danny Caxton, who neither stood nor offered to shake hands.

'Get to the point, then.' Caxton's voice was raspy, but strong and clear enough to make him still a presence to be reckoned with. 'I'd like to get this silly business over and done with. The sooner the better.'

'Us, too,' said Banks.

For a moment, Banks felt his resolve falter, then he couldn't help but notice how Caxton's gaze lingered on Winsome's breasts and slid lasciviously down over her thighs and legs. Despite the drooping shoulders, general emaciation, scrawny wattles, wrinkles and obvious signs of wear and tear, he appeared relatively spry for an eighty-five-year-old. The years had taken their greatest toll on his face, Banks thought. Once a handsome man, with what Banks's father had scathingly referred to as matinee-idol looks, he was now more an example of Dorian Gray in reverse. Somewhere, perhaps, hidden away in an attic, was a painting of that handsome young man, but here was the lined and jowled reality, ravaged and wrinkled with the sins of the years. He was like an ageing bird of prey without its plumage.

No matter how much wealth Caxton had accumulated, he clearly hadn't spent anything on plastic surgery or dental care. His teeth were like yellowing fangs hanging from pale receding gums. They gave his smile the bared-teeth quality of a wild beast. His eyes were glaucous, rheumy and milky blue, and the network of red and purple veins on and around his nose showed a predilection for the bottle. Liver spots dappled the backs of his hands. Only his hair showed professional attention. A healthy silvery-grey in colour, cut short and simply combed diagonally from a straight side parting, it contrasted nicely with his tan. It had to be expensive to look that good and that easy. He was wearing a long-sleeved shirt and tan chinos despite the heat. Through the glass table, Banks could see that his big toenails had thickened and tapered into claws, just like that bird of prey's.

'The incident we want to ask you about occurred during your summer season in Blackpool in August 1967,' Banks went on.

'Alleged incident,' corrected Feldman.

'Oh, the incident took place all right. All that's alleged is your client's part in it.'

Feldman inclined his head.

'Do you remember that season, Mr Caxton?'

Caxton made a steeple of his fingers and rested it under his chin, as if deep in thought. 'I had many a summer season at Blackpool and elsewhere,' he answered finally. 'Eventually, they all sort of blend into one. You can't expect me to remember every one of them. You'll discover when you get old, Superintendent, that your powers of recall won't be what they were.'

'I thought it was yesterday old people can't remember,' Banks said. 'Not years ago.'

Caxton gave a harsh laugh, more like a phlegmy cough. 'Often it's both.'

'Especially if you don't want to.'

'Tut-tut,' said Feldman.

'Let's say, for the sake of argument, that I was in a show in Blackpool that summer,' Caxton went on. 'I'm sure it wouldn't be too hard for you to find out. What of it?'

'Do you remember signing autographs outside the stage door after a weekend matinee?'

'That was a fairly regular occurrence. One has to keep one's public satisfied.'

Banks consulted his notebook. 'Saturday, the nineteenth of August.'

'It's possible. Like I said, I can't remember one summer from another.'

'As you said, it wouldn't be difficult to check the records, Mr Caxton,' said Banks. 'In fact, we've already done that, and you were in the line-up of that show that season, and there was an afternoon matinee that Saturday. It finished at four o'clock.'

Caxton spread his hands. 'Well, if you say so.'

Banks could sense Winsome getting restless beside him. The young man came back bearing a tray of tea and a jug of iced water, with cups and glasses.

'Bernie, would you play mother?' Caxton asked. 'I'm afraid my old joints make bending and pouring rather difficult.'

Bernie poured, breaking the silence only to ask about milk and sugar. Banks and Annie accepted iced water. It was hot in the conservatory, the sun's heat magnified by the glass. Banks hoped the antiperspirant he had applied that morning was as good as it said on the label.

'Let's get back to Blackpool 1967,' Banks said. 'That day, signing after the matinee, do you remember a young girl who expressed an interest in getting a start in show business?'

'There were always young girls around,' said Caxton, with a chuckle. 'And plenty of them thought they had what it took to get into show business. I was hosting *Do Your Own Thing!* You might remember it, Superintendent, though I imagine your charming young companion here would have been far too young. And perhaps even in another country.' He smiled at Winsome and Banks noticed that she didn't react, just jotted things down in her notebook again. Caxton shrugged. 'So what? I got a lot of interest from young people.'

'This one was fourteen.'

'They didn't have their ages stamped on their foreheads. You know as well as I do that a girl may often look and behave far more advanced than her actual years.'

'In this girl's account, you took her back to your hotel room and raped her.'

'I did what?' Caxton spluttered. 'Did I pick her up and cart her off like a Viking raider?'

'You asked her to accompany you in a chauffeur-driven car. A Bentley or a Rolls.'

'I never had time for Rolls-Royce. Far too ostentatious for my taste. It must have been the Bentley.'

'The one you have in your garage today?'

'Don't be absurd. I replace them quite often'

'You sent your assistant for her.'

'And she came willingly? With someone she didn't know? Tut-tut.'

'She didn't know what was waiting for her.'

'Superintendent Banks . . .' Feldman wagged his finger.

Caxton sighed and took a sip of tea. 'Superintendent, Sergeant, I have some idea of where you're going with this, but I have to say I have never raped anyone in my life. I've never had to. I have been blessed by knowing a multitude of beautiful, willing women of all ages, all creeds and colours.' He spoke pointedly to Winsome. 'I'd like to say shapes and sizes, but I have been far more particular about those qualities.' He gave a mock shudder. 'I can't abide obesity, and those anorexic creatures you see on the catwalks today leave me cold. I can honestly say that I've never had to beg for it, and I've never had to take it by force. And as far I can possibly know, I have never knowingly canoodled with anyone under-age or caused anyone harm.'

'Our information tells us different.'

'Then perhaps your information is wrong. It was a long time ago. It's easy to be mistaken about things. To misremember.'

'Not something like this, I shouldn't imagine. Rape. She was a virgin.'

'Aren't they all? Then why was nothing done at the time?'

'It was.'

'And?'

'Nothing came of it.'

Caxton spread his hands and grinned his wolfish grin. 'I rest my case.'

'We still have to investigate.'

'I understand. And I'll tell your superiors you did your best.'

'It's not over yet. What about those paintings in the hall?'

'What about them?'

'Classical rape scenes, for the most part. Is that something that interests you especially?'

'Oh, come, come. Surely you can't arrest a man for his taste in art? Not yet.'

'Nobody's arresting you.'

Caxton glanced at his lawyer. 'Well, that's good, because I'm beginning to get a bit bored. Bernie?'

'Would you get to the point, if there is one, Superintendent,' said Feldman. 'Mr Caxton is a busy man.'

'At his age?'

Feldman raised an eyebrow.

'Do you deny that you raped a girl on the date in question?' Banks went on.

Caxton's face reddened with anger. 'Of course I do. Do you think I don't know why all this has happened? It's that business with Jimmy, Rolf and the rest. It's brought them all out of the woodwork. I'll bet you a pound to a penny it's the newspapers after a story, or someone with a story to sell to them. They're all after money.'

'Them?'

'Tarts. Sluts. Especially the ones who weren't good-looking enough to get a fella. Haven't you noticed it's always the ugly cunts who cry rape?' As he spoke, spittle showered from his mouth but fortunately stopped short of Banks and Winsome.

'Danny, I wouldn't, if I were you,' said Feldman, tapping him rhythmically on his arm.

'Well, I'm not you.' He wagged his finger at Banks. His chair legs screeched on the floor. 'Let me tell them how things were. They have no idea. We were knee deep in willing girls. Couldn't move without bumping into one. What would you do? Only if they were willing, of course, and by God were they willing.'

Banks's resolve had returned fully by now. In fact, it was even stronger than it had been the previous evening when he had replayed his conversation with Linda Palmer. He would have to tread carefully from now on. 'And not underage?'

'Naturally they weren't. Goes without saying. It was just too easy. Sometimes I really felt sorry for those poor young lads who wasted away pining for a taste when I had so much I didn't know what to do with it. The puny boyfriends. They didn't stand a chance against real men like me.'

'Danny!' said the lawyer.

'None of them ever gave you any trouble, said no?' Banks asked.

Caxton frowned. 'Not so as I remember.'

'And your memory's that good, is it?'

'For my age.'

'What was your driver called?'

'Eh?'

'The chauffeur? What was his name?'

'I can't remember petty details like that. Mike or Steve or Frank or something. I've been through a few drivers in my time. Never did learn to drive. Whoever he was, he'll be dead by now.'

'Do you remember the Majestic Hotel?'

'Lovely old place. Gone now, I suspect?'

'Long ago. You had a sort of private entrance, if I'm not mistaken.'

'It wasn't private. They just allowed me certain privileges. We used the staff entrance and the staff lift.'

'That's the way our witness remembers it. Why?'

'Why what?'

'Why did you feel the need to smuggle her up in the staff lift? So nobody could see you?'

'Smuggle her? I never smuggled anybody in it. You make me sound like one of those people-traffickers.'

'Well, why did you use it, then?'

'There were always fans waiting in the hotel lobby. Autograph hunters and what have you. It was a celebrity hotel. A lot of us in the summer shows stayed there. The staff didn't like it, the celebrities getting mobbed and so on. It was a discreet hotel. Easier all round if we took the back way.'

'Yet she left by the front, when you'd done with her.'

'I don't know what you're talking about. If it had happened, the police would have been round fifty years ago, wouldn't they?'

'Who was the other man in the room, the one who asked the victim to get into the car? What was his name? His function?'

Caxton's expression suddenly became guarded, and a hint of anxiety crept into his tone. 'What are you talking about? There was no one else in the room.'

'Which room? When?'

'Whatever room you're talking about. Ever.'

'When you shared your prize with another man?'

'Don't be insane. Why would I share anything? Are you trying to say I'm a queer or something?'

'Are you? I don't know,' said Banks. 'I must admit, you don't seem the sharing type. But I'm afraid our witness has a clear memory of this other person. He was younger than you, apparently, so there's every chance he's still in fine fettle today. Who knows, maybe the years have worn away at him and he's ready to talk. Maybe his conscience has got the better of him. Was he there on other occasions, too? Other times with young girls? We heard he seemed rather reluctant, as if he was pushed into it. Maybe trying to impress you or something. What were you doing, Danny? Showing off. Throwing a little titbit his way. Who is he? Who were you hanging out with back then? We'll find him, Danny, don't worry about that. Then we'll have a witness. Maybe we'll even track down the chauffeur and some of the hotel employees. Some of them must have been young at the time. A bellboy, maybe. And then—'

'That's enough,' said Feldman.

Banks gestured to Winsome and they both stood up. 'For once,' Banks said, 'I find myself actually agreeing with something a lawyer says. Don't bother to show us out. We'll be seeing you again soon, Danny.'

Caxton didn't look so cocky now, Banks thought. In fact, he seemed deep in thought, and worried thought, at that. Banks felt the lawyer's eyes burning into his back as he and Winsome walked away, no doubt keeping an eye out in case they decided to steal the silverware or a painting. He thought he heard Caxton's raspy voice saying something about making some calls.

Outside at the car, Winsome leaned forward and rested her palms on the bonnet to take a deep breath.

'What is it?' Banks asked. He could see that she was shaking.

'Sorry, guv. I feel sick. That man. Who does he think he is? I feel like I've been slimed.'

Banks couldn't help but laugh at those words coming from her mouth. 'Sorry,' he said. 'I never took you for a *Ghostbusters* fan.'

Winsome gave him a lopsided smile. 'It was my dad. He had the video. Practically wore it out. Family tradition. Every Christmas. I wouldn't mind, but it's not even a Christmas movie.'

'Come on, I'll take you for a drink, and after that we'll pay a little visit to the ex Mrs Caxton in York. I'll bet she has some interesting stories to tell.'

The Unicorn wasn't one of Annie's favourite pubs, being too cramped, run-down and unfriendly for that, but it did have the advantage of being just across the road from Eastvale General Infirmary. Burned-out A & E doctors drank there when their shifts were over, and exhausted nurses dropped in for a quick bracer before heading home to face yet more domestic drudgery. It also attracted the occasional errant pupil from Eastvale Comprehensive, just down the hill, not necessarily over eighteen. As long as they kept to themselves and didn't cause any trouble, the landlord wasn't bothered, nor were the police. The Unicorn's other advantages were that, during the day, it was quiet, with no games, jukebox or yahoos, and the landlord kept a decent pint of Black Sheep. Smoking had long since been banned in pubs, but Annie could have sworn that the Unicorn still stank of stale tobacco smoke and that the gloss brown of its ceiling was the result of years of accumulated nicotine and tar.

Annie and Gerry found a table by the bay window easily enough. One of the legs was too short, so Annie folded up a beermat and stuck it underneath. Someone had carved a heart and initials into the wood. The carving had been there so long, had so many drinks spilled on it, that it had almost faded into the table. Annie wondered if 'KP' still loved 'HB.'

'You're having a double brandy, no argument,' she said to Gerry, and proceeded to drop her bag on her chair and head for the bar. 'I don't suppose you're hungry?' she asked over her shoulder. Gerry shook her head. Annie was starving, so she ordered a packet of salt and vinegar crisps along with her pint of bitter.

Back at the table, she opened the crisps and offered the packet. 'Help yourself.'

'No thanks.' Gerry's luxuriant red tresses were securely fastened back in a ponytail, which showed off her high fore-head with its intricate blue tracery of veins just below the surface, the delicate bone structure of her pale, lightly freck-led face, the green eyes.

'So how are you really?'

'I'm fine. Really.' Gerry took a sip of the drink and coughed. A hint of colour came to her cheeks.

'Not exactly VSOP, I know,' said Annie. 'But it'll do the trick.'

'Really, I'm all right. I don't need mothering.' She put the glass on the table.

'Mothering?' Annie spluttered. 'Christ, Gerry, all I'm trying to do is show a little concern, and you accuse me of mothering.'

'Sorry, I didn't mean it like that.'

'How else am I supposed to take it? I'm just about old enough to *be* your bloody mother if I'd had a teenage preg-nancy, which I didn't.'

Gerry smiled. 'I didn't mean that at all. It didn't bother me, really. The post-mortem. True, I felt a bit faint when Dr Glendenning made the first incision, but it's fascinating, really, once you get a really good look at someone's insides. I wanted to be a doctor when I was younger. I used to love *ER* and *Casualty* and *Holby City*.'

'Christ,' said Annie. 'I'm practically old enough to remember

Emergency Ward 10. I'll guarantee you that Alan does. They turn my stomach, medical dramas.'

Gerry laughed.

'And more to the point,' Annie went on, 'I'm used to things like gallbladders and lungs being in the right places.'

Gerry wrinkled her nose. 'Yes. It was a bit of a mess, wasn't it?'

'A bit of a mess? There's an understatement if ever there was one. Her spleen was where her liver was supposed to be.'

Gerry picked up her glass again and took a swallow. 'Don't,' she said.

'I thought it didn't bother you.'

'Not at the time, but thinking about it . . . There's no need to keep reliving it. I won't forget in a hurry. At least we can be thankful she wasn't pregnant.'

'I don't know. It might have pointed us towards a motive. Someone did a real job on that poor girl. Can you imagine it? Kicking her head and stomach like that? *Stamping* on her. We've got to find whoever did this. And fast.'

'What did you think of the scars on her wrist?'

'Sad to say,' said Annie, 'it's not all that unusual in young girls.'

'Suicide, or just . . . you know . . . a cry, like the doctor said?'

'Can't tell. Maybe someone even did it to her. Some sort of torture. But I'd go with the doc for now. It's not like Doc Glendenning to make wild guesses, so I'd say, given his experience, that he's seen that kind of thing before, and he knows a hawk from a handsaw. Off the cuff, I can only add that I don't think it was a really serious attempt to kill herself, or she'd probably have tried again and succeeded.'

'So how much closer are we?'

'Well,' said Annie, after a long draught of beer, 'we might not know who she is yet, or where she's from, but we've got the artist's impression, along with her stomach contents

– kebab and pizza – tattoos and a birthmark. And the doc reckons she ate about two or three hours before she was killed, which means sometime between eleven and midnight. It's not the sort of meal you'd have in a sit-down cafe, I reckon, so it's most likely takeaway.'

'The stomach contents don't help us much more than the tattoos,' said Gerry. 'It seems like every takeaway sells just about any junk food you can possibly think of in the same place these days. I know places where you can get fish and chips, tandoori, burgers, pizza, kebabs, falafels, chop suey and currywurst. All from the same fryer and oven.'

'Maybe so,' Annie said, 'but there is one thing worth considering. Places like that are far more common in urban areas than around here, say.'

'But we've got one here, in Eastvale, near where I live. Why couldn't she have started out from here?'

'She could have, I suppose,' said Annie. 'I know the place you mean. The student area, right? We'll check it out. But the spot where the body was found is only, what, fifteen minutes' drive from Eastvale. If she ate her last meal two or three hours before her death, what she was doing in Eastvale the rest of the time?'

'Partying?'

'Maybe. She didn't need to have set off immediately after the meal.'

'So she *could* have started here.'

'Yes. But no one local has been reported missing as yet. We need to extend our area. I know I'm making wild generalisations, Gerry, but I'm also trying to be logical about it. I still think kebab and pizza places are more prevalent in urban areas, so I'm thinking that if she didn't start out here, maybe she started out in the north-east, maybe Tyneside or Teesside.'

'That's a huge area,' Gerry said. 'And most of it's off our patch. Besides, if she had her last meal between eleven and midnight and was killed between two and two-thirty, it doesn't take two or three hours to drive from Teesside or Tyneside to where her body was found.'

'They could have stopped somewhere for a while or partied before they left, as you suggested earlier. And it's a smaller area to consider than the whole country. I'm just saying it's somewhere to start, Gerry. It's a massive job, but if we can get CCTV footage from the major roads in the area for before and after two a.m., we're in with a chance. We can work out the most likely routes and check all vehicles within our time period. But we also need to know who she is. Get a list of the tattoo parlours and kebab and pizza outlets in the north-east.'

'Fair enough. But maybe they started even further north and stopped somewhere en route for the food? Ate in the van.'

'Maybe,' said Annie. 'But I don't think there are a lot of kebab and pizza takeaways between Teesside and where she was found. Certainly few enough to check out quickly. Have you got a better idea?'

'No,' said Gerry. 'Sorry. I just don't know ... it's all so sketchy.'

'You don't need to be sorry for playing devil's advocate. It sharpens the thinking. And I agree it's sketchy, speculative. But we need a plan. We've got to do something. Let's not forget that the poor girl was abused, and that took more than fifteen minutes.'

'But it didn't have to happen in the van, is what I'm saying.'

'True,' said Annie. 'But if not, why was she naked?'

'Maybe the van was just to dump her after whatever had happened.'

'So what do you suggest we do first?'

'Schools, colleges, tattoo parlours and kebab and pizza takeaways in Eastvale and points north-east, like you said, boss.'

'Right. You've got it.'

'What do you make of the tattoos? Any chance there?'

'Tats like hers are ten a penny these days,' said Annie. 'Nothing artistic or distinctive, just off the peg. But we'll get some photos run off. Someone might recognise the combination, locations. And the patrol officers and PCSOs can start asking around the parlours – Teesside, Tyneside.'

'There's a tattooist right here in Eastvale, too.'

'How do you know that?'

Gerry said nothing, just looked away and blushed.

'You didn't!'

'Just a little one.' She held her thumb and forefinger in a close pincer shape.

'Show me.'

'No way! Not here.'

'Where is it?'

'I'm not telling you.'

'Christ, you're the quiet one, aren't you? Did your boyfriend put you up to it?'

Gerry sipped more of her brandy. 'Boyfriend? Chance would be a fine thing. I don't have time, what with the exams, computer studies and the job and all. No, it was my treat to me on getting the posting to Eastvale.'

'To each her own. So first we'll ask around about the tats and the takeaway, starting here. They were professionally done, even if they are common designs, so we might get lucky with some artist recognising his or her handiwork, or remembering the birthmark.'

'I still can't get over how young she was,' said Geraldine. 'Just lying there on the table like that, so vulnerable.'

'Obviously old enough to get involved with some nasty people.'

'Come again?'

'Well, you don't think all this just happened to her by accident, do you?'

'You're not trying to say she was on the game or something, are you?'

'I don't know about that,' said Annie, 'but I don't think we're dealing with a complete innocent here. The doc found semen in her vagina, anus and oesophagus.'

'You don't have to remind me,' said Gerry, sipping more brandy. 'She was raped.'

'He said the odds are that it didn't all come from the same person, but there's no telling how many as yet. We'll know after Jazz has done the DNA testing.'

'She was gang-raped?'

'It's likely. But the rapists didn't kill her,' Annie went on quickly. 'That was someone else, later, in a different vehicle, after she'd walked a quarter mile back up the road. It was the broken rib piercing her heart that most likely killed her, the doc said, though she'd probably have died from her other injuries eventually. Remember, the doc also said from his examination of the footmarks that it looked very much as if she was kicked to death by just *one* person. She may have been raped by the men in the van, but she was still alive when they threw her out into the ditch. So what does she do?'

'She starts walking home.'

'Right. Makes sense, doesn't it? The poor lass is stark naked, and in pain from the sexual assault and the tumble into the ditch, so she wants to get help, even get to hospital, perhaps. Or home, as you say. Maybe she sees a light on in the Ketteridge house, but she can't climb over a wall and a barbed-wire fence in the state she's in. Maybe she's hoping for a gate or something, some means of entry. Whatever. She's lost. She starts walking back in the direction they came from – the van came from – and they've gone on ahead. Where are *they* going? Don't forget, if you turn right at the bridge at the bottom of Bradham Lane, you'll soon get to a roundabout that'll get you to Leeds, Bradford and points south in no time.'

'You know,' Gerry mused. 'We're only assuming she was naked when they kicked her out of the van, but maybe she wasn't. Maybe it was the other person who took her clothes, the killer.'

'Good point,' Annie conceded. 'But I reckon if those blokes in the van were having sex with her, she probably had her clothes off, or most of them. And I doubt they'd have given her time to put them on again before they chucked her out.'

'Makes sense. Could they have come back and finished her off?'

'Apparently not,' said Annie. 'At least that's not what Mandy Ketteridge heard. And I keep going back to the unlikelihood of some whacko happening along and killing her.'

'You still think it was someone she knew?'

'Yes. Don't forget, Mandy Ketteridge said she thought the second vehicle turned around and went back the way it came.'

'Maybe the victim didn't see who it was, or if she did, she didn't think she had anything to fear from him. Maybe she thought it was a friend. She was disoriented, remember. Hurt. Naked. On drugs as far as we know. She heard a car. She thought she'd be rescued. It must have been the first thing that came into her mind. Joy. Relief. I mean, how do you think you'd feel if you'd just been through what she'd been through?'

Annie swallowed and turned away. Gerry had no idea, of course. As far as Annie was aware, Banks was the only one in Eastvale who knew she had been raped several years ago, before her transfer there, by fellow detectives after a promotion party. She remembered exactly what she had felt like, and she had fought tooth and nail. She would also know how long it took several men to rape a woman if she hadn't managed to fight her way out after the first attacker.

Annie took a long slug of Black Sheep. 'Right. She's hurt, heading away from where her attackers went. Another car comes. She's hoping for help, wherever he's going. It stops a few yards beyond her. As you said, she must have thought she'd found help. A Good Samaritan.'

'Hmmm, maybe,' Gerry said. 'But it turned out to be some psycho killer who decided to beat her to death? We're back to that again.'

'No,' said Annie. 'There was nothing psycho about it. That's my point. And why would a psycho bother to turn around and go back the way he came? Wouldn't he be more likely to just carry on down Bradham Lane?'

'Depends where he was going.' Gerry frowned. 'What are you getting at? I don't understand. Someone followed her right from the start of the journey, from before she was raped?'

'Or someone knew where she was going and followed at a distance. That would explain how the second vehicle could be ten or fifteen minutes behind the first, as Mandy Ketteridge said it was. It makes sense if the killer *knew* they were heading down Bradham Lane. *Had* to take Bradham Lane to get where they were going from the road they were already on. If he knew all that, I'm thinking he may have held back a little while before following them down the lane so they wouldn't see his lights behind them.'

'So you have them going from the north-east to West Yorkshire?'

'It's a possibility, isn't it?'

'But how could whoever's in the second vehicle know they're going to throw her out of the van?'

'He doesn't. But when it happens, and he sees her walking towards him, he seizes his opportunity. Maybe he can't believe his luck. We don't know what was in his mind, what he was hoping for, or expecting to happen. The thing is, Gerry, I'm saying that it was most likely someone she knew who killed her. Someone who wanted her dead for a reason. It wasn't a random sex killer attack.'

'We don't know that whoever was in the second vehicle didn't rape her, too.'

'According to Mandy Ketteridge, it didn't stop that long, but she heard raised voices, more like an argument than a sex attack.'

'Is she in any danger?'

'Who?'

'Mandy Ketteridge. Remember, she asked about it, seemed worried?'

'I shouldn't think so,' said Annie. 'Nobody but us knows what she saw and heard.'

'But if they did know, or suspected? They might have seen her light on. It's a loose end. We don't know who or what we're dealing with, how far they'd go.'

'Now you're making me paranoid. We'll have the patrols pay extra attention. I still don't think she's in any danger, but it wouldn't do any harm to keep a close eye on the place.'

Gerry thought for a moment, swirling the brandy in her glass. 'Let's say you're right about the killer knowing the victim,' she said. 'How does that help us?'

'If it was someone she knew, then perhaps there was a motive. If there was a motive, once we know who she was, it gives us a better chance of finding out who had it.'

'What motive? So she couldn't report the rape?'

'I don't know. Maybe she knew too much about something?'

'Or she was in thrall to someone, a pimp, whatever, and disobeyed orders, was made an example of,' said Gerry. 'Or it was family, an honour killing, something like that?'

'As far as I can tell, she wasn't Middle Eastern.'

'There's other kinds of honour killings,' said Gerry. 'Funny term, really. There's no honour in it at all, is there?'

'Come on,' said Annie. 'Enough of this. We'd better get back to the station and see if there are any developments.'

Gerry knocked back the remainder of her brandy and pulled a face. She teetered a little when she stood up to leave. 'You'd better not be drunk,' said Annie. 'Not on one double brandy. Or you might pass your exams, young lady, but you'll never make it as a DS.'

At the same time as Annie was soothing Gerry with brandy, Banks had been as good as his word and bought Winsome a small whisky and soda in Whitby, sticking to Diet Coke himself. After that he had driven them across the moors to York while Winsome dozed for an hour in the passenger seat. Even the Alabama Shakes didn't keep her awake. Nor did she hear the Rolling Stones doing 'Stray Cat Blues' from their 1971 show at the University of Leeds. Banks hadn't realised it was on the playlist, and he felt uncomfortable when Jagger started singing about a thirteen-year-old girl. It reminded him that those days had, indeed, been different, though Jerry Lee Lewis had been hounded out of the country for marrying his thirteen-year-old cousin.

When they finally arrived at the ex Mrs Caxton's flat in a converted convent not far from York city centre, they found that her day had hardly been anywhere near as abstemious as theirs.

The woman who answered the doorbell was short and plump, with a fuzz of pinkish-white hair over chipmunk cheeks and a small, pinched mouth. The tight T-shirt and tartan slacks she wore didn't do her any favours. But she probably didn't care about that. She had a glass in her hand, and Banks could smell the gin from where he stood.

'Mrs Caxton?' he asked, identifying himself.

'As was,' she said. 'Then Mrs Braithwaite, but the second one was no better than the first, so I've gone back to my maiden name – Canning. But you can call me Carol. Don't stand out there in the hall, or you'll have the neighbours talking. Nosey lot, they are. Come in, make yourselves at home. Is this about Danny?'

'Why do you ask?' said Banks, as he and Winsome followed Carol Canning into her living room. The large picture window framed a view of the main road, where traffic slowed for a large roundabout. The flat was cleaner and neater than Banks would have expected from the state of Carol Canning so early in the day. Maybe she had someone to come in and 'do' for her, or perhaps she was just a fastidious, house-proud drunk. Maybe the drink was her way of celebrating a day's house-work. Whatever the reason, the mantelpiece was dust free, and the wood surfaces shone with recent polish.

'Well, nobody's interested in little old me any more, my second husband wouldn't say boo to a goose, but Danny always was a bit of a lad, to say the least. He sailed a bit close to the wind, if you catch my drift. Besides, you called me Mrs Caxton. It's been a long time since anyone called me that. What is it? Tax evasion? Not that I care. I don't get a penny from him. Not any more.'

'It's not tax evasion,' said Banks.

'Sit down. Tea? Something stronger? Gin?'

'Tea would be really nice.'

Carol Canning headed for the kitchen. Winsome looked at Banks and widened her eyes. Banks smiled at her. Carol seemed to him the sort of drunk who could hold her liquor; at least, she didn't wobble when she walked, and her speech wasn't slurred. A steady drip throughout the day, Banks guessed, causing and maintaining a gentle buzz. She returned several minutes later with a tray bearing a rose-patterned china teapot with gilded edges and two matching cups and saucers. There were also similar bowls of sugar and milk. Banks, who preferred his tea in a mug, accepted milk and sugar and took the proffered saucer. Not a trace of a tremor in Carol Canning's hand. Banks could hardly get his finger through the handle of the cup. He noticed that the level of gin in Carol's glass was considerably higher than it had been before she went into the kitchen.

When everyone had been served, she sat on the sofa, lit a cigarette, which she attached to a long ivory holder, put her legs up and stretched her smoking arm along the back, holding the gin close to her breast. It might have been the nineteenth century, and she might have been reposing on a chaise longue. 'Now do tell,' she said. 'Don't tease. You haven't come all this way just for the view.'

'No,' said Banks, trying to hold his teacup delicately, without snapping off the fragile handle. 'It is about your ex-husband. The first one.'

'So what has Danny boy been up to now?'

'Now?'

'A figure of speech.' She wagged her finger and spilled a little gin. 'You policemen! I can see I'm going to have to watch what I say.'

'Sorry. Just habit. Well, you'll hear about it soon enough, so I might as well tell you that your ex-husband has been accused of a rape in 1967, and that other similar incidents are being investigated.'

'1967?'

'Yes.'

'We were divorced in 1965.'

'Yes. But were you ever aware of anything like that while you were married to him?'

'I wouldn't have put it past him. Danny was always rather forceful, shall we say. I mean, his idea of foreplay was, "You awake?"' She laughed. 'He liked it rough – but that's not to say he ever hit me or anything – and he liked it often and anywhere. I always assumed he had other women, but I'd never have imagined that he had to rape them. He was very attractive, was Danny. Lots of women fancied him and I'm sure plenty of them were only too willing to spread their legs.'

'These were young girls.'

She chewed her lip. 'How young?'

'Underage. Fourteen. The one we talked to.'

She put her cigarette hand to her mouth. A half inch of ash dropped on to the front of her T-shirt. She ignored it. 'Oh my God.'

'That surprises you?'

'No, no. Not particularly. But it does shock me.' She took a hefty slug of gin. 'As much as I'm capable of being shocked these days.'

'But it doesn't surprise you?'

Carol Canning thought for a moment, a little pale, took a gulp of gin, then whispered, 'Nothing about Danny surprises me. He was a law unto himself, that man. What he wanted, he took.'

'He wanted young girls?'

'Christ, I was only sixteen when he took me. And there was no hesitation on his part. I didn't even have time to say no.'

'He raped you?'

'He *took* me. I wasn't unwilling and I wasn't a virgin. I was a little bit tipsy. I don't think I wanted to say no. It was flatter-ing, getting attention from a star like Danny Caxton. See how naive I was? There was a time when I was flattered by the attention of celebrities. It took me long enough to learn better. You wouldn't find a bigger pack of deviants outside an institution.'

'Well, this fourteen-year-old girl wasn't flattered, and she says he raped her.'

'Is this for certain? Are you sure she's telling the truth, and not just out for what she can get?'

'Sure as we can be. At least, we're investigating the allega-tion. Why should she lie?'

Carol snorted. '*Men*. Why *wouldn't* she lie? If she was ashamed of what she did, or regretted it too late? Got a bit pissed, and things went too far. Women do that all the time.'

'Do what?'

'Cry rape.'

'We don't think that's what happened,' Winsome said.

'But you're not sure, are you, love? And you have no evidence. Besides, they're all coming out of the woodwork now, after Jimmy and Rolf. They can smell the money in it, you ask me.' She turned back to Banks.

'Did you know any of Mr Caxton's friends?' he asked.

'Danny didn't have any friends. Just hangers-on. They came and went.'

'Do you know any who hung around longer than others? Or any from 1967?'

'I told you, we were divorced by then. I have no idea who his cronies were.'

'You must have been very young.'

She smiled flirtatiously. 'Flattery will get you anywhere. We were all young once.' She looked at Winsome. 'Some of us still are. I was nineteen. We'd been married two years. I suppose it was '62 when we first met. My fifteen minutes.'

'You must have heard things about him, though?'

'I can't say I paid a lot of attention. I had an exciting enough life to live. You know about his background, don't you?'

'Some things,' Banks said cautiously. 'What do you mean?'

'Well, it wasn't all public knowledge. He had a hard time of it when he was young, did Danny.'

'You mean being taken away from his parents?'

'Partly that,' said Carol Canning. 'But it wasn't until much later that he found out what really happened, around the time we were married, in fact.'

'What do you mean?'

'What happened to his parents.'

'It says in his official biography that they both died in the war,' said Winsome.

'That's true enough, love. At least, his mother died in a concentration camp.'

'And his father?'

'He was a member of the Volksdeutscher Selbstschutz.'

'What was that?' Banks asked.

'It was a paramilitary group made of up ethnic German Poles. Danny's father was half-German. They basically did all they could to help the German war effort, including massacring fellow Poles. For years Danny thought his father had died in the camp with his mother, when it's not entirely impossible that he had helped put her there. One day an old family friend called by, a camp survivor. He knew Danny's family. You can imagine how upsetting the news was for him. Of course, he was famous then. He felt he needed to keep it quiet. He was ashamed. It seemed unsavoury. I suppose it helped that he couldn't really remember his parents – after all, he hadn't seen them since he was three – but even so, it's a devastating thing to happen to someone, and no matter what he's done, Danny isn't without sensitivity.'

Banks could imagine how much it must have hurt and confused the young man. Perhaps if anyone were looking for a trigger to Caxton's later behaviour, that might have been it, though from what Carol Canning had said, he was already a man used to getting his way sexually, even if it meant being a bit rough. Still, something like that could rip your soul in two.

'What happened to him? The father?'

'Nobody knows. He might have died in the war or ended up living to a ripe old age in Germany – east or west – after it was all over. One thing's for certain, he'll be dead by now. Danny never talked about him again in my presence. I remember his expression when he was told the news. Face set like stone. Pale as a ghost. And he didn't argue, didn't contest it. He just left the room. When he came back, hours later, he acted as normal, as if nothing had happened. Cracked a joke or two. That was Danny.'

Banks reconsidered his direction. 'Let's go back a bit,' he said. 'You didn't sound surprised at the accusation when I first mentioned it.'

'Am I surprised Danny shagged a fourteen-year-old? Not at all. He always liked them young. Am I surprised he was a bit rough with her? No. He never was a patient or considerate lover. Am I surprised you're making such a fuss about it after all this time? Yes. Those were different times.'

'And stars like Danny Caxton were subject to different laws?'

'In a way. Yes. They were gods. And you know what the gods got up to.' She drank some more gin. 'Have you asked her why she took so long to report this . . . incident . . . or whatever it was?'

'She didn't. She reported it at the time and nothing was done.'

A triumphant and unpleasant grin split her features. 'Seems like it's down to you lot, then, doesn't it, ducky?'

'I'm not saying the police weren't at fault. We'll be checking out that aspect of the case, too.'

'I'll bet you will. You could probably save yourself the trouble, you know.'

'Oh, yes? How?'

'Well, think about it. Danny was a big star. People liked to be around him. Bask in his glory. He had charisma, you know. Tons of it. People came under his spell. Important people, like senior coppers, judges, politicians, royalty, for all I know. Or people who relied on him for their jobs, to keep raking in the money. You don't kill the cash cow just for a quick slice of beef, do you? And the others, the coppers and their like, they liked to be seen with him, liked to be able to impress their mates by saying they'd been down to Danny's for the weekend, rubbed shoulders with Mick and Keith, and, by heck, you should have seen the crumpet. He played golf with the chief constables. Gave generously to the Police Widows and Orphans Fund and a few others. Someone always owed him a favour, belonged to the same club, was a mate, depended on him for their livelihood or status. He was clever with people like that.'

'Manipulative? A user?'

'Of course. But without seeming so obvious. He was a charmer, was Danny, when he wanted to be. When he wanted something. If he committed the occasional indiscretion, odds were there'd be people to cover it up, people who didn't want any grief to fall on him.'

'You're saying he bribed his way out of an investigation?'

'I'm saying he didn't have to. He was golden, was Danny. Untouchable.'

'Rape isn't a simple indiscretion, Mrs . . . Canning . . . and Danny wasn't particularly charming when he wanted to have sex with the girl we've just talked to.'

Carol made a dismissive gesture. 'He always got what he wanted, one way or another. There's no doubt he was screwed up. But he's not stupid. He might not have had much formal education, but he taught himself.'

'The point remains,' Banks went on, 'that the girl *did* report the assault, the rape, to the local police at the time, which makes me inclined to believe that it did happen.'

'And they did nothing. What I said before still stands. She got pissed and went too far. Regretted it in the morning.'

'Then why would she bother going to the police and raking it all up? Surely that must have been painful for her. Nobody knew. Why not just get on with her life and chalk it up to inexperience?'

'I don't know. Guilt? Shame? Maybe she wasn't too bright. Maybe she got pregnant.'

'She didn't.'

'Don't tell me Danny used a rubber Johnny. That'd be a first. He wouldn't know how to put one on.'

'She didn't get pregnant.'

Carol Canning drank some more gin, and her eyes seemed to blur out of focus, then, very slowly, under a puzzled frown, they sharpened again and she took off on a different tack. 'On the other hand,' she said. 'Neither did I.'

'What?'

'Get pregnant. I thought it was me, but maybe he was shooting blanks. I mean, I had three with Kenny. Kenny might have been no great shakes in the bedroom department, but he had the right stuff, apparently. Danny just had to touch me and I came like the dickens, but Kenny just had to look at me and I'd get pregnant.'

'Didn't you go to a doctor?'

'With Danny? No. We didn't care that much, really. We were having too much of a good time to want kids. Even when we were married we didn't see that much of each other. I was still touring then, first with the girls, then solo. And if Danny was playing the rear end of a horse in Christmas panto in Leeds, I was Widow Twanky down in Brighton. It was a crazy life.'

'And if you had got pregnant?'

'There were ways of dealing with it, even then.'

'Why did you split up?' Winsome asked.

'I don't really see as it has anything to do with your investigation, but we just drifted apart. We really did. It was easy, so easy we never even noticed it happening.' She waved her cigarette arm theatrically in the direction of both of them. 'I mean, he went one way – variety shows, lousy pop songs, quiz programmes, bad movies – and I went another – Granny Takes a Trip, psychedelia, dope, acid, country weekends with the Maharishi, the whole shebang. Even us pop girls had a bit of fun, you know. I made a solo album, a folky sort of thing, like Vashti Bunyan, but it went nowhere. I had a nice voice. They all said so. *New Musical Express, Melody Maker, Record Mirror*. Even Danny said I had a nice voice.'

Where had Banks heard that before? Linda Palmer. Perhaps it was a line Caxton used with all the girls. Suddenly, Banks remembered what he had been racking his brains over since they had arrived. The Tri-Lites. Carol Canning had been one of the original Tri-Lites, so named before the term had been hijacked for lights of three different wattages. They were a girl group popular in the early sixties. He wouldn't have known that to look at her now, of course, and he had been a bit too young back then to appreciate their obvious charms, but her mention had jogged his memory. They had enjoyed a period of chart success from about 1961 until 1965 when their sort of music started falling out of fashion. They wore knee-length dresses and had bouffant hairdos, all trying to copy Helen Shapiro, Kathy Kirby or Susan Maughan. Banks remembered seeing them once or twice on *Top of the Pops*. In the mid-sixties they tried to imitate the American sound popular at the time, but they were no match for Tamla Motown. Banks remembered that Carol had tried to go solo in the late sixties, jump on the hippie bandwagon, but her career had quickly foundered.

'The Tri-Lites,' he said.

'Oh, don't. Please. For my sins. They were wigs, you know. The big hair.'

'Fooled me.'

'And awfully hot onstage, or under the studio lights. I don't think people ever noticed how much we sweated doing a show. We were all pretty ripe when we got off. Stripped right down and jumped in a lukewarm bath as soon as possible. As often as not with some randy young lad from one of the bands.' She winked. 'You know what they say. When the music's over, it's time to have fun.'

'Never heard that one,' said Banks. 'I thought it was "turn out the lights".'

'Don't you turn out the lights when you want to have fun, Superintendent?'

'And after the solo album?' Banks asked. 'What then?'

Carol Canning stared into space again for a while. At first Banks thought she was miffed at his lack of response to her flirting, but he realised that she was mired in difficult memories. 'Oh, those were the lost years, ducky. Next thing I knew I was married to Kenny, and it was 1975. All Hot Chocolate and Bay City Rollers. Our day was over. Though I still think we could have given Abba a run for their money.' She got to her feet, still remarkably steady, Banks thought, sang a few bars of 'Dancing Queen' and lit another cigarette. 'God, this is so depressing. Let's all have a big drink, and I'll put some real music on, shall I? Aretha or Dionne or something. Definitely *not* the fucking Tri-Lites.'

Winsome gave Banks an anxious look, and he glanced at his watch. 'I'm afraid we'd better be off now,' he said.

'You're no fun. You're going to leave an old lady alone with her memories and her gin?'

'Needs must.'

She waved her glass at them and some of the gin slopped over the side, dribbled down her hand and splashed on the front of her T-shirt to join the cigarette ash. 'Now see what you've made me do.' She pouted. 'Go on, then. Off you go. They all do in the end.'

Banks and Winsome took their leave. As Winsome got behind the wheel, she turned to Banks and said, 'I know it's only the second day, guv, but already I have to confess I'm getting sick to death of this case and these people.'

Banks had expected something like that. He wondered if Annie would have been able to keep quiet as long as Winsome had in Carol Canning's company. He doubted it. She wasn't quite as sensitive as Winsome, and not as well behaved. She usually gave as good as she got, or thought she was getting. 'My sentiments exactly,' he said. 'Give me a down-to-earth honest criminal any time. The more godawful these people are, the more we owe it to Linda Palmer to make a good case against Danny Caxton.'

'Yeah,' Winsome said. 'I suppose so. I suppose you're right.'

'And cheer up. You know what the woman in the movie said: "Tomorrow's another day."'

5

After a glass of grapefruit juice, a mug of green tea and a bowl of muesli, Annie was ready to set off for work. She was hoping there would be something from forensics that morning, and an identification of the victim would also be welcome. When the news came on her car radio, it was no surprise to hear that one of the main stories was about the unidentified young girl found murdered on a leafy lane in Yorkshire, and the other was about Danny Caxton being interviewed on a matter of historic sexual abuse. As yet, the media had only scant details about both cases. One of the things they didn't know, and were at all costs not to find out about, was that there had been a second car in the 'leafy lane' on the night of the girl's murder. For the time being, it suited Annie for the rapists to think they were suspected of murder and the murderer to think he was home free. That way the rapists might panic and perhaps make a mistake, and the killer would carry on blithely unaware while the police closed in on him. At least, that was the theory.

After they had drawn a blank in the Eastvale tattoo parlour and takeaway, Annie had told Gerry to work on the assumption that the victim was being transported from the north-east to some point south of Eastvale by a route off the beaten track. She had also assumed that the victim was *from* the north-east, but she had realised, lying awake in bed the previous night, that the vehicle might have been carrying the girl *home*. Someone might have picked her up in Middlesbrough or Sunderland, for example, and been in the process of driving her back down south, to where she lived, when things had gone wrong and the driver had taken a detour down a quiet country lane and dumped her. Raped and bruised, but alive. But if that were the case, why was she walking back the way she had come?

Annie ignored the throng of media and made her way up to the squad room. Neither Winsome nor DC Doug Wilson was in, but Gerry sat at her desk working on the computer, hair held back by a tortoiseshell Alice band, which looked surprisingly cool on her. She maintained good posture, Annie noticed, unlike herself, who bent over, hunched and round-shouldered, as she hunted and pecked. Gerry seemed poised, ergonomically perfect, as if being at a computer keyboard were the most comfortable position in the world, everything at the right height and the right angle. And, of course, she touch-typed like a pro, eyes on the screen all the time.

'Anything yet?' Annie flopped into her chair, put her feet up on the desk and took a sip of the coffee she had picked up at the Starbucks on Market Street. She was trying to give it up, hence the green tea, but the lure of a latte was just too much at the start of the working day. Only one, though. That was her rule.

'Still nothing,' said Gerry, pausing at her labours. 'The lab's finished with Roger Stanford's work clothes. Nothing there, as we suspected. We've also run checks on his background. Nothing. I think we can scratch him from our list. I've been in touch with Cleveland, Northumbria and the Durham Constabulary, and they'll offer us all the help we want. They're appalled by what happened, of course. They've already got patrol cars out to check up on the tattoo parlours and kebab and pizza places.'

'Good. How about CCTV?'

'That's a bit more interesting,' Gerry said, reaching for a file folder. 'Though nothing to get too excited about. The nearest cameras service the big roundabout on the south-west edge of Eastvale, the end of Market Street. You'd turn off at the third exit for Bradham Lane, which is about two miles west.'

'OK. So we can find out who went that way.'

'Right, guv. But this is where it gets interesting. After the end of Bradham Lane, a mile or so west, there's another roundabout, where you'd take the first exit if you were heading for Harrogate and West Yorkshire.'

'Cameras?'

'Yes.'

'So if we find the same car on *both* roundabout cameras, separated by however long it takes to travel down Bradham Lane, and if the timing is right, then we might be on to something?'

'Yes.'

'Better stick at it then. Anything from missing persons yet?'

'Nothing. Either nobody's missed her yet or she makes a habit of disappearing for days at a time. I've also initiated enquiries at schools and social services. Oh, and you might not have seen this yet.' Gerry tossed one of the morning tabloids towards Annie's desk. 'Page two.'

On the front page was a huge photograph of Danny Caxton receiving his MBE, circa 1985, and on page two was a short article about the mysterious naked girl found dead in the Yorkshire Dales. Beside it was an artist's impression of the victim, without broken teeth and swollen lips. Annie hadn't seen it yet. 'She scrubs up nicely,' she said, shaking her head. 'A pretty young girl. Jesus Christ, what a waste.'

'What do you think?'

'It's good.' Annie tapped the newspaper. 'Someone might actually recognise her from this.'

The door opened and the diminutive Jazz Singh stood there in her lab coat, brandishing a buff file folder. 'Before you ask,' she said. 'I worked late last night, as did everyone in toxicology. This is a particularly nasty one and whatever you need, you know . . .'

'Thanks, Jazz,' said Annie. 'What've you got for us?'

Jazz sat down in Doug Wilson's empty chair. 'We're still waiting for the DNA results to process,' she began, 'but it looks as if there were three distinct samples of seminal fluid in the girl's body. All secretors.'

Annie's jaw tightened. Three. The magic number. Gang bang. It was three men who had tried to rape her once. She flashed on the image of the naked girl being assailed from all sides, in all orifices, by three men turned to animals by lust. Maybe they had jobs, families, loved their mothers, but that night, whether under the influence of drugs or not, they had become inhuman, bestial, and had violated and humiliated a vulnerable young girl.

'How can you tell how many there were if they were all mixed up?' she asked.

'We have our little secrets. You use Y-STR to separate them. The Y chromosome. The male line. And STR means short tandem repeats. They're—'

Annie held her hand up. 'All right, all right. Sorry I asked. You've blinded me with science.'

'That didn't take long.'

'*Three* men, you say? Christ.'

'Yeah, I know,' said Jazz, as if reading Annie's thoughts. 'What can I say? I only deliver the news. I should have DNA profiles before the end of the day, then at least we can check them against the database.'

'They won't be there,' said Annie. 'They never are.'

'Don't be so negative. At least we've got three shots this time.'

'True. Anything else?'

Jazz pulled out some sheets of paper. 'Preliminary tox results show a fair bit of alcohol in her system—'

'Enough to make her drunk?'

'Oh, yes. Tipsy at any rate. I don't know how well she could hold her booze, but Dr Glendenning said her liver and kidneys show an unusual amount of damage for someone so young.'

'That's because someone booted them into her lungs,' said Annie. 'Maybe we should be thankful she was pissed. She might have felt less pain and fear.'

'She wouldn't have felt much at all,' said Jazz. 'We also found significant traces of ketamine in her system. The girl was off her face.'

'Enough to go along willingly with what they wanted?'

'Impossible to say for sure, but highly likely. Definitely high as a kite. Probably no sense of judgement. Even without the booze she'd have been gaga. A lot depends on when she took it, or was given it. It's fast-acting, but it doesn't last more than a couple of hours if you ingest it. The doc didn't find any needle marks on her skin, so we're assuming she took it orally. I assume you're both aware of the effects?'

Annie glanced over at Gerry, who shook her head. 'Remind us,' she said. 'DC Masterson here failed drugs 101.'

'Hallucinations, sense of detachment from the body, depersonalisation.' Jazz paused. 'From what we can tell, it was a high dose, around a hundred milligrams.'

'What does that mean?' Gerry asked.

Jazz picked up another sheet of paper. 'Have you heard of the K-hole?'

'Vaguely,' said Annie.

Gerry merely looked puzzled.

'It's a state some users enter into when the dosage is somewhere between seventy-five and a hundred and twenty-five milligrams. People have described it as like entering an alternate universe or another dimension, a black hole in the soul.

You leave everything you know behind, including yourself. Loss of identity, loss of bodily awareness, sensation of floating, euphoria, loss of time perception.'

'Sounds like fun,' said Annie.

'As I said, I don't think she would have felt any pain. With any luck, she might have had no sensation at all, been somewhere else entirely, not really aware of what was happening to her.'

'Until later,' said Annie. 'It may explain why they kicked her out of the van.'

'Yes,' Jazz agreed. 'But it can also cause amnesia. You forget it all like you forget a dream. If you come back at all, that is. They say it's a state very close to clinical schizophrenia.'

No matter how high or depersonalised the girl had been, Annie doubted that she had been completely unaware of what was being done to her in the van.

'Well, we'll never know what she felt, will we?' said Gerry, 'So there's not much point in speculating. But now we know she was raped by three men, and she had been plied with alcohol and ketamine, we've got a bit more to go on, haven't we? Her murder could be drug-related.'

Annie smiled. 'Ever the practical one, Gerry. Ask the locals to check known dealers – especially in ketamine. But it hardly narrows down the field much, does it?'

'Same general area?'

'For the time being. If we draw a blank we can expand the search.'

'I said there were traces of sperm from three distinct sources,' said Jazz. 'Not that she was raped by three men.'

'You didn't see the body,' said Annie. 'But we'll bear that in mind.'

'The dental records and tats photos are still doing the rounds,' Gerry added. 'We might get something from them, though it doesn't appear she visited a dentist very often.'

Annie turned to Jazz. 'Thanks for getting this done so quickly,' she said. 'And we'll keep our fingers crossed there's a hit with the DNA database.'

'Even if there isn't, I should have a bit more information on the assailants for you later. Pity DNA doesn't indicate home address.'

Annie laughed. 'It would certainly make our job a hell of a lot easier. Thanks again.'

'It's about time we had that celebratory drink,' said DCI Ken Blackstone. 'Congratulations on the promotion, Alan.'

They raised their glasses and clinked. Banks sipped some of his Sam Smith's and forked up a piece of black pudding and smoked bacon Scotch egg. Blackstone was eating a prawn and Marie Rose sandwich washed down with a glass of chilled California blush.

'I'm not sure congratulations is the right word for it,' Banks said. 'But thanks, anyway.'

Blackstone scratched his head. 'What do you mean? Too much paperwork?'

'That, too. But . . . that's not why I wanted to see you. The drink, of course, but . . .'

'Something on your mind?'

'My first big case as a superintendent.'

'Yes?'

'Danny Caxton.'

Blackstone put his sandwich down. 'Oh, bloody hell. They certainly chucked you in at the deep end.'

'That's an understatement. Though I must say, having talked to both the accuser and the man himself, I'm a lot more keen than I was a couple of days ago.'

They were sitting opposite one another at the end of a wooden bench in the narrow alley outside Whitelock's, one of Leeds city centre's oldest pubs, and usually one of the most crowded. That lunchtime was no exception. Summer students sat on nearby benches smoking and idling over their pints, shop girls from the Trinity Centre gossiped over a gin and orange or white wine spritzers, and office clerks chatted over a quick half of bitter. The used plates, emptied of their beef in ale pies, burgers, hot dogs or cheese and chutney sandwiches, were piling up. The staff could hardly keep up with the serving, let alone the clearing away. The buildings were high on both side of the narrow alley, letting in no sun, but the heat certainly had everyone wilting, Banks included. Blackstone remained immaculate and cool in suit, shirt and tie. With the glasses, bald spot on top and tufts of hair above his ears, he was getting to resemble Philip Larkin or Eric Morecambe a bit more every time Banks saw him. He had also put on a bit of weight, Banks noticed. Though the alley was crowded, there was a gap between Banks and Blackstone and the group of students, German by the sound of them, sitting next to them. And it wasn't too noisy to have a conversation.

Banks had spent the morning with Winsome going over the itemised lists of stuff the search team had taken from Caxton's house the previous evening and sending out inquiries for lists of his friends, employees and associates in the late sixties. There was nothing so far from the search, only a bit of mild Internet porn, but there were diaries and appointment calendars that might prove useful in pinning down his movements at critical times, and pre-digital photographs that might link him with some of his victims. He had left Winsome to continue the task while he drove to Leeds.

'There were always rumours about him,' Blackstone said. 'You know he lived not too far from here for a while?'

'Yes. Otley, wasn't it?'

'That's right. Had a nice big house after his first flush of fame in the early sixties. Before my time, of course, but there were rumours of parties. Orgies, I suppose. Quite the "A" guest list, too, if the stories are to be believed. High-ranking coppers, judges, politicians, a bishop or two.'

'Well, he certainly got his immunity from somewhere. What were the rumours?'

'Mostly that he liked them young. I mean, he wasn't that old then, himself.'

'Underage?'

'Never heard that mentioned specifically.'

'Unwilling?'

'I think everyone assumed the girls threw themselves at him.'

'That's what he told us. One of the accusers who's come forward lives near Eastvale. I've been assigned the investigation.'

'Lucky you. Any hope?'

'Maybe. A glimmer.'

'So what do you want from me?'

'She used to live here. In Leeds. She was on her holidays with her family in Blackpool when the assault took place.'

'What does she say?'

'That Caxton and another man raped her in a hotel room.'

'How did they get her there?'

Banks explained as best he could to Blackstone what Linda Palmer had told him. 'She's not clear on everything,' he added. 'It was a long time ago.'

'You're telling me.'

'She says she reported it when the family got back home. Here. Her mother went to the police station with her.'

'That would've been Brotherton House, back then. Top end of the Headrow.'

'I know,' said Banks. 'There's got to be paperwork somewhere, Ken. That's the first thing we need to track down. Proof that she reported what happened, proof that nothing was followed up.'

'Might be tougher than you think. The paper trail might be somewhere, maybe. But the question is, where?'

Banks sipped some more beer. It tasted good but didn't do a lot to slake his thirst. Maybe he should have asked for a pint of chilled lager on a day like this. 'Computers?'

'I'm not sure anything that far back has been entered. In fact, it most likely hasn't been. Let me look into it. I know a good archivist. It'll give me an excuse to ask her out for lunch or something.'

'Always happy to be of help in the romance department.'

'And what about you?'

'What about me?'

'You know. The love life.'

'What love life?'

'Like that, is it? I thought you had a lovely young girlfriend. Italian, isn't she?'

'I did. Oriana. It just didn't work out, that's all. She was too young. Then either she was too busy or I was. You know the sort of thing. There was never any talk about . . . you know . . . any commitment or anything. We had fun, that's all.'

'So no pain?'

'I wouldn't quite say that. I listened to *Blood on the Tracks* and *The Boatman's Call* a few too many times after she left. Drank a bit too much Laphroaig. Felt sorry for myself. But did I slit my wrists? No.'

'With me it's always *In the Wee Small Hours* and Macallan eighteen-year-old.'

'Yeah, that's a good combination, too. I always said you had class.'

'So there's nothing new on the horizon?'

'Not so far as I can see.'

Blackstone gestured to Banks's almost empty glass. 'Another?'

'No. Better not. I have to drive back. I'll do a bit of

shopping while I'm here first. Walk it off.' One thing Banks wanted to do was go to Waterstones and buy Linda Palmer's latest book of poetry, along with *Dart*, the book she was reading when he talked to her. And maybe *Ariel*. They might give him a bit more insight into her character. Besides, he might also enjoy them. He would also make time to go to HMV and pick up the new Sviatoslav Richter box set, his deferred present to himself on his promotion and salary increase. If they had it in stock, of course. He still missed the old Classical Record Shop. He had been listening to a lot of solo piano music in the long summer evenings – Angela Hewitt, Imogen Cooper, Mitsuko Uchida and other contemporary pianists playing Bach, Schubert, Chopin and Mozart, mostly – but Richter was a new discovery for him. He had enjoyed the 1958 Sofia recital and was looking forward to listening to some of the live New York recordings he had read about in *Gramophone*.

'If I'm going to attempt to find something in the archives,' Blackstone said, 'I'm going to need to know what it is. Is that a problem?'

'Not at all. As far as I'm concerned you're an essential member of the investigative team as of now. You know as well as I do that victims' identities are always sacred in cases like this.'

'I've been there. You don't think anyone escaped the fallout from the Savile business around here, do you?'

'I suppose not. Leeds lad, wasn't he?'

'For our sins. And you also know that if you're dealing with something along those lines, there's a good chance any written records of what happened might have disappeared over the years.'

'I know that, too. But it doesn't hurt to look.'

'Not you, it doesn't. You're not the one who'll be getting a lungful of archive dust.'

'Surely you've got more hygienic storage facilities these days?'

'I wouldn't count on it.'

Banks lowered his voice. 'The complainant's name is Linda Palmer. She was fourteen at the time.'

'Tough one,' said Blackstone.

'She's a survivor, though,' Banks went on. 'Become a successful poet, as a matter of fact.'

'Poetry?' Blackstone pulled a face. 'Not really up my street.'

'Mine, neither,' said Banks. At least it didn't used to be, he thought. He had read that morning some excerpts in his anthology from Milton's *Paradise Lost,* and the final lines, the expulsion of Adam and Eve from the Garden of Eden, still reverberated in his mind: 'They, hand in hand, with wandering steps and slow, / Through Eden took their solitary way.' There was something deeply tragic about it that was as much, if not more, in the solemn music of the syntax as in the meanings of the words themselves. One thing he was quickly coming to realise as he worked his way through the anthology was that even if you didn't understand a poem, which was frequently, you could still enjoy its music. 'She's been very successful,' he said. 'She's smart and articulate. She doesn't seem broken at all.'

'Sounds like you're smitten, mate. Attractive, too?'

'That, too. But mostly she's just an interesting woman who went through a terrible ordeal a long time ago. But she's dealt with it. She hasn't let it ruin her life.'

'Why didn't she pursue it back then?'

'She was ignored after that first interview. Her mother wanted to forget all about it. They never even told her dad. Years passed.'

'And this business in the newspapers has brought it all back?'

'That's right.'

'You believe her story?'

'Yes.'

'Good enough for me, then.' He took out a small notebook, not the official one.

'She said they went to Blackpool the last two weeks of August,' Banks said. 'The twelfth to the twenty-sixth. And the assault occurred after the Saturday matinee at the end of the first week. That'd be the nineteenth of August. I looked it up.'

'And she reported it when?'

'First week after they got back. She can't remember exactly what day, but early in the week, probably Tuesday or Wednesday. That'd be the twenty-ninth or thirtieth of August 1967.'

'Remember what you were doing then?'

'Probably listening to *Sergeant Pepper's Lonely Hearts Club Band*,' said Banks. He had a sudden flash of memory. The summer Sunday afternoons sitting on Paul Major's front steps listening to the Beatles' new album on the old Dansette. Banks, Paul, Graham Marshall, Dave Grenfell and Steve Hill. Was that what he was doing while Linda Palmer was getting raped? Steve, Paul and Graham were all dead now, one from cancer, one from AIDS and one from murder.

'Why didn't she report it in Blackpool, after it happened?' Blackstone asked.

'I don't know,' said Banks. 'I imagine she was confused, upset, in shock. I think she wanted to pretend it never happened, hide it from her parents.'

'I'm just thinking that if it went through us, someone would have probably passed it on to Lancashire.'

'I'll have Winsome get in touch with them, again. Ask them to try harder. But in the meantime—'

'Don't worry. I'll have a root around for you.'

'Thanks, Ken. You're a pal.'

'Muggins, more like.'

Excerpt from Linda Palmer's Memoir

I have been praised for my 'unflinching gaze,' my 'clarity of perception' and my 'fearless imagination' as a poet, all of which is ironic, in some ways. Sometimes I feel very much the phoney, far more the blinkered coward unwilling to face up to the tragic events of my own life. But we don't, really, do we? Not while they're happening. We get through them somehow – the rape, my mother's, father's and husband's deaths, the loss of an unborn child, the lingering aftermaths of all our sorrows. It's only when they're over that we have to face up to them, when they have become memories. And memories can hurt far more than the events themselves. They can also be untrue. Perhaps the reviewers are right in other ways, though, as I have no fear of expressing things the way I feel them. You probably think I'm tough. If only you had known me then.

I'm not saying my account won't be 'true' as far as I can possibly make it so, just that it has gone through the black hole of time and memory and you may have to indulge my occasional lapses. I will try not to twist the truth, or augment it, but I may comment on it. I may also drift into stream of consciousness from time to time. I hope that doesn't put you off.

I'm starting with this preamble because I imagine myself writing this for you, a policeman used to facts and forensics, reason and evidence. But I think imagination plays a far greater role in your work than many people realise. You even read poetry. That surprised me. Wordsworth. Who would have thought it? You said I should try to write down what happened, that writing might help me to remember, but I can hardly become the 'me' I was at fourteen. Memory doesn't work like that; at least, mine doesn't. I can only imagine me then from where I am now, if that doesn't sound too T.S. Eliot. It doesn't mean I don't or can't remember. It doesn't mean that all this is a lie. It just means that I'm looking back from a great distance. It's not that things are tiny, as if I were staring through the wrong end of a telescope. Not at all. When I close my eyes, the figures are as large as any on a TV screen. I can see details, even recall smells and textures. But they may not match the past exactly. If I were to draw an outline of what I see on a sheet of tracing paper and place it on top of the original scene, the lines wouldn't quite coincide, some would meander or go off at tangents, the positions would be out of true, the proportions hopelessly mismatched and misshapen. Mad geometry.

Remember, these things happened a long time ago, so the details melt and distort like a Dalí watch, but the feelings are still true. I wonder what use my feelings will be to you, but I will continue as best I can. I should also tell you right now that I can't tell a story in a straightforward way. First this happened, then this. Just the facts, ma'am. It's not me. If I could do that I'd probably be making a fortune writing popular fiction. I suppose that's what you're used to. But I get distracted, sidetracked. I digress. In a strange way, I feel I'm writing this as much for myself as for you. It's the only way I can write. I do aim for honesty, however uncomfortable it may be. I shall try to tell the truth, and perhaps if we are both patient, some of it may emerge.

In the first place, I want to be clear that I don't think the incident blighted my life. I don't think I've lived a blighted life. I've been lucky, on the whole. I've had periods of great happiness and joy, much success and acclaim. My marriage was a blessing and my children remain a joy. There have been years when I haven't given a passing thought to what happened in Blackpool when I was fourteen, until all this recent fascination with historical abuse, which makes me I feel I have to stand up, put my hand up and say, 'Yes, it happened to me, too.' Solidarity with other victims? Perhaps. But true, nonetheless. So, to it.

It was summer and we were going on our annual holidays. Two weeks in Blackpool. Every year the same. Same boarding house, breakfast and evening meal included. But this time, for the first time, my best friend Melanie and her parents were coming with us. They lived on the same estate in Leeds, just around the corner from us, and Melanie and I were in the same form at Silver Royd. We were hoping that, as there were two of us, we'd be allowed to roam a bit, let off the leash, while our parents got to do the things they wanted, like go to the pub and sit on the beach in deckchairs with their knotted hankies on their heads and magazines protecting their sleeping faces from the sunshine, should we be lucky enough to have any.

On the whole, my parents weren't too controlling. Two years ago on holiday, my dad had even let me go and see the Beatles at the ABC as long as Mum went with me. He had even queued and got the tickets for us but wouldn't have considered going, himself. It was 'fab,' as they used to say. Mostly it's just a blur of adrenalin, but I still remember when Paul sang 'Yesterday' for the first time anywhere, ever. Tears just streamed down my cheeks as I listened to those sad words. What I could hear of them, at any rate. Mum never said much, but she was pale and shaky when we left, and I'm not sure she ever got over a theatre full of teenage girls screaming and crying and jumping on their seats and wetting themselves. I didn't do that, of course, but I suppose what I'm saying is that I was a typical teenager, perhaps even more innocent than most. Paul was my Beatle then, but a few years later it was the bad-boy John.

With Melanie, the holiday would be different. We would wander the Golden Mile, play the one-armed bandits, watch the mechanical hand drop the trinket it had grabbed just before it reached the chute. Perhaps we would be allowed to visit the Pleasure Beach after dark. We would flirt with boys, ride the Big Dipper, wear KISS ME QUICK hats, visit all the joke shops, buy itching powder and whoopee cushions, examine the racks of cheeky postcards outside the gift shops without being dragged away by our mothers or fathers. (Q. 'Do you prefer long legs or short legs?' A: 'I like something in between.') We could be just like pretend grown-ups. We hadn't even brought our buckets and spades. We were too old for toys like that. We had put away childish things and were about to embrace the grown-up world. At least that was the idea. I wasn't to know how the grown-up world was soon going to embrace me.

And what did we look like? Typical sixties teenagers. In those days, I wore my blond hair down to my shoulders like Marianne Faithfull, with a parting in the middle and a fringe at the front, but I should imagine we were dressed conservatively and sensibly, and my mother certainly wouldn't let me wear one of the miniskirts that were fast becoming all the rage. I remember the arguments. 'You'd look no better than a common trollop, young lady.' I was never sure which was meant to be the worst, a 'trollop' or 'common'. We might have been wearing jeans some of the time, but most likely we were wearing the same sort of thing we wore at home, bright summer dresses, skirts halfway down our calves, cool cotton blouses, that sort of thing. But we looked nice. I'm sure we looked nice. And innocent. At least nobody could say I was asking for it because of the way I dressed.

And so, after the usual chaos of packing and making sure everything was turned off, unplugged and locked up, we met Melanie and her parents at the bus stop and set off for the station.

At the meeting that Friday evening in the boardroom, the whiteboard was covered with photos of the Bradham Lane body taken from all angles, as well as the artist's impression of the girl's face and close-ups of her tattoos and birthmark. Alongside were pictures from the crime scene and a timeline, carefully drawn up by Gerry on the computer.

Annie had brought Banks up to speed just before they started the meeting, and he took his seat with the others, including Gerry, Doug Wilson, Stefan Nowak, Vic Manson,

Jazz Singh and assorted CSIs. Winsome had gone home, as this wasn't her case, and she had plenty of homework to do on Danny Caxton. That beady-eyed bloke from the press office, Adrian Moss, who had visited her in the morning with AC Gervaise, was also present. He had been prowling the corridors a lot lately, as if he were up to something. He reminded Annie of a snake-oil salesman, not that she had ever met such a creature.

Annie surveyed the expectant faces, knowing how hard they had all worked since the body had been found on Wednesday morning. Now it was almost the weekend, and most of them would have a couple of days rest and some time to spend with their families, a brief respite from the world of violent death. Not Annie, and probably not Banks, either, she thought. This was the kind of case that put its hooks into you. She didn't know how Banks felt about his high-profile investigation yet, but she knew him well enough to hazard a guess that he wasn't too thrilled. That was being kept as much under wraps as hers for the moment. There were no meetings and little squad-room gossip, though Danny Caxton was making a splash in the media.

Gerry began by describing the CCTV searches for possible cars and vans. 'We've made a start,' she said. 'DC Wilson is coordinating the team watching the CCTV and ANPR feeds. But it'll be slow going. There's a lot of it. We're also checking Bradham village itself and all the farms and villages in the immediate area, as well as having a close look at events in Eastvale that night.'

'Quite a job, then?'

'Yes, ma'am. There wasn't a lot of traffic at that time of night, of course, but there was more than you might expect, especially over a two- or three-hour period. Seems that the route our vans took cuts a big corner off if you want to get to Harrogate and West Yorkshire, especially if you want to avoid the A1 with all the lorries and roadworks. It's a bit slower, of course, but some drivers aren't in that much of a hurry. The main problem isn't the volume of traffic, though. It just takes time to narrow things down, find the drivers, check their stories. We have to follow up on every car and van. And the quality of the images isn't always as good as one would hope. According to Mandy Ketteridge's statement, we believe the murder took place between two-fifteen and two-thirty in the morning, so we're starting by working on a time spread between one and three a.m. Naturally, we'll extend that if we get more information.'

'Anything stand out yet?' Banks asked.

'There's a couple of builders' vans,' Gerry said. 'One white, the other dark blue, or black. We think the girl was taken and raped in a van of some sort before she was dumped by the roadside. At least she was dumped from it, even if she was raped elsewhere. The problem is, the number plate on the white van is impossible to read.'

'No name on the side, or logo?'

'No, sir. Not on either.'

'OK. Keep at it,' Banks said.

'And Gerry,' Annie added. 'As we think the second van might have turned back—'

'We'll be checking for that, too, though there are a few out-of-the-way routes over the moors that can get you back to Eastvale by a different, and CCTV-free, route.'

'Bugger,' said Annie. 'But if he did take a different route, away from the cameras, it seems to indicate some degree of premeditation, or at least self-preservation after the fact.'

'Lots of people know they're on candid camera everywhere they go these days,' said Banks. 'If he'd just killed someone, he'd probably be extra cautious, so that's a good call.'

'I would have thought he'd also be panicking,' said Annie. 'Unless it was something he was used to. I don't know about you, Gerry, but I think if I'd just gone too far and killed someone, I'd be crazy with fear. I wouldn't be thinking clearly.'

'Perhaps,' said Gerry. 'But we've no way of knowing. I suppose it affects different people differently. It doesn't mean he was a cold-blooded killer, just that he maybe felt a sense of calm and clarity after he'd done it. Relief, maybe.'

'Sexual?'

'That's possible, too. Lord knows there are enough men who get off on violence against women.'

Annie summed up what little else they knew so far and invited Stefan and Jazz to provide an update. Stefan spoke about cars and tyres, using the photos on the whiteboard as a guide, and explained how there just wasn't enough information from the skid marks to run against a database search for make and model. He also explained how the traces of blood and the girl's muddy footprints led him to his theories about the sequence of events, though there were, unfortunately, no recoverable footprints from the killer, only signs of a scuffle by the roadside. They were working on identifying footwear marks made on the girl's body, he said, but he stressed that they were partial and would be unlikely to lead to the actual footwear the killer had been wearing, should he still be foolish enough to have it in his possession. There were, however, one or two scuff marks and scratches unique to that footwear. The one thing he was reasonably certain of was that there had been no one with her on her ten- or fifteen-minute walk from where she had been dumped to where she had been killed, so it seemed that whoever had kicked her out of the van while 'My Silver Lining' was playing had gone on his way. It also appeared as if there had been only one killer.

'Maybe they were working in concert,' Annie suggested.

'What do you mean?' Banks asked.

'Maybe it was prearranged. Someone knew she was going to be tossed out of the van, and whoever it was in the other van following for the specific purpose of killing her.'

'I suppose it's possible,' Banks admitted. 'But it's a bit elaborate, don't you think? Why go to all that trouble when the people in the van could just as easily have killed her before they dumped her?'

'Maybe they weren't supposed to know she was going to be killed? It's not any more unbelievable than some psycho just happening to pass by.'

'True enough,' said Banks.

Then Jazz Singh took over.

'I've been working with the DNA for a while now,' she began, 'and even though we've got no hits on the database, I'm sorry to say, I've come to a few conclusions. As you know, we found samples of semen from three males in the girl's orifices. The men clearly didn't use condoms, unless all three broke, so we can assume they're confident or stupid. Or both. Either way, it's to our advantage.'

'They most likely don't expect anyone to be searching for them,' said Banks. 'Especially if, as Annie suggests, they didn't kill the girl. Either she was willing, or they raped her and gave her graphic warnings of what would happen to her if she talked.'

'Agreed,' said Annie. 'And I'd lean towards the latter, given the amount of trauma they inflicted on her. Which leads me to believe they had confidence of some control over her even when she was out of their immediate presence.'

'Right,' said Jazz. 'She knew them. Maybe they knew where she lived. Again, to our advantage. Now, in addition to having good-enough samples to match with any suspects we might find, there are one or two things I can tell you about the three men already, using an ethnic inference test. It's not infallible, and it can only be used as an estimation. It won't stand up in court. In fact, I don't think the information should leave this room. However, it might help you with your investigation. A comparison of Y-DNA markers to those in a database indicate the three men were all of Asian heritage, from the Indian sub-continent, most likely Pakistan. I can study other databases and haplogroups, but I'm not sure that will help you any further at this point.'

'Pakistan?' said Adrian Moss in disbelief.

'Of Pakistani descent, yes, but they may never have actually *been* there. They could be as English as you and me. I'm simply talking about ethnic origins.'

'But living here?' Moss asked.

'The DNA doesn't tell us where they're living, but I suppose we can assume that they are here, as their semen was found in the victim at the crime scene. I doubt they sent it via airmail. I've started a familial search, but that's yielded nothing so far. No criminal brothers, mothers or fathers. I can dig further and uncover genetic disorders or high risk of developing certain medical conditions in future, if you want, but it becomes expensive and time-consuming, and I don't see what good it does us.'

Adrian Moss looked at Jazz. 'Are you sure about the ethnic origin?'

'Yes. Why? Doesn't it help?'

'It's a fucking media nightmare is what it is,' he said. 'Excuse my language.'

'I'm not too sure about that,' said Annie. 'I think it's a terrific lead, Jazz. Well done. For a start, it points us in a specific direction. We could be dealing with a grooming situation gone wrong, for example. Wasn't it the case in Rotherham, Rochdale, Aylesbury and all the other places that those involved in grooming were men of Pakistani heritage exploiting white girls?'

'Yes,' said Banks. 'But I still think we ought to keep an open mind. Don't jump to conclusions. It wasn't necessarily a grooming gang that did this. They could have been friends of hers, for example, or people pretending to be friends. Or students. Kids today hang around with all kinds of ethnic groups. They're not racist, most of them, except your BNP types. And Pakistanis aren't genetically predisposed to grooming young girls for sex. After all, it's not something we haven't been doing for years already – and by we I mean ethnic Brits and other Europeans. It's not a specifically race-related issue.'

'It becomes one when most people caught at it these days are of Pakistani origin,' Annie argued. 'And they weren't caught before because everyone – including us – turned a blind eye because we were scared of upsetting the Muslim community. And nobody believed the victims. Remember that buried report from West Midlands in the news not long ago?'

'Can't you all hear what you're saying?' Adrian Moss cut in. 'This is dynamite. Any one of those words or theories. As soon as the media get anywhere near this, they're . . . we're . . . we're . . . I mean, for Christ's sake: Rotherham, Rochester, Pakistanis, grooming. It's a public relations nightmare waiting to happen. We'll be accused of racism. Worse, of *Islamophobia*.'

'You're here to prevent that, aren't you?' said Annie, smiling sweetly at him. 'And take heart, Adrian, we're hardly dealing with devout Muslims, are we? Think about it. Alcohol, ketamine and possible gang-rape were involved, and the last I heard they're a big no-no as far as Islam is concerned. Whoever gang-raped the girl or beat her to death don't believe in any deity I'd care to know about. They rape underage girls, sell them for sex.'

Moss groaned and put his head in his hands. Annie wasn't sure whether it was 'gang-rape' or 'sell them for sex' that caused such a reaction. 'Whatever you do,' he pleaded, 'just don't mention grooming to the media. At least not yet, not until you have absolute proof and I've had a chance to smooth the way. Even then, please clear it with me first.'

'Don't worry, Adrian,' said Banks. 'We'll be keeping as much as we can back. We'll keep both you and the CPS in the loop. We don't even know the victim's identity yet. And there's something else we should keep in mind.'

'What?' asked Annie.

'They may have groomed her and even raped her, but they didn't kill her.'

'We can't be certain about that,' Annie said.

'Possibly not. But from what you've told me, and Jazz's analysis bears this out, all we really know is that the victim had rough sex with three men of Pakistani descent, and it seems they tossed her naked out of a moving van in the middle of nowhere. The murder took place *after* that. Beyond that, it's all speculation.'

'I'm sorry,' said Jazz. 'But we got nothing from the murder scene, nothing from the killer except scuffs in the grass and the shoe or boot impressions Stefan's working on.'

'But they still threw her out of a moving vehicle,' Annie insisted. 'That's attempted murder, for a start. And I happen to think our speculations are very reasonable given the circumstances.'

'Maybe they did it for a laugh,' Banks argued. 'Kids can be irresponsible. And cruel. And that wasn't what killed her. Or the sex. She walked for about ten minutes back along the road before someone stopped and did the killing.'

'Fair enough,' said Annie. 'You're the boss. So what exactly does this new information tell us?' She went to the whiteboard and took up a red marker, noting down the points as she talked. 'I know it's mere speculation, but we have assumed the van was travelling from the north-east. Most likely it was heading for West Yorkshire, or maybe Greater Manchester. We might look more closely at communities with a large Asian popula-tion. There are bound to be a few in Teesside or Tyneside, not to mention West Yorkshire and Greater Manchester.'

'I agree that's it's a useful lead,' said Banks, 'and we have to work with it. We also need to keep quiet about it until we have more to go on. The three men probably lived in an area with a high Asian population. If you tie that in with the kebab and pizza takeaway, or tattoo parlour, for example, you might be able to narrow it down even further. But we still need to find out who the victim is. That's what's most likely to lead us to our suspects.'

Annie sat down dejectedly. 'The drawing's in the papers and on TV. It'll be shown again tonight and over the weekend. I don't know what more we can do. Someone has to recognise her.'

'Maybe that's the problem,' Banks said.

'What?'

'Somebody does recognise her, and that's why they're not talking.'

'Scared?'

'Look how badly she was beaten,' Banks said. 'It sends a message. Anyone who does know who she is very likely knows who did it, and why. If she's got any sense, she's got to be scared to death of him, or them.'

'Then we need to find this person as fast as we can,' said Annie.

'Well, this is nice,' said Annie, raising her glass. 'Cheers.'

In the early evening, Banks and Annie were sitting outside at the Queen's Arms, in the market square, food on order and pints of Timothy Taylor's in front of them. Luckily for them, Adrian Moss had done his Pied Piper act and spirited the media away from the market square into the press room for a spot of disinformation. The evening light was soft and warm, the shadows slowly lengthening, and the limestone was almost the colour of Cotswold stone. The square was quiet. Most people were at home having dinner with the family, Banks thought, or getting ready for a night on the town.

'Cheers,' he said. 'You do realise that what Jazz just told us makes your job rather . . . delicate?'

'"Delicate"? Is that what promotion does for you, makes you use words like "delicate"?'

'That's not fair.'

'I know. And I'm sorry. It just slipped out. It just doesn't sound like the old you, that's all. It sounds more like Adrian Moss.'

'I almost feel sorry for poor Adrian,' said Banks. 'He's certainly copped for it, hasn't he? Two major media bombshells in a week. I'm actually relieved that your latest bit of news will keep him occupied more than anything I might do next.'

'Charming. Maybe I'd feel sorry for him, too, if he wasn't such a wanker.'

'Adrian has his own agenda, and it's my guess that right at the top of it is Adrian Moss.' Banks smiled. 'See. I'm not so different from who I was before. I've just got more responsibility.'

'And power.'

'That's a laugh.'

'Didn't you read that report where they said not to let misguided fears about offending cultural sensitivities get in the way of nailing the bastards who exploit children? Or something along those lines.'

'I read it,' said Banks. 'And I agree. But that doesn't mean you have to go charging in like a bull in a china shop with all guns blazing. Softly, softly.'

'Softly, softly, my arse,' Annie replied. 'And don't mix your metaphors. Though the image of a bull with an AK 47 is most amusing. I don't give a damn whether they're brown, blue or yellow with green spots. If they drugged and raped that girl we're going to get the bastards for it.'

'I'm with you on that, Annie,' said Banks. 'It just makes things more . . . delicate. That's all I said. I can tell you exactly what's going to happen. Soon, the chief constable will give us all the lecture about not rocking the boat and respecting community values, Islam in particular.'

'Oh? So it's all about the chief constable's comfort levels, is it?'

'You know it isn't.' Banks paused. 'You're going to have to act as SIO on this investigation, you know. Not officially. I mean, not as a DI.'

'Promote me to DCI then. Your old office is still empty, isn't it?'

Banks smiled. 'I would if I could. Believe me, whenever I get a chance I put a word in the right ears. But you've got to improve your chances by setting an example. As I said, even though I'm SIO on paper, you'll be doing the job yourself if this Caxton thing goes as it should. It's "delicate", therefore a little tact with your success would go a long way to convincing the brass you're worth promoting, that you can handle the big time.'

A young girl delivered their meals. She couldn't have been much older than the victim, Banks thought. They thanked her and made a start before getting back to their conversation. 'How's the veggie lasagne?' Banks asked.

'Probably a lot better than your curry of the day.'

'Oh, I don't know. Tastes all right to me.'

'What is it?'

'Dunno, really. Curry. Of the day. Anonymous.'

Annie poked his arm. 'OK, I take your point about tact. But isn't it exactly because of that attitude you're expressing that this grooming business got out of hand to start with? Being "delicate"? Treating everyone except the victims with kid gloves? Coppers and social workers so frightened of offending any ethnic or cultural group that they can't do their jobs properly? Victims so convinced they won't be believed that they don't even bother to report crimes?'

'That's a part of it,' Banks said. 'Along with the breakdown of the family unit, overcrowded housing, immigration policy, Margaret Thatcher, the death of God, Cameron, the drug culture and the sexual revolution. Might as well throw UKIP in there, too.'

'Well, we have to throw them somewhere. But aren't we going down the same path? Not the UKIP path, but like the others, too touchy-feely and inclusive and diverse to do anything?'

'Not if we can help it. I'm just saying we're going to have to tread carefully. We can't go shouting out to all and sundry that three British Pakistanis are responsible for everything that happened to that girl. The rape, yes, but we can't be sure about the murder. I'm not saying what they did is minor, or that they should get off lightly, but don't lose sight of the fact that we're after three rapists and one killer, here, whatever their colour, and though I'd guess the killer knows who the rapists are, they don't necessarily know who he is. And we don't know what ethnic group he belongs to. You're right. It shouldn't matter. Only that we know he's a killer.'

'You don't really think the girl went along with the three men willingly?'

'I don't know. She might have done, if she knew them. If your theory is right, she might have gone with them because they'd groomed her. She might have thought that she had nothing to fear, that they were just going to have a bit of fun. Then things got out of hand, perhaps because of the ketamine. But from what I read in the post-mortem report about her injuries, and I mean the sexual injuries, I doubt that she went along with what they did. On the other hand, as Jazz said, if she was off her face on ketamine, who knows what was going through her mind? If Gerry's on the right track, you might get a lead from the CCTV.'

'Maybe,' said Annie. She picked up a forkful of lasagne. 'Eventually. What about your case? Danny Caxton. Do you believe the accuser after all this time?'

'I think so,' Banks said. 'You know, she was about the same age as the Bradham Lane victim when it happened. And she was raped, too. In her case, by two men. She also lived to tell the tale. She went willingly to the hotel with Caxton, drank a glass or two of champagne, then things turned ugly. That's what I mean. Maybe your victim got willingly into the van for the drugs, booze, music, party time, whatever, and then things turned nasty. There's no evidence that she was abducted or anything like that.'

'Quite the opposite,' said Annie. 'She was ejected. On the other hand, the three men *could* have abducted her from the street somewhere first. I just wish we knew more.'

'It'll come,' said Banks. 'Danny Caxton is a nasty piece of work, I can tell you that much.' He finished his pint. 'Bugger it,' he said. 'That went down well. I'm going to have another.'

'Drinking and driving?'

'I'll get one of the PCs to drive me home.'

'Ooh, flexing our superintendent's muscles are we? Remember what I said about power?'

'Damn right. If you've got it, flaunt it. That's what I say.'

He went inside to get himself another pint and an orange juice for Annie, who was at least willing to stick with him for a while longer, even if she wasn't drinking. It was that time of evening when the place was almost deserted inside. Pat, the Australian barmaid, clearly had the night off, and Cyril had one of his playlists on: Marianne Faithfull singing 'Summer Nights'. Very appropriate. Banks got the drinks and went back outside. The square was starting to fill up a bit now, young couples, families, some groups back from long walks, ready for the evening meal and few pints. Other pubs had tables outside, and he could hear conversations and laughter from all sides. Music. It was Friday night. The weekend starts here.

Annie smiled when he handed her the drink. 'I'll give you a lift home,' she said. 'How's that for an offer?'

'Best I've had all day. But it's out of your way.'

'That's just the kind of person I am. Now, tell me about Danny Caxton. He seemed so nice on telly. I mean, in an avuncular sort of way. I didn't fancy him or anything.'

'Yeah, he's everybody's dirty uncle. He's arrogant, foul-mouthed and he has no sense of remorse. It wouldn't surprise me in the least if he's raped dozens of young girls over his career.'

'Well, there's an open mind for you.'

'Oh, I'll keep an open mind, all right. And he'll get a fair trial, if it ever comes to court. The odds are probably in his favour. It's the other bloke that interests me at the moment.'

'What other bloke?'

'I told you there were two rapists. According to Linda, the other was a bit younger than Caxton, and Caxton seemed happy to share the spoils with him. I'd like to know why. And who he was, of course. And what's happened to him.'

'Is there a way to find out after all this time?'

'I think so. Linda Palmer remembers seeing a photograph of the same man some time after her ordeal, maybe in October 1967, though she can't remember where she saw it. She says she's certain he wasn't famous, so I'm just wondering if she saw it in the local newspaper or something. At least that's a place to start.'

'But the rape took place in Blackpool.'

'That's because Caxton was in a summer show there. He actually lived near Otley at the time, just outside Leeds, and according to our records he appeared in panto at the Bradford Alhambra that Christmas. *Puss in Boots.*'

'Christ, I used to *hate* pantos,' said Annie.

'I wouldn't have imagined you got to very many, living in the artists' colony and all.'

'It was my uncle and aunt. They always worried about me not having a normal childhood, and that was one of the ways they remedied it, by taking me to the panto in Newquay every Christmas. *Normal*. Panto. I ask you.'

Banks laughed.

'Maybe she saw him on telly or in a pop music magazine?'

'I don't think so,' Banks said. 'She seemed adamant that she didn't know him and hadn't seen him before. I don't believe he was a public figure. I think he may have been some sort of aide to Caxton. I would imagine panto would provide just as good a hunting ground as summer season, so we'll be trying to track down any incidents there, too. If I could find the photo she saw, maybe she'd recognise him, then we'd have an ID, at least.'

'How would you do that?'

'I'd get an idea of what newspapers or magazines a four-teen-year-old might have seen in 1967 and come up with a pile of photocopies for her to sort through. Something like that.'

'Talk about a long shot.'

'Or maybe I'll just start with the local paper and get lucky. Who knows? That's the sort of thing that happens with these cold cases. Everything's a long shot. Sometimes it seems as much about understanding the times as well as the characters involved.'

'1967? You ought to be good at that. One of your best years, wasn't it?'

Banks smiled. 'It was a very good year, but I was still just a kid, a bit too young to enjoy all the new freedoms people were talking about. Not that they ever reached Peterborough. But musically, it was great. The Summer of Love. The Doors, Jefferson Airplane, Pink Floyd, Love, Cream, Hendrix. *Sergeant Pepper*. Magnificent.'

'Well, you can listen to all your old records and relive it.'

'Not a bad idea, at that,' said Banks. 'There was a dark side to it all, though, and I have a feeling that's where I'll be finding myself.'

'Don't we always?' said Annie. 'Don't we always?'

6

It was Monday morning, five days since the unidentified body had been found on Bradham Lane, and the eight-mile stretch was still closed to traffic in the hope that Stefan's team would unearth some significant clue that had so far eluded their efforts. Fortunately, the lane was so little used that there was no immediate clamour for its reopening. A couple of cyclists had written letters to the local paper, but that was about all. Everyone else who had used it as a pleasant and convenient alternative had returned to the A1 temporarily without complaint.

Every day the media gathered at both ends of the lane, but the scene was well guarded, with the mobile crime unit blocking the top end. One or two hardy reporters had tried sneaking across the fields to take photographs, but the vigilant eyes of the officers guarding the inner scene, the immediate area in which the body had been found, had spotted them in time. Even so, a few long-distance shots had appeared, the kind that have to be published with a circle added to pinpoint where the crime happened. Desperate for any sort of crime-scene image, one less reputable newspaper had even published a shot of a similar spot on a different road and claimed it as the place where the battered and broken body of the young girl was discovered. Both the cyclist who had found the body, Roger Stanford, and the Ketteridges on the nearest farm, had come under media siege at one point or another. As Stanford seemed on the verge of a nervous breakdown and Mrs Ketteridge lived in fear of losing her baby, the local police had seen all the interlopers off and posted guards around the farm and Stanford's house.

The investigation had naturally slowed down over the weekend, especially as the budget allowed for little or no overtime. In the meantime, information wasn't exactly pouring in. The CSIs had made no more headway and Jazz Singh had done about as much as she could with the DNA.

Late that morning, Gerry was sitting at her computer in the squad room when the telephone rang. She picked up the handset and announced her rank and name. It was one of the community support officers working the Bradham Lane case, calling from the mobile crime scene unit. 'Sorry to bother you, DC Masterson,' she said, but I've got a caller on the hotline who insists on speaking to the person in charge of the investigation.'

'That would be DI Cabbot,' said Gerry. 'Or DCI Banks.'

'They're not around. I rang you because the caller sounds a bit spooked. Young. Can I put her through? Maybe you could talk to her?'

'Put her through.'

She waited a few moments, and a small, scared voice came on the line. 'Hello? Hello? Do you know about the girl in Bradham Lane, the one whose picture was on telly?'

'I'm DC Masterson,' said Gerry. 'And I'm working on the case. Do you know who she is? Can you help us?'

'I don't know. Is the drawing a good likeness? Have you actually *seen* her?'

'I was there when she was found,' Gerry said. It was more or less true. 'Yes, I saw her. It's a good likeness.'

'It is her, isn't it? Was she, I mean . . .?'

'Are you OK?'

'I'm OK. Yes. It's just that she was my best friend. It's *her*. It looks like her. I haven't seen her for days. And they . . .'

Gerry felt her blood turn cold. 'Who?' she said. 'Who are they?'

'I can't. They'll kill me, too.'

'It's all right, love,' Gerry said, as gently as she could. 'Can you tell me who she is, then?'

'Yes. It's Mimsy.'

'Mimsy?'

'Mimsy Moffat.' The caller paused. 'We used to tease her about that,' she said. '"All mimsy were the borogoves." She loved *Alice*. I remember when we talked about starting a band. We were going to call ourselves Mimsy and the Borogoves.'

Gerry knew 'Jabberwocky'. She had been a big Lewis Carroll fan when she was at school, and she still read the *Alice* stories once a year. 'That's a cute name. You can sing and play instruments?'

'No. It was just blethering.'

'You said "we". "We used to tease her." Who else?'

'Just me, really.'

'Can you tell me where Mimsy lived?'

'On the estate. Number fourteen Southam Terrace.'

'Where's that? What estate?'

'Wytherton Heights.'

'Wytherton?'

'Teesside. Near Middlesbrough.'

'OK. My name's Gerry. What's yours, love?'

'I'm sorry. I can't tell you. Nobody must know.' Then she hung up, or switched off her mobile. Gerry immediately hit redial but her call went through to a generic answering service, the kind you get with a pay-as-you-go mobile when you don't bother to personalise it. She left her name and mobile number just in case, then returned to her computer screen and clicked through to Google Maps.

Wytherton was an area that clung like a boil to the arse of Teesside between Stockton and Middlesbrough, and

Wytherton Heights was a sprawling square mile of council estates fringed in the north by a forest of sixties tower blocks and to the south by the main Wytherton Road. Town Street bisected the estate about a quarter of a mile up from Wytherton Road. Southam Terrace, Gerry discovered, lay somewhere near the middle of the largest section.

What little information Gerry could find on the estate told her that it was a mix of post-war council housing. Some people who lived there had bought their houses from the council in the eighties or later, and there were a few older private houses scattered around the edges, mostly turned into student bedsits to service the nearby college. The Google Maps satellite images showed a mix of domestic architecture, from the grime-encrusted back-to-backs and through terraces to sixties brick council houses, maisonettes and old tower blocks. The aerial photographs she managed to dredge up showed higgledy-piggledy streets straggling west of a wasteland of abandoned factory yards with high fences scrolled with barbed wire, or walls topped with broken glass. To these, west of the houses, by the canal, stood a modern shopping centre.

Gerry didn't think she was a snob, but she had been brought up in a nice Georgian semi in a suburb of Liverpool called Crosby, not far from the Irish Sea. She had attended Merchant Taylors' Girls School before reading law at Cambridge. Her mother was a schoolteacher and her father a solicitor and, needless to say, her decision to join the police after university had caused a family row or two. She wasn't certain why she had done it, herself, only that she knew she didn't want an academic career, and she didn't want to be a lawyer. She thought that in the police she might at least get the chance to use her initiative now and then, find a little excitement, even danger, and that every day would be different. She could also use her IT skills. And Gerry wasn't without ambition. If she did the right courses and was successful in her fieldwork, she knew fast-track promotion was a strong possibility for someone like her. The sky was the limit. She knew it sounded silly, and maybe joining the police was the wrong way to go about it, but she might even one day end up running MI5, like Stella Rimington, whose books she enjoyed. One of her friends had been recruited at Cambridge, and she remembered feeling jealous that she hadn't been singled out, too. Perhaps it was because she wasn't reading politics or Middle Eastern languages.

No matter how much she tried to be 'one of the lads', though, she knew she was posh when it came right down to it. Places like Wytherton Heights gave her the creeps. A big godforsaken ugly splodge of urban hell stuck between the beauties of the North York Moors and the Yorkshire Dales National Park, it might as well have signs saying NO GO AREA in big letters all over it. Perhaps she was showing her upper-middle-class upbringing, but she wouldn't be surprised if it was the sort of area that boasted a tattoo shop or two as well as a kebab and pizza takeaway. As for whether it was home to a large Asian population, she had no idea, though she could soon find out.

Gerry felt immediately guilty for being so judgemental. She had always prided herself on being a nice, decent, thoughtful person, kind to all and sundry, but perhaps her short time in the police had changed her. DI Cabbot could be cynical at times, so perhaps some of that was rubbing off on her. One glance at the Wytherton Heights estate onscreen was enough to tell her that she wouldn't like visiting it.

But this wasn't the time for self-analysis, she thought, getting to her feet. Like it or not, it was time to pick up her boss from County HQ and whisk them both up to Southam Terrace, Wytherton Heights. Maybe it would turn out to be a much nicer place than she thought.

★   ★   ★

The Wakefield office of the West Yorkshire Archive Service was unfortunately not a modern air-conditioned building, being instead housed in the old Registry of Deeds office, a 1930s building on Newstead Road. Ken Blackstone handed over the form he had filled out, and after he and Banks had shown their warrant cards, Ms Brindley made a quick search to locate the occurrence book. She soon came back with the volume they wanted and placed it on the table in front of them.

'It would have been the end of August or beginning of September, 1967,' Banks said. 'I don't know the exact date, but it was before school started again.'

It didn't take long to locate the brief, neatly written entry of the thirtieth of August 1967, at 2.35 p.m. Reading the unadorned entry, Banks could only imagine what that day had been like for Linda Palmer and her mother, perhaps agonising over whether to go, frightened, embarrassed, sitting on the bus to town not knowing what to expect. As it was only an occurrence book, not a statement, there was very little detail. The complainant was identified as 'Linda Palmer' and her mother's presence was also noted. They had come with a 'crime complaint', which was further described as 'indecent and unlawful' in the description. There was no mention of rape, and Danny Caxton was not named. Detective Inspector Stanley Chadwick had talked to the complainant, but when it came to further action and result, there was nothing. Blackstone flipped forward a few pages to see if he could find anything else, but all the entries were similarly brief. They would need the case files or individual notebooks to find out any more, and they were gone, if there had, indeed, ever been any. Destroyed years ago, most likely.

Disappointed, Banks asked Ms Brindley if she would make a copy of the entry in question. It wasn't much, but every little helped at this point.

'As you can see,' she said, 'the occurrence book is rather large and heavy. It's very awkward to fit in the photocopier. I'd suggest you use your mobile and take a digital photo, if that's acceptable?"

'Of course.' Banks took out his mobile, positioned it carefully and took three photos, just to make certain. 'Is there any way of finding out if anything came of this?' he asked when he had finished.

'Not without the records, no, and I'm afraid we don't have those.'

'I know,' said Banks. 'Is there *anything* else?'

'Well, let me see. We do have the court registers, so if anything went to court it would be listed in there.'

'As far as we know, it didn't,' said Banks. 'But thanks, anyway.'

'No problem.' Ms Brindley smiled and asked them if there was anything more they required.

'No, thanks,' said Blackstone. 'You've been a great help. Thanks very much.'

Ms Brindley inclined her head briefly then drifted away. Banks and Blackstone made their way outside again, where it was marginally cooler than inside.

They found a pub with a beer garden not far from the cathedral and sat down at a table in the shade next to two young women struggling to control three small children, who already appeared to have ingested a surfeit of sugar. The pretty mother with the ring in her nose and a stud in her lower lip gave Banks a long-suffering glance, and he smiled at her.

It was a chain pub, but that was OK with Banks. At least it meant they would get their food quickly. Blackstone passed him a laminated menu. They both decided on the steak and mushroom pie special, and Blackstone went to get some drinks – Coke, as they both had to drive later – and put in their order at the bar. While he was away, the eldest of the children at the next table, perhaps about three, tottered over to Banks, grinning and slobbering drool down the front of his bib. The girl with the stud in her lip swept forward and picked him up with one arm in a surprisingly gentle and graceful motion, smiled sweetly at Banks and apologised.

When Blackstone got back, Banks raised his Coke. 'Cheers. I didn't notice you pursuing young Ms Brindley with quite the vigour I would have expected from you.'

'Didn't you notice the ring on her finger?'

'Afraid not.'

'Big sparkler. Probably zircon. Third finger of her left hand. Wasn't there the last time I saw her.'

'Too late, then.'

'Story of my life. Cheers,' said Blackstone. 'I see from the news you've got a media circus on your hands up in Eastvale.'

'Tell me about it. I'm sneaking around like a mischievous schoolboy. Our Media Relations Officer is about ready to blow a gasket. The mere mention of "Pakistani" sends him into conniptions.'

'Pakistani?'

'Annie might have a grooming case on her hands involving members of the British Pakistani community. Not a word, mind you.'

'My lips are sealed.'

'We think the girl was raped by three men and beaten to death by another on a remote country lane in our neck of the woods. Gerry's just discovered who she was, and her home happens to be on a council estate that's conveniently located just on our side of the county border.'

'Nasty. I don't suppose this Caxton business helps with the media relations, either?'

'Oh, Adrian loves that,' said Banks. 'That's his wet dream. It's the race thing that's got his knickers in a twist.'

The food came and they paused for a while to eat in silence. The pastry on Banks's pie was soggy and the meat more gristle than steak. One of the other young children at the next table threw some cutlery on the grass and let out a piercing scream. Banks winced. The young woman picked up the spoon and smiled at him again.

'I'm sorry we couldn't get much from the archive,' Blackstone said.

'That's OK. I didn't expect anything more. There is one interesting piece of information, though.'

'Oh?'

'"Chiller" Chadwick. I've come across him before on another old case. Always had my suspicions he was bent, but I could never prove it.'

'I don't suppose he's still around?' said Blackstone.

'Died of a heart attack in March 1973, if I remember rightly.'

'I think I know the case you mean,' Blackstone said. 'Wasn't that the rock journalist connected with the murder at that Brimleigh rock festival in 1969? Chadwick would have been the SIO back then, right?'

'That's right,' said Banks. 'Linda Lofthouse, the Mad Hatters, Vic Greaves, all that lot. Seems a lifetime ago.'

'1969?'

'Our case. The journalist. 2006, wasn't it? 1969 seems several lifetimes ago, and as for 1967 . . .'

'The Summer of Love.'

'That's right. Not for Linda Palmer, though. You know, Ken, there are a few leads in this that might not be too cold. I remember from the other case, we located Chadwick's oppo, a DS Enderby, and he also had a DC called Bradley. I talked to Chadwick's daughter Yvonne as well. There's a chance he might have mentioned Linda Palmer or Danny Caxton to one of them. From what I heard about him, he struck me as a hard man, and not beyond a verbal or a beating, but I don't think he was the kind of person who'd have liked being anyone's fool, or in anyone's pocket. Even Caxton's.'

'It's worth a shot, isn't it?' said Blackstone. 'Tracking them down. His daughter. This DC Bradley.'

'Definitely. I've got their addresses back on the old case records in Eastvale. At least from 2006. But first I've got something I'd like you to do for me, if you can spare a couple of lads for a few hours.'

'My team is at your command,' said Blackstone.

Banks explained about the photo Linda Palmer remembered seeing and suggested starting with the *Yorkshire Evening Post* for October 1967.

'Those old newspaper morgues are more complicated than you'd think,' said Blackstone. 'I suppose you know the old YEP building's been knocked down and they've moved to Whitehall Road?'

'Yes.'

'The thing is, they always stored their photos by theme, not date, and I expect they still do.'

'We'd need to go through the complete issues,' Banks said. 'The photo might be part of a story and we'd need to know that story. We don't know the theme. Surely they're on microfiche somewhere? Old newspapers are fragile, aren't they?'

Blackstone considered for a moment. 'I think your best bet is Leeds Central Library. They've got a Local Studies Department that has all the old YEPs on microfilm. It shouldn't take too long to scroll through them. Would it be a problem, getting your victim to Leeds?'

'I can't see why,' said Banks.

'Then there's no reason you shouldn't do it tomorrow.'

'That soon? Can you get it organised?'

'Sure. I know some of the staff there. We use the facility often. I'll have a word, let them know to get it set up. October 1967?

Banks pushed his plate of half-eaten pie aside. Blackstone followed suit. 'If it's going to be that easy, we might as well throw in September and November as well, if that's no problem.'

'Not at all. Early afternoon good?'

'Fine with me. Thanks, Ken.'

'Right, then. You know where the place is?'

'I ought to do.'

'I'll ring you in the morning, tell you who to ask for.'

'In that case,' said Banks, 'I'll put off interviewing Bradley and Chadwick's daughter until Linda's had a chance to examine the photos. Who knows, I might have a few more things to ask them about if we get lucky on this.' He finished his Coke and stood up. 'Shall we?'

The young woman with the children gave Banks a weary smile as they left.

Blackstone nudged him. 'You could have been in there, mate. I saw the way she was eyeing you. Ready-made family.'

Banks laughed. 'Just what I need right now.'

Wytherton was about a forty-five-minute drive from Eastvale. At the heart of the Heights estate, Southam Terrace was a narrow, potholed street of through terrace houses blackened by years of industrial smoke. The council might well have restored the Victorian town hall to its former sandstone glory, but nobody had bothered sandblasting the streets of Wytherton Heights. Even the sunlight didn't do much to brighten up the sooty facades and grimy slate roofs. Gerry parked her lime-green Corsa across from the Moffat house, and she and Annie walked over the hot tarmac. The smell of warm tar provoked in Annie a sudden memory of sitting by the roadside on hot summer days when she was a child, picking off chunks of softened tar and rolling them into balls.

The gate was closed, peeling green paint in need of a touch-up, and beyond it two children played on a postage-stamp lawn littered with bright-coloured plastic toys. The children, one about two, the other about five, looked up suspiciously from the structure they were building of different-coloured interlocking blocks.

'That's nice,' said Annie, crouching. 'What is it, a castle?'

'Prison,' said the five-year-old, and sniggered.

'They learn young around here,' Annie muttered, standing up. 'Mum and Dad in?'

'Dunno.'

Gerry knocked on the door, and they waited almost a full minute before anyone answered. They could hear the TV playing loudly inside, some overexcited sporting commentary, but nothing else. Eventually the door opened and a man in a grubby string vest stood in front of them. 'Yeah? What is it?'

Annie flashed her warrant card. 'Mr Moffat?'

'No. Lenny Thornton.'

'Is Mr Moffat at home?'

Thornton scratched his head. 'Well, he was here maybe ten years or so ago, but it'll be the missus you're after. Well, the girlfriend. You know. Her name's Moffat.'

'Mimsy?' said Gerry.

'Bloody hell, no, pet. That's her young lass. Sinead's her mother.' He had a strong Geordie accent. Annie was used to hearing it, but she could see Gerry struggling to understand.

'Is Sinead Moffat in, then?' As Annie spoke, she and Gerry were edging forward into the front room. Lenny Thornton edged back politely as they moved forward. Eventually they were able to shut the door behind them. The closed curtains let in a faint glow, but the main source of light was a large flickering TV screen showing an international football game. Maybe there was a big tournament on somewhere that Annie hadn't heard about, but she thought it more likely the game was a repeat. When she saw who was playing, she knew it was. She had watched it several days ago.

'Sinead's out,' said Thornton, 'but you's welcome to a cuppa, if you's like.' He subsided into a well-worn armchair, lit a cigarette and gestured to a teapot and a cluster of stained mugs on the table under the window. 'Kettle's in the kitchen.'

'No, thanks.' Annie glanced around the room. It was untidy, with stacks of magazines and articles of clothing strewn here and there. An unpleasant odour hung about the place: cigarette smoke, old socks and boiled cabbage. Then there was Lenny Thornton.

There are some men, Annie thought, such as Daniel Craig and Aidan Turner, who should be shirtless as often as possible, but Lenny Thornton wasn't one of them. His hairy belly drooped over his belt, little squares of fat pushing through the net of his string vest, and his man-breasts wobbled when he moved. He could also do with a shave and a haircut, and probably a wash, too. A tin of Carlsberg Special Brew rested on one arm of his armchair and an ashtray on the other. Annie also noticed, as her eyes adjusted, that there was another person in the room, a man with long, greasy hair and a lined unshaven face, who might well be dead for all the sound he'd made or movement he'd shown. Annie thought he resembled a zombie biker in the dim light. 'Who's that?' she asked.

'That's Sinead's brother,' Lenny Thornton answered. 'Hasna moved from that chair in ten years. Except to go to the local, that is. Say hello to the polis, Johnny.'

Johnny gave what sounded like a grunt without taking his eyes away from the football game. The door on the other side of the room was open, and Annie could see through the kitchen and the open back door to the yard beyond, with its high brick wall and latched wooden gate. A bicycle without wheels leaned against the wall. She knew without looking that beyond the gate would be a narrow cobbled alley, and on the opposite side another backyard exactly the same. People used to have their WCs out there, but most had got indoor toilets these days and only used the old outhouses as storage sheds. At least a light breeze blew in through the open door. There were two hard-backed chairs at the table by the window, and Annie decided they were probably the safest place to sit, after she had moved a pile of old *Racing Posts* from one of them.

'Do you know how long Sinead will be?' she asked.

'No telling with her when she goes out and about.'

'Do you know where we can find her?'

'Could be anywhere.'

Annie pressed on. 'And Mimsy?'

'Your guess is as good as mine. Her name's Mimosa, by the way. Sinead says she named her after a posh drink she had at a wedding once. But everyone calls her Mimsy. 'Cept Sinead, that is.'

'Any other children?'

'She's got an older brother.'

'What's he called? Buck's Fizz?'

'Come again?'

'Never mind.'

'Albert, he's called. After his granddad. Silly name for a kid these days, I'd say.'

Albert and Mimosa, Annie thought. It sounded like a good stage name. What act would they perform? Magician and assistant? 'Where's Albert?'

'He's out an' all.'

'So there's just you and Johnny here?'

'That's right, hen.'

Annie sighed. 'Lucky us.'

'So why don't you just tell us what you want, then you can go about your business and we can get back to the footie.'

Annie glanced at the screen. 'I've seen it,' she said. 'Croatia win 3–2 in extra time.'

Thornton glared at her. 'You can be a right bitch, you know that, love?'

'I've been called worse. Look,' Annie went on, softening her tone. 'I've got a serious job to do here, and you're not being very helpful.'

'I can't tell you people are here when they're not, can I? That'd be lying. You're not asking me to lie to the polis, now, are you?'

'OK, but I'm sure you could give us some idea of where Sinead is?'

'I told you. I don't know where she goes.'

'What does she do? Has she got a job?'

'Job? Nay, lass, none of us has a job. Everyone knows there's no work around these parts, even the tarts what work at the Job Centre. Hasn't been for years. The old uns'll tell you it was Thatcher shutting down the steelworks and engineering factories. Even Johnny over there's never had a job in his life, and he won't see t'other side of forty again. *Job?*'

So Mimsy Moffat was probably third-generation unemployed, Annie realised. She thought for a moment, then opened her briefcase and slipped out a copy of the artist's impression. He had tried to make Mimsy appear as alive and unblemished as possible, and succeeded to a large extent. She showed the image to Lenny Thornton. 'Could this be Mimsy?'

Thornton squinted, then took the sheet of paper to the window and inched open the curtains to let the direct light fall on it. 'That's her,' he said, handing it back. 'To a tee. It's bloody good, that is. Who's been drawing her, then? Is it one of her own?'

'She draws?'

'Aye. Anything and everything. She'd draw the bloody kitchen sink if there was nothing else around.' He glanced from Annie to Gerry, and Annie thought she could see fear in his eyes. 'What's going on?' he asked. 'It's never good news, having the polis around. Is something wrong?'

'It's not one of Mimsy's drawings,' Annie said. 'Don't you watch the news? Read the papers?'

Thornton sat down again. '*Racing Post*, some days. And Johnny won't have the news on. Says it's all lies and government conspiracies. We just watch Sky Sports. Look, love, come on, you're making us nervous.'

Annie sighed. 'Mr Thornton, I'm sorry to have to tell you this, but we think Mimsy's dead. That's why we're here. That's why we're asking questions.'

Thornton turned to her, slack-jawed. 'Dead? What do you mean you think Mimsy's dead?'

'We believe she was murdered last Tuesday night. Have you seen her since then?'

'No. No, I haven't. But . . . murder? Our Mimsy? Who'd want to murder her? Johnny, will you turn that thing down?'

Johnny did something with the remote and the volume quietened a little.

'That's what we'd like to find out,' Annie said. 'We really need to talk to Sinead.'

'But you can't think she had anything to do with it.'

'I'm not saying she did. But she's Mimsy's mother. She'll have to be informed. And someone will have to come to Eastvale Infirmary and identify Mimsy. We'd prefer her mother to come if at all possible.'

'Eastvale?' Thornton lit a cigarette. His movements seemed to be in slow motion, mechanical. Annie realised he must be in shock, for all his apparent bravado. She didn't think she could have broken the news any more gently. 'Mr Thornton? Are you all right? Do you want me to call someone for you? Doctor? A neighbour?'

Thornton waved his cigarette. 'Nay, nay. I'm all right, hen. Just give me a minute for it to sink in, like. Our Mimsy. Murdered. What happened? Who did it?'

'Somebody gave her a beating. We don't know who.'

Johnny still hadn't reacted at all, and Annie doubted that he had even heard what she had said. She decided against trying to involve him for the time being. He was Mimsy's uncle, and he was certainly weird, but there was no more reason to expect him to move out of his chair now than Thornton said he had in the last ten years. Johnny could wait.

'When did you last see Mimsy, Mr Thornton?' Annie pressed on.

'I can't remember.'

'Come on, Mr Thornton. Try a bit harder. Please.'

Thornton furrowed his brow. 'Few days ago, I suppose,' he said finally.

'She does live here, doesn't she?'

'When it suits her. She comes and goes. You know what they're like.' He let his head rest in his hands for a moment and rubbed his whiskered face. 'Sorry, hen. I'll miss her. She was a breath of fresh air around here, you know, when she was home.' Then he got to his feet, knocking the Carlsberg Special Brew tin off the arm of the chair as he did so. Beer spilled over the threadbare carpet. 'I need something a bit stronger than that,' he said, taking a bottle of Johnnie Walker out of the cupboard and pouring himself a large glass before he returned to his armchair and took a gulp. Annie noticed that his hand was shaking.

'Technically, she's your stepdaughter, Lenny?'

'Technically, me and Sinead aren't actually married.'

'How long have you been living here together?'

'Six years.'

'Common law, then. As good as. How old was Mimsy?'

'Fifteen. And her brother Albert's eighteen. Christ. Albert. He'll be gutted. They're both Sinead's by her first husband.

Les Moffat.' He nodded towards the window. 'The two wee uns out there are mine and Sinead's.'

'How many children altogether?'

'Just the four.'

'Where is Albert?'

'He said he was off to go clubbing with some mates in Manchester. That were last Thursday.'

'Do you know who these mates are? An address?'

'Just mates of his.'

'Where's Les Moffat these days?'

'No idea. Down south, somewhere, I think.'

'So she stopped out a lot, Mimsy?'

'Aye. I suppose you could say that.'

'Nights as well?'

'It were all the same to her.'

'Where did she go?'

'Search me. She never said. Mates. And asking Mimsy anything she didn't want to tell you was like banging your head against a brick wall.'

'Did she have a boyfriend?'

'Not as far as I know. She might have had. I honestly don't know what she got up to.'

'Didn't you worry about her?'

'No sense worrying, is there? *Que sera, sera.*'

'What about friends? Who did she hang out with?'

'Just her mates as far as I know. That's what she said if you ever asked her owt.' He tried to mimic a young girl's voice. '"I've been with my mates", "I'm going out with my mates."'

'Know any of their names?'

'Nah. Just, you know, they're local kids.'

'From school?'

Thornton reached for his cigarettes. 'I suppose so. Where else do kids meet other kids?'

Gerry seemed uncomfortable, and Annie remembered that she came from a nice clean comfortable middle-class home and went to a posh school. She wasn't used to this rough and ready way of life, the smells, the untidiness, the laissez-faire attitudes, the lack of discipline, the poverty. Annie had grown up in a messy and poor artists' commune and lost her mother at an early age, but her childhood had not been without love, care and comfort. This, she thought, looking at Lenny and Johnny, is what becomes of certain people when they feel disenfranchised, get put down and ignored all the time and come to feel there's no useful way through life for them, that nobody cares and nothing's going to change for the better. The most extreme do what Johnny was doing and sit catatonic in their chairs, day in, day out. For the rest, there are drugs, drink, violence, crime or just simple apathy broken up by the distraction of video games, sex and mobile phones. Life is something to be got through. Days are hurdles, weeks are rivers to cross, months lakes and years oceans. Annie wondered if life had been like that for Mimsy, too.

'Do you know where any of Mimsy's friends live?' she asked, without much hope.

'No. Just here and there, around the estate, you know.'

'Is there somewhere they hang out, some place in particular?'

'Probably at the shopping mall or down on the Strip,' said Thornton.

'The Strip?'

'Used to be the old Wytherton Town Street. It's got a few shops and cafes, couple of pubs, little parks, places to hang out. The name's a joke, like. The Strip. Las Vegas. There's a bookie's, but that's as close to a casino as you'll get down there. But it's changed a lot. Too many Pakis for my liking. It's like they've taken over everything. You might find some of her mates there if they don't mind too much who they hang out with. It doesn't really come alive until after dark. In daytime you'll most likely find them at the shopping mall, hanging around the fountain, or painting each other's toenails in someone's house.'

'How far away is this Strip?'

'Mile or so. There's a bus goes from the next street over.'

Annie made a note. They could check out the shopping mall first, then come back later and see what they could find out on the Strip. In the meantime, their priority was to find Sinead Moffat. 'So you've no idea where Mimsy's mother is, Mr Thornton?'

Thornton drank some more whisky and took a deep drag on his cigarette. 'You might as well know,' he said. 'You'd find out, anyway. Sinead's a junkie. She goes off with her junkie friends and they spend all day on cloud fucking nine I don't know where.'

'Do you know their names?'

'No. They never come here.'

'You don't share this life with her?'

'No.'

Annie could see from his arms that he didn't inject heroin, at any rate. 'So Sinead is a heroin addict? That's what you're telling me?'

'That's right. Oh, she's all official. Registered and all. And right now she's on methadone and going for counselling at the treatment centre, so. For all the good it does.'

'What do you mean?'

'Tried it all before, hasn't she? She always goes back.'

'But she shouldn't be shooting up with the others at the moment, not if she's on methadone?'

'She shouldn't be, no. When she's clean, when she's . . . oh, Christ, she can be the sweetest thing. She tries. My God, she tries. It just breaks your heart. I'm sorry. I really don't know where she is. She went to the clinic for her dose. Then she was supposed to go for counselling. If she was feeling all right, she might have gone shopping in the town centre. Middlesbrough, like.' Lenny Thornton had tears in his eyes. They had welled up so much that Annie was sure they would start to flow down his whiskery cheeks, but they didn't; they just clung there stubbornly, moist and heavy, on the bottom rims of his eyelids.

Annie handed him a card. 'I'm really sorry for your loss, Mr Thornton. You should be with your wife at a time like this. Will you try and get in touch with her and phone me when she comes back? And keep her here until I can get here?'

'Aye, pet. I'll try. This'll do her head in.'

'Did you know that Mimsy cut herself?' Annie said, raising her arm and pointing. 'Her wrist.'

'Aye, that were a couple of years back. Nowt serious, like.'

Annie assumed he was speaking of the physical injuries, not the psychological problems behind them. She nodded and stood up. Gerry needed no bidding to follow suit. 'Did Mimsy have her own room here?' Annie asked.

'That she did.'

'Mind if we have a look? Just to see if there's anything.'

'Top of the stairs on the left,' said Thornton.

Annie led the way upstairs and saw the door was half open. They both slipped on their latex gloves, and Gerry pushed on the door. The hinges creaked as it opened. The first thing Annie noticed was that Mimsy had been tidy for a teenager. Much more so than Annie herself had ever been. She didn't know about Gerry. She probably sat all her dolls in a neat row on a bookshelf and arranged the books according to the Dewey decimal system. Or perhaps it was simply that Mimsy wasn't here very often. The striped wallpaper was peeling up there, just as it was in the living room.

Mimsy Moffat didn't have much to keep tidy. The bed, a narrow single, was made, and there were clothes in the laundry hamper. Annie had been expecting the usual teenage posters on the walls – One Direction, Justin Bieber – but the only one was a poster advertising *Swan Lake* showing a beautiful ballerina appearing to float in mid-air above the water. The small chest of drawers was filled with underwear, make-up, socks, tights and a few pieces of cheap jewellery – earrings, a heart pendant with no photos inside, a charm bracelet with only a tiny pair of shoes on it. There were also a few T-shirts, clean and neatly folded. In her bedside drawer were a hairbrush, a box of Kleenex, a packet of paracetamol and a box of tampons. Nothing out of the ordinary.

A small desk stood under the window, which looked out on the backyard and the other backyards across the alley. On it lay a flat oblong tin of Lakeland colouring pencils and an 8 x 11 WHSmith sketchbook. Lenny Thornton had said that Mimsy liked to draw. Annie rifled through the pages, stopping here and there to admire a composition. Some were sketches of the uninspiring view from the window, others clearly more subjects from the imagination: magical creatures, half-deer, half-woman, flitting through forests at night, a stormy sea with tall-masted wooden ships tossing in the waves, a far-off mountain peak beyond a barren, red and orange landscape under a grey and purple sky, very *Lord of the Rings*, with a halo of fire at the summit. There were also some copies of the Tenniel illustrations to the Alice books. The one thing they all had in common was that they were very good. Perhaps a bit primitive in technique, but lacking nothing that couldn't be learned by someone with the basic talent in a few months. If Mimsy Moffat were the artist, she had been talented indeed. Annie put down the sketchbook and wandered over to the small bookcase.

There were few books, mostly Mills & Boon romances, Martina Cole and bulky collections of illustrated fairy tales by Hans Christian Andersen and the Brothers Grimm, along with children's books like *The Water Babies*, *Tales of Beatrix Potter*, *The Wind in the Willows* and not surprisingly a reproduction of *Alice's Adventures in Wonderland* and *Through the Looking-Glass* with the John Tenniel illustrations. The wardrobe held a couple of denim jackets, a winter coat with fake fur collar, various leggings, distressed shorts and jeans, some miniskirts and cheap print dresses, along with a few pairs of shoes, including sandals, no-name trainers and two pairs of court shoes. There was no mobile phone or computer. No stereo system, CDs, iPods or the like. No purse or handbag. No TV. In many ways, it was a spartan room, and Annie was hardly surprised Mimsy didn't spend much time there. Though no doubt it was spartan exactly *because* she hadn't spent much time there. But where had she spent her time, and what were the attractions there?

'Gerry, would you go ask Mr Thornton for a bin bag and permission to take the contents of Mimsy's laundry basket? Who knows, we might find something in her pockets, or stains with DNA to match the samples Jazz took from her body.'

Gerry went out and after a few moments came back with a black bin bag. 'He says he doesn't care what we take,' she told Annie. 'The level in that whisky bottle's gone down a fair bit, too.'

'People deal with bad news in their own way,' said Annie. 'Any word from Johnny?'

'Nothing. I think there's something seriously wrong with him.'

'You're probably right about that. Brain damage would be my guess.' She glanced around the room again. 'Anything else you think we should take?'

'Maybe the hairbrush?' said Gerry. 'Just to make sure about DNA.'

'Good point.' Annie put the hairbrush in one of the smaller plastic bags she carried in her shoulder bag, then put Mimsy's dirty laundry in the bin bag and labelled both.

Downstairs everything seemed much the same except, as Gerry had noted, the level in the whisky bottle. The football game was still on, fast approaching extra time, Johnny hadn't moved, and Thornton was lighting another cigarette. 'We'll be off, now,' Annie said. 'Are you sure there's nothing we can do for you before we leave, Mr Thornton?'

'Nay, pet. Just leave me be. I'll be all right. Johnny and me, we'll be all right.'

'Are you sure you don't want us to call someone?'

'I don't know as I want to talk to anyone right now,' said Thornton. 'But thanks, hen. You'd best be on your way now, all right? Find out what happened to our Mimsy.'

'You will give me a ring when Sinead comes back, won't you? We'll arrange to have her brought to Eastvale and back home again.'

'I'll ring,' Thornton said. His voice sounded throaty. He turned just as they opened the door. 'Would you mind sending in the wee ones in as you leave?' he said. 'You never know what's going to happen to them out there.'

It was the first thought he'd shown for his own children, Annie realised, taken aback by the request. Grief affects us all in different ways, she told herself, and who was she to judge Lenny Thornton? She knew next to nothing about his life. She shielded her eyes from the onslaught of sunlight and watched as the children actually obeyed her instructions and went inside. Maybe they thought there was a treat in store for them.

'Come on, Gerry,' she said. 'Let's have a little shopping trip.'

Excerpt from Linda Palmer's Memoir

Let it be a steam train, then. I remember my excitement as it chugged out of Leeds City station, all straining hooks and cables, the whole thing creaking and rattling like the chains of Marley's ghost, the way only a steam train can, almighty exhalations of smoke exploding from its funnel as it built up momentum, the speed quickening, faster and faster, settling into the regular, rocking clickety-clack rhythm as it escaped the confines of the city. Soon green fields full of sheep and cows flashed by, a tiny village, a lonely farmhouse, a river. A cyclist waiting at a level crossing waved to us, then bent to adjust his bicycle clips. Perhaps I'm already being free and easy with the details, but I'm sure you get the picture. It helps to get me in a mood to go on, and even invented memories can summon forth true ones.

I do recall that the compartment was stuffy, and Melanie's father opened the windows on both sides. I spent much of the journey reading *Lorna Doone*, carried away with the romance of it all, and Melanie had her head buried in the latest copy of *Jackie*. Occasionally we sneaked glances at each other and pulled faces. Our parents sat quietly, Mother reading her *Woman's Weekly*, Dad just puffing his pipe, gazing out the window, wool-gathering. Melanie's parents had their heads bent over a crossword puzzle. It was all very Philip Larkin, the bicycle clips, the smell of warm carriage cloth, framed tourist scenes on the carriage walls: Torquay, Brighton, Sunny Prestatyn. Through Huddersfield and Hebden Bridge we chuffed and clanked, tall mill chimneys and the dark satanic mills themselves, many still functional at that time, then up into the Pennines we rolled. Rills trickled in deep green clefts down the hillsides. Here and there stood a brooding, isolated farmhouse. I wondered about the people who lived there. Made up stories about them. The magical world their children had discovered in a cave under the waterfall, the witch who lived in the cottage deep in the woods and kidnapped children who strayed too deeply into the shadows.

Before long we had left Preston behind and it was time to play 'Spot the Tower'. You knew you were almost there when you could see Blackpool Tower, that smaller but nonetheless proud replica of the Eiffel Tower, in the distance. Melanie saw it first, and I was miffed. Usually it was me. I always had a feeling that my mother and father let me win, but there was no such indulgence with Melanie. Soon it was time for our fathers to heft the suitcases down from the luggage racks and our mothers to remind us not to forget anything. A few spots of rain streaked the grimy windows as we entered the outskirts of Blackpool, but that was all right. We could smell the sea air.

The rain didn't last. In fact, I'm at a loss to remember whether it even materialised beyond those few stray drops. Whatever happened, I remember that first day was as sunny and bright as the rest of the days that first week. It must have rained, though. It always rains on seaside holidays. The summers of childhood were surely never as warm and sunny as I remember them.

So what did we do that first afternoon and evening? I don't remember. Oh, I'm sure we went straight to the boarding house, found our rooms and unpacked. Perhaps it was already teatime. Melanie and I were sharing a room, which was all right with me, as we both liked to stay up late and read or listen to the pirate stations, if we could pick any up, or Radio Luxembourg on our trannies under the bedclothes.

As I remember, the room was much the same as the year before, only this time with two single beds crammed in: boring flower-patterned wallpaper with the squashed fly still on a rose petal, a window looking out on the backyard, a pipe running down one wall that rattled and clanged every time anyone ran a tap or flushed the toilet, a chamber pot under each bed, and a bowl and jug you could fill with water for washing and brushing your teeth. The toilet and bathroom would have been down the hall, as usual, shared by everyone on the floor, use of hot water strictly regulated, dinner at 6 p.m. on the dot, or you were out of luck. It wasn't the kind of place that encouraged one to stay indoors, no matter what the weather. You never lost sight of the fact that you were an interloper in someone's home, tolerated out of necessity, perhaps, but never entirely welcome.

Maybe we went for a walk on the prom that first evening, or took one of the open trams along the front. We might have even ventured on the beach, removed our sandals, pulled our dresses up over our knees and gone for a paddle. Perhaps we even shared a bag of cockles or winkles, digging out the poor creatures from their shells with pins, like little gobs of snot. Perhaps, though I doubt this happened so soon, we strolled the Golden Mile and played in the amusement arcades. Though I can't remember what we did, I do remember the sense of excitement I always had at the start of a holiday, of new places to be discovered, new experiences, new adventures, new possibilities. The sea air was always intoxicating, always full of promise. This time, with my best friend Melanie by my side, I was sure it would be even more exciting than usual.

7

Lenny Thornton was as good as his word, and he phoned Annie at a quarter past nine that evening to inform her that Sinead had come home. Annie then called Gerry, who picked her up in the Corsa, and they set off for Wytherton Heights for the second time that day. After talking to Lenny Thornton they had visited the shopping mall but had drawn a blank. There were no young people around, and the store workers and security guards could tell them nothing except what a nuisance the kids were, and how they scared away legitimate customers. No, no one had ever seen young girls with older Pakistani men. Most of the Pakistanis shopped in the Asian market at the other end of the Strip.

It was another sultry evening, the heat still clinging and clammy, streetlamps haloed with eerie light. The estate was in shadow and already dark, as many of the lamps were out; they had either been vandalised or the council just couldn't be bothered fixing them when they stopped working. The light was on in the front room of 14 Southam Terrace, and when Annie knocked on the door, Lenny Thornton answered briskly. He'd put on a T-shirt and jeans since their previous visit, but otherwise nothing much had changed. Johnny was asleep in his armchair, mouth open, snoring loudly. The TV was tuned to a golf tournament. No wonder Johnny was asleep, Annie thought.

'He took it badly,' Lenny said, nodding towards Johnny.

Annie wondered how he could tell. 'So I see. You said Sinead's at home?'

Lenny gestured towards the stairs. 'In her room. Go easy, won't you, hen. She's a bit fragile. It's still early days with the methadone.'

'Don't worry. Seen anything of Albert yet?'

'Not yet, no.'

Annie and Gerry went upstairs. The bedroom was dimly lit by an orange-shaded bedside lamp that cast shadows over the walls and ceiling as they entered. It was a bare room, with just a wardrobe, dressing table, chest of drawers and a small TV set on a table opposite the double bed. Maybe it was because of the rose-patterned wallpaper and soft lighting, but it seemed more of a woman's room to Annie, and she couldn't imagine a man like Lenny Thornton here in the bed. None of her business.

Sinead lay propped up on her pillows, smoking, staring into space, an overflowing ashtray on her belly. Her mascara was smeared, and she had clearly been crying. A number of screwed-up tissues lay on the bedspread and floor around her. The room smelled of skin moisturiser and cigarette smoke.

Annie had seen junkies of every variety over the years, from some she was positive were dead to others so clear-minded she couldn't believe they were drug addicts, and she quickly guessed that Sinead Moffat was closer to the latter type. Not many people knew it, but a heroin addict who got her regular, quality-controlled doses of the drug could often function almost normally, hold down a job, raise a child and so on. It was the desperation of no fix, no money to feed the habit, the uncertain quality of the stuff and the aura of crime in squats, dirty needles and dingy flats where the addicts congregated that caused the problems. You just had to think of the opium addicts of the nineteenth century, like Coleridge and De Quincey, to see both the range of achievement and the depths of despair that were part and parcel of a junkie's life. But now, according to Lenny Thornton, Sinead was on the methadone cure. Methadone suppressed opioid withdrawal symptoms, and because it was an opioid itself, it also blocked the effects of drugs such as heroin and morphine. It worked for some people, and many prisons had extensive methadone treatment programmes.

Gerry took a chair by the door. Annie sat on the edge of the bed and took Sinead's hand. Sinead didn't resist but her hand felt dry and lifeless as a sheet of paper. 'I'm very sorry,' Annie said. 'Do you want to see the artist's impression?'

Sinead sniffed and nodded. Annie showed it to her. Sinead traced her index finger over the image, then passed the drawing back to Annie and turned aside. 'That's Mimosa,' she said. 'I've got a better likeness, if you can use it.' She opened the drawer of the bedside table, shuffled through a stack of photos and handed one to Annie. 'Taken last year. She hasna changed that much.'

It was a close-up of a young girl with short blond hair parted on one side, so that a long lock curved over her left eye, almost covering it. Her face was free of make-up, her complexion smooth and pale, and it was clear that she was destined to become a true beauty, if only she had lived. She had the ghost of a smile on her face, as if an amusing thought had just passed through her mind. Annie also thought it was the kind of face that men would find attractive.

'I took that,' Sinead added. 'We went to Filey for the day. I was doing good on methadone and Mimosa . . . well, Mimosa was being the kind, attentive daughter.'

'It's good,' said Annie. 'May I borrow it? I promise I'll let you have it back.'

'Please do,' said Sinead. 'It's the best one I've got.'

'How are you doing?' Annie asked.

Sinead took a drag on her cigarette. 'As well as can be expected. If you mean am I high, I don't know if Lenny told you, but I'm on the methadone. Everything feels a bit far away and muffled, but I'm here, and I'm hurting. I can't believe my little girl is gone.'

'Lenny said he thought you might be with your addict friends when we called earlier.'

Sinead managed a weak smile. 'He would. But I wasn't. I really am going to make it work this time. I went to the clinic, then spent some time with my counsellor, and after that, just to cheer myself up, I went shopping and treated myself to Pizza Express with my friend Carolyn.' She pointed to a few packages in the corner. 'Haven't even got around to opening them yet. What happened to my Mimosa?'

Annie swallowed. The last thing she wanted to do was tell Sinead Moffat what had been done to her daughter. Even the scant details on the news, which Sinead clearly hadn't seen, were bad enough. 'We think she was murdered,' she said.

'But how? Why?'

'That's what we're trying to find out.' Annie pressed on quickly ahead, skirting the question of how Mimsy had been killed. Lenny Thornton could tell her that Mimsy had been 'beaten', if he remembered. 'We're going to need you to come to Eastvale to identify your daughter. But it's late now. We can send a car for you tomorrow morning, if that's OK?'

'I can see her then?'

Annie knew that the staff there would have cleaned Mimsy's body up as best they could for identification, but it would still be a great shock. 'Yes. Tomorrow. Is it OK if I ask you a couple of questions now?'

'OK.'

Annie looked over to Gerry, who had taken out her notebook.

'When did you last see your daughter?'

'I think it was after the weekend, you know, the one before this. She came by for a while on Monday, changed her clothes, had something to eat. Same as usual.'

That was the day before she had been killed, Annie realised. 'Did you talk about anything in particular?'

'No.'

'Do you know where she'd been, where she stayed when she wasn't here?'

'No. There was a mate called Jade. They hung out a lot together.'

'Boyfriend?'

'I wouldn't be surprised.'

'But no one she talked about?'

'No.'

'How long had things been like this?'

'About six months.'

'And you weren't worried?'

'Of course I was. I'd been there, myself. Teenage girls are secretive. You must remember that yourselves? But I knew there was no point goading her or nagging her. If there was something bothering her, she'd tell me when she was good and ready.'

'Did she seem worried or upset by anything?'

'No, she was as cheeky as ever.'

'What were you doing on Tuesday evening?'

'Me. You don't think—'

'We need to know where everybody was,' Annie said.

'We were here, all of us. Just a normal evening in.'

'All of you being you, Lenny, Johnny and Albert?'

'Not Albert.'

'Where was he?'

'You'll have to ask him. Probably in the pub with his mates. Paul and the others. But he wouldn't hurt Mimosa.'

'We're not saying he did, Sinead. We just need to know these things. Didn't he come home that night?'

'He rarely comes home. So rarely you could hardly call it his home.'

'Where does he stay? Girlfriend?'

'He may have one, but he's more one for the lads, is Albert. I don't mean he's gay or anything. Heaven forbid. He just likes his ale and a bit of pushing and shoving, you know, like lads are. He often stays at Paul's. That's Paul Warner. They more or less share a flat on the edge of the estate.'

'Would you say that you and Mimsy were close?' Annie began.

'Mimosa. I always called her Mimosa. Everyone else called her Mimsy, but I called her Mimosa. Some people thought it was a silly name, but I've always thought it's beautiful.'

'Sorry. Mimosa. Would you say you were close?'

'I always liked to think so, but not recently, no. Not especially. Maybe when she was little, but times have been hard over the past few years, since she's been more grown up. Things happened. I've let my family down. Made mistakes. I couldn't control her lately. I never knew where she was or what she was up to.'

'You said she was secretive?'

'More so these past few months than she used to be. Yes.'

'Her father left several years ago, right?'

'That was one of the good things that happened.'

'Any idea where he is now?'

'Australia wouldn't be far enough.'

'Is that where he is?'

'No. I've no idea. Haven't seen or heard from him in more than ten years.'

'And after he left?'

'There were others. Men. I wasn't a good mother. I made some bad choices.'

'Did any of the men bother Mimosa?'

Sinead turned away, but Annie could tell she was nodding, even with her head buried in the pillow. She touched her shoulder. 'Sinead. Did anyone interfere with her?'

'One of them. Just one. I walked in on them one night, right there in her room. He was making her toss him off, the filthy bastard. She was only eight. She didn't know what was going on, it was supposed to be a game for her, but she wasn't happy about it. I went ballistic, threatened to call the police and everything.'

'Did you? Call the police?'

'No.'

'Why not?'

'Because things were bad enough already.' She faced Annie. Her light brown eyes were flecked with amber. 'I'm sorry, love, but nothing good's ever come of calling the police around here. There was other stuff. Stolen goods in the house. Drugs. If I'd got the police involved they'd have given us more grief than they'd have given him.'

'What did you do, then?'

'I shoved all his stuff in a case and chucked it out of the window. He ran off and never came back.'

'We'll need his name.'

'Mallard. Eddie Mallard. I wouldn't be surprised if he's on your books.'

'And what about Lenny?'

She managed a half smile. 'Lenny's all right. A bit rough and ready, but his heart's in the right place. He never hurt Mimosa and he takes good care of me.'

'When do you think you and your daughter started drifting apart?'

'When she was about thirteen. She was sullen and depressed. It was just a difficult time for her. Self-image and everything. I suppose I should consider myself lucky she didn't suffer from anorexia or bulimia.'

'Any particular reason?'

'Not that I could fathom. Hormones, I suppose. She got very moody, started stopping out. Just till late at first, then all night.'

'Is that when she cut herself?'

Sinead gave Annie a sharp glance. 'You saw that?'

'Hard to miss.'

'Yes, it was around that time.'

'Was it serious? I mean, did Mimosa really try to kill herself? Did it bleed a lot?'

'No. It wasn't deep. I talked to her. I've . . .' Sinead held up her arm and pulled her sleeves up over her wrist. There were the same sort of criss-cross scars as they had seen on Mimsy. 'It was a long time ago. But I told her I understood. I knew she was unhappy, miserable. She thought everybody hated her, and she'd never have a boyfriend or anyone to love her. Some of the other kids at school made fun of her.'

'Why?'

'Do they need a reason? Her name? Her family? I wasn't a good mother. I didn't know what to tell her except everything would be all right. But it wasn't enough.' She gave a little shiver. 'I wasn't always there for her. And Lenny and Johnny are harmless, like I said, but they were no use to Mimosa. No use at all. She was thirteen. She needed a mother, and I failed her.'

'Did talking help?'

'I don't think so. Not by then. I couldn't get through to her. They grow up so quickly these days. Then they're gone.'

'Sinead, Mimosa didn't have to be gone. Someone took her. That's why we're here. We want to find out who it was and make sure they don't do it to anyone else and that they pay for what they've done.'

'How can they pay? What's the price of my daughter's life?'

'It's the only price the law allows. I can't change that.'

'No, love. No, you can't. Oh, what does it matter who did it? She's gone. It was my fault. I've been trying, honest I have, but it hasn't done any good, has it? Sometimes I think she was born under a bad sign.'

'What do you mean?'

'I know what her problem was, where it came from. There were older men sniffing around, even when she was thirteen.'

'They took advantage of her?'

'What do *you* think? She had that sort of sexy innocent thing going. She couldn't see it herself. That's why it's so powerful, because it's unconscious. Believe it or not, I used to have some of it myself, back in the day. It's good for nothing but trouble.'

'Was there anyone in particular?'

Sinead chewed on her lower lip for a moment, then said, 'Once. Yes.'

'Was it before or after the self-harm?'

'After. He was supposed to be her counsellor or something. I found them in his office one day when I made an unexpected visit. I'm not proud of it, but I went ballistic on both of them. I told her to get out. We had a terrible fight. We said things you can't ever take back.'

'She was underage,' Annie said. 'He was committing a crime. Did you call the police?'

'You don't get it, do you? We *never* call the police. They're the last bloody people we'd call. Sorry. But I did tell the social and I'm sure his bosses fired him.'

'Do you remember his name?'

'Sorry. They'll know down the social.'

'OK,' said Annie. 'She kept on living here after that?'

'Where else could she go? She was only a kid. We don't have any family up here. But she used the place like a hotel, came and went as she pleased with hardly a word to anyone when she was here. The social came round and tried to make things work, but . . . well, they've got a lot on their hands, too.'

'How did you get on after that?'

'Not too bad, I suppose. She calmed down a bit for a while.'

'What about Lenny? Couldn't he do anything?'

'The big soft lunk? Nay. He wasn't her father, and Mimosa never tired of letting him know it. He loved her, in his way – and I don't mean owt dirty by that – but he couldn't tell her what to do. And our Johnny . . . well, you've seen him, poor beggar. His brain's addled with booze and pills from way back, when he was in that motorbike gang. There was the accident, too. Hurt his head. He's not been the same since. As if I've got any room to talk. I spent most of my time on the nod when our Mimosa was out gallivanting till all hours. Now it's too late.'

'And more recently? Do you think she was doing drugs?'

'Maybe. I warned her, of course, but she just sneered and said something about the pot calling the kettle black. Not heroin, though. I think I'd have been able to tell. Pot, most likely, maybe ecstasy?'

'Ketamine?'

Sinead frowned. 'I don't know about that. I don't even know what that is. I mean, I wouldn't have known what to look for.'

'Did Mimosa herself have a thing about older men?' Annie asked. 'You know, father figure, that sort of thing?'

'She thought most boys her own age were shallow and only interested in one thing. I tried to tell her that *all* men were only interested in one thing, but I don't think she listened. Yes, she'd usually go out with older boys, men sometimes. She felt more comfortable with them. Maybe she needed a father figure, I don't know about all that psychological gobbledygook. Christ knows, Lenny's not much use, and her real father was worse than useless.'

'I was in her room earlier,' Annie said, 'and I saw a sketchbook with some pencil drawings in it. I know a bit about art, and they're very good.'

'She was mad about drawing. Yes, she was good. I once read somewhere that artistic talent skips a generation. Her granddad – my dad, Albert – was a bit of a hippie and a wonderful artist. He painted concert posters and album covers and stuff. But me and Johnny, forget it. And forget our Albert, even though he's named after his granddad. But Mimosa. She had it, all right.'

'My dad's an artist,' said Annie. 'I grew up in a sort of artists' colony near St Ives.'

'Lucky you,' said Sinead, flashing her a weak smile. 'Did you inherit any of his talent or did it skip you?'

'I can draw a bit, but not as good as Mimosa. Did she and her brother get along? Share stuff?'

'They didn't see much of each other, but when they did they were fine. He loved her, I'm sure of it. He'll be gutted when he finds out.'

'We'd appreciate it if you'd let us know when he turns up.'

'I've tried to phone him, but his mobile's dead or turned off. Albert's got nothing to do with this, I can assure you.'

'That's not what I'm saying. But maybe he knows something that might help us. Will you let us know?'

'All right.'

'We couldn't find a mobile phone or a laptop computer or anything in Mimosa's room.'

'She always had her mobile with her. Not that she ever used it to call us. It was one of those cheap pay-as-you-go things.'

'Do you know the provider?'

'No idea.'

'What about a laptop?'

'No. She didn't have one of those. We couldn't afford one. All she had she carried in that pink canvas shoulder bag she always took with her. You know the sort of thing it had . . . I don't know what you call them . . . like butterflies and stuff stuck on.'

'Appliqué?'

'If you say so, love.'

'What else did she have in her bag besides the mobile?'

'Oh, you know, the usual stuff. Her purse, what little money she had. Ciggies, of course. And her precious sketchbook and pencils. They had to be a certain kind, the pencils. And the sketchbook was smaller than the one in her room. More portable.'

'Did you ever open it?'

'Once. But she caught me at it and hit the roof.'

'Why? What was in it?'

'She said it was private. That's the funny thing. It wasn't like dirty pictures or anything. It was nothing really, just sketches of people she'd seen on a bus or in cafes, faces, and local street scenes, a market, drawings of buildings, someone's garden, cats and dogs. That sort of thing. She drew whatever caught her eye.'

Damn, thought Annie. That sketchbook might be a useful aid to finding Mimosa's abductors, and her killer. If she drew everything, there was a chance she had done a few portraits. She might even have sketched her killer. But there had been no sign of a pink shoulder bag at the scene. No doubt it had remained behind in the van with her clothes. The rapists would have destroyed it all by now, if they had any sense.

'Nearly finished,' she said, noticing Sinead's eyelids start to become heavy.

'It's all right, love. I shouldn't think I'll get much sleep tonight.'

'Did you ever see Mimosa with any Asians?'

'What . . .?'

'Did she hang around with Asians, specifically Pakistani?'

'Like I said, I don't know who her friends were. I mean, it wouldn't surprise me. They're everywhere now. But I never saw or heard anything. I don't think she really liked them much. She got into a bit of trouble for calling them names. Why?'

'It probably doesn't matter.' Annie patted Sinead's arm and stood up. 'You get some rest if you can,' she said. 'We'll see you in the morning. OK?'

'OK.'

Downstairs, they said goodnight to Lenny and Johnny. Lenny murmured something back through his haze of smoke, but Johnny was still dead to the world, anaesthetised by booze and brain damage. Or golf.

Outside the Moffat house Annie and Gerry sat in the car to collect their thoughts for a few moments.

'What's the bet she's back on heroin again tomorrow?' said Gerry. 'The real stuff.'

'I don't think so,' said Annie. 'I think she really wants to give it a try this time. But this is a hell of a setback, that's for certain. She's just lost her daughter. Besides, if heroin gives her a bit of comfort and takes away some of the pain for a while, who are we to judge her?'

'But it's not a solution. It's only a temporary escape.'

Annie regarded the innocent young DC for a while. In the shadows, Gerry seemed no more than a young girl herself. 'You're right, of course,' Annie said tiredly. 'But sometimes temporary relief is better than no relief at all. How do you expect someone like Sinead to deal with this sort of loss and grief? It'd be enough to turn me to heroin. God knows I came close with those painkillers I was on after I got shot.'

'But can't we do something for her? For all of them?'

'Of course,' said Annie. 'And we can bring about world peace and put an end to hunger and child prostitution while we're at it, too. Get real, Gerry.' Annie started the car. 'Come on, let's have a ride down to Sunset Strip and see what's shakin', man. Who knows, there might even be a drink in it.'

While the shopping mall they had visited that afternoon had been shiny and new, and mostly empty, the Strip resembled a dilapidated badly lit movie set for a summer night on the main drag in the deep south of America. It wasn't so much the people, but the garish colours of the neons, streetlights and brightly lit shop windows all just a little distorted in a haze of pollution and humidity. Outside the Wytherton Arms an older crowd stood drinking pints and smoking and talking while a younger group weaved through the traffic and went into the balti restaurant across the street. People queued outside the chippie next door to the pub and stood around to eat out of their cardboard boxes when they'd been served.

Shops and businesses lined both sides of the half mile or so between the overpass to the east and the canal to the west, all with grilles that could be lowered after closing time, some with their plate-glass windows protected even while they were open for business. At the far end, near the overpass, Annie could make out the outline of a small mosque with its minaret. The various payday advance and cheque-cashing merchants were all closed and barred for the day, though their signs remained lit. Among the other businesses were a bookie's, two charity shops – Oxfam and British Heart Foundation – a halal butcher's, an off-licence, a nail bar, the balti restaurant and takeaway, an exotic greengrocer, a newsagent, a heel bar, Cash Generator, a hairdresser's and a minicab office. Next door to the latter was a kebab, pizza and burger takeaway with a couple of tables out front where two youths in white shirts sat smoking and drinking Coke from the can, legs stretched out across the pavement so that anyone walking by had to step over them. Over the road was an old cinema festooned with garish Bollywood movie posters. There was no tattooist, as far as Annie could make out. Just by where they parked, it looked as if a couple of buildings had been demolished and replaced by a swatch of balding grass and a couple of benches. No one was sitting there. Mingled smells of cumin and coriander infused the air.

'I'd put the Krook lock on, if I were you,' Annie said.

Gerry put the clamp on her steering wheel. 'See that?' she said, as they got out of the car. 'Sunny's kebab and pizza takeaway.'

'Burgers too,' Annie added. 'Hungry?'

Gerry pulled a face. 'Not that hungry.'

'Foodie snob.'

Just as they started to walk away from the car, a police patrol car pulled up by the side of the road and two burly uniformed officers got out, hitched up their overloaded belts and approached.

'Evening, ladies,' said the tallest one.

Annie noticed Gerry reaching for her warrant card and just managed to grasp her wrist in time. She wanted to see how this panned out. 'Evening, officers,' she said. 'Problem?'

The officer pointed back at their car. 'You can't park there,' he said.

Annie glanced over her shoulder. 'Why not? I don't see any signs or anything.'

'Do you see any other cars parked nearby?'

'No. That's why we parked there.'

'It's a double yellow line.'

'There's only one line there,' Annie said, looking at her watch. 'And it's well after eight o'clock.'

'Reg, isn't that a double yellow line you see there where that puke green Corsa's parked?' he asked the other officer.

'Certainly is, Bill.'

'The outer one's a bit faint, love. Sorry about that. Hard to see in the dark. The council doesn't get around here very often to paint them. You'll have to move on or I'll write you a ticket.'

'I don't think so,' Annie said. She could sense Gerry's nervousness beside her, but she still wanted to know how far these cops would go, and why.

'What brings you out here to this godforsaken part of the world, ladies?' Bill asked.

'We're after a tattoo parlour,' said Annie.

Bill eyed her up and down. 'Oh, yeah,' he said. 'Where you going to have it done, then?'

'Somewhere you'll never see it.'

'There's no need to be like that. Besides, there's no call for that sort of place around here.'

'Why not? A tattoo parlour would fit in perfectly.'

'Wrong colour,' said Bill. 'Tattoos don't show up well on these people's skin.'

'You guys,' Annie said. 'You'll have me in stitches.'

'You know, I'd be careful if I was you,' Bill said, thrusting his face closer towards Annie's. So much so that she could smell beer on his breath. 'Couple of nice ladies like yourselves. It's a dodgy neighbourhood, this is. You can see for yourselves the kind of people that hang out here. We don't want any trouble. Now, why don't you just get back in that illegally parked car and drive away before we get serious about this.'

'*Get serious?*' said Annie.

Bill sighed theatrically. 'We don't really want to take you in unless we have to.'

'Too much paperwork,' Reg added.

Even Gerry laughed at that. 'Take us in?' she said. 'Over a car that's parked perfectly legally? You've got to be kidding. I'd like to see you try.'

'Ey up, Reg, it speaks,' said Bill.

'Is this how you treat all visitors to the street?' Gerry asked.

'We don't like strangers around here, love, no matter how posh they sound. Don't get very many.'

'You know, Bill,' Annie said softly, 'you sound just like a bent sheriff from a bad Western.'

Gerry gasped and Bill took a step back, his face turning red. 'What did you say?' He reached for Annie.

Annie stood her ground. 'You heard.'

Bill grabbed her by the elbow. 'Right,' he said. 'That's it. You're coming with us.'

'No we're not,' said Annie, swiftly extricating her arm. He'd squeezed it tightly, and it hurt, but she wasn't going to show weakness and massage it in front of him. She pushed down the sense of panic and images of the rape she had endured a few years ago. These men seemed like mirror images of the ones who had done that. Bill moved forward with surprising speed, but Annie stepped back just as quickly, and he stumbled a little as he lurched forward.

'Why, you little bitch.'

'Bollocks to you,' said Annie, and she pushed past them and carried on walking, Gerry trotting along beside her.

'Hey! Wait a minute!' Bill and Reg walked after them. Annie turned to see Bill's hand on the baton at his waist. He was breathing hard. 'We're not finished with you two yet. Where do you think you're going?'

'What's it to you?'

That seemed to confuse Bill for a moment. He looked at Reg. 'We've got a right pair here,' he said, then turned back to Annie. 'Hop it, the both of you. We'll let you off this time. We don't want any trouble. Just get back in your car and piss off out of here. You don't belong. Is that clear? It's for your own good, believe me. No-go area, this is, and we don't want to spend the rest of the night mopping up after you two tarts. Believe me, if you're out for a bit of fun you've come to the wrong place.'

Annie took a deep breath and walked towards them. As she did so, she reached for her warrant card. 'Know a better one, do you?'

Bill pulled out his baton. Annie held her hands out, palms up. 'Whoa, wait a minute, son. You're making a big mistake here.'

'Am I?'

Annie thrust her warrant card at him. 'Yes. See. Get out of jail free card.'

Bill stared at the warrant card and turned pale. 'Fuck me, Reg,' he said. 'It's a DI.'

'*She*'s a DI,' said Annie. 'Is this the way you behave towards all your visitors?'

'We don't get a lot of tourists,' mumbled Bill.

'I'm not bloody surprised, the way you treat them.'

'Ma'am.'

'I wouldn't be seen dead here myself if I didn't have a job to do.'

'A job? We don't know anything about no job.'

'That's because it's a surprise visit.'

'Who to?'

'That'd be telling.'

Bill puffed out his chest. 'This is our patch. You owe us the courtesy of letting us know you're coming and why you're here.'

'Spot check,' said Annie. 'We go around the country checking out police officers for courteous service and politeness. You two scrotes have just failed.'

'But you ... you didn't tell us who you were. You didn't identify yourselves.'

'Shouldn't matter,' Annie said. 'We're posing as members of the public.'

Gerry took out her notebook.

'What's she doing?' Reg asked.

'I'm making a note of your numbers,' said Gerry. 'I'd like your names as well.'

'Bugger off.'

'All right. Be like that. We'll make do with the numbers.'

'It's not our fault,' said Bill. 'We've got orders. It's a dangerous street. People get mugged here and stuff. We're only trying to protect the public.'

'By pulling your baton?' said Annie.

'That was a—'.

'Mistake? Yes, I know. A big one.'

'Look around you, for Christ's sake,' Bill went on. 'What do you see?'

'A lot of people out enjoying a nice summer evening?'

Bill lowered his voice. 'Pakis. That's what.'

'So what?'

'Well, you can't trust 'em, can you?'

'And you can't touch 'em, either,' Reg, suddenly emboldened, added. 'Racism, that is. That's why we warn people off. It'd be more than our job's worth to take one of 'em in.'

Annie moved closer, took the artist's impression of Mimsy from her bag, and thrust it in front of Bill's face. 'Know her?'

Bill studied the sketch. 'Bloody hell! Is that the girl that's been in the news all weekend?'

'Bingo. Give the man a cigar. Do you know her?'

Bill looked at Reg, and they seemed to have a silent conversation.

'Better if you tell the truth,' Annie said.

Finally, Bill bit his lip and said to Reg, 'It's the Moffat girl, isn't it?'

'It could be her,' said Reg.

'We know that now,' said Annie. 'You could have saved us a lot of time.'

'How?'

'This likeness has been in the papers and on TV for a few days now. Surely you must have received copies for distribution at the station?'

'It's just not a good likeness,' said Bill.

'What do you mean? Her mother and stepfather recognised her, for Christ's sake. You recognised it just now.'

'Yeah, well, maybe we're specially observant. She doesn't usually look like that.'

'She looks a hell of a lot worse than that right now, I can assure you,' said Annie. 'Have you seen her recently?'

'Around the Strip sometimes, sure. She's usually wearing make-up and she wears her hair different, that's all. And tarty clothes.'

'It's not her face you notice, if you know what I mean,' said Reg.

Annie rolled her eyes. 'Nudge, nudge. God give me strength. So now you do recognise her, where and when did you last see her?'

'Not for a while now. Over a week or so.'

'Do you remember the last time you saw her?'

'Not specifically, no. We see a lot of people on the Strip.'

'Who was she usually with?'

'Just her mates, you know, young girls like her.'

'Any place in particular?'

'That kebab and pizza place down there,' said Reg, pointing. 'It's run by a Paki, but the food's not bad if you like that sort of thing. You get hungry on night shift, or maybe you don't remember. And there's a minicab office next door, they use that sometimes.'

'Who does?'

'The kids. But the Strip's not a place many white kids hang out. The Strip. You'd likely see them more often at the shopping mall playing with their mobiles, texting and sexting and Instagramming and stuff.'

'She's a troublemaker, that one,' said Bill. 'Gob on her like the Tyne Tunnel. It's no wonder she came to a sticky end.'

'*Sticky end*,' Annie repeated, not even trying to keep the disbelief out of her tone. 'This girl, whose name is *Mimosa* Moffat, by the way, was tossed out of a moving car on a country lane on *my* patch after being repeatedly raped, then beaten to death by one or more persons unknown. We know she came from around here, so is it OK if we ask a few questions around the neighbourhood? It's all right. We don't require your help unless you happen to have seen a suspicious van parked on the street here last Tuesday night.'

'We weren't on duty last Tuesday.'

'Right. Thanks for your help. You can get back to playing with your todgers in the patrol car now, if you like.'

'Now, hang on a minute, love,' said Bill. 'There's no call for—' But Annie and Gerry walked away, towards the kebab and pizza takeaway.

Before they were out of earshot Annie turned and said, 'And don't you fucking dare give us a parking ticket.'

Banks and Linda Palmer met in a pub he had discovered high up in the moors north of Lyndgarth, oddly named the Low Moor Inn. Banks had expected it to be empty on a Monday night, but the place was jumping – well, Banks thought, about as much as a place like the Low Moor Inn could ever jump. It was full of local farmers mixed with coast-to-coast walkers slaking their thirsts after a long day in the hot sun. The pub offered bed and breakfast, so a few of them would be staying for the night, which explained why there were so few cars in the car park.

The Low Moor Inn was one of those old Dales pubs with thick stone walls to keep out the howling wind, though there was no wind that night, and the huge fireplace was dark and empty, like the jaw of some mythical beast. It was still muggy outside, but inside the pub a pleasant chill came from the thick stone. They were the sort of walls that hoarded winter and emanated its chill throughout summer. Framed paintings of local scenes hung here and there, some of them for sale, with prices written under them. The lighting was dim, and despite being crowded, the pub was reasonably quiet, conversations hushed, laughter muted by the strange and ancient acoustics. The bar was of dark polished wood with rows of coloured bottles behind reflected in the long mirror, and a brass footrest ran along the bottom. It was polished so bright you could see your face distorted in it. Wooden chair legs scraped on the rough flagstone floor, and the round wobbly tables were scarred by many a cigarette end. Linda was already waiting when Banks arrived, a glass of white wine in front of her.

'How on earth did you find this place?' she asked, looking around in admiration.

'Just got lucky,' said Banks. 'They don't do food in the evenings, though.'

'That's all right. I'm not hungry.'

'Another white wine?'

'I'd better stick with this,' said Linda. 'Driving.'

Banks got himself a pint of Daleside bitter. It was his first drink of the day, he realised, and the day was almost over. He had expected to have a brief telephone conversation with Linda about tomorrow, but she had seemed on edge and said she needed to get out of the house for a while, so he had suggested they meet at Low Moor.

'It does seem a bit off the beaten track,' said Linda. 'Are you worried you're being followed? Or that I am?'

'Something like that. After all, you're the celebrity. Someone might spot you.'

Linda laughed. It was a silky, musical sound. 'Well, thanks for the compliment, but I've never known anyone recognise a poet in the street.' She glanced around. 'Or even in a pub. Maybe it happened to Heaney and Larkin, but not me. Not even Carol Ann Duffy, I shouldn't think.'

Banks hadn't heard of Carol Ann Duffy, so he kept quiet about that. 'I'm sorry to drag you all the way up here,' he said. 'Can't be too careful these days.'

'You didn't drag me anywhere. I told you, I needed to get out for a while.' Linda tilted her head and looked at him. 'I was getting a bit stir crazy. Besides, would it be the worst thing in the world?'

'What?'

'If they see us together. Find out who I am. The media.'

Banks took a sip of beer and considered what she had said. 'No,' he said. 'I don't suppose it would. Though it could make things difficult for the Crown Prosecution Service down the line. But they're pests, the media. Once they latched on, they would never leave you alone. They're like mosquitos. Not only are they annoying, but they need your blood to breed. You could say goodbye to your peace and tranquillity for a while.' Adrian Moss would probably love a high-profile victim as well as a high-profile suspect, but that wasn't Banks's concern. Moss's job was to get the most out of the media for the police while getting the least out of the police for the media. He had already thrown the TV a bone in the shape of the search of Caxton's home, but even he would draw the line at throwing Linda Palmer to the wolves. Maybe. 'And you can be sure they wouldn't go easy on you,' Banks went on. 'They wouldn't be sympathetic and understanding. They'd dig up every boyfriend you've ever had and ask you some tough questions, maybe even insinuate that you led Caxton on, or you're making it all up in the hopes of selling more books.'

'It's very sweet of you to think about me. But I know what the media are like. Don't forget, I came to you. And I came into this with my eyes wide open, fully aware that it might bring about some infringements of my privacy and put me in an awkward position.' She smiled. 'Not to mention disturb my peace of mind. I've been jotting things down, as you suggested. It's remarkable the things I remember. Or think I remember. I've not been sleeping very well.'

'I'm sorry to hear that.'

'I've no wish to get fixated on an incident from my past, however traumatic, but the more I immerse myself in that two-week holiday and its aftermath, the more details nag away at me.'

'As a detective, it's those details I'm interested in,' said Banks.

Linda took a sip of her wine, then asked, 'Have you spoken with Caxton yet? I saw the police raid on the news.'

'Yes, quite dramatic, wasn't it? I spoke with him just before it.'

'And?'

'Naturally, he denies everything.'

'Denies that anything happened?'

'Denies that he ever *forced* anyone to have sex. Denies that he would ever have *needed* to force anyone to have sex.'

'Arrogant prick. Does he even deny that he was in Blackpool that week, that I asked for his autograph, that he invited me to his hotel?'

Banks held up his hand. 'Linda, stop. You know I can't talk to you in detail about this yet. If it were to get to court and it came up that I'd coached you in any way it could damage the case. I can interview you as a witness and him as a suspect, but that's as far as it goes. It's a delicate balance. All I can say is that he says he doesn't remember you.'

Her mouth opened and shut. 'He doesn't remember me?'

'That doesn't mean—'

Then Linda started to laugh. 'The most soul-destroying, ugly, painful experience in my life, and he doesn't even remember. Well, there's irony for you.'

'What else would he say?'

'And there's me feeling disappointed at not being remembered by my rapist. I should feel better for thinking he's lying?'

Banks could think of nothing to say. He was used to comforting a different, more normal sort of victim. Linda Palmer was all over the place, up one minute, down the next. And what was he to say? That there had been so many victims, how could Caxton be expected to remember one from another? That he was just lying, that it was part of his denial? She knew all that.

'I'm sorry,' she said. 'You must forgive me. I'm afraid this has all sort of jumbled up my emotions. I don't know what I'm feeling from one minute to the next.'

'I can understand that,' said Banks. 'Best to stick to what's going to help us.'

'The facts, ma'am, just the facts?'

Banks smiled. 'Something like that.'

Linda stared into her glass. She seemed tired, Banks thought. Bags were forming under her striking dark blue eyes, a pallor on her skin. Banks noticed her hands, the long tapered fingers, nails bitten down, a chunky pewter ring, a silver bangle around her left wrist and a little black-faced Swatch watch with a chequered band on her right. She was wearing jeans and a tan suede jacket over a white blouse, and she carried a shoulder bag to match her jacket. 'Here,' she said, reaching into the bag, which she had set on the empty chair beside her. 'I've got something for you.' She brought out a book with her name on it, called *Mnemosyne's Children: Selected Poems, 1985–2012* and handed it to him. 'I've published a new collection since then, but I thought this might be a good place to start. If you want to, that is. I hope this won't be construed as trying to bribe a police officer.'

Banks took the book and thanked her. 'Bribe? With a book of poetry? To do what?' Then he realised he'd implied an insult or a slight. 'I don't mean it's not worth anything or not a good bribe or—'

'Please,' Linda said, laughing. 'No more, or your foot will be so far down your throat you'll choke. I know what you mean. It was a joke.'

'Anyway, I know about the new book. I bought it in Leeds the other day. I haven't had a chance to read it yet.'

'I'm glad you didn't buy this one, then.'

'Mnemosyne,' said Banks. 'Isn't that memory?'

'Indeed. Consort of Zeus, mother of the Muses.'

Banks opened the book and saw that it had been signed on the title page: 'To Alan Banks, the copper who quoted Wordsworth.' He'd never had a book inscribed to him before. 'Thank you,' he said, feeling a little embarrassed. Then he hesitated, not sure whether to share his current enthusiasm, then decided what the hell. 'Actually, I've been working my way through an anthology of English poetry. I read Gray's "Elegy Written in a Country Churchyard" this morning.'

'More titles than you can shake a stick at,' said Linda. 'What did you think of it?'

'Interesting. I liked it, the tone, the sentiment, I suppose. I must confess, though, I sometimes have trouble understanding what's being said. Maybe it's the language, or maybe I'm just thick.'

She smiled. '"A poem should not mean but be." Someone said that once. I can't remember who. But I always find it useful to fall back on when I fail to understand something. Wait till you get to the Romantics. Or you could skip forward to them.'

'That would be cheating.'

'Then cheat. So what? Be a devil. I don't think reading in chronological order contributes a great deal to the love or understanding of poetry. You could even chuck a few translations in the mix. Rilke, Baudelaire, Akhmatova.'

Banks tapped her book. 'Well, maybe I'll cheat and jump forward to this,' he said.

She toyed with the stem of her wine glass.

'I wanted to talk to you again about the other man,' Banks hurried on. 'It could be important. You say you think you saw a photo of him some time after you'd reported what happened?'

'Yes. I just can't remember where.'

'Did you read many newspapers in those days?'

'At that age? No, I read *Jackie* and *Melody Maker* and *Photoplay*.'

'You liked going to the pictures?'

'Twice a week. We had a lot to choose from then. Lyric, Crown, Clifton, Western, Palace – and they were all within walking distance. There were the Odeon, the Gaumont, the Tower, the Majestic and the ABC in town if you had to see something as soon as it came out. And lots of other local fleapits if you were willing to get a bus to Hyde Park, Headingley or Harehills. The local cinemas all showed double bills, too, so you could easily see four films in each a week. More if you wanted to go to a different cinema every night. Melanie and I looked old enough to get into X films at some of them when we were fourteen. We loved horror – Hammer, Christopher Lee, Vincent Price, Edgar Allan Poe, all that stuff.'

'I remember doing the same,' said Banks, then he paused. 'It doesn't really matter, but you just told me you looked old enough to get into X-certificate films when you were fourteen. Were you often mistaken for someone older?'

'I see what you mean,' Linda said. 'Might Caxton have thought I was older? Yes, maybe. Though I told him my age. I suppose he might have assumed I was lying. Though why, I don't know. Girls of fourteen usually add something when they lie about their age, rather than subtract a year or two, the way I do now. I don't think he cared. He wanted me, so he forced me. It was rape whichever way you look at it, my age or my lack of consent.'

'As I said, it doesn't really matter if he says he thought you were twenty-five. It's just the kind of thing the media might seize on.'

'I'll be sure to keep my childhood secrets from them.'

'So you didn't read the newspapers. Did you watch the news on TV?'

'It was on sometimes, if my dad was watching, but I can't say I paid much attention. I saw the papers at news-stands, and we had the *Yorkshire Evening Post* delivered at home every day, so it was lying around the house. I'd see the front pages, I suppose. Sometimes read the sports page, if Leeds United were playing.'

'You were a fan?'

'They were golden back then.'

'Do you have any recollection whether it might have been a minor celebrity you saw, someone on the fringes of Caxton's world, maybe in another show in Blackpool at the same time? Or could it have been a sports personality, someone like that?'

'Either is possible, I suppose,' said Linda. 'But I honestly can't remember. As I said, I think I might recognise the same photo if I saw it again. My mind works with patterns like that. But can I remember where I saw it? Or the context? No. Maybe a newspaper. I'm sure I didn't see it on TV. And it was about a month after Caxton and the other man raped me. I'd say late September at the earliest. Most likely sometime in early October.'

Banks leaned forward. 'OK, so here's what I've got in mind. We're going to start by going through microfiche editions of the *Yorkshire Evening Post* from September 1967. You'd be surprised how little time it'll take if you don't have to do a lot of reading. Will you have a good look at the pictures and tell me if you recognise anyone?'

'I'll try. Where are these microfilms?

'Leeds Central Library. I'll pick you up tomorrow after lunch, say about one. OK?'

'Fine with me.'

'And if that doesn't work out, we can always move on to other sources. I suppose it's possible he was in *Melody Maker* or *Photoplay*. Then there's the nationals. You must have seen them sometimes, too?'

'I suppose so. Maybe when I passed a news vendor or something, but we didn't get any at home except the *People* and the *News of the World* on Sundays.'

'A right collection of villains you'd find in those,' said Banks. 'And that might take a bit longer to set up.'

'I don't think there's any hurry, do you?' She seemed to hesitate.

'What is it?' Banks asked.

'Something I've been wanting to ask you. Just tell me if I'm being impertinent or if it's classified or anything.'

'OK. Fire away.'

'I've been thinking about that poor girl found dead on Bradham Lane.'

'Do you know the place?'

'I use it often if I'm heading south from Eastvale. It's a lovely detour, far nicer than the A1. But it seems such a lonely, forlorn place to die. I saw the artist's impression in the paper. She was very young, wasn't she?'

'About fifteen, we think.'

'And you've no idea who she is, how she got there, or why?'

'I—'

Linda held her hand up. 'I understand. You can't talk about it. That's OK. I'm sorry.'

'All I can tell you,' said Banks, 'is that she was naked and we believe she was raped repeatedly, beaten to death and left by the side of the road. That much has all been in, or more or less implied by, the press.'

Linda put her hand to her mouth. 'My God, the poor child.'

'And we do know who she was. We just found out.'

'How terrible for her parents.'

'Because of her age, she won't be identified by name in the media, but that artist's impression has already been in all the papers and on TV, as you know, so plenty of people have seen an image of her. Obviously some of them will know who she was, so it wouldn't surprise me if there's a leak before long.'

'It hardly matters to her, does it, but her family . . . What you said about the media.'

'We'll do our best to protect them.'

'I'm sure you will,' said Linda. 'I'm sorry. I didn't mean to pry.' Clearly upset, she gathered up her things. 'I must go,' she said. 'Are you coming?'

Banks still had half a pint left in his glass. He could easily have left it, but he was strangely comfortable in the cool, stone pub, and he never minded being alone with his thoughts. 'No,' he said. 'I'll hang on and finish my drink. Maybe read a poem or two. You head off. Thanks for coming.'

'Until tomorrow afternoon, then.'

'Tomorrow.'

Banks hunched over the rest of his beer, Linda's book on the table in front of him, and thought for a moment. Linda Palmer was obviously feeling a lot of empathy for the dead girl, Mimsy. However different their backgrounds and the circumstances of their suffering, he also felt that the two girls would have understood each other. Linda was hardly groomed over time, as it appeared Mimsy Moffat may have been, but she was given cigarettes and champagne and promised a spot on *Do Your Own Thing!* by someone loved and trusted by the whole country. Mimsy was most likely abused by people she thought were her friends. Perhaps Mimsy was far more knowing and sophisticated at fifteen than Linda had been at fourteen, but when it came right down to it, that didn't matter. Their fates had been similar: both had been betrayed and violated at a very early age, but only one had lived.

He opened the book Linda had given him and turned to a poem called 'Memory':

It can cut breath
into corpses,
image the womb
and frame things
which are not;

yet it cannot transfer
to the minute the exact angle
of that branch's bending,
nor measure its dance.

Itself but for a moment,
outside falls in:
drawn away
from the natural breeze
into space thick as blood,

the vivid, fleshy
shadow sways
inaccurate and
permanent, against
a changing sky.

It seemed to relate to what they had talked about, Wordsworth's idea of perception and imagination somehow being involved in the creation of memory, and perhaps Linda's own thoughts about how memory transforms rather than presents an accurate snapshot of experience. He sensed a certain distance and detachment in the poem – she wasn't confronting the thought or experience head on, viscerally – but he liked how the sound and imagery of her language seemed to fill out the idea behind the words. It wasn't something he could paraphrase, but perhaps, he thought, that was what a good poem should do: express something that could be expressed no other way. That was why so much of it was so damn difficult to understand. Like most people, he probably tried too hard to translate it into rational meanings instead of letting it perform its magic. Not mean, but be.

Well, perhaps the book had given him some insight into poetry, but he wasn't sure whether it had given him any into Linda Palmer. She remained an enigma to him. He had no doubt that all the feelings were still there, or the memory of them, even after all this time – rage, humiliation, shame, guilt, fear – but they were preserved under an obsidian veneer. It remained to be seen how thick that veneer was.

Banks closed the book, glanced at his watch and finished his pint. Time to go. He took one last look around the cosy bar. He'd like to have another, linger a little longer over Linda's poetry, but he was driving, and he knew it would be a long day tomorrow.

Annie and Gerry stepped over the outstretched legs of the two youths and walked through the open door of the takeaway. They had already smelled the tomato sauce, peppers, onions and grilled meat and spices from a distance, but the aroma was even stronger inside, with hot cooking oil added to the mix. The small space was brightly lit. There were only two small wobbly Formica-topped tables as the business was clearly predominantly takeaway and customers weren't encouraged to hang about.

One man stood behind the counter talking to another in a cook's white uniform. The grills and ovens were off to one side, mostly hidden, and the wall behind the counter housed displays of crisps and chocolate bars. A glass-fronted fridge stood to one side filled with a selection of fizzy drinks.

The man behind the counter smiled and asked, 'What can I do for you two lovely ladies?'

'See, at least someone around these parts has some manners,' Annie said to Gerry. She smiled sweetly back at the man. 'I'll have a slice of margherita please, and my friend here will have a doner kebab.'

'Coming right up, my lovelies.'

He was good-looking, Annie thought. Late thirties or early forties, she guessed, tall, with earthy brown eyes and an athletic frame. He wore his hair cropped, like Banks, and had a neatly trimmed beard turning a little grey around the edges. The other man in the cook's garb went over to his station and prepared to heat up some pizza and kebab. He was more well padded than his workmate, and probably a year or two younger, with a smoother, lighter complexion and slightly longer, greasy hair.

Gerry was making a face and mouthing, '*Calories.*'

'It's all right,' Annie whispered. 'You don't have to eat the bloody thing.'

'Not from round these parts, are you?' the man asked. 'I'm Sunny, by the way. This is my caff. Sunny's Kebab and Pizza.'

'Nice to meet you,' said Annie. 'No, we're not from around here.'

'Thought I hadn't seen you before.'

'Do you live nearby, Sunny?'

Now he started to appear suspicious. 'Who's asking?'

Annie showed him her warrant card.

'Fuzz,' he said. 'I should have known.'

'*Fuzz?*' echoed Annie with a wide-eyed glance at Gerry. 'Fuzz? Nobody calls us fuzz any more.'

Sunny shrugged. 'It's the nicest word I know.'

'I'm confused,' said Annie. 'What have we ever done to you that fuzz is the nicest word you know for us? Just a few moments ago you were calling us "my lovelies". Now some women might find that offensive, but my friend and I don't mind, do we Gerry?'

'Always nice to be called lovely,' mumbled Gerry. 'Better than fuzz.'

'We get harassed all the time. Insulted. Threatened. One of my friend's sons got beat up just walking home from the mosque the other night. My friend down the Strip had a brick thrown through his window not so long ago. Did you lot do anything to help? No. You should have seen the trouble he had getting anything out of the insurance company.'

That was hardly a problem of racism, Annie thought. Nobody can get money out of an insurance company. But there was no point arguing. She had worked in racially sensitive areas, and she knew the score. Eastvale wasn't one of them, but Wytherton clearly was. It was a delicate exercise in political correctness and positive discrimination. You really had to know your catchphrase of the day and jargon of the moment. Annie took the drawing out of her bag. 'What my partner and I would really like to know is whether you've seen this girl around here.' She held up the image.

Annie could have sworn that an expression of shock and fear flashed across Sunny's face before he said, rather too quickly, 'No. I've never seen her before.'

Annie gestured to the cook. 'What about your friend?'

Sunny called him over. His name was Faisal, and he was more surly than Sunny. He glanced at the drawing and shook his head.

'He doesn't know her, either.'

'We hear she came here for takeaways.'

'Lots of people come here. I can't remember every customer I've ever served.'

'No, but she's an attractive girl, don't you think? What about last Tuesday?'

'No. I told you. We don't know her. If she came here, she wasn't a regular. Maybe she came once and didn't like our food. It happens, believe it or not.'

'Funny that,' said Annie, leaning on the counter.

'What is?'

'Well, we know she lived around here. In fact, we've just come from her mother's place up the road. And one of the local coppers tells us your food is popular with the young people from the estate.'

'Lots of people live around here. They don't all eat here.' He pointed across the street. 'Maybe she preferred fish and chips?'

'Maybe so. But this girl was murdered last Tuesday night, Sunny, and do you know what the pathologist found in her stomach contents when he did the post-mortem?'

'What?'

'Pizza and kebab. Now, what do you think of that?'

Faisal placed their orders on the counter without looking their way, and Sunny put the boxes in a paper bag. 'That's sick, that is,' he mumbled. 'Here. Take it. On the house. Just go away.' He handed Annie the bag.

But Gerry placed some money on the counter. 'We'll pay,' she said. 'Keep the change.'

'And, do you know?' Annie held up the bag as they were leaving. 'Our CSI people are very clever these days, just like on telly. They can match anything with anything if they've got a sample.'

8

One of the responsibilities Banks had yet to face in his new job was administering a bollocking to officers under him. He'd done it often enough over the years as a DCI, mostly on an informal basis, but as detective superintendent and head of Homicide and Major Crimes, it was his job both to stand up for and to discipline his team. So his heart sank when Superintendent Carver from Wytherton strutted into his office early on Tuesday morning with a complaint. He had known last night that it would be a long day but he had never imagined it would start like this.

Though Banks was a detective and Carver wore a uniform, that didn't count for anything; in rank, they were equal. But Banks could tell by Carver's arrogant manner that he clearly felt coming from a tough urban patch made him somehow superior to these lowly sheep-shaggers on the edge of the largely rural Yorkshire Dales. Carver was all brass, bulk and Brylcreem, slathered with an aftershave that smelled like a tart's window box. He wedged himself into a chair by the conference table and began his litany of woes. Before he could get too far, Banks sent for Annie and Gerry, who had just got back from taking Sinead Moffat to identify her dead daughter at the mortuary. They turned up a few minutes later, coffees in hand.

'Sit down,' said Banks. 'Superintendent Carver here has brought some very serious complaints to me regarding you two. What do you have to say for yourselves?'

'We'd like to hear what we've been accused of first, sir,' said Annie.

'You ought to know by now,' Banks said, 'that it's a matter of courtesy to inform the officer in charge of a neighbouring policing area when you intend visiting his patch.'

'It wasn't a planned visit,' said Annie. 'We received an anonymous phone call identifying the girl found dead on Bradham Lane and we—'

'You should still have informed Wytherton Police Station of your visit. But that's the least of the problems. I have it on the authority of Superintendent Carver here that you intimidated two of his patrol officers on the street. PCs Reginald Babcock and William Lamont.'

'Intimidated? That's a laugh.'

Carver glared at her.

'Would "played silly buggers with" describe the incident more accurately?' Banks asked, with one arched eyebrow.

'Last night we returned to Southam Terrace on the Wytherton Heights estate to talk to the girl's mother, a recovering heroin addict who wasn't home during our first visit.'

'So this was your *second* unannounced call on Wytherton in the same day?'

'Yes.' Annie glanced at Carver. 'Apologies for not ringing ahead. Perhaps we should have said we were coming, but we thought we had more important matters to deal with at the time. Sometimes you just get caught up in the momentum of an investigation. The case was breaking fast after several days of getting nowhere.'

Carver inclined his head in acceptance of the apology.

'When DC Masterson and I got out of our car,' Annie went on, 'we were approached by the two officers in question. DC Masterson made a note of their numbers if—'

'I know who they are,' growled Carver. 'Reg and Bill are two of my best men.'

'Then I'd hate to meet any of the others,' said Annie.

Carver gave her an appraising glance. 'I imagine you would,' he said. 'I've been having a word or two about you, and it seems your record is hardly unblemished, not without incident.'

'That's out of order,' said Banks. 'DI Cabbot was—'

Annie touched Banks's arm. 'No, boss,' she said. 'It's fine. Let him go on. I'm interested to hear.'

Carver coughed and fiddled with his tie. 'It's just that your attitude to male police officers might be seen as prejudiced.'

'Am I prejudiced against men?' Annie said. 'Is that what you're saying? Maybe I am towards some, but that prejudice doesn't necessarily extend as far as every thick sexist oaf on the force or I'd have a hard time indeed doing my job. Your men tried to bully and intimidate us.'

'That was because you didn't announce your presence as police detectives.' Carver's expression took on a distinct sneer. 'Not because they're rapists or bullies. Not all men are, you know.'

'Listen to yourself,' Annie said, her voice rising. 'Just listen to yourself.'

It was Banks's turn to touch Annie's arm. 'OK, DI Cabbot, Superintendent Carver, that's enough of that from both of you. Let's agree to differ and leave personal slights behind us. Is that OK, Superintendent?'

Carver bristled. 'Go on, DI Cabbot,' he grunted. 'We're listening.'

'We were approached by the officers in question, who informed us that we couldn't park where we were because it was a double yellow line.'

'And?' said Banks.

'There were no double yellow lines, just a single.'

'But as I understand it, the officers were simply enforcing what they knew to be a parking law for that stretch of road,' Banks countered.

'There were no signs about not parking there, either. They said one of the lines had faded over time, and the council hadn't got around to repainting it yet, which I thought was a load of bollocks.' Annie looked at a smirking Superintendent Carver. 'I'll bet they found time this morning, though.'

'Why didn't you just do as you were instructed and move on?' asked Banks. 'Better still, why didn't you tell them who you were and why you were there?'

Annie bit her lower lip. She knew that in one sense she had behaved the way she had because she had wanted to provoke the officers, to push them, test their behaviour. But she also knew that she had been sticking up for herself and Gerry, as members of the general public, trying to strike a blow against big hulking men who get pleasure from pushing women around. 'It was their attitude,' Annie said. 'Their manner was confrontational right from the get-go.'

'So you didn't like their attitude,' mocked Carver. 'Funny, that's exactly what they said about you.'

'Well, they would say that, wouldn't they?'

Banks smiled, but Annie's Mandy Rice-Davies imitation didn't get her far with Carver. Perhaps he was too young to remember the Profumo affair.

'In fact,' Carver continued, pulling at the sharp crease in his uniform trousers, 'they went on to say that you two were both abusive and belligerent. That at one point you—'

'Now hold on a minute,' said Annie. 'It was one of your men who grabbed me by the elbow and pulled his baton. Not us.'

'Because he was provoked.'

'Provoked, bollocks,' said Annie. 'He did it because he's a bully.'

'The officer said you were reaching into your bag. He thought you could have been reaching for a knife or even a gun. It's a dodgy area. Drugs and stuff. They have to be careful. Every night they go out on patrol they could face some serious threat to life and limb. That's why they might seem a bit more aggressive than some.'

'And I thought it was just in their nature,' said Annie. Gerry shifted uncomfortably in the chair beside hers.

'Again, I'd like to know why you didn't simply identify yourselves as police officers from the start,' said Banks. 'That would no doubt have prevented all these problems from arising, including the parking.'

'I didn't see why we should have had to,' protested Annie. 'We weren't asking for special treatment. As far as I was concerned, we had broken no laws. We were simply two women parking a car – legally, as far as we were concerned – and walking down the street minding our own business when those two brutes came over and started hassling us for no good reason. The fact that we didn't introduce ourselves as fellow officers only means they thought we were members of the public. And members of the public deserve to be better treated than we were. I'm sorry if you don't like to hear it, but those two officers set out to bully and humiliate us from the start. Anything we did, whether you call it "intimidation" or whatever, was by way of defending ourselves.'

'Including insinuating that one of my men was "bent"?' asked Carver.

'I said he reminded me of a bent sheriff in a bad Western. He did. I don't think that constitutes calling him bent.'

'Semantics,' said Banks, again suppressing the laughter. 'Let's put the incident with the officers aside for the moment. As if that wasn't bad enough, I understand the two of you then went on to inflame the local Asian community.'

'We most certainly did not,' said Annie. 'I don't know who told you that, but whoever it is, he's a liar.' She held Carver's gaze as she spoke. 'Mimosa's family told us that she sometimes hung out on what they called the Strip, a half-mile stretch of Wytherton Town Street between the overpass and the canal bridge. Mimosa's stepfather told us he didn't like it because there were too many Asians around, but it's the nearest place where there's anything happening at night, and most kids aren't as bigoted as Lenny Thornton. They like to hang out on the street, especially on warm nights. As Mimosa was from Wytherton Heights and our DNA specialist has informed us that the samples of semen taken from her body were Pakistani in origin, that's why we went there in the first place after talking to Sinead Moffat.'

'What do you think about that, DC Masterson?' Banks asked, turning to a terrified Gerry.

'It's true, sir, what DI Cabbot says. We didn't set out to inflame anyone in the community, and I don't believe we did. As DI Cabbot said, we were following a perfectly valid lead about the murdered girl.'

'Did you find the place swarming with young girls?'

'No,' said Annie. 'But considering that Mimosa Moffat has been dead for almost a week, it'd hardly be business as usual, would it?'

'Even so, it's a thin lead, or so it seems to me,' said Banks. 'I understand that certain accusations were made?'

'No accusations,' Annie replied. 'I showed the two men behind the counter in a kebab and pizza takeaway an artist's impression of the dead girl. They said they didn't know her.'

'And then?'

'I wasn't sure I believed them. After all, if she hung out on the Strip and she ate kebab and pizza, there was a good chance she'd been in their takeaway, wouldn't you say, sir? It's the kind of place young people hang out, especially if they're under the legal drinking age. I might have mentioned her stomach contents as I left, just to make them think a bit.'

'There are dozens of such places around,' said Carver.

'Not as close to where Mimosa Moffat lived,' said Annie. 'Not in her own neighbourhood. And an area she was known to hang out in. And the PM did find—'

Carver waved his hand. 'Even so. That was still no reason to strut into my manor and start harassing racial minorities. Wytherton is a balancing act. And the fact that the dustmen are on strike and we have a heatwave at the moment doesn't help, either. Tensions are high.'

'Well, that explains the smell,' said Annie. 'But as for harassing racial minorities, come off it, sir. In the first place, the Asians didn't seem to be a minority in the area, and in the second, I didn't harass anyone. Nor did DC Masterson. Maybe I didn't wear kid gloves, but I treated them all in exactly the same way I treat everyone else I question in a homicide investigation.'

'Well, if that's the way you go around—'

'Did you discover anything more on this Strip?' Banks cut in. Carver glared at him.

'No. Apart from the smell. We talked to the guys in the minicab office next door, but that's all. Everything else was pretty much closed, and there weren't a lot of people about. None of the ones we talked to admitted to knowing Mimosa. It was if she didn't exist. I got the feeling that someone's got these people scared, or well trained, sir. They—'

'This is pure balderdash,' fumed Carver, getting to his feet. 'Just because you couldn't get any leads in your investigation, you accuse a whole community of being involved in a cover-up. If they said they didn't know her, it was probably because they didn't. I suppose you think my officers are part of the conspiracy, too?'

'I never said that, sir,' Annie answered. 'But if the cap fits . . .'

'You certainly implied it. Don't you think your time might have been better spent asking them if they had noticed anything, instead of pestering local cafe owners and businessmen?'

'That's enough of that, Superintendent Carver,' said Banks. 'Let's leave implications out of it for the moment. Sit down.'

Carver didn't look happy, but he subsided into his chair.

'And we did ask Reg and Bill if they'd noticed anything,' muttered Annie. 'Or if they recognised Mimosa Moffat.'

'By which time you'd already alienated them.'

'Did they, by the way?' Banks asked him. 'Notice anything?'

'No,' said Carver. 'I talked to them about it once we knew why your officers were nosing around. And none of my men saw anything on the night in question, either. Reg and Bill weren't even on duty. But the fact remains,' he went on, 'that Wytherton is a racially sensitive community. The place is like a tinderbox. It could go up at any moment. You don't go marching into such an area and start pushing people around and making arbitrary insinuations. If you go in there at all, you go there with all your facts straight – and preferably with specific names, warrants, evidence, the lot.'

'More than if they happened to be white?'

'Damn right,' said Carver.

'We didn't push anybody around,' Annie said. 'I don't get it. Is this some sort of positive *non*-discrimination?'

'Think about it, DI Cabbot,' said Banks. 'Call it post-colonial guilt, if you like.'

'Even that doesn't explain it.'

'Then just accept it.'

'It's simple,' said Carver. 'It's pragmatic, a matter of simple practicalities. Let me explain. Your average whites don't make too much of a fuss if you hassle them. The Muslim community pulls together and makes a noise about it. No matter that they're mostly third-generation Pakistanis in Wytherton – their grandparents came over in the fifties – and that they often embrace Western culture and seem just as English as you and me. Maybe their grandparents brought the old religion with them, but it started to fade with their children. These days, they're either westernised or . . . well, you know, attracted by the other extreme. Luckily that doesn't happen too much around Wytherton. Either way, they feel themselves to be different, singled out, as easily demonised, especially when it suits them, and they make a noise about it. And when they do, guess who has to deal with it.' He pointed his thumb at his own chest. 'Wytherton is a split community. We've got the Muslims mostly to the south of the Strip in Lower Wytherton, though they're spreading slowly into the north, and Wytherton Heights is mostly white. There are also areas where whites and British Pakistanis live side by side and have done for years. The boundaries are constantly changing. If we went in and came down hard on the Muslim community for no good reason, we'd have pitched battles on Town Street. Is that what you want to see, DI Cabbot?'

'No,' said Annie. 'But we didn't go in hard, and it wasn't for no good reason. Besides, I don't believe the men we're dealing with are Muslims in any real sense of the word. Muslims don't do what was done to Mimosa. Muslims don't rape and kill young girls. Well, they do, actually, some of them, but we'll leave that aside for the time being. And they don't exactly have an enlightened attitude towards women, while we're at it, but if you point that out to some people, they just accuse you of picking on it as an excuse to demonise them because they don't believe the same things you do. We may be wrong, but we think – I think – that Mimosa and probably some of her friends were being groomed. And we think it's happening on your patch. Whether you simply ignored it or hadn't a clue, I have no idea, but I should think they've suspended operations for the time being. What I want is justice for Mimosa Moffat, a fifteen-year-old girl from the Wytherton Heights estate who was gang-raped by three men of Pakistani descent, according to DNA evidence, and beaten to death by a person or persons unknown on *my* patch. If that means upsetting a few people in the community, so be it. Boo-bloody-hoo. Besides, the nearest any of that lot have been to Pakistan is the nearest Karachi Curry House.'

'Irrelevant, DI Cabbot,' said Carver. 'Are you on some sort of personal vendetta? Is that what's preventing you from seeing the bigger picture? Because if—'

'That's enough, Superintendent Carver,' said Banks. 'We take your point, but we do have a murder investigation to carry out. It seems you're running a slack ship, as far as I can tell. The artist's impression of Mimosa Moffat – done, by the way, because her face was beaten to a pulp – was circulated throughout the country, including Wytherton. Someone clearly isn't doing their job right.'

'I resent that.'

'Resent away. How would *you* suggest we approach the problem?'

'Well, you've got all the facilities, and your minds are made up, so you hardly need my advice.'

Banks could tell that Carver was annoyed that he had a difficult area to police, while Homicide and Major Crimes was housed at the more peaceful Eastvale Police HQ and had a mini forensic lab attached. But Banks could hardly help it if Carver were trying to pass his manor off as Fort Apache, the Bronx. 'Humour me,' he said. 'What about CCTV on the Strip?'

'You can try,' said Carver. 'But there isn't very much. Besides, it was over a week ago. They'll have recorded over the hard drives or DVDs or whatever they use by now. You might try questioning some of the local shopkeepers.'

'I get it,' said Banks. 'Basically, not much chance of finding out if there was a car or a van parked near the kebab and pizza takeaway and the minicab office a week ago?'

No.' Carver shot Annie and Gerry a withering glance.

'So where do you suggest we start?'

Carver puffed up his chest. 'I don't know how you go about doing things down here, but I'd suggest you start by taking the Moffat house apart. We've had cause to pay more visits there over the years than we have to the entire Muslim community.'

'Well, that's no surprise if you're too frightened to say boo to them, is it?' said Annie. 'You can't have it both ways.'

'Let Superintendent Carver speak,' said Banks.

'Thank you,' said Carver. 'Let me tell you about the Moffats. When it came to handing out brain cells they weren't exactly at the front of the queue. By now they're second-generation unemployed, third, if you discount Albert Senior's artistic pursuits. He never did a day's work in his life either, just sat around smoking joints and splashing paint on canvas. Albert and his common-law wife Maureen moved there in the late sixties and had Johnny and Sinead about five years apart. The family was called Kerrigan back then, no Moffat on the horizon for a while. Touch of the Irish about them, a background of wandering navvies and horse traders. Albert Kerrigan bought 14 Southam Terrace in the eighties when Mrs Thatcher made it possible for less well-off people to buy their own council house in the hopes they would become more law-abiding and house-proud.'

'Spare us the political lecture, Superintendent Carver,' said Banks.

Carver harrumphed and went on. 'We know things didn't turn out that way. And, I might add, the police at the time strongly suspected that Albert Kerrigan used money acquired through the sale of illegal drugs in the house purchase.'

'Let me guess,' said Annie. 'They couldn't prove it.'

'That's right. Kerrigan claimed he'd sold a painting to get the money, but I couldn't imagine anyone paying six grand for the rubbish he turned out.'

'And you're an art expert, too,' said Annie. 'Wonders never cease.'

Carver went red.

'Shut it, DI Cabbot,' said Banks.

Carver cast her the evil eye and went on. 'I was only a constable on the beat back then, patrol cars, but I had plenty of first-hand experience of the various Kerrigans and Moffats over the years. Sinead Kerrigan married Leslie Moffat in the late nineties, and Mimosa and Albert were born around the millennium, just three years apart. Les Moffat was a small-time crook. A bit of housebreaking, the occasional mugging after dark in Middlesbrough town centre. He could be violent when he wanted to, and he buggered off when the kids were still little. That was around the time Albert Kerrigan died of a brain tumour. Only in his fifties. I blame the drugs.'

'And his wife?' Banks asked.

'Maureen? Drifted off with some Travellers. Never been seen since.'

'Which leaves Sinead, Lenny, Johnny and the kids,' said Banks. 'Were any of the children ever fostered out or taken into care?'

'No,' said Carver. 'They always managed to avoid that fate. God knows how.'

'What about Sinead's brother?' Banks asked. 'I heard he's a bit . . .' He glanced at Annie.

'Doolally,' she said.

'Johnny's five years older than Sinead,' said Carver. 'He rode with a local biker gang involved in drugs and all kinds of nastiness until he smashed his bike up on the A19 one rainy day. Never been the same since. Just sits in his chair. Which suits us fine.'

'What happened after Les Moffat left?' Banks asked.

'Mama Sinead is left behind looking after the whole family. After Moffat, there was a string of men, bad choices for the most part, junkies, criminals and unemployed layabouts all. That's when she developed her drug habit, and she wasn't averse to a bit of soliciting to support it. Then Lenny Thornton came on the scene in 2009, and she soon had two kids by him. We've had our run-ins with Lenny. He's settled down these days, but he specialised in car theft after a childhood of joyriding. Then when the security locks got too complicated for his tiny brain, he moved on to fencing stolen goods. But he wasn't very good at it. After a short stretch inside, he seemed to go straight. We've had nothing on him for two or three years now. And that, my dear friends, is the Moffats of Southam Terrace. And when you start feeling all warm and tingly inside about Sinead Moffat getting her act together, doing the methadone cure, think again. She may well be trying to kick her heroin habit at the moment, but don't let that fool you. Judging by all previous attempts, she'll be back on it in no time, and turning tricks, if any man in his right mind will pay her for it.'

Banks gave him a dirty look. 'Watch it, Mr Carver,' he said. 'That was uncalled for.'

'Sorry,' said Carver.

'Are you suggesting that one of the family killed Mimosa?' Annie asked.

'All I'm saying is it's a good place to start. Better than Sunny's Kebab and Pizza. You could do worse than have a chat with the social and school authorities, too. Wytherton Comprehensive. Lovely place. Shoo-in for Oxford.' He paused. 'You admit you don't know who actually murdered the girl. All I'm saying is look close to home. Isn't that the way it usually is? Her brother Albert's a yobbo for a start. He's broken a window or two on the Strip in his time, usually after a skinful of ale. He wouldn't like it if he'd heard she'd been shagging Pakis.'

'I won't tell you again, Mr Carver,' said Banks. 'There's no room for that sort of crudeness here. A bit more respect.

According to our forensic evidence, the girl you're talking about was *raped*.'

'Doesn't mean she hadn't done it willingly at some point. Perhaps you'd like me to assign a couple of my local CID officers to help you with your enquiries in Wytherton?' Carver went on, pushing his luck.

'We can handle it,' said Annie.

'I don't think that will be necessary,' said Banks. 'It's a Homicide and Major Crimes case. We may consult on occasion, should the need arise.'

Carver gritted his teeth. 'If you say so.'

'I think that's all for now,' Banks said. 'You know your next actions, DI Cabbot, DC Masterson. Tear the Moffat house apart and find Albert Jr.'

It was another warm day in Wytherton, though much less muggy, and the smell of decomposing rubbish polluted the air. The dustbin men had been on strike for over a week now, Gerry had learned, and there seemed to be no end in sight. She had spent a good part of her morning on the phone and discovered that Les Moffat, Mimosa's birth father, had died of liver disease two years ago and that Eddie Mallard, the ex-boyfriend of Sinead's who had molested Mimosa, had been stabbed in a prison brawl four years ago. She had also got through to one of Mimosa's teachers, who told her that Mimosa was naturally bright but didn't apply herself enough. She could have done a lot better if she had tried, but then, Gerry thought, couldn't we all. There had been attendance issues lately and Mimosa had paid more than one visit to the head teacher's office. She had also been warned over the using of racial slurs. That seemed odd to Gerry, but perhaps if Mimsy was in a relationship with a group of Asian groomers then it was a form of camouflage.

The social service offices were housed in a flat-roofed, modern one-storey building on the other side of the canal, just across the bridge, over from the new shopping centre and about half a mile from the Strip. Beside it was a small square of tufty, dried-out grass where a few young people lounged, shirtless and listless, smoking joints or cigarettes, drinking from plastic water bottles or cans of lager. Gerry felt the sweat sticking her white silk blouse to her skin as she went through the front doors into the reception area.

A bored woman sat behind a glass partition like a ticket-seller at a railway station. Without looking up from her keyboard, she said, 'Take a number and wait over there,' as if it were for the hundredth time that day.

Gerry flashed her warrant card, and the woman pointed to a desk wedged into a corner. 'Over there,' she said. 'See Alicia. She deals with all police matters.'

Alicia glanced up as Gerry approached. She was probably mid-thirties, plump with short curly dark hair and a badge with her first name below a smiley face. A place of mixed messages, this, Gerry thought.

Gerry showed her warrant card again. The woman examined it closely and gestured for her to sit down, making it clear who was in charge. Gerry sat on the moulded orange chair, trying to avoid a bit of old chewing gum stuck near the left edge. There was noise all around, chatter, computer printers, keyboards, ringtones. Not much laughter. The squad room was bad enough sometimes, but Gerry wondered how anyone could get any work done with such a din going on. Like anything else, she supposed, you got used to it.

'What's it about?' the woman asked.

'I'm here to see someone about a girl called Mimosa Moffat.'

'Who?'

'Mimosa Moffat.'

'Just a minute.'

The woman tilted her computer screen towards her, hit a few keys and frowned as she scrolled up and down. 'Moffat,' she said eventually. 'Address?'

Gerry told her.

'I'll see if the case officer's in his office. Hang on a minute.' Alicia picked up the phone, pressed a couple of buttons and waited. Eventually, someone answered and a brief exchange followed. Gerry could hardly hear a word because of the ambient noise. When Alicia put the phone down, she told Gerry, 'Ciaran will see you now. His office is down that corridor over there, first right, second left. Got it?'

'Got it,' said Gerry. 'Name on the door?'

'Ciaran O'Byrne.'

The corridors beyond the open plan area formed a maze, and even with clear and simple directions, Gerry almost missed the second turning. She finally found the name on the door, knocked and answered the call to come in. Ciaran O'Byrne stood up to shake hands when Gerry entered. He was probably about her age, late twenties, skinny, bearded and casually dressed, mostly in black. The small office was so filled with filing cabinets and piles of papers that it was hard to find anywhere to sit. It was also like an oven. Gerry noticed there were no windows, just a sort of grille high in the wall, which was made of perforated plywood panels. A grinding, coughing noise came from inside the grille, but Gerry couldn't feel even the slightest waft of cool air.

'Just clear those papers off that chair,' O'Byrne said. 'You can dump them on the floor.'

Gerry picked up the papers and set them gently beside the chair, then sat down.

O'Byrne leaned back in his chair, tapped a pencil tip against his lower lip and said, 'What can I do for you? Alicia said it was something to do with the Moffats.'

'That's right. Mimosa Moffat, in particular.'

'She's not a bad kid, really, isn't Mimsy. Better than some. I must say I haven't seen her for a while, though. I hope she isn't in any trouble.'

Gerry felt gobsmacked. 'Er . . . no . . . I mean, that is . . . you haven't heard?'

'Heard what?'

'Mimosa was killed last week. I'm from the county Homicide and Major Crimes. We're investigating the case. The local police said we should talk to you.'

O'Byrne dropped his pencil and sat up straight. 'What? She what? Bloody hell.'

'Mimosa was murdered. Raped and murdered on a country lane just outside Eastvale about a week ago. Her picture has been on the news and in the papers all week. An artist's likeness, at any rate. We only found out who she was yesterday through an anonymous phone call.'

O'Byrne rubbed his cheeks and eyes. 'Oh my God. I'm so sorry to hear that. And I must apologise for my ignorance. This job's depressing enough as it is. Any chance I get, you'll find me fishing in Upper Teesdale or walking the Dales, not watching the news or reading the papers.'

'I thought someone might have told you.'

'I'm sure someone would have, eventually. Just not yet. My God. Mimsy Moffat. What happened to her?'

Gerry gave him an edited version of the details, skipping the points the team had decided to keep to themselves.

'What is it you want from me?' he asked. 'I have to say, first off, that I wasn't especially close to Mimsy.'

'Why not? Weren't you her case officer?'

'Case officer? No. Whatever gave you that impression? I work mostly with Sinead, and sometimes Johnny, not Mimsy. She didn't have a specific case officer.'

'Why's that?'

'Didn't need one. Sinead has a drug problem, as you probably know already. Has had on and off for years. It's caused
her a number of other problems, bad judgement and child
neglect not being the least of them. Her common-law husband
and her brother haven't always been able to step into the gap,
so to speak. We – I – have kept an eye on Sinead. Try to help,
make sure the kids aren't suffering, the little ones especially,
Tammi and Mike.'

'And they weren't?'

'Not as I'm aware. Mimsy had a few problems at school,
poor attendance, disruptive behaviour, talking back, and the
like. She was excluded more than once, but that wasn't much
of a cause for concern. None of us really liked school, did
we?'

Gerry actually *had* liked school, but she wasn't going to tell
O'Byrne that. She'd liked the learning and the sports, and had
particularly excelled at hockey and field events, not to mention
all the academic subjects except geography. 'She was only
fifteen,' she said. 'She should have been attending whether she
liked it or not.'

'Short of dragging her there . . . Look, Mimsy was a bit of a
tearaway, and she didn't respond well to authority. She liked
to think she was different, not part of the ordinary crowd.
Typical rebellious teen in some ways but she was also naive.'

'Did she have learning difficulties?'

'Not as such. Short attention span, mild dyslexia. That's
about all. It was more of an *attitude* problem.'

'Did you notice any recent changes in her behaviour?'

'Not really. But I haven't actually really spoken with her for
a while.'

'You mentioned Leonard Thornton earlier. What about her
uncle Johnny?'

'Johnny's disabled.'

'You take care of him, too?'

'Lord, no. He has his own NHS carers. All I do is coordinate to some extent, make sure the left hand knows what the right hand's doing.' He leaned forward and rested his hands on the desk. 'I'm sorry, but I don't know what it is you want from me. To the best of my knowledge, and the department's knowledge, none of the children were being abused or mistreated. There were some negligence issues, and we worked with the family on them. But there has never been any doubt that Sinead and Leonard Thornton have been fit parents, despite the occasional lapse. No matter what some people think, we try to avoid intervention unless we feel it absolutely necessary.'

'Is there anything you can tell me about Mimosa's life? Her problems. Her friends. What she got up to. We still have a lot of blanks to fill in. Let's start with her friends. Some names would help.'

'I wish I could, but I'm afraid I don't know.'

'OK. Her problems?'

'Well, her biggest problem is a drug-addicted mother. I know that Sinead's on a methadone programme at the moment, but we're not a hundred per cent certain it will do the trick. She seems determined, but it hasn't worked before, and frankly, this terrible news about Mimsy . . . well, I'm not sure what it will do to her. Though I got the impression they fought a lot, I also think it may have been because they were like as two peas in a pod. Not the heroin, of course but in some respects of character. But Sinead's problems mean the kids – Mimsy and Albert in particular – weren't subject to the usual parental discipline and control. As I said, they're not bad kids, really, but Mimsy has run a little wild, which is only to be expected under the circumstances, and Albert got probation for vandalism a while back. He's lucky he didn't get done for hate crime as well, as it was a halal butcher's window he chucked the brick through. Also lucky for him he was drunk at the time. It's a turbulent neighbourhood.'

'Did you ever have any direct contact with Mimsy?'

'Briefly. When she self-harmed about eighteen months ago.'

'Was there any particular reason for what she did?'

'As usual in cases like that, there were a number of factors at work. I think mostly she was lonely and felt unloved, and she wanted to make her mother notice her. Sinead was going through a particularly difficult time then.'

'A cry for help? Did it work?'

'Sinead understood. She'd been there herself. She'd done exactly the same thing in her own teenage years. She rallied herself for Mimsy's sake. That was the first time she signed up for the methadone programme. At least she started trying. And Mimsy went for counselling.' He picked up his pencil again and started twisting it in his short stubby fingers. 'Didn't last long, mind you. I'm afraid the counsellor . . .'

'The counsellor abused her. Yes, Sinead mentioned something like that.'

'He wasn't one of ours, of course. He was private. Well, assigned through the NHS, but you know what I mean.'

Like most people employed to serve the public in some way, O'Byrne reacted first by trying to cover his own arse and that of his department. *Not our fault. Not part of our mandate.* How often had she had heard those words prefacing an excuse for not doing anything, or for doing the wrong thing? 'She was what, all of thirteen at the time?'

O'Byrne looked sheepish. 'Yes.'

'Then you know as well as I do that he raped her, no matter how consensual their arrangement was.'

'I've told you Mimsy was a bit of a tearaway, uncontrollable, something of a wild child. She was probably trying to assert her freedom, show she was a grown-up. And she could be manipulative when she wanted.'

' It sounds as if she could be manipulated, too,' said Gerry. 'Are you trying to exonerate this counsellor? Are you saying she led him on?'

'No. No. Not at all. But so many girls her age think they're so sophisticated, when deep down they're actually not. I'm just saying I don't think he threw her over the desk and had his way with her.'

Gerry couldn't think of an appropriate response to that. She moved on. 'I'll need his name.'

'John Lewton. He was disciplined, naturally. Terminated. Struck off. He can't practise any more. I believe there were even steps towards criminal prosecution but bargains were made. As I understand it, he left the country not long after.'

'For where?'

'Spain. Apparently he owns some property there.'

Gerry would check the story out, of course, and make sure this John Lewton hadn't suddenly reappeared in Mimsy's life.

'I know you can't talk about these things,' said O'Byrne, 'but have you any idea who did this or why?'

'We don't. Not at the moment. You said you didn't know who Mimosa's friends were in the neighbourhood, but we'd like to talk to someone her own age she might have confided in. Is there no one you can think of?'

'No. I'm sorry. But I'm sure she wasn't in a gang. We monitor gang activity closely.'

'What about the young girls hanging out on the Strip with older Pakistani men?'

O'Byrne's eyes turned towards the grille and he sighed. 'That thing never works,' he said. 'Aren't you too hot in here? I am.'

'Very.'

'Come on. Let's go for a walk.'

They left by the back door, beside which was a narrow footpath leading to the canal. From there, you could follow the towpath for some distance.

'I often come out here when I just want a little break or to cool down,' he said as they walked. 'It's not especially pretty, but at least it's outside.'

It certainly wasn't pretty, Gerry thought, with a factory belching smoke beyond the towpath, white suds floating on the filthy brown water, and the all-pervading smell of rotting garbage. There were also small piles of black bin bags spilling rubbish here and there, along with broken prams and wheel-less bicycles. Gerry thought she saw a rat scuttle from one bag to another. She didn't even think it was much cooler by the canal, but it was certainly nice to be out of that oven of an office.

'I mentioned the young girls hanging out with the Pakistanis on the Strip. The local police don't seem to know much about it, or think much of it. Does it go on? Have you noticed anything like that?'

'I'm afraid not. I don't have any reason to go there. I don't live around here. Soon as it's time to go home, I'm gone.'

'Very sensible,' said Gerry. 'But it's a divided area, I hear. There's a large Muslim community, mostly people of Pakistani descent.'

'True,' said O'Byrne. 'But we don't have a lot to do with them.'

'Why's that?'

'They don't want us putting our noses in their business. They take care of their own families in their own way, according to their own customs, traditions and laws. I mean, some of our staff are from the community, and they have special ties, of course. They've occasionally been involved in certain domestic issues, but as a rule, by far the most of our work comes from the largely white estates.'

'I see,' said Gerry. 'And you find it easiest not to help?'

'Not to *interfere*. Yes. Best for everyone, all round.'

'So you leave them to their own vigilante brand of justice?'

'I'd say justice is your job, not mine. Wouldn't you agree?'

'No matter what they do?'

O'Byrne managed a weak laugh. 'Do? They don't do anything that anyone else doesn't do. Besides, we're not the police. I'll bet your police up here have far less trouble with them than with the local white population. Binge-drinking, vandalism, shoplifting, drugs, graffiti and the like. Some of those kids are just out of control, and their parents aren't much better.' He paused. 'Believe me, we try to be sensitive to issues of race and cultural differences, and we try to be colour-blind. It's an awkward balance, and I'd be the first to admit that it doesn't really work and we don't always get it right. We're only human, after all.'

'Have you talked to members of the community, people from the mosque, the imams?'

'No. But I know what their answer would be.'

'What?'

'If they do these things, they can't be true Muslims, there-fore, they're not our problem.'

'That's a bit short-sighted, isn't it?'

'Tell that to the imam.'

'It's just that we have reason to believe that Mimosa might have been connected with some Pakistanis, and there seem to be a lot of them in the neighbourhood. Running the shops and businesses along the Strip, for example. A takeaway, mini-cab firm, balti restaurant and so on. We know she ate kebab and pizza shortly before she died. Coincidence?' Gerry real-ised she was pushing it a bit with this. All they really knew was what Dr Glendenning had found in her stomach and what Jazz Singh had got from the DNA: that her last meal consisted of pizza and kebab and that she had had rough sex with three men of Pakistani descent. There was nothing to indicate that the men came from this area, or that she had eaten her last meal on the Strip. Still, Gerry believed that Ciaran O'Byrne needed a bit of a kick up the arse, and as often as not in her business the roots of a crime began on the victim's own door-step, so it wasn't an unreasonable assumption.

'Well, there are lots of places you can get kebab and pizza, and there are Asian communities all over the country.'

'Yes, but Mimosa lived *here*.' Gerry paused. 'I must say, you seem remarkably unconcerned. Don't you get it? We're talking about a fifteen-year-old girl in your care who was raped and murdered.'

'I've told you, Mimsy wasn't in my care.'

'But you have a close connection with the family, with her mother particularly.'

'But not because of Mimsy. Yes, well, I try to do my job. Things were difficult, but they were coping. Mimsy didn't need to be taken away and handed over to foster parents or put in a home. She could take care of herself. At her best Sinead was there, and Leonard Thornton is a decent bloke, despite all appearances to the contrary.'

'Maybe. But he didn't keep a close eye on Mimosa.'

'Surely you can't blame Leonard for what happened to her?'

'I'm after finding out who did this to her. Then we'll see about blame.' Gerry took a deep breath. 'Mr O'Byrne, I find your wilful ignorance about this whole matter astonishing, not to mention disturbing. Didn't you read about what happened in Rochdale, Rotherham and the rest? Isn't it required reading for the social services? Can't you see what's going on in front of your eyes? There's every possibility that Mimsy, and no doubt other young girls, were being groomed. They're what, thirteen, fourteen, fifteen? Alienated. Neglected. Lonely. Unloved. Some of them with learning difficulties. These men offer them some material comforts, a packet of crisps, a mobile top-up, a free fizzy pop, then friendship, companion-ship. Then come the demands. The sex with friends, with strangers.' She pointed. 'It could be happening right there, less than half a mile down the road on the Strip and you don't know about it. Now a girl is dead.'

'You've no proof that any of this is happening in Wytherton,' said O'Byrne. 'It's all conjecture. And even if there is some truth to it, you can't blame us. Nor can you blame Mimsy's death on it. We do our best, but we're drowning under the flow of shit from these estates. It's like standing with your finger in the dyke. You lot don't do anything to help, either. It's not our job to arrest criminals. It's yours.'

'It's your job to protect the children and let us know what's happening.'

'Nobody wants to get involved in a race war here in Wytherton. There's already plenty of tension around here. The English Defence League and the British National Party are active. Windows have been broken.'

'Including one by Albert Moffat. Is he a member of either of the groups?

'Not as far as I know.'

'Besides, isn't race war a bit alarmist? Who said anything about that? Surely there are ways of handling these things without starting a race war?'

O'Byrne stopped walking and faced her. 'Yes? And how? Tell me how. What do you do, walk in and say "Stop it, fellows, leave our poor little white girls alone"?'

'You could at least report it to your bosses, or to the police. You could at least give the possibility some serious consideration and talk about it.'

'I've already told you we have no evidence of such things going on. Do you? And as for the local police, I've told you how much use they are. You must know that yourself, from what you've said. You can report your concerns to them until you're blue in the face, but it'll go nowhere. As far as they're concerned these girls are the dregs from the council estates. These girls are making their own lifestyle choices. They decide who they want to go out with, who they want to sleep with. If they choose to be sluts, so it goes. They get no better than they deserve.'

'Written off at thirteen? Sexually assaulted by her psychological counsellor. A man who was supposed to heal her. Did Mimsy deserve to be raped and murdered?'

'Don't be ridiculous. Of course she didn't. I'm speaking generally. They grow up quickly around these parts, in case you didn't know.'

'So you do have concerns, then?'

'I always have concerns in my job. All I'm saying is that as far as I know, so far, they don't involve grooming.'

'So everyone ignores the problem, turns their backs and thinks it will just go away?'

'If you think you can cure all the world's social ills, then go ahead. I used to think that when I first took this job.'

'And now you're a dyed-in-the-wool cynic at what, twenty-eight? I'm just surprised to find it still going on after the revelations of the last year or so.'

'It was going on long before Rotherham or Rochdale, and it'll be going on long after. Whether it's reached Wytherton or not.'

'Don't sound so pleased about it.'

O'Byrne started walking again, hands deep in the pockets of his jeans. 'I'm not. That wasn't fair. You don't have to be so snarky.'

'Maybe I do,' said Gerry after a while. 'Let me just ask you this, Mr O'Byrne. Did you have *any* idea what was going on? Did you ever see young white girls hanging around with older Asians just around the corner from here, maybe when you went out for lunch? Didn't it seem in the least bit suspicious after what you've read in the papers or seen on the news? Oh, sorry, I forgot, you don't pay any attention to the news because it's too depressing, and you leave this neighbourhood the minute the buzzer goes.'

'I do my job, as I told you, but it's not my life. And I didn't see any such thing. Whatever was going on, they obviously kept a low profile, and I should imagine it was mostly done after dark, not at lunchtime.'

'They'd hardly need to worry about daylight with social workers like you around.'

'That's insulting.'

'Maybe so, but not as insulting as your ignoring the problem. You knew Mimosa was involved, didn't you? But you didn't do anything. Why was that? You were afraid of being branded a racist, sent on a diversity training course?'

'You don't know what you're talking about. I had no idea what was going on. If indeed anything *was* going on. You haven't even proved that to me yet.'

'Haven't I? Well, I'm getting fed up of your evasions and excuses. First of all the local police, now you. The very people who should be looking out for girls like Mimosa. What is it with this place?'

'Those girls are already lost,' said O'Byrne. 'Like you said, they'd do anything for a packet of crisps or a can of alcopop. Whatever it is they're doing, it's their own choice. Why can't you just accept that?'

It was Gerry's turn to stop in her tracks. 'The dregs from the estates, eh? If you really believe that, Mr O'Byrne,' she said, 'then you're in the wrong job.' Then she turned and walked back up the towpath towards the bridge, her face burning with anger.

Banks had been wondering what to play on the journey from Eastvale to Leeds. His first thoughts had been maybe Bob Dylan, Patti Smith or Leonard Cohen. After all, Linda was a poet, and so were they. Or perhaps he should play nothing at all in case she wanted to talk. In the end, he asked her if there was anything she liked in particular. She thought for a moment, then said she'd always been a huge Bowie fan. Banks put on *Pin Ups*, not perhaps Bowie's most popular album, but one which satisfied Banks's love of old sixties music and Linda's love of Bowie. The startling segue from 'Rosalyn' to the shimmering portamento that opened 'Here Comes the Night' still sent a shiver up his spine every time he heard it, like the opening chords of the Small Faces' 'All or Nothing'. He didn't turn the volume so high that they couldn't talk if they wanted to, but Linda seemed distant, lost in her own thoughts. Occasionally she pointed out a song she particularly liked – 'See Emily Play' or 'Sorrow', for example – but mostly she remained silent, staring out of the side window at the passing landscape of the Vale of York. They turned off at Wetherby, made their way past the outer ring road and into the city centre, and Banks managed to find a parking spot near the Merrion Centre, just behind the library. They walked across Millennium Square, which was crowded with people sitting out at the cafes enjoying the fine weather.

The library and art gallery were on the Headrow, next to the town hall, housed in another grand Victorian building. Inside and out, the library complex was also an architectural delight, with its magnificent stone staircases, parquet floors, marble pillars, tiles and mosaics. A reviewer had once complained that the ceiling in the reading room was so magnificent it would distract people from actually reading. Both Banks and Linda had been inside before, so they didn't stand and gawp as much as some visitors were doing, but made their way straight to the office where Ken's contact, Marian Hirst, was waiting for them.

Marian was a short trim woman with no-nonsense grey hair and a pair of black-rimmed glasses that hung on a chain around her neck. Her nose was beak-like and her eyes dark and lively. Banks couldn't help thinking that she couldn't look more like most people's image of a librarian if she tried.

'DCI Blackstone told me you were coming,' she said, with a distant trace of a Scottish accent. 'He uses the service often himself. I've got everything prepared for you in a little office here. Now, you know how to work the machine, I assume?'

Banks nodded. He'd used a film reader before.

'Everything is clearly labelled, so you'll know exactly where you are.'

'Is it possible to get copies?' Banks asked.

'Not as you go,' she said. 'But if you put in a request our staff can provide one for you.'

She led them across the intricate parquet floor, her shoes clicking and echoing from the high ceiling as they walked, and entered a small room. Three boxes of film roll sat on the table beside the reader.

'Make yourselves as comfortable as you can,' Marian said. 'I'll be off about my business. And by the way, Ms Palmer, it's an honour to meet you. I'm a great fan of your poetry.'

Banks noticed Linda blush as she muttered her thanks.

'I see some people recognise you,' Banks said when Marian Hirst had left them.

'No doubt your friend told her I was coming.'

'I shouldn't think so. Ken knows better than to blab your name around. Besides, he wouldn't know an ode from an oud.'

Linda laughed. 'Hmm. I think this is a one-person job. Why don't you just show me how to set up the rolls then go and have a look at the Atkinson Grimshaws or something? I don't want you hovering over my shoulder the whole time.'

Banks showed her how to operate the reader, and as soon as she was satisfied she could manage by herself, she shooed him away. He had no real idea how long it would take, but he reckoned he'd give her an hour, for starters, which allowed him plenty of time for a coffee and Kit Kat in the Tiled Room cafe, where he made a couple of phone calls and checked his email. There was nothing much new. According to Winsome, the media crowd was growing outside Eastvale HQ now that they knew Mimosa Moffat was the Bradham Lane victim and that there were rumours of grooming. Annie had set off for Wytherton to meet up with Gerry and talk to Albert Moffat, who had finally turned up.

After that, Banks did take a few minutes to go and see the Atkinson Grimshaws in the art gallery before heading back to see how Linda was doing. He wasn't a great fan of art galleries and was far more comfortable with music and literature than with the visual arts, but Grimshaw's moody quayside and oddly lit nighttime city scenes were a delight. An hour and ten minutes had passed by the time he checked his watch, and he walked back next door to the library. He hadn't got far when he saw Linda wandering down a broad stone staircase, holding on to the bannister. She was glancing around, the other hand clutching the neck of her blouse, as if searching for someone. Him, perhaps.

'Linda,' Banks called out, heading towards her. She seemed as if she were ready to fall down the stairs, and he felt like reaching out his arms to save her, but she held on as she turned and caught his eye. He could tell by her expression and her pallor that she had been successful.

'I saw him,' she said, still clutching the cotton of her blouse at her throat with one hand. 'I found him.'

'Show me,' said Banks, taking her arm and leading her gently back up the staircase to the viewing room.

Linda pointed towards the viewer as if it were something she couldn't bear to touch, and Banks leaned forward to study the head-and-shoulders photograph of a handsome young man in a dark suit. According to the brief story, his name was Tony Monaghan, and his picture was in the newspaper because he had been found murdered in the public conveniences in Hyde Park, Leeds, on the twelfth of October 1967.

'There's something else,' Linda said. 'Something else I saw

when I was looking through. I didn't see it at the time, but . . . You have to see it first.' Linda fiddled with the machine. 'As I said, I haven't seen this one before today. I went ahead a bit to see if there was anything else about the man I recognised and I saw this. Here. The end of October. Look.' She moved away.

Banks leaned over. The photograph showed a number of high-ranking police officers standing around one central figure, who was handing over an oversized cardboard cheque, a big cheesy grin on his face. 'Superstar Danny Caxton presents Chief Constable Edward Crammond with a cheque for £10,000 for the Police Widows and Orphans Fund.' The story went on to say how Caxton had helped raise the amount through personal appearances and telethons, and how he valued his relationship with the local police, what a wonderful job they did, and so on. It was dated the twenty-seventh of October, just over two weeks after Tony Monaghan's murder and two months after Linda's rape.

It was clearly the photo of Danny Caxton that had upset Linda Palmer the most, but the picture of the man who had raped her after Caxton nearly fifty years ago intrigued Banks even more. *Tony Monaghan*. Perhaps he was now investigating a murder in addition to a rape.

9

The Bay Horse was a sprawling modern chain pub on the estate, sitting beside a cluster of local shops – greengrocer, butcher, newsagent and hairdresser. When Annie and Gerry walked in that Tuesday afternoon, the place was almost deserted except for a lone figure in jeans and a black T-shirt sitting hunched over his pint in the far corner. Some music Banks would probably recognise was playing softly in the background – maybe Dire Straits, Annie thought – but other than that the pub was quiet.

When they got a little closer, he looked up at them, and Annie could see that his eyes were red-rimmed, as if he'd been crying. He had a skinhead haircut and was stockier than Annie had expected, with elaborate tattoos on the muscles of his arms. She could see some similarity in features to the images of Mimosa she had seen, the cat-like slant of the eyes, the full, slightly pouting lips. On Mimosa it would all have been sexy as hell in life, whatever her age, but it made Albert's features seem a little too feminine. If he had more hair, Annie thought, he might even be quite handsome.

Lenny had told them he had just given the news to Albert about Mimosa and left him in the pub, that he had wanted to sit alone for a while and digest what he'd heard. Annie leaned over and said, 'Albert? Lenny told us you were here. We're the police. We need to ask you a few questions. Is it OK if we sit down?'

Albert looked from one to the other. 'Might as well,' he said.

Annie nodded towards the almost empty glass. 'Another?'

'Thanks.'

Gerry went to the bar and came back with a pint of lager for Albert and two diet bitter lemons for herself and Annie.

'We'll try and make it brief and painless,' Annie said. 'We're really sorry about your sister. I understand you've only just heard about what happened?'

'Yes.'

'Where were you?'

'Manchester, clubbing with some mates. I went there on Thursday and came back this morning.'

'Drive?'

'Nah. Train.'

'When did you last see Mimosa?'

'The weekend before. Sunday, I think. Maybe Monday.'

'And you weren't worried about her? I mean, she'd already been missing two days before you left for Manchester.'

'That wasn't unusual. Not for our Mimsy. Besides, I'm not always at home myself.'

'What did you do last Tuesday night?' Annie asked.

'I stopped over at Paul's. We'd had a bit to drink, like, watched some DVDs and crashed out.'

'What time was this?'

'Dunno. We met up in the pub earlier. Not this one. The Hope and Anchor, near his place. We left there about tennish, I suppose.'

'And went to Paul's?'

'Yeah. That's Paul Warner. He's my best mate.'

'You stay there often?'

'Paul says I can crash whenever I want. He's got one of those let-down couches. It's pretty comfortable. And a power shower. Cool.'

'What about work, Albert? Don't you have to go to work in a morning?'

'I'm unemployed. Paul lets me work with him sometimes. Odd jobs, like, you know, fetching and lifting.'

'What does this Paul do?'

'He's got his own business. Painting and decorating. Odd jobs on the side. He's good at fixing things. Tellies and computers and sinks and stuff.'

Annie heard the barman greet a regular. Albert sipped his lager and stared into the cold pale liquid.

'What was your relationship with your sister like?' she asked.

'Relationship?'

'Yes. How did you get along?'

'Do you have a big brother?' Albert asked.

'Me? No,' said Annie.

'I do,' said Gerry. 'He's five years older than me. He used to tease me like hell, but once when I was about ten he rescued me from a gang on my way home from school. They were shoving me around and getting rough with me.'

Albert glanced at her and nodded. 'You understand, then,' he said. 'The problem with Mimsy was that she never knew when to keep her gob shut.'

'Bit of a mouth on her, had she?' said Annie.

'You can say that again. Not always, mind. She could be sweet and gentle as anything. Quiet, even. But when the mood took her. She was no fool, wasn't Mimsy, and she didn't suffer fools gladly.'

'That can make for a hard life,' Annie said.

Albert looked at Gerry again. 'So you'll know what it was like,' he said. 'Having a big brother and all. I love our Mimsy, and I'd have done anything for her, but she was a kid and she wasn't part of my life in that way, so I probably treated her like crap some of the time. I mean, we didn't have much in common, we didn't hang out or anything.'

'You didn't share any parts of your life?' Gerry asked.

'I used to let her come and help sometimes, when I was working with Paul.' He turned away. 'Maybe we'd even let her have a lager and lime when we'd done, like, if it was thirsty work. There's no harm in it, is there?'

'I don't know,' said Annie. 'We hear Mimosa liked a drink.'

'She did and all.'

'But you don't know where she went in her spare time,' Annie went on, 'what she got up to?'

'No. Some people would probably think she was too young to be let loose like that, but you see it a lot these days. Kids as young as twelve, thirteen, fourteen, getting up to whatever they want with no questions asked.'

'Did Mimsy stop out all night?'

'Sometimes, sure.'

'Do you know where?'

'I never asked and she never said.'

'Is there anything you can tell us that might help us find her killer, Albert?'

Albert looked Annie in the eye, then leaned forward and spoke with a ferocity that made her flinch. 'Do you think those Pakis did it?'

'Which ones would that be?' Annie asked.

'That lot down on the Strip.'

'What do you know about them?'

'Nothing. 'Cept they're old, and she shouldn't have been hanging out with them. You can't trust them, can you? They're not like us. They do things different.'

'What did you see?'

'Our Mimsy getting in a taxi outside that minicab place next door to that takeaway. She was with a fat Paki, an older bloke in a suit. All tarted up, she was, too.'

'Did you recognise the man?'

'No. He wasn't anyone I'd seen in the takeaway or the other shops. I mean, I've got nothing against them, really, but what was our Mimsy doing getting in a minicab with one of them?'

'Did you ask her?'

'Last time I saw her. When we were walking down the street.'

'What did she say?'

'Told me it was none of my fucking business what she did, and they were a lot more fun to hang out with than the sad bastards at school.'

'Did you tell your parents, your mother?'

'I didn't tell anyone, did I? Why should I get her in trouble. I'm no snitch. But I told her she should stay away from them, that they were up to no good.'

'What did she say to that?'

'She just laughed and said what did I know.' He paused. 'I'm not a racist, really, but it's not right, is it? Blokes like that hanging about with young girls like Mimsy. It surprised me, really, when I saw her, like, because I thought she . . . well, I thought we agreed on certain things.'

'On Pakistanis?'

'Yeah. Immigration. Them coming and taking over. That sort of thing.'

'Have you seen any Pakistanis with other young girls?'

'No. I mean, not really. You know, you'll see one or two of them down the Strip, in the takeaway or waiting for a minicab, but I never took much notice. I mean, anything you need around the Strip you have to get from them. They've got it all sewn up. Except the chippie, and that's run by the Chinks. But they don't live around here.'

Not a racist but . . . Annie thought. The number of times she'd heard that. 'I understand you got probation for throwing a brick through a halal butcher's window,' she said.

'I was pissed, wasn't I?'

'But why that particular window?'

'Dunno. It was just there.'

'When did this incident with Mimosa and the taxi occur?'

'Week before last. Wednesday or Thursday.'

About a week before she disappeared, Annie calculated. 'And next time you saw Mimsy was on the Sunday or Monday after that?'

'That's right.'

'How did she seem? Was she upset, worried or anything? Was there anything different about her?'

'No. Same as usual.'

'Any marks on her? Anything like that?'

'No. She just got pissed off when I mentioned I'd seen her with the Paki, that's all. And, yeah, she was wearing some new trainers, fancy Nikes. I asked her where she'd got the money for them, and she told me she'd saved up.'

'Did you believe her?'

'No reason not to.'

'Did she have a part-time job? A summer job?'

'No.'

'Did Lenny or Sinead give her any pocket money?'

'Shouldn't think so.'

'Where do you think she got the money for new trainers?'

Albert shrugged. 'Dunno. She'd saved it out of the bits and pieces she earned helping out me and Paul? But it must have taken her a long time. He doesn't pay either of us much. Bit of a skinflint, is Paul. Maybe some bloke gave it to her. You haven't told me. Did they do it? Do you think it was the Pakis?'

'We don't know who it was yet, Albert, so don't take it into your head to do anything stupid.'

'Are you calling me stupid?'

'No, I'm not. I'm just telling you not to do anything foolish. Leave it to us to find out what happened.'

'Right. As if you lot would ever do anything if it was Pakis. You'd be too scared of being called racists.'

'Albert, no matter what you think, we're out to catch a murderer here, and we'll use whatever it takes to do that, whoever the murderer turns out to be. You have my word on that.'

Albert stared at her, then picked up his pint. The new customer started playing one of the machines near the door. Sirens and bells filled the air. 'There's something else,' Albert went on. 'Not specifically to do with Mimsy, but a Paki mate of mine – he's OK, by the way, none of that religious mumbo-jumbo, and he's a loyal Boro fan – he says he heard that some of the older blokes had been messing with white girls. You know, like that Rotherham thing.'

'Did he say anything more?'

'No. Just that.'

'When was this?'

'A few weeks before I saw Mimsy getting in the taxi.'

'Did you make any connection between what he told you and what you saw?'

'Connection?'

'Never mind. What's his name?'

'Ali.'

'Do you know where he lives?'

'Somewhere south of the Strip. But we have a drink in the Wytherton Arms now and then. You could probably find him in there most nights. Like I said, none of that religious non-drinking mumbo jumbo for Ali.'

'If you happen to bump into him before we have time to find him, would you give him this and ask him to call me?' Annie said, handing Albert her card.

'I don't want him to think I've been talking to the polis.'

'Albert. It's for Mimosa.'

Albert took the card reluctantly. 'I'll think about it.'

'How did it end, this last talk with Mimosa? Did you stay friends?'

'I suppose so. It's her life. I just told her if she needed anything, like, all she had to do was ask. She gave me one of her friendly pecks on the cheek, said something about her knight in shining armour, and that was that.'

'That was you? Her knight in shining armour.'

Albert managed a thin smile. 'Yeah. That's what she called me sometimes.' He looked at Gerry. 'I saved her from bullies too, once or twice, when she was about ten. It sort of stuck.'

'Mimsy was bullied?' Annie asked.

'For a while, yeah, at school.'

'Why?'

'Who knows. She was just different, that's all. And, like I said, she was mouthy.'

'But it stopped?'

'Far as I know.'

Annie paused, as much to let Gerry catch up with her notes as anything else. Albert drank some more lager and Annie sipped the tart bitter lemon. A pint would have been so much better. 'Do you remember that incident with the psychological counsellor?' she asked.

'Do I ever. Mum really laid into Mimsy that time. Him, too. I think she knew she'd fucked up a lot in her own life, and she saw Mimsy making the same mistakes, same bad choices. It just set her off.'

'Was Mimsy doing drugs then?'

'Some, maybe. Pills and dope and stuff.'

'Ketamine?'

'K? That's crazy stuff, isn't it? I don't know. I wouldn't think so. Mimsy liked a good time, she didn't want to go apeshit barking bonkers.'

'Have you seen or heard of this counsellor since?'

'No. They fired him. I heard he'd buggered off to Spain or somewhere. Too good for him. Ought to send him to the fucking North Pole stark bollock naked. Good riddance.'

'Is there anything else you can tell us, Albert?' Annie asked. 'Anything at all. Was there anyone you know who'd want to do Mimosa harm?'

'Not that I know of. Except maybe the Pakis, if she pissed them off.'

'OK.' Annie glanced towards Gerry, who put her notebook away. 'If you think of anything, and I mean anything, that may help us catch your sister's killer, no matter how unimportant it seems, give us a call. Right?'

'Right,' said Albert.

'And try to get in touch with Ali. Want a lift home?'

'Nah. Thanks. I think I'll just stay and have another. Let it all sink in.' He rubbed his eyes. 'I just feel like numb, like.'

They met in Banks's office shortly after his return from Leeds: Banks, AC Gervaise and Adrian Moss. Banks could have done without the latter, but he seemed to be all over the place like a dirty shirt these days. The station was still under siege, cameras clicking and questions shouted every time anyone came in or went out. The clamour seemed as much to do with Mimosa Moffat as it did Danny Caxton. Now that Mimosa had been identified, a phalanx of media had headed up to the Wytherton Heights estate to get the story from the horse's mouth, so to speak. No doubt viewers of the evening news and readers of tomorrow's newspapers would be treated to Lenny Thornton's or Albert Moffat's opinion on the local Muslim community and Sinead's feelings about her murdered daughter. Only Johnny Kerrigan would remain silent.

Winsome, Banks knew, had been hard at work since he had phoned her from Leeds with the identification of Linda Palmer's mystery man. She had been on the phone and the Internet to amass as much information as she could about Tony Monaghan's life and death and had gathered it together in a small file, which Banks had just finished reading. At the moment, Winsome was in the squad room trying to squeeze out more information and was due to join them shortly.

For his part, Banks had stayed on in Leeds for a while after Linda had found the photographs. He had offered to arrange transport back to Minton-on-Swain for her, but she said she'd like to do a bit of shopping and visit some friends, then she'd take the train back in the evening. Banks first visited Ken Blackstone at Elland Road, where they had trawled through various archives and records, mostly in vain, coming up with an interesting titbit about the long-dead Chief Constable Crammond, but not much else.

The problem, as Blackstone pointed out, was that it seemed the records had been systematically expunged at some point over the last fifty years. There were no surviving witness transcripts, though supposedly every homosexual with a passing acquaintance with the Hyde Park public convenience would have been questioned, along with a number of undercover police officers and officers placed on surveillance at various periods in the roof of the structure, where they had been able to spy on whatever was going on below. Another quick visit to the Wakefield archive had produced only the stark entry in the occurrence book: 'No further action.' What it all added up to, Banks still didn't know, and he was hoping a bit of a brainstorming session back in Eastvale would go some way towards correcting that situation.

The basic facts, culled from newspapers, were that the man Linda Palmer identified as her second rapist had lived in Hampstead. Only twenty-six years old when he was murdered, Tony Monaghan worked for a London advertising agency, Philby, Leyland and Associates, based in the West End, and he was up in Leeds on company business during the time the incident occurred. At the time of the murder, Monaghan had been wearing a bespoke suit from a Savile Row tailor and a lilac shirt. That had, no doubt, sealed his dismissal as a 'queer'.

Monaghan's body had been found in the public conveniences at Hyde Park in the student area of Leeds. He had been
stabbed to death, and his wallet was missing. The prevailing
theory was that he had been on the prowl, looking for rough
trade, and had found it. The public conveniences were a
notorious spot for homosexual encounters, and though homosexual acts between two consenting adults in the privacy of
their own homes had been legalised in the Sexual Offences
Act that summer, the legality did not apply to public toilets or
public acts of lewdness.

According to the date in the occurrence book, the investigation had been dropped after less than two weeks, and
Monaghan's body would have been released for burial. Nothing
more of interest appeared, and the photo that had caught Linda
Palmer's attention was the only visual record still existing.

'It's as thin as the Caxton investigation as far as evidence
goes,' Banks said, after pushing the file aside. 'There's hardly
any forensics, nothing to say whether he had been sexually
active, sexually assaulted or what. Nothing to indicate that he
was even gay. One of the papers speculated that it might have
been a mugging, with Monaghan a stranger to the city and all,
maybe not knowing the reputation of those toilets. But
muggers rarely kill. There's also some speculation that whoever
he picked up was psychologically confused about his sexual-
ity and became violent when Monaghan made a pass. It's also
possible he was a "queer" hater or someone who saw himself
on a crusade against indecency. Don't forget the law had just
been passed. It was controversial and it must have set off any
number of nutters.'

'What's the link with Caxton?' asked AC Gervaise.

'We don't have one yet,' Banks said. 'Apart from Linda
Palmer. Winsome's still digging.'

'Was nothing else mentioned in the press or the police
investigation?'

'No. Nobody dug deeply enough.'

'Is Ms Palmer sure this is our man?'

'Certain,' Banks said. 'She was shaken up by the whole thing. She got no impression that he was gay, of course, but she admitted she wouldn't have known much about such things back then.'

'But he *did* rape her?'

'Yes. She said she remembered he hesitated, seemed nervous. But there could be many reasons for that. And just because a man rapes a woman, it doesn't mean he's not gay.'

'Point taken.'

'Where do you want to go with this?' Adrian Moss interjected.

Banks glanced at Gervaise. 'Nowhere yet,' he said. 'Not until we've actually got somewhere to go.'

'You want to keep it under wraps?'

'For now, yes. As much as we can.'

Moss made a note. 'OK. Good.'

'We don't know what we've got,' Banks went on. 'We don't know if it's a lead or a red herring. If Linda Palmer says she's sure it's the man who raped her with Caxton, I, for one, believe her, but even so, it gets us no further. I mean, it's not as if he's still alive to identify Caxton, and we're not here to investigate his murder. It's bad enough having to investigate a fifty-year-old rape, but add a murder in the mix and it'd be damn nigh impossible.'

'You might be surprised, Alan,' said Gervaise. 'The one might actually illuminate the other.'

'There's that, I suppose.' Banks scratched his cheek. 'I must admit, I *was* hoping it would turn out to be someone who might still be alive, but that was probably reaching a bit.'

'Don't you think it's too much of a coincidence that this Monaghan was murdered such a short time after assaulting Ms Palmer?' asked Gervaise.

'I do,' said Banks. 'And I also think it's fishy that Caxton was photographed handing a cheque over to Crammond just over two weeks after Monaghan's murder, only days after the investigation stopped. But just at the moment I can't come up with a good reason as to how all these are linked. Was Monaghan simply in the wrong place at the wrong time? Did he pick up someone who, for whatever reason, stabbed him to death? What was he doing in Leeds, for a start? If we knew even that it would be something.'

'He was on business, wasn't he?' Gervaise said.

'That's what it said in the paper. He was in advertising.'

'What about his old firm?'

'Philby, Leyland and Associates? No longer in business,' Banks said. 'Winsome checked. She's still trying to track down other ex-employees.'

'Advertising must have been an exciting occupation back then,' Gervaise said, 'if it was anything like *Mad Men*.'

'I think it attracted its fair share of hip young creative types, that's for sure,' Banks agreed.

'A lilac shirt,' said Moss.

Banks looked at him. He was wearing a dazzling white shirt, old school tie and pinstripe suit. 'Indeed,' he said. 'Your point, Adrian?'

'Oh, nothing really. I mean, maybe back then, in the dark ages, so to speak, a police detective might well have taken such an article of clothing as a sign of . . . well . . .'

'Gayness?'

'Yes. And when you add the fact that Monaghan worked in advertising, a flamboyant and creative business, and the place his body was found, then . . . well, it's hardly surprising, is it?'

'No force would put a great deal of its resources into an investigation of that sort back then,' said Banks. 'No more than they would into the murder of a prostitute, as we discovered from the Yorkshire Ripper case. But even so, there should have been *something*, if only for form's sake.'

'Was there any information as to whether he was actually murdered in the toilet itself, or whether his body was brought from elsewhere?' AC Gervaise asked.

'No,' said Banks. 'So far it seems everyone assumed that he was killed where he was found, but any forensic information and exhibits, if there were any, have disappeared.'

'No forensics?'

'Nothing. I should imagine there was a lot of blood, though, given that he was stabbed.'

'So he goes in the cubicle with whoever he picked up,' Gervaise said. 'The other bloke's standing behind him. They get ready to do whatever they're about to do, and the other bloke takes out a knife and stabs him, then slips his hand in his inside pocket for his wallet.'

At that moment there came a light tap on the door and Winsome entered, carrying a folder with her.

'I hope you've got something for us,' Banks said, 'because we're getting so desperate for leads here AC Gervaise has taken to crime fiction.'

Winsome sat down and poured herself the remaining splash of coffee. 'I think you'll like this, guv,' she said. 'Tony Monaghan was first employed as a PR consultant and publicist by Danny Caxton in 1966.'

'I thought he worked for an advertising agency in London?'

'He did, but they contracted him out. Apparently he did such a good job on his first assignment that Caxton asked for him by name.'

'How on earth did you discover this?' asked Gervaise. 'The agency's been defunct for years, Alan says.'

'I have my methods, ma'am,' said Winsome.

'Come on, DS Jackman, give.'

Winsome managed a brief smile. 'Yes, ma'am. Well, first off, I pushed Danny Caxton's management company for that list of employees we've been after. I'd asked them before, but they were dragging their feet, going on about how many there were and how long ago it all was. I don't think they were stalling particularly, just that it was another job on their table and there was nothing in it for them, I suppose, so why hurry? The secretary I spoke with this time was quite chatty. Must be a slow day. She seemed to find no reason to keep it from us, and when I expressed a sense of urgency, she faxed it to me. Monaghan's name appeared, along with Philby, Leyland and Associates. I rang her back and asked her for more details about him, and she told me she didn't know much, but it wasn't unusual to hire freelancers or subcontract publicists from specialist firms. It happened a few times in Danny Caxton's career. Monaghan was with him on and off from May 1966 until his death in October 1967. Monaghan took a break at home in London after the Blackpool summer season, and he headed back up north again to work with Caxton on the panto he was appearing in at the Bradford Alhambra that Christmas. Monaghan was married, by the way. I'll see if I can find anything out about the widow. Anyway, the secretary I talked to knew nothing about Monaghan's death – she wasn't even born then – though she did say that most of the office knew they once had an employee who'd been murdered way back in the mists of time.'

'I suppose you would remember something like that,' Banks said. 'Excellent work, Winsome. Now we have a concrete link between Monaghan and Caxton.'

'Yes, but it hasn't exactly taken us anywhere, has it, guv?' said Winsome.

'I don't know about that. An employee of Caxton's, some-one who led Linda to the car and back to the hotel, who raped her in the hotel room, along with Caxton, and two months or so later he's murdered in a mysterious and gruesome way. Don't tell me that's just coincidence.'

'And the murder was never solved,' Winsome added.

'The murder was never even investigated,' Banks said. 'Just like Linda Palmer's original complaint. Sounds like orders from on high to me. We have the photo of Caxton with then chief constable, Edward Crammond, and old gossip has it they were close, dinners together, golf club, even a cruise. Was Danny Caxton golden, or what?'

Banks could hear Adrian Moss's sudden intake of breath. Phrases such as 'orders from on high' were anathema to him. 'Never mind, Adrian,' he said. 'I'm sure you'll find the right direction to spin it.'

Moss glowered at him.

'And nothing showed up in any of the documents we've seen,' Banks went on, 'or any of the press reports. Nothing else to link Monaghan to Caxton. It was all kept quiet, if indeed anyone knew at all.'

'That's some cover-up,' said AC Gervaise. 'But surely your DI Chadwick must have known?'

'Possibly,' Banks agreed. 'At least, I assume he would have been the one to get the order to cease and desist. But seeing as he's long dead, we can hardly ask him, can we?' He paused for a moment. 'But we can do the next best thing – talk to his oppo DC Bradley. He's alive, at least he was when I talked to him ten years ago about that pop festival murder. I was going to talk to him and Chadwick's daughter about the lack of investigation on Linda's case, anyway. Now I've got a bit more to ask them about.'

AC Gervaise sniffed. 'Seems this DI Chadwick has left quite a legacy.'

'Yes,' said Banks. 'I could probably make a career out of just working over his cold cases.'

★   ★   ★

Yvonne Reeves still lived in a bay-window semi on the outskirts of Durham. A light breeze ruffled the thick foliage of the trees that shaded the street and gave some shade from the sun. Yvonne ushered Banks and Winsome into the living room, which had been redecorated since Banks's last visit. It seemed brighter and airier than he remembered. Yvonne didn't offer tea but sat down opposite the two visitors and folded her hands in her lap. She wore black trousers and a cotton print top and seemed to have lost bit of weight since his last visit. Banks remembered her being more full-figured. She wore her grey hair cut short, and its thinness, along with that of her body, made Banks wonder whether she was suffering from a serious illness. She seemed on the ball, though, and didn't appear to be lacking in energy. There were a few more lines on her face than last time, though that was only to be expected. She would have been fourteen in 1967, Banks had calculated, the same age as Linda Palmer, though she looked older. They might have even known one another, as they had both grown up in West Leeds.

'I seem to remember you were here about one of my dad's old cases a while ago, weren't you?' she said.

'Going on for ten years back,' said Banks.

'Is it that long?'

'Just about.'

She looked at Winsome. 'I don't remember you, love.'

'I was just a wet-behind-the-ears DC back then,' Winsome said, with a sideways glance at Banks.

Yvonne smiled and turned back to Banks. 'So what is it this time?'

'Another of your father's old cases.'

'I'm sure I told you last time that he didn't bring his work home – except for what we talked about last time, when I was involved with those hippies and the Brimleigh Festival murder. But that was only because of me.'

'I know,' said Banks. 'It's an even older crime than that.'

'When?'

'Summer of 1967.'

Yvonne stared out of the window as if lost in memories. 'My goodness. I must have just turned fourteen then.'

'That was my estimate.'

She shot him a sharp glance. 'And what do you expect me to remember?'

'I don't know. Maybe nothing. A local girl about your age was sexually assaulted. The incident happened in Blackpool, but she lived near you in West Leeds. She went to Brotherton House with her mother, and your father heard her complaint. It was entered in the occurrence book. Then there's nothing more.'

'It can't have gone anywhere, then, I suppose.'

'No. But it's resurfaced recently, and I was wondering why it was never investigated when it was first reported.'

'Is that the Danny Caxton business I've seen on the news?'

'That'll be it. Yes.'

'Bloody hell!'

'Do you remember? Did your father ever mention Caxton?'

'He was a popular name in our house.'

'Your father knew him?'

'He'd met him. But my mother was the fan. I thought he was a bit naff, myself, but I was just a precocious fourteen-year-old.'

'So was his victim.'

'Do you really think he did it?'

'Did you have any idea of the things Jimmy Savile was doing?'

'I've read about some of them,' said Yvonne. 'You're right. I always thought he was a creep, but I'd no idea what kind, the depths . . . Rolf Harris, too. I quite liked "Tie My Kangaroo Down, Sport". And Bill Cosby in the States. Who would have thought it?'

'So why not Danny Caxton?'

'That's poor reasoning, Mr Banks.'

'Alan. I didn't mean it that way. I just meant, why should it be so unbelievable? We're gathering evidence. The case is getting stronger. But with something like this you've got to build a strong solid structure, as you can imagine.'

'I don't know what you hope for from me. Danny Caxton never touched me.'

'Did you ever meet him?'

'Me? No.'

'We're interested in anything you can remember, really,' said Winsome. 'A word, a gesture, anything. We know it was a long time ago, but something important might have stuck in your memory about that period.'

Yvonne looked at her. 'You know, love, it's a funny thing about memory, especially as I get older. I can sometimes remember specific days, maybe even arguments Dad and I had about – oh, some boy, or some skirt I was wearing being too short, or music I was listening to being too loud. Sometimes he seemed remote and distracted – a lot of the time he was like that. I don't ever remember him being much of a talker. Now I look back, I sometimes think it must have been his job getting him down. What a funny thing memory is.'

Banks remembered lines from another of Linda Palmer's poems: 'In no time at all, we alter what we / see – not nature, but nature exposed / to our vision.' She was right about the constant dance of memory and imagination, perception and creation, history and fiction. How easily the one was transformed into the other, or *by* it, sometimes to such an extent that we actually believed a thing had happened the way we remembered it, when it hadn't happened that way at all. He gave up pursuing the thought. It wasn't a fruitful line of inquiry for a detective.

'How did Caxton and your father meet?'

'I don't really know the details, but apparently there was a big do at work, something to do with a donation to a police charity by Danny Caxton. He was always doing things like that, collecting for charity and stuff. They had a special gala ball or something, a dress-up job, and even though Dad was only an inspector, he got invited and he got to take Mum, too. Well, she was made up. Had to buy a new dress and everything. Our place was a madhouse for a week before.'

'Do you remember when this was?'

'It might have been around the time you're talking about, 1967. There were pictures in the papers and everything. The chief constable, Crammond, was well in with Mr Caxton, or so my dad said. And come to think of it, he did say something about a case, some colleague of Mr Caxton's being found dead.'

'Did he say anything more?'

'No. Just that it was bad timing, you know, for the charity ball and everything.'

'Do you remember anything else about the summer or autumn of 1967, especially anything to do with Danny Caxton?' Banks asked.

'Not about Mr Caxton, no. Except Mum was thrilled to meet him, of course. She said they shook hands – he even kissed the back of her hand like a real gentleman – and he had such a lovely smile. No wonder they called him "The Man with the Big Smile". He even said, "Do your own thing!" You remember, that was his catchphrase.'

'I remember,' said Banks.

'We seemed to argue a lot that summer, Dad and me. I was just starting to get excited about all the new music and the gatherings and stuff. Hendrix, Cream and so on. I wanted to wear flowers in my hair and go to San Francisco. My dad thought it was all stupid, of course. But there was something in the air, something different, something magical. Maybe it was just me. I suppose fourteen-year-old girls can be impressionable. But I was right in a way, wasn't I? I mean things did happen – well, I told you about some of that last time you were here, I remember 1969 better. I was sixteen then and far more up for it.'

'Was there anything in particular about your father's state of mind in the period we're talking about?'

'He was grumpy a lot. I thought it might have been because of all the hippies starting up and all those demonstrations and marches. And the drugs. It made his job harder. Though I think most of that came later. But I suppose it wasn't an easy time for the police, having lots of freedom-loving people taking mind-expanding drugs, and anarchists and communists on the streets ripping up cobblestones and whatever.'

Banks suppressed a smile. It was rare that anyone gave a thought to the policeman's point of view, in his experience, but trust it to be a policeman's daughter, whether she embraced hippiedom or not.

'I do remember one argument we had around that time,' Yvonne went on. 'He said it was all very well for me to go on about miniskirts and mascara and listen to the Rolling Stones, but if I had to deal with some of the things he did, I'd never want to go outside again.'

'Did he say what?'

'No. I can't remember, but I just assumed he meant his job. You know, junkies, dead bodies and stuff. He was always going on about what a dangerous world it was out there. I mean, the thing with Linda Lofthouse was later, so it wasn't anything to do with that. But he seemed frustrated. More than usual. He even fought with Mum once or twice, which was rare. He almost never lost his temper with her.'

'Do you remember the circumstances of this particular argument?'

'No. It was years ago. I was doing my homework, but they were quite loud and I couldn't help overhearing. I suppose the fact that they were having a row made me want to listen. Mum said something about it being a good thing because it meant he wouldn't have to go and mix with all those queers, and I just remember that he got angry and said that he was hamstrung and couldn't do anything. He said something about his effing boss, too. Funny, I only remember that because he swore, which he rarely did at home, and I had no idea what "hamstrung" meant. It was the first time I ever heard the word. I had to look it up in the dictionary.'

'Do you remember when that was?'

'No. I mean, not specifically. Around the time you're talking about. It was probably September or October, as I was back at school, but I don't know for sure.'

'Before the ball?'

'Around then.'

It sounded to Banks as if Chadwick had been complaining to his wife about not being allowed to investigate something to do with gays, perhaps because his boss had intervened, and if the timing was right, it could well be the Tony Monaghan case. But which boss? There had been many officers above Chadwick at the time. Edward Crammond? It would be useful to find out who Chadwick's other senior officers were and see if any came up in the names of 'friends and acquaintances' Winsome had gathered so far from Caxton's past. 'Did your father ever say anything about homosexuals?'

'What do you mean?'

'That summer, the Sexual Offences Act had just made homosexuality legal for adults over twenty-one in the privacy of their own homes. It was a transitional time. It caused a few problems for the police.'

'What? You mean you could no longer beat the shit out of people for being gay?'

'Something like that.'

'Sorry. I didn't mean *you* specifically, but you've got to admit your lot didn't exactly have a spotless record when it came to respecting minority rights – whether sexual orientation or race.'

'Yvonne, you're right. But I don't want to argue about that today. Mostly we do our best. Your father did his best. You know that. But sometimes there's a rotten apple. Maybe the police force attracts prejudiced bullies to a certain extent. I've met a few in my time. But not everyone's like that.'

'Oh, I know that,' said Yvonne, with a pout that made her look thirty years younger for a moment. 'Sorry, I'm just being provocative. Dad certainly wasn't like that. I don't think he was a rotten apple at all. A bit strict, yes. Conservative, square. He didn't like the hippies and all that, but I never once heard him say a bad word about coloured people or gays. And he wouldn't hit them or harass them just because he didn't approve of them. He liked to pretend to be a crusty right-wing curmudgeon when I was defending the workers and the students and so on, but I believe at heart he was a liberal. He believed in a fair deal for everyone. He hated privilege. He didn't really want to go to Caxton's ball, you know. He only did it for Mum.'

'Did he ever say anything about gays?'

'If he did, I don't remember. Only that argument I told you about, when Mum mentioned queers.'

'Did he ever mention the name Tony Monaghan?'

'Not that I heard.'

'Do you remember anything at all about a body found in the public toilets at Hyde Park up by the university?'

'I remember it vaguely, but I don't remember when, or any details. I mean, when you're a copper's daughter you probably do pay a bit more attention to such things than someone else would. But I wasn't really interested in crime stories. True or fictional. I do know those toilets were supposed to be a hotbed of gay activity. Everybody knew that. There was a rumour going round at school that the police used to hide up in the ceiling there and watch through peepholes to catch the gays at it.'

'Maybe it's true,' said Banks, smiling. Many public conveniences did serve as meeting places for homosexuals, he remembered. His father had always warned him to stay away from certain public loos, even in Peterborough.

Yvonne laughed. 'I couldn't see my dad up there spying on people through a peephole. He was tolerant on the whole. Except with me, of course.'

Banks stood up, and Winsome followed suit. 'Well, maybe he had that in common with a lot of fathers. Thanks, Yvonne. You've been very helpful.'

'I have?'

'Well, we know more now than we did before we came, so I'd call that a successful visit, wouldn't you?'

'I suppose so.'

Banks handed her his card. 'In case you remember anything else. Call me any time.'

'I'm afraid I didn't follow your advice very well, did I?' said Annie glumly swirling the last of her Shiraz in the large wine glass. 'A little tact. Softly, softly.'

'No. You did the bull in a china shop with all-guns-blazing approach.'

'I didn't think so, but since that bastard from Wytherton had his say, you probably do.'

'It doesn't matter,' said Banks. 'You were playing silly buggers with two oafs. Fair enough. You've had your fun, now just put it behind you and get back to work.'

'Christ, what a day,' said Annie. 'Now Sinead Moffat hates me, too. She blames me for the search. And I'm pissed into the bargain. And I'm going to have another one.'

'My pleasure.' Banks poured the wine.

'Ta,' said Annie. 'What's that we're listening to? It sounds a bit like Jeff Buckley.'

'It's Tim Buckley,' said Banks. 'His dad. *Blue Afternoon.*'

'His dad? Get away with you.'

'It is. He died young, too. Drug overdose.'

'All your lot did,' said Annie.

'I saw him once,' Banks said. 'Knebworth Festival, 1974. It was one of the last gigs he did. Fantastic.'

They were sitting in the wicker chairs in Banks's conservatory after a dinner of Marks & Spencer lasagne and Caesar salad, with dressing that came in a sachet, a bottle of Shiraz almost empty on the table between them and the lightest of breezes blowing though the open windows. The sun had gone down, but there was still a bluish glow in the sky behind Tetchley Fell. Banks had caught up with Annie in the corridor outside an interview room after he had got back from talking to Yvonne Reeves. It had been a long day, and Annie had looked drawn and haggard, so he had invited her to dinner, stopping off at M&S on the way.

Maybe Annie deserved the opportunity to let off a little steam, Banks thought. It was a complex case she was on, and the death of a child – which Mimosa Moffat was, when you came right down to it – got to even the most hardened officers. The fact that Annie had, herself, been raped some years ago, and was still recovering from a recent shooting incident, made her even more vulnerable. But Banks was still convinced that she was more than up to the task. Not only that, but that she was the best person for it.

'What's wrong with me, Alan?' she said when he had emptied the last of the bottle into her glass 'Am I a racist? Is that it? Do you think I'm a racist?'

'I don't think you're a racist, Annie. It's just complicated, that's all. What do you think those mothers in Nigeria are thinking about, the ones whose daughters were kidnapped by Boko Haram?'

Annie squinted at him. 'What? I can't even begin to imagine what hell they're going through, worrying if they're ever going to see their daughters again, scared about what's been done to them.' She gave a shudder. 'It doesn't bear thinking about.'

'Exactly. It doesn't matter what colour they are, does it? They're mothers going through hell, like any mother here would whose child goes missing, and children suffering. I know it sounds like a cliché, but we're all just people. Good 'uns, bad 'uns and in-between 'uns, most of us.'

'"If you prick me, do I not bleed?"'

'You've got it.'

'But why is this race business all so complicated?' Annie went on, waving her glass at him. 'It drives me round the bend. I don't know what I'm supposed to think or say. Is grooming girls for underage sex supposed to be OK in their culture, like female genital mutilation or honour killing? Are we supposed to *respect* it all, no matter what, just because it's their culture, like the Scots with their bagpipes and haggis? I mean, I don't even like bagpipes and haggis. It's not *my* bloody culture, I can tell you that. So does that make me a racist? And who do we blame? Society or the kids? Whatever happened to morality? Good and evil? Right and wrong?'

'Outdated concepts, I'm afraid,' said Banks. 'But I think you're getting way too many things mixed up here. What's acceptable to one group isn't necessarily acceptable to another. And there's a big difference between haggis and bagpipes and female genital mutilation.'

Annie tipped her glass at a dangerous angle and narrowed her eyes. 'I know that. I *know* that. I'm just trying to make a point, that's all. Am I supposed to think all these things are OK because they're sacred to some culture or ethnic group or medieval religion? Am I supposed to be *inclusive*? Is it all part and parcel of our *diversity*? Would I be *divisive* if I disagreed?'

'Probably,' said Banks. 'But calm down. You're letting this get to you way too much.'

Annie sniffed. 'I think anyone who performs female genital mutilation should be hung, drawn and quartered, bagpipes should be exiled to one of the inner circles of hell, and as for haggis, well, the jury's still out on that one.'

Banks laughed. 'That's because you're a vegetarian.'

'They have vegetarian haggis, you know. Boil in a bag.'

'What's it made of?'

'I don't know. The inner organs of turnips and cabbages or something. But am I wrong about all this?'

'We both know,' said Banks,' that for every Asian who does something like this, you could find thousands who are decent, hard-working, law-abiding members of the community.'

'But it's not those people we're dealing with, is it? It never is. We deal with the worst, like whoever raped Mimosa. The dregs. We take the decency of the majority for granted.'

'True enough,' said Banks. 'But what else can we do except try to protect the good guys and catch the bad guys? Look on the bright side. Danny Caxton, for example. For years he got away with abusing underage girls, but now we're coming down on him and people like him.'

'Thanks to Operation Yewtree. But don't you think even that's gone a bit over the top? I mean, famous people are getting arrested just for touching someone's arm or giving them a hug forty years ago, for crying out loud. Teachers are scared to touch children. I know I'm one to speak, given what happened to me and all, but I've never usually had much trouble removing an uninvited hand from my knee and telling its owner to bog off.'

'Maybe there's always some sort of overcompensation for letting things slide for so long,' said Banks. 'Like positive discrimination. Some people complain that jobs are given to women or to blacks just because they're women, or black, for example. It's our nature to try to make amends. And the Jimmy Savile business encouraged a lot of women to come forward and speak out. Don't forget, either, that many of the victims had come forward before, at the time of the incident, and been ignored. Women like Linda Palmer. That's down to us. Not you and me specifically, but the force. We've made mistakes. That's why Adrian Moss seems to be wringing his hands most of the time these days. But the point is, it's happening. Same with grooming gangs. Sure, they got away with it for far too long in Rochdale, Rotherham, Manchester, Oxford, Aylesbury. Now it's Wytherton. Fair enough, too many people are still ignoring it, including us and the social, but you're coming down on them.'

'With my hands tied behind my back, it seems.'

Banks smiled at her. 'Annie, I have every faith that you can do it, even with your hands tied behind your back.'

'You know,' Annie said, 'the more I think about it, the more I'm sure that bastard Carver is bent.'

'He's probably just trying to do a really difficult job. It can't be easy, policing a divided community like Wytherton.'

'No, it's not that. Those two coppers, Bill and Reg. I know I goaded them a bit, but they were ready to beat the shit out of us, Alan. Now, who runs a station where it's OK for patrol officers to do that for no reason than someone being mouthy?'

'Zero tolerance,' said Banks.

'Bloody hell, you've got an excuse for everything, don't you?'

'Not an excuse, but maybe a reason. And I'm not saying I agree. I'm just saying that's probably their philosophy.'

'Yeah, well, you can keep your zero tolerance if it means bashing me on the head with a baton.' She took a hearty swig of wine.

Banks thought for a moment. 'I suppose they'd say they were defending their patch. It can't be an easy beat, Wytherton. And we come in like some invading army. No wonder Carver defends them.'

'Me and Gerry? An invading army?'

'You know what I mean.'

'That man Carver's a stuffed uniform,' said Annie.

'But why was he so unhelpful?' said Banks. 'That's the point. You'd think he'd have a bit more about him. Have some idea what's going on in his manor.'

'He turned a blind eye.'

'I don't know,' said Banks. 'But I can't help finding myself wondering if there isn't something he's trying to keep under wraps.'

'Like what?'

'Those two coppers who gave you a rough time— ...'

'Reg and Bill. Pair of pillocks.'

'Right. They weren't on duty the night Mimosa Moffat took her last ride, were they?'

'They said not.'

'What if Mimsy was a problem? Their problem.'

'Problem? Mimsy? What are you talking about?'

'But what if she was?' Banks said. 'I'm just thinking out loud. What if they were involved somehow?'

'You mean Reg and Bill were having sex with underage girls?'

'Exactly. It's not beyond the bounds of possibility, is it? Maybe they found out what was going on, and that was their price for turning a blind eye? Maybe Mimosa threatened to blow the whistle. I know there's still a lot of loose ends, like nobody knowing she was going to be walking up the lane and so on. But as a working theory, does it hold water? Maybe they were planning on killing her at the other end of her journey, later, away from their own patch.'

'Reg and Bill? But they said they didn't know what was going on down the Strip. Even Carver didn't.'

'Why couldn't they be lying? I doubt that it would have been hard for them to get hold of a car we couldn't trace. One of the cars on the CCTV was stolen, wasn't it?'

'True,' said Annie. 'But Reg and Bill?'

'It wouldn't be the first time police officers have lied to protect themselves. I'm merely suggesting that maybe you should have another chat with them. Find out exactly where they were last Tuesday between one and three in the morning.'

'Carver will love that,' Annie said.

'Fuck Carver. It's our case. Work around him.'

'You know, you might have a point. And the more I think of it, the more I'm convinced those two blokes in the takeaway were lying. You should've seen their faces when I said we'd be able to match the food we'd bought with the victim's stomach contents.'

'You told them that?'

'Yeah. So?'

'Well, we can't, can we?'

'Maybe not exactly, unless we matched the DNA with a goat or a lamb they'd been serving. But it put the wind up them, I can tell you that.' Annie clinked glasses with Banks and slopped a little wine over the rim of hers on to the carpet. 'Oops,' she said. 'It's red, too. Sorry.'

'Forget it. How does Gerry feel about all this?'

'The poor kid's terrified she's going to be sent back on probation or something. You know, I like Gerry a lot, but she can be a bit of a mouse. She's a bit too "golly gosh" and "jolly hockey sticks" for me sometimes.'

'It's a matter of background,' said Banks. 'She went to a posh school, didn't she?'

'Think so.'

'There you are, then. Give her a chance. She'll probably be chief constable one day. Playing fields of Eton and all that.'

'I don't think it was Eton. It was Merchant Taylor, or some such place.'

'It's just a saying. "The Battle of Waterloo was won on the playing fields of Eton."'

'What's it mean? Who said that? David Cameron?'

'It's supposed to have been the Duke of Wellington, but it may well be a misquote. People who go to public school are destined for great things. Leadership. That's the point.'

'If you say so. The old boys network? And the old girls?' Annie drained her glass and waved it. 'Can we have another?'

Banks got to his feet. 'I'll open another bottle if you want.'

'Can I stop here for the night? I'm too pissed to drive and I can't afford a taxi all the way to Harkside. I'd probably be sick, if I had to go in a car.'

'I've got an early start in the morning, but the spare room's made up.'

Annie hesitated for a moment, then she said, 'I don't need the spare room.'

Banks went to get another bottle of red from the rack in the kitchen, then he went into the entertainment room to put another CD on. What had she meant by that remark? He wondered. Was it some sort of come-on? Any romance they had shared had fizzled out long ago, and he had thought neither of them was foolish enough to want to rekindle it, to mix work and sex again. Now this? But Annie had had way too much to drink. She was upset, confused, and he wasn't going to take advantage of her.

Tim Buckley had put him in a late sixties mellow mood, so he flipped through the classics: the Grateful Dead's *American Beauty*, Joni Mitchell's *Blue*, CSNY's *Déjà Vu* and the rest. Or should it be *Astral Weeks*? *Harvest*? *Songs for Beginners*?

David Crosby's *If Only I Could Remember My Name*? In the end he went for Love's *Forever Changes*.

When he got back to conservatory with the wine, Annie lay sprawled in her chair, fast asleep, glass clutched to her chest, mouth open, snoring gently. Banks refilled his glass, then put his feet up and settled down to enjoy the breeze and listen to 'Alone Again Or.'

10

The following morning it was still warm, but the sky had become overcast when Banks went to pick up Winsome and head for Leeds. Annie had looked rough at breakfast, and they hadn't spoken much. Banks didn't suppose that sleeping on the chair in the conservatory had done her much good. Whether it was her intended meaning or not, she certainly hadn't needed the spare bedroom.

The ex-detective constable Simon Bradley, Winsome had discovered on the computer before they set off, still lived in the same stone-built detached house off Shaw Lane in Headingley that Banks remembered from his previous visit. Banks rang him, and he agreed to see them whenever they could get there.

After an uneventful drive down the busy A1 listening to a live Jerry Garcia Band CD, Banks and Winsome pulled up in the quiet, leafy street near the end of 'Dear Prudence'. Beyond the green gate, the garden was in full bloom. Banks didn't even know what half the flowers were called, but the riot of shape and colour certainly created a joyous effect. It had been almost ten years since he had last visited, but he remembered the garden had been Mrs Bradley's pride and joy. It seemed that it still was.

Simon Bradley opened the front door on the first ring. 'Detective Superintendent Banks. Glad you could make it so quickly. Good to see you again. Come in, come in.' He glanced at Winsome. 'My, my, things have changed since the old days.'

Winsome gave her best toothy smile, curtsied and said 'Why, yes, mastah, dey surely have.'

Bradley laughed. 'Cheeky minx, isn't she?'

'You don't know the half of it. I wouldn't mess with her if I were you. And call me Alan, please. And the cheeky minx is DS Winsome Jackman.' Banks felt Winsome nudge him in the ribs, not hard enough to hurt, as they followed Bradley into the living room, from which French windows led out to a neatly mown back lawn, complete with a small gazebo, garden shed, outdoor grill, bird-feeder and patio with a green table and matching moulded plastic chairs.

Bradley turned to Winsome. 'Please let me apologise. I really didn't mean anything by what I said back there. I just sometimes feel like a bit of a dinosaur. Old habits die hard.'

'Indeed they do,' said Winsome. 'That's all right, sir. I've been learning a lot recently about how things were back in the day. It's an education.'

'I'll bet.' Bradley clapped his hands. 'Outside or in? No air conditioning, I'm afraid. Only an old fan.'

'Seeing as the weather's still holding up,' said Banks, 'let's try outdoors.' The sky was still cloudy, and Banks could still feel that sort of electric crackle in the air that presaged a storm. He hoped it wouldn't hit before he and Winsome could set off back to Eastvale. Sometimes you got enormous hailstones in a summer storm, and visibility could quickly dwindle to practically nothing in no time.

'Excellent. Pam's just making a pot of tea. She'll be out with it shortly.'

As they walked through the living room, Banks noticed that the floor-to-ceiling collection of first-edition crime fiction he remembered from his previous visit was still there.

'Pam complains endlessly about the books and the space they take up,' Bradley said, 'but what can I do? She came up with a one in, one out scheme, but I'm afraid it's not working too well. Some of these people just keep on writing. And it's not just the collecting, you know. I do read them all.'

'But surely you must find their stories a bit different from the reality you remember?'

'You're not a fan?'

'I can't say I am. I've read a bit of Christie and Doyle, of course, but I don't really think anyone was expected to believe that their exploits in any way reflected reality. I prefer spy thrillers, myself.'

'Oh, I'm definitely with you on espionage fiction. Le Carré, Eric Ambler, Len Deighton, Alan Furst. Among the best. But do you know, that whole realism bit never really bothers me in the least. Sure, they get the procedures and the lingo wrong, but that's not such a terrible thing. And the lingo changes all the time. I bet I wouldn't understand a word if I found myself back in the old cop shop again. No, as long as the stories are gripping and the cops are interesting characters, I'm fine with it. What do you think, DS Jackman?'

'I'm afraid I don't have much time for reading,' Winsome said. 'But when I do, I prefer non-fiction. History. Biography. Nature writing. That sort of thing.'

'Admirable.'

'And when I read crime fiction,' Winsome went on, 'I prefer mine hard-boiled and American. Chandler, MacDonald – both of them – and Hammett. When men were men and dames were broads.'

Bradley gave a little bow. 'Of course. What exquisite taste.'

Banks gave Winsome a quizzical look, but she gave him inscrutable back. They sat at the patio table, and almost before they had made themselves comfortable, Bradley's wife Pam came out to say hello and serve tea, saying she hoped Earl Grey was all right, but she always thought it more refreshing than Darjeeling on a warm day. Banks had often wondered why tea could be so perfect for such weather, but it was. They thanked her, and she disappeared back inside the house.

Bradley must be about seventy now, Banks calculated, but he was still in good shape. He had lost a bit of hair since the last visit, but he hadn't put on any weight, and nor did he seem any more stooped or stiffer with age. With his sharp-creased white trousers and short-sleeve V-neck pullover, despite the heat, he resembled a cricketer at start of play, though it was probably regular rounds of golf, not cricket, that kept him in shape. Maybe a little tennis, too. Banks made a note to get more exercise, though he knew he probably wouldn't do it. Two five- or six-mile walks a week and regular shorter strolls near his cottage seemed to suit him fine. And he still had the kind of metabolism that kept him trim no matter what he ate or drank.

'This is one of the things some people find hard to believe in detective novels and on TV,' said Bradley gesturing to the cups of tea and plate of biscuits. 'The tea or coffee. Especially Americans. Seems too genteel and twee to them, I suppose. I don't think their coppers are quite so well treated when they come calling.'

'I could just imagine someone offering the Continental Op a cup of tea,' Winsome said.

They all laughed.

'But it happens all the time here,' said Banks. 'Sometimes I think we ought to have toilets installed in our cars.'

Bradley put his cup down, tilted his head to one side and stroked his cheek with his index finger. 'Unless I'm very much mistaken, it seems that having worked for DI Chadwick is going to haunt me for the rest of my days.'

'Remind me how long you worked with him.'

'I was a DC for Chiller from 1966 to 1971, when I transferred to Suffolk CID.'

'Chiller?' said Winsome.

'Nickname,' explained Bradley. 'He was a bit of an icy sort of character. Cool in the extreme, and I don't mean in the "hip" sort of way.'

'And DI Chadwick died in 1973?' Banks said.

'Right. We didn't really keep in touch after I left. I just heard through the grapevine, which could be slow in those days.'

'Was there a rift of some sort?'

'Not at all. It was just our way. I moved on. Chiller let go with both hands.'

'How's your memory of 1967?'

'How could I forget? It was the year that hippies suddenly became a worldwide phenomenon. Oh, they'd been around a while, probably since '65 or so, even in Leeds, but '67 was the break-out year, when the newspapers all got in on the act. San Francisco. Wear some flowers in your hair, and so on. Chiller hated the buggers.'

'The Summer of Love.'

'Ah, yes. The Summer of Drugs, we called it. You have to remember, I was a bit of a young fogey, too.' He smiled at Winsome. 'Pinstripe suit, short hair, shirt and tie. DS Enderby was the one who drew Chiller's wrath by letting his hair grow over his collar. Have you talked to him yet this time, by the way?'

'I don't think he'll be able to help us,' said Banks. 'He only worked with the two of you on the Linda Lofthouse murder, didn't he?'

'That's right. He was from your neck of the woods. North Yorkshire.'

'Well, this is a West Yorkshire matter, or West Riding, as they used to call it.'

'OK. Shoot, and I'll see what I can do.'

Banks told him first about Linda Palmer's visit to Chadwick and the complaint he had seen in the occurrence book. While he talked, Bradley listened intently, taking an occasional sip of tea. When Banks had finished, there was a brief silence.

'Danny Caxton,' Bradley said. 'There's a blast from the past.'

'Still around.'

'Yes, I've been hearing about him on the news now and again. Hence the interest, I assume?'

'Well, I think there's a certain kind of justice in proving someone's long-ago crimes when they've been so arrogant and so bullying they think they've got away with them.'

'But it was a different age,' Bradley argued. 'The sixties. Especially '67.'

'That's what everyone seems to say. Believe it or not, I've considered that argument, and the times. I enjoyed the late sixties. The permissiveness was great for young people, but I don't think it extended as far as rape.'

'You believe this woman's story?'

'I do. There are others, too, with similar tales to tell. But this one's my case. I just want to know if you can remember anything about that period in Chadwick's career, if he said anything to you about it. I know it's a long time ago, but some little thing might have stuck in your mind.'

'I remember him saying there was a complaint about Danny Caxton,' Bradley said. 'I remember that well. It was a hot summer's day, like we've been having up until now. I never saw the girl who made the complaint and, as I said, as far as I know, it never went anywhere. She came in with her mother, I think.'

'So there was no investigation?'

'Not as I remember. Chiller said it was something to do with Blackpool, so not really our case.'

'He said that?'

'Yes.'

'The incident – alleged incident – took place in Blackpool a bit more than a week before the complaint was registered in Leeds.'

'I certainly never heard any more about it. I assumed he'd passed it on to Blackpool or West Lancashire CID. It would have been their call.'

'We've checked and double-checked, and we can't find any record with Lancashire. There's only the occurrence book entry with the Leeds police. They don't remember anything about it.'

'Then it can't have gone any further. I mean, it's hardly surprising Blackpool wouldn't want anything to do with it. Summer season's big business there. Lots of name stars. Lots of paying customers. Mustn't upset the apple cart.'

'Could it have been buried?'

'That's possible,' Bradley admitted, scratching his cheek. 'Things did go astray on occasion, and there wasn't exactly anything to bury, was there, if as far as it went was an occurrence book entry? As I said, it was another time. Different rules. Besides, Danny Caxton was a big shot around the station. Rubbed shoulders with the chief constable. I think even Chiller got to go to one of his dinner dances, but not the lowly likes of yours truly.'

'Too bad.'

'Oh, I don't know. I wasn't a fan, myself. More of a Mantovani man.'

It was certainly true about the different rules back then, Banks knew. The advent of the PACE rules in the eighties along with the updating or repealing of many old acts had changed policing a great deal. On the other hand, Banks thought, there were bent coppers taking bribes to look the other way and lose evidence today, just as there were back then. Maybe it was a bit harder to get away with it these days – so many watchdogs – but it still happened. And sometimes orders came from above to look the other way if a notable person was involved, especially if said notable person had something on notable police persons. That was human nature, and it could only be tempered by rules and law, not completely controlled. You could slide about on the moral scale as much as you wanted, or you could convince yourself that you were certain what was right and what was wrong. Whichever way Banks thought about it, however, ignoring a fourteen-year-old girl's claims of having been brutally raped came under 'wrong'. But he realised there was no sense in arguing moral relativism or the tenor of the times with Bradley. The man had been a lowly DC, and it had been nearly fifty years ago. As he said, another age. Best stick to trying to prise out a bit more information.

'Caxton lived in Otley at the time,' Banks said. 'And he was a local big shot. Charity events and the like. Prime high-ranks territory out there, isn't it? Lawnswood? Bramhope? Poole?'

'You think he put the kibosh on it? I'm not saying it couldn't have happened that way,' Bradley admitted. 'But it's more likely there was simply no substance to the complaint. No leads. Nothing to investigate. If the case was buried, though, the orders would have had to have come from higher up than Chiller.'

'How did he seem about it?'

Bradley scratched his temple. 'He was a bit broody for a while. He had his moods, did Chiller. I suppose it could have been something to do with that, you know, being told to lay off. He wouldn't have liked that. Very much his own man, was Chiller. I would imagine that whether or not he thought Caxton might be guilty of such a thing, he'd have liked to have had a look into it himself, just to satisfy his curiosity. But there was nothing he could do by himself, going up against someone like Caxton against orders. That's the stuff of fiction and, for all his courage, he valued his job.'

'So he took it seriously?'

'I'd say he was disturbed by it, yes, but I still think he would have found it hard to believe such a thing of a bloke like Caxton.'

'What did you think of him?' Banks asked. 'Caxton. I mean, when you heard his name in connection with a possible sexual assault.'

'I didn't know him, of course. Never met him. But I suppose I thought, nah, never, not him. He'd even been in the station once or twice, so I was told. And he was hardly ever off telly in those days. It'd be like thinking your Uncle Ted was a perv.'

'Many a person's Uncle Ted was a perv.'

'You know what I mean. Familiar. Friendly. Cosy.'

'It's a good disguise, don't you think?'

'So it would appear now.'

'Do you remember anything else from around that time?' Banks asked. 'Anything DI Chadwick might have said? Or anyone, for that matter? The super? The chief?'

Bradley pursed his lips. 'I had little truck with any rank higher than Chiller's, so no to that last part. As I remember, it was around my first anniversary with Leeds CID, the end of my first year working with DI Chadwick. As I said earlier, we had a fair bit of the Summer of Drugs stuff going on, so we found ourselves liaising with the Drugs Squad a lot. There was also the Sexual Offences Act, or the Queer Act, as we called it. You might remember that the House made homosexuality legal between consenting adults in private sometime during that summer. A lot of poofs seemed to take that as open season, and we had more work than ever. I do remember the first murder investigation I ever took a big part in, earlier that summer. A prostitute found floating in the canal down by The Calls. Posh now, with all those fancy restaurants, boutique hotels and flats, but it was a proper warren of crime back then.

She'd been stabbed twelve times and dumped there. Foreigner. Polish. I never saw the body, like, only came in later for the legwork.'

'Did you ever find out who did it?'

'No. We never did. We suspected the pimp, but he had a cast-iron alibi, of course. There was some speculation later that she might have been one of the Ripper's first, before the "stone in the sock" murder in 1969. Amazing what you can do with hindsight. But we'd never heard of the Ripper then, and prostitute murders were all too common.'

'And all too rarely investigated,' said Banks, remembering his days in Soho in the eighties. *'Plus ça change.'*

'Limited resources and too long a list of suspects. What can you do? You know as well as I do that most killers are related or in some way close to their victims. And stupid. Normally it doesn't take you more than a day or so to run them down. But there are some – prostitutes, stranger murders, random killings, clever buggers, gang hits – they're a little harder and call for more resources.'

'Do you remember the murder of a bloke called Tony Monaghan, found stabbed in the public toilets in Hyde Park? This would have been a bit later than the Caxton business. October.'

Bradley's expression turned grim. 'Oh, yes,' he said. 'I remember that one, all right.'

At least Gerry hadn't teased Annie about appearing at work in the same clothes she had worn the day before. Maybe she hadn't even noticed. Or perhaps she was just being polite. As Annie was suffering through a three extra-strength paracetamol hangover, she was thankful for small mercies. Banks had seemed in good spirits when they had met briefly over morning coffee before she set off for the station and he drove off to Leeds.

Before they left to talk to Paul Warner, Gerry filled Annie in on the previous evening's developments. The only new information was that DC Doug Wilson had found Albert's mate Ali in the Wytherton Arms. Unfortunately, Ali proved uninformative when questioned about what he had told Albert about older Pakistanis and underage girls. It was just a rumour, or so he told them. Such rumours were always doing the rounds.

Annie was also more than happy to let Gerry drive her to Wytherton later that day, where they found Paul Warner's flat on the second floor of an old detached house on the north-western edge of the estate. She understood it wasn't a part of the estate, wasn't a council house, but was privately owned and rented.

Paul Warner answered the ring and led them up the carpeted staircase. The hall and stairs seemed recently renovated, and Annie fancied she could even smell fresh paint. At first glance, he wasn't what Annie had expected. Here was no tattooed skinhead, but a tall, slim, handsome young man with spiky blond hair, casually dressed in a red polo shirt and ice-blue jeans. The living room was a surprise, too: uncluttered, light and airy, walls painted in ivory and cool shades of blue-grey. The ubiquitous flat-screen TV dominated one wall, opposite the three-piece suite, and the window looked out on the main road below. On the other wall was a large bookcase. Banks would probably examine every title, DVDs and CDs too, but Annie just cast a swift eye over them, enough to see that Warner favoured books on history, war and politics, along with a bit of DIY, that he liked action and superhero films and had a box set of Beethoven's symphonies and Schubert lieder. No metal or grunge. She walked over to the window. Over the road was a row of shops – the usual newsagent, minimart, chippie and betting shop – and the pub, the Hope and Anchor, which had seen better days, stood on the corner. Beyond lay the industrial sprawl of south Teesside. If you looked to the far left, Annie noticed, you could see the start of the open countryside, green fields and rolling hills. The sky had turned a bit threatening, she thought.

'Nice,' she said, turning around. 'I'm impressed.'

'Thank you. I like it,' said Warner. 'Please, sit down, both of you. Is this is about Albert's sister? It's terrible what happened to her. I really feel for him.'

'When did you hear?'

'Last night. Albert told me. He came around in a hell of a state.'

Gerry and Annie sat on the broad sofa. It was as comfortable as it looked. Gerry took out her notebook.

'I must say this is a cut above the usual bachelor pad we see in our line of work,' said Annie. 'I assume it is a bachelor pad?'

'I'm not married, if that's what you're asking.' Warner cast Gerry a sidelong glance and Annie noticed her blush a little. Well, she was about his age, she guessed. Mid-twenties or thereabouts. Significantly older than Albert Moffat. She wondered if Moffat looked up to Paul as some sort of older brother figure. There wasn't much for him to look up to in Lenny and Johnny at home.

'I'm not sure I can be of any help, but I'll try,' Warner said as he leaned back in one of the armchairs. 'I'm not averse to helping the boys in blue.'

'We're girls, Paul,' said Annie, 'in case you haven't noticed. And as far as I can see, neither of us is wearing blue today.'

Warner laughed. 'Sorry. Just a common saying, that's all. My apologies. I can see I'll have to be on my toes with you two.'

'Only if you've got something to hide.'

'Well, that remains to be seen, doesn't it? I'll try to be as open with you as I can, but first you have to tell me what you want to know.'

'We want to talk about your pal Albert Moffat,' Annie said.

'OK.'

'How long have you known him?'

'About two years.'

'Where did you meet?'

'Pub.'

'Which pub?'

'The Hope and Anchor, the one on the corner there.' He pointed towards the window. 'I'd just moved into the area, and we got talking.'

'Where did you move from?' Annie asked.

'Birmingham.'

'May I ask why?'

Warner shifted in his armchair. 'Why does anybody move anywhere?' he said. 'For a change, I suppose. And to get away from Birmingham.'

'You and Albert Moffat became friends right away?'

'Yes. I suppose we did.'

'What do you have in common? I must say you seem strange bedfellows.'

'It's true that Albert doesn't always make a great first impression on people, but he's not as stupid as most people think he is. He's a bit shy, lacking in confidence, maybe. He's also a laugh, especially after a few jars. And he has a good heart. He could probably have done a lot better for himself, given the chance, but you have to understand, Albert didn't have the advantages, his upbringing and everything.'

'And you did?'

'I went to a decent school, yes. Pure luck. And I found it easy to do well there, pass exams and stuff.'

'University?'

'I tried it for a year. Warwick. Politics and history. I do find the subjects interesting, but I'm afraid I'm not much of an academic.'

'What about Albert's racism?'

'Racism?'

'Well, he seemed anti-Asian when we talked to him.'

'Oh, that. You get that a lot around here. People get scared when they see too many dark faces around, don't you think? Although sometimes I think Albert has a point, however crudely he makes it.'

'Oh?'

'Don't sound so surprised. I'm not a dyed-in-the-wool fascist. I don't worship Hitler and go around beating up Pakis or anything like that. I do happen to have some strong opinions about Europe, immigration policy, migrants, the economy and so on. All Albert lacks is subtlety and intellectual depth in his opinions. I've done a bit of background reading in politics, even though I didn't continue with it. Albert's even less of an academic than I am.'

'Yet you still spend time with him. An educated and well-read young man like yourself. How did the relationship develop?' Annie asked.

'I don't know. How does anything develop, really? I lent him a few books. Albert *can* read, you know, and he's not too proud to ask questions about things he doesn't understand. We'd usually end up in the Hope and Anchor or the Coach and Horses, maybe with a few other locals, talking politics or whatever, whether we should stay in Europe or get out, how we should deal with the migrant camps in Calais, curbing immigration quotas, whatever, then sometimes we'd come back here with a six-pack or two and talk and watch DVDs. It's a lot cheaper to drink at home.'

'You were moulding his character? Sort of like Pygmalion?'

Warner smiled. 'Well I'm hardly Henry Higgins, and I can't see Albert as Eliza Doolittle, but I suppose in a way I might have been moulding him, yes. But not in a really overt way. I mean, I never forced any of my values or opinions on him, just tried to get him to think more deeply about the ones he had, about what he felt. I had a mentor once, when I was about his age, one of my tutors at university, and I learned the value of having someone to look up to. That's all, really. I don't think he's got a lot going for him at home.'

'Is that what you did last Tuesday?' Annie went on. 'Go to the pub then come back here?'

'Yes.'

'What time?'

'We met up in the Hope and Anchor about eight.'

'Until when?'

'About ten, maybe a little later.'

'Was anyone else with you?'

'Only in the pub. There were about five or six of us.'

'Did you all leave around ten?'

'I don't know. People sort of went their own ways. Albert and I came up here for a few more bevvies, a couple of the lads drifted home, others stayed in the pub.'

'Right. So how long did you stay here drinking? I assume you were drinking?'

'Yes. I suppose we stopped up talking and watching DVDs until about two or three in the morning, maybe later, then we crashed out.'

'What did you watch?'

'That night? *A Bridge Too Far*. Oldie but goodie. Albert can't watch anything he wants at home because they have the TV permanently locked on Sky Sports. Albert's not a big golf fan.'

'So Albert Moffat was with you all Tuesday night?'

'Well, not exactly *with* me. I don't swing in that direction, and neither does Albert. But here, yes. He slept on the sofa, like he usually does if he stops over.'

'He stays here often?'

'Whenever he wants.'

'And in the morning?'

'Lazy sod didn't wake up until nearly eleven.'

'Would you say you and Albert were both drunk by the time you crashed out?'

'Probably. Almost certainly. I had a hell of a headache the next morning.'

Annie felt like saying she knew what he felt like, but that was pushing the empathy with a witness too far. 'Too drunk to drive?'

'Definitely.'

'Do you own a car?'

'I've got a little Citroën van. For work, like.'

'Where do you keep it?'

'Outside on the street.'

'Were you with Albert in Manchester over the weekend?'

'No, we don't live in each other's pockets. And I'm not a great fan of clubbing. The music drives me crazy, that pounding beat and monotonous repetition.'

Annie gestured towards the bookcase. 'Yes, I noticed you have more refined tastes.'

Warner narrowed his eyes. 'Don't miss much, do you? It was something I picked up from my mentor a while back. Not that I don't like pop stuff. I do. I just gained an appreciation of finer things. I'd never listened to classical music before, and when I did I found I liked it.'

'Did you know Mimosa, Albert's sister?' Annie asked.

'Of course. I've been round to Albert's place a few times. Sometimes she was there. But she was Albert's kid sister. I wouldn't say I really *knew* her well.'

'Were they close?'

'I think so. He was protective towards her. I mean, it was a difficult family, so I would imagine they relied on one another a lot. They were separated by the age difference, of course, as well as gender. But she could be quite mature for her age.'

'So you've talked to her?'

'On occasion, yes. She helped us with jobs once or twice. Just little things like passing a can of paint up a stepladder or something. She seemed to appreciate having somewhere to hang out other than home. I can't say I blame her, having met the family.'

'Was this recently?'

'No, not for a while now.'

'What was she like?'

'Mimsy? Probably not much different from most girls her age, though I can't say I have much experience to go on. I don't have any siblings. I suppose she spent most of her time thinking about make-up and dreaming about pop stars and the like. But she was always pleasant enough when I saw her. She seemed bright. More so than Albert, I'd say.'

'In what way?'

'She was quick to grasp your meaning, even when you were being ironic. She was naive though, I think, in some ways. Not very well read. But talented. A good sketch artist. At least to my untutored eye.'

'Would you say she was easily manipulated?'

'I wouldn't know. I never saw anyone try to manipulate her. I imagine she would be keen to please. She lacked confidence and made it up by being a bit mouthy, but I got the feeling that she'd been let down a lot in her life and she wanted to make a good impression.'

'Albert said she didn't suffer fools gladly.'

'I doubt she did. I can't say I saw any evidence of it, but if she felt slighted or put down she could certainly let you have a mouthful.'

'Did Albert tell you about Mimosa hanging out with a Pakistani bloke down on the Strip?'

'What? No. Why would he tell me something like that? Even if it was true. Was this recently?'

'Maybe he thought you'd help him do something about it? You wouldn't approve, would you? Didn't you say you agreed with him about immigrants?'

'Not exactly. And my approval doesn't come into it. I don't approve of mixed marriages, as a matter of fact, but they were hardly about to get married, were they?'

'Who?'

'Mimsy and this person you're talking about.'

'Have you heard of grooming?'

'Yes, of course. It's hard not to these days, isn't it?'

'Would it surprise you to hear that we think it might have been going on along the Strip, and that Mimosa, and perhaps even some of her friends, had been groomed?'

'Good God, that's awful. And the police haven't done anything?'

'We've only just found about it,' Annie said, feeling as if she were apologising. 'We're not even certain we're right yet.'

'It's an appalling thought. I had absolutely no idea that anything like that could have been going on. I suppose it wasn't something I thought could happen here, not practically on my own doorstep. I saw the news about Rochdale and all the rest, of course. But they all seemed so far away from Wytherton in so many ways.'

'Unfortunately not,' said Annie. She glanced at Gerry, who put away her notebook, and they got up to leave. 'I think that's all for now,' Annie said, holding her hand out to shake. 'Thanks for your time, Paul.'

Warner shook. 'Of course. If there's anything else . . .'

'Naturally. We'll be in touch.'

When they got outside, Gerry noted down the licence number of the white Citroën Nemo. PAUL WARNER, PAINTING AND DECORATING was written on the side above a phone number, which Gerry also copied down. 'He's certainly an odd one, isn't he?' she said.

'Indeed he is,' said Annie. 'A real fish out of water. But I think he's given Albert Moffat a convincing alibi.'

'Any particular reason you remember the Tony Monaghan murder?' Banks asked.

'It was my first body, for a start, and a nasty one at that.' Bradley screwed up his face with the effort of memory. 'I won't forget it in a hurry. The smelly toilets, being cooped up in that tiny space with the body and all. It made me gag. Hard to believe it's an Indian restaurant now. It was still early days for me, remember, and it took me a good few times before I could approach a murder scene with a settled stomach. A queer murder. They were usually easy enough to solve, too, but we got nowhere with that one. Not that we didn't work hard at it, whatever you might think. At least at first.'

'I don't think anything. Tell me about it.'

Bradley looked up at the clouds, as if for inspiration, then said, 'We got a call to the public conveniences in Hyde Park. Very public and very convenient, if you know what I mean. The new act may have made homosexuality legal, but you still got a lot of rent boys and the like trawling for trade in these sort of places.' He glanced at Winsome. 'Don't get me wrong. I'm not homophobic, any more than I'm racist. I was all for making it legal, but some of the creatures that crept out of the gutter, or from under stones, were enough to make your skin crawl.'

'This victim wasn't a rent boy,' said Banks.

'No. He wasn't. Not in this case. He was in his late twenties, as far as we could tell, nicely dressed, wearing a wedding ring. Stabbed, as you say. Eight or nine times, as I remember. We thought maybe he was a prospective customer who'd tried it on with the wrong person. I mean, some people did just go there for a piss, you know, if they didn't know any better. And he was a stranger to the area, up from London, so I remember.'

'Was robbery a motive?'

'We certainly considered it. Pockets emptied. Maybe even a drug deal gone wrong. There was plenty of that around, too.'

'So you couldn't identify him at first?'

'No. Only later, when we asked around. He had a card from a hotel in his top pocket – something the killer must have missed. That led us to the Queen's Hotel in City Square, and then to his room. We found out he was from London. His name was Tony Monaghan. He worked for an advertising agency.'

'Philby, Leyland and Associates,' said Banks. 'How far did you get with that investigation?'

'Not far at all, beyond identifying the body and noting the cause of death. We interviewed a few people we knew were habitués of that particular public toilet, but we didn't get anywhere with them. We talked to a few people at the hotel, but nobody knew anything about him. He hadn't been staying there long and he was on his own. We even canvassed some of the students who lived nearby. One lad told me he was on his way home from a party late on the night in question, and he saw two men carrying a third slumped between them, as if he was drunk, like. He said he thought it seemed funny because the two men didn't look like students – you get plenty of drunkenness and that sort of thing around the university – but they were like thugs, like boxers or all-in wrestlers. "Two burly bald blokes without necks", was how he put it, if I remember correctly. He didn't like the looks of them, so he got out of the way sharpish, like, before they saw him. The timing matched, but we couldn't get any further with it. There was no CCTV back then like there is these days. And it was a filthy night, raining and all, so the lad could have been mistaken. We did our best to carry out a thorough search of the park for a murder weapon or any other trace evidence, but we found nothing, and if there had been any trace evidence the rain would have washed it away.'

'But the two men *could* have been carrying Tony Monaghan's body towards the toilets?'

'They could have been.'

'What did you do?'

'I took the student's statement. That was it. We had a twelve-year-old kid stabbed and dumped on some wasteland near Leeds Parish Church, so we gave all our attention to that. It was a nasty one. Kid, and all.'

'Did you solve that?'

'Oh, aye. Eventually. Stepfather confessed early in 1968. He'd been abusing the boy and he'd threatened to tell. It was a busy time. There was plenty of other stuff we worked on. Robberies, drugs, assaults, prostitution rings and so on, but these are the ones that stick in your mind over time.'

'True enough. Did you get the student's name?'

'I did, at the time, but I can't remember it now.'

'Was there a post-mortem on Monaghan?'

'I'm sure there was,' Bradley said. 'But . . .'

'What?'

'Well, it's funny, but a while later, sometime the following year, I tried to locate some of the Monaghan files, including the PM report.'

'Why did you do that?'

'A similar case. Similar MO, at any rate. There was no gay angle, though, and it turned out to be a complete red herring. Bloke stabbed near a notorious public convenience. But it was the wife. Found out his dirty little secret and followed him there.'

'It was the similarity in method and location that sent you looking for the Monaghan files?'

'Yes. But I couldn't find them, couldn't find any post-mortem report, nothing.'

'So within a year or so of what you admit was a superficial investigation, all traces of the crime had been somehow expunged from your files?'

'The files themselves had been taken. That's the only explanation for it.'

'Did you challenge DI Chadwick on it?'

'I asked him if he knew where they were, but he said he didn't. He was evasive. Said something about the chief constable taking an interest.'

'Edward Crammond?'

Bradley gave Banks a sharp glance. 'You do work fast. Yes, Chief Constable Edward Crammond. A right bastard. And a reputation for hobnobbing with the rich and famous.'

'Including Caxton?'

'Indeed. You know what became of him, don't you?'

'Yes,' said Banks. 'Both he and Chief Superintendent McCullen were dismissed for accepting bribes from a prominent Leeds drug dealing gang in 1974. We found it in some old files.' Banks thought he heard a distant rumble of thunder. He looked towards Winsome and indicated that she should pick up the questioning, as they had determined on the drive down. After all, she had done most of the background work on the Monaghan case so far.

'Did you find any link between the young girl's complaint and the Tony Monaghan murder?' Winsome asked.

Bradley seemed surprised by the question. 'Nay, lass. There weren't none. Not as I recall.'

'Whose decision was it to take no further action on the Monaghan murder?'

'That would have come from high up, just like with Caxton.'

'Chief Constable Edward Crammond?'

'Very likely.'

'Why would he have the files removed?'

'I don't know.'

'Can you guess?'

'Aye,' said Bradley. 'Same as you can. And no doubt we'd come to the same conclusion.'

'How did you experience it?' she asked. 'Down in the trenches. How was it put to you? I mean, I'm not long beyond being a mere DC myself, so I do have a clear memory of what it's like down there, even now. I've still no idea what the brass are thinking.' She glanced at Banks. 'Not even him, half the time. I just get on with my job, do what I'm told.'

'Aye. That's the way it was then, too.'

'So if someone told you that was it, forget it, the case was closed, that's exactly what you'd do, no questions asked?'

'Of course,' said Bradley. 'Unless you're Philip Marlowe or someone. You know as well as I do they don't have to give you a reason.'

'Was that how it happened?'

'As far as I can remember,' said Bradley. 'One day I was talking to Monaghan's employers in London about the reason for his visit, the next thing Chiller came in and told me the case was over and done with. I asked him if that meant we'd got someone for it, but he just said no and walked out. End of story. Then, like I said, the files disappeared.'

'How did he seem when he told you this?'

'Chiller? Proper pissed off, if you'll pardon my language.'

'Weren't you curious about what happened?'

'Course I was, love. But I valued my job. And even if I'd wanted to, I didn't have time or the resources to go gallivanting about following up personal investigations. That sort of thing only happens on telly.'

'So that was the end of Tony Monaghan. Stabbed in a public toilet.'

'If you care to look at it that way.'

'What other way is there?'

'Some lifestyles are more dangerous than others. If you hang around notorious public toilets looking for rough trade you're taking a risk.'

'But Monaghan was a stranger in town,' said Winsome. 'How would he know?'

Bradley tapped the side of his nose. 'They knew. They all knew. There's a network.'

Banks finished the last of his tea. It was cold and slightly bitter. 'Simon,' he said, 'did you have any reason at all to think there was something fishy about the Tony Monaghan murder?'

'What? You mean other than the student's statement, being asked to drop the case and the files disappearing?'

'Well, that made two in a row that got quickly dropped, unless I'm missing something. Close together, too.'

'But they were different. I mean, I never really thought about the Caxton thing like that.'

'Like what?'

'Like the way we were talking about it earlier. Orders from above. You know. I never connected the two at all. I just assumed the girl must have been making it up.'

'And Monaghan?'

Bradley glanced out over the back garden. It wasn't as colourful as the front, but it was clearly well tended and cared for. 'It just didn't feel right,' he said eventually.

'In what way?'

'I don't know.' Bradley gave a little shiver and tapped his stomach. 'Haven't you ever had that feeling, a sort of gut instinct? You just *know* there's something wrong – what the Americans call hinky – and you can't quite grasp it.'

'Did you ever have any reason to think Tony Monaghan might *not* have been a homosexual?' Winsome asked. 'Despite where his body was found. That his death might have been staged in some way?'

'Well, I did for a while, when I took the student's statement, but the more I thought about it, the more I thought he might have been mistaken.'

'Did you ever come across any evidence to prove that Monaghan *was* a homosexual?' Winsome asked.

Bradley thought for a moment. 'Well, no, not really.'

'You knew he was married?'

'He was wearing a wedding ring, and we found out just a day or two later that he had a wife, yes. But none of that really counted for anything. There were plenty of homos who were married. Especially then. They felt it gave them some sort of immunity, or maybe they were in denial. We just made the assumption that he used his business trips around the country to satisfy his perverse cravings.'

'Did you talk to Monaghan's wife?'

'I didn't. No.'

'Did DI Chadwick?'

'I don't know. If he did, he didn't say anything to me about it.'

'But it is possible that Monaghan might not have been gay, isn't it?' Winsome persisted.

'I suppose so. But what was he doing there?'

'Maybe it was as you said earlier. Maybe he just needed to use the toilet. Did you find out where he'd been that evening? Had he been drinking? Dinner with friends? Business colleagues? I mean, if he'd had a few pints, it would make sense that he'd need to relieve himself. Where was he coming from? Which direction was he heading? Back to the hotel? Why was he walking alone?'

'We didn't get to ask all those questions. Who could we have asked them of? We didn't get time to trace his movements.'

'So maybe the student was right, after all. But didn't it bother you? You said you talked to his employer in London. Did you find out what he was working on up north?'

'No. They said they respected their clients' confidentiality. I argued with them, but it was no good. They said I'd have had to get a court order, and the whole investigation came to a halt before I could do anything like that.'

'Did you ever wonder why?'

'Of course I did.'

'Come up with any ideas?'

'Not really.'

'Would it surprise you to find out that Tony Monaghan was in Leeds because he worked for Danny Caxton, who was appearing in pantomime in Bradford that Christmas?'

Bradley flinched as if he'd been kicked. 'I'd bloody well say it would, yes. Where did you find that out?'

'It came up in our inquiries,' Winsome said. 'So you've got two cases now, only weeks apart, both nipped in the bud, and both starring Danny Caxton. What do you think of that?'

'I don't know what to think. If I'd known at the time—'

'Oh, come on, Simon,' Banks cut in. 'Surely you've got a bit of imagination.'

'Well . . . I suppose, you know, if Monaghan was queer and he was connected with someone high up—'

'Like Caxton? Or a senior police officer?'

'Maybe the chief constable. Or a local politician, bigwig, whatever. Well, if there was a such a connection, maybe a little influence had been brought to bear. They'd want to keep something like that quiet, wouldn't they, legal or not.'

'Do you think DI Chadwick knew about this connection?'

'No. I very much doubt it,' said Bradley. 'I think they kept him as much in the dark as they did me. Like I said, he seemed pissed off at being told to give it up. See, there was always one thing that rankled.'

'Oh?' said Banks. 'And what was that?'

'It was the body. I mean, it was gruesome enough, and all, no doubt about that.'

'So what was wrong?'

'The position, partly. It just didn't seem right, Chiller thought, didn't seem natural he would have fallen the way he had.'

'But you don't know for certain that's what happened?'

'It's what the pathologist said at the scene. Course, we never got a proper post-mortem report. Not that I ever saw.' He shook his head slowly. 'Look, I'm bloody gobsmacked by all this. Are you *sure* you're right?'

'We only have a few facts, Mr Bradley,' said Winsome. 'That's all. What we've told you is true as far as it goes. Obviously, we need to know a lot more. Can you think of anything else?'

'Just something Chiller said. I wouldn't have known because it was my first, like.'

'What was it?'

'There wasn't enough blood. If he'd been killed where we found him, he wouldn't have fallen the way he was lying and there would have been a lot more blood.'

'Did the pathologist remark on this?' Banks asked.

'I think so. It's a long time ago. But if he did, it was in a sort of offhand way, like it might not mean anything, or there might be a simple explanation. I've since found out that not all knife wounds bleed a lot. The cut ends sort of form a seal. But one of the thrusts had severed a major artery, the femoral. There should have been more blood. But, like I said earlier, the weather was foul and we certainly didn't find any traces of blood in the park.'

'So DI Chadwick suspected that your student might have been right about what he saw, and Tony Monaghan was killed elsewhere and dumped in the toilets?' Banks said.

'I'm not sure he actually came out with it like that, but yes, it seems that way.'

'Which brings a whole lot of assumptions into question,' said Banks, giving Winsome the nod to get ready to leave.

'Simon, I know it's not easy, remembering,' he said. 'But do you think you could write down what you've just told us, and anything else you can remember about the case?' Banks gave him a card. 'You can email it to me, if you like. Or fax it.'

Bradley took the card. 'Yes. Yes, of course.' He smiled at Winsome. 'Nice to meet you, lass.' He stood up and shook their hands. 'Let me—'

'Don't worry,' said Banks. 'We can find our way out. Thanks.'

As they were leaving, Banks glanced behind him. He had noticed a cabinet by the wall, and he saw a pale Bradley open its door and take out a bottle of dark amber liquid. Just before he closed the front door behind him, he heard Bradley call out, 'Pam? Pam? Where's the bloody glasses, love? I need a drink.'

Excerpt from Linda Palmer's Memoir

We found the Coffee Cellar on our third day, the second having been spent mostly on the beach. It was a scorcher, and we slathered ourselves in Ambre Solaire and just lay there on towels on the sand letting the rays tan us. Those were the days when it was called suntan cream rather than sunblock. You could even buy stuff that would give you a tan if you just rubbed it on, but you ended up orange and obviously fake.

The Coffee Cellar was a bohemian establishment. At least, that was what Melanie said. She liked to use words like that. You walked down some narrow wooden stairs in the dark, moved aside the beaded curtains and there you were, all dim shaded lights, brick walls pied with saltpetre, fishnets on the ceiling and upturned barrels for tables. There was a boy in a striped shirt working a hissing espresso machine behind the wooden counter. French posters hung on the walls – mostly cafe and cabaret scenes. I didn't recognise them at the time, but in my student days I came to know the familiar Toulouse-Lautrec and Renoir prints so popular in beatnik cafes of the fifties and sixties. Half naked can-can dancers, prostitutes, absinthe drinkers, decadent poets sitting around outside Left Bank cafes arguing about philosophy.

The music was good, or so we thought. A lot more adventurous than the usual cafe fare. More 'Whiter Shade of Pale' and 'Light My Fire' than 'Puppet on a String' and 'The Last Waltz'. And we could smoke down there. Melanie and I smoked Sobranie Black Russians, Pall Mall filter tips, Peter Stuyvesant or those funny pastel-coloured tubes. We wouldn't be seen dead with Woodies or Park Drive. We felt very grown-up and sophisticated in our coffee bar, smoking our exotic cigarettes, but perhaps to the boy behind the counter we just looked like two fourteen-year-olds trying to act grown up. He was always nice to us, though, and he even gave us a free biscuit each with our coffee one morning. I'd been smoking for about a year by the time I was fourteen, as had Melanie, though at first it had made me sick, and I had to work at it to get it right. We were secretive about it, of course – our parents would have killed us if they had known. I noticed my mother sniffing once or twice when we sat down for the evening meal, but when she mentioned the smell of smoke, I told her we'd been for a Coke at one of the seafront cafes in the afternoon, and the smoke must have got in our hair or clothes. You could smoke everywhere then.

That first week, Melanie and I fell into a routine: Coffee Cellar, amusements arcades, pier, Golden Mile and beach. Most evenings we spent at the Pleasure Beach, though it never got really dark enough for the full impact of bright lights at that time of year. We didn't usually go to the Coffee Cellar in the evenings. We tried it once, but it was full of a different crowd, people in black polo neck jumpers with their hair over their collars. Even a couple of berets and beards. No stools left. They were an older crowd, too, and they looked at us as if we were just kids, which I suppose we were.

It might have been the Summer of Love in San Francisco, and even in London, for all we knew, but we were in Blackpool, where it was just a normal summer. I'd heard *Sergeant Pepper's Lonely Hearts Club Band*, I remember, and I didn't know what to make of it, though I thought 'She's Leaving Home' was one of the saddest, most beautiful songs I'd ever heard. I wanted to be a songwriter as well as a singer and famous actress. What can I say? I was fourteen. I suppose here I'm trying to explain why I walked so naively into what happened on Saturday, and that was certainly a part of it, my desire to be a singer and songwriter. *Do Your Own Thing!* might have been mostly for the boring old grown-ups, but they did occasionally have someone on with a guitar, like Donovan, who sang his own songs. Why not me?

And I was also at that time an inveterate autograph hunter. I don't suppose it's a very popular pastime these days, but it certainly was in the sixties. It seems to be the sort of thing no one does any more, like having a pen pal or trainspotting. I mean, having an email pal and writing down diesel engine numbers doesn't make it, does it? And stars are either too inaccessible or so busy pretending to be just like you and me that you wouldn't even think of asking them for their signatures in a little book. Then you get people like Russell Brand signing his autograph on young girls' bare breasts.

Back then, you could buy all kinds of fancy autograph books with different coloured pages and golden edging between fake burgundy leather covers or William Morris designs with autographs engraved on the front in gold leaf script. They had their own shape, what you'd call 'landscape' in these days of computer printers. Even my dad had an autograph book – he showed me it – and he had Nat Gonella and Harry James and lots of people I had never heard of who were famous in his time.

Mine wasn't as full, and I do confess to writing away on occasion with a stamped addressed envelope and receiving a signed photograph in return. Or sticking in a scrap of paper I happened to have with me at the time. Blackpool was always good for autographs because of all the summer season shows there. Since I first started collecting, when I was twelve, I got Frank Ifield, Helen Shapiro, Jimmy Tarbuck, Les Dawson, Adam Faith, Sandie Shaw, Marty Wilde, Heinz from The Tornados, Des O'Connor, Cilla Black, Scott Walker, Tommy Cooper, Gerry Marsden, Paul Jones, Gene Vincent and Karl Denver. I could've got the Bachelors once, too, if I'd waited longer, but I was too near the back of the crowd.

Maybe I was stupid to get in that fancy car with Danny Caxton, but my autograph hunting took me to him and my artistic ambitions caused me to go with him to the hotel.

Gerry kicked off her shoes and went over to turn on the shaded table lamp. It wasn't quite dark yet, but it was getting there. It had been a long day, and all she wanted to do was put her feet up with a good book and a cup of herbal tea. First, though, she went into the bedroom and changed out of her work clothes. She felt a bit sticky from the day's humidity and thought a shower might help – one of her little luxuries was that the flat came with a power shower – so she got straight in before she could talk herself out of it. Coming out feeling and smelling clean with her long hair still wet and hanging over her shoulders, she put on tracksuit bottoms and T-shirt and walked through to the small kitchenette to put the kettle on.

The flat she rented on the fringes of Eastvale College campus was a sort of attic that took up the top floor of an old house. Not exactly a penthouse, but she had a nice view beyond the streets of student housing and the college itself to the woods and hills in the west beyond. She could even see the meandering silver line of the River Swain as it made its progress into Eastvale from its source high in the hills. The living room was spacious and comfortable, with a dormer window, sofa and two armchairs, the bedroom adequate, the en suite a delight and the kitchenette all right if all you wanted was tea and toast. There was no cooker, but there was a hotplate for fry-ups, not that she ever ate those. Mostly she ate out, and lightly at that. It was a student area so there were plenty of cheap cafes and takeaways of every variety – even kebab and pizza combined.

Gerry opened the window and felt the merest hint of a breeze. She could hear the sound of a student party from across the street – the occasional whoop over pounding dance beats. They wouldn't go on too late, they never did, except at the end of term. Now it was mostly just summer students. The threatening sky that had dogged most of the day and presaged a storm seemed to have broken up without coming to fruition, and she could see a half moon through a rent in the cloud cover and, here and there, a bright star shining through a thin veil of cloud.

She made her tea and sat in the comfortable armchair she liked best for reading. With some Chopin nocturnes playing quietly in the background, she picked up her Kindle and started reading *Fifty Shades of Grey*. It had taken her two years to get around to it after an acquaintance in her Pilates class had recommended it, and it took her about fifteen minutes to press 'Home'. It wasn't just the bad writing, she didn't get the point of it. She wasn't a prude, though it had been a while since she'd had a boyfriend. That was because she didn't have the time, not lack of inclination – now her life was all studying for exams, courses, and work work work. There was simply no room for a boyfriend, and she was not the kind of girl to favour one-night stands or the casual fuck-buddy arrangement. Sometimes she felt sad and lonely, but mostly she loved her job and its possibilities so much she didn't mind too much. She scrolled through her small collection for something else to read and decided on Elena Ferrante's latest in the Neapolitan series. She had followed the adventures of Elena and Lila right from the start.

Before she could get very far, her mobile buzzed. She had to hurry to get it out of her briefcase and just managed to press the on button before the call went through to answering.

At first there was a disconcerting silence, then a small voice said, 'Is this who I spoke to before?'

'It's me,' said Gerry.

'You gave me your number.'

'Yes. Are you Jade?'

'Who told you that? It's not my real name.'

'What's your real name?'

'You can call me Jade.'

'What is it, Jade? What can I do?'

'You said to ring if I . . . if I ever just . . . you know . . . wanted to.'

'That's right. Is something wrong?'

'Nothing's changed. Everything's quiet. But I'm going away.'

'Where to?'

'I don't know yet. Far away from them. I've got a few ideas.'

'What do you want from me, Jade?'

'I want to talk to you.' There was another pause, shorter this time. 'There's things I want to tell you before I go. Things about me and Mimsy.'

'Tell me.'

'Not on the phone. Can you meet me somewhere?'

'Can you come to me? In Eastvale?'

'No. I've got no money, for a start. And I might be seen. I'm safe where I am.'

'OK. Say where.'

'Up on the estate, right on the eastern edge, there's a couple of terraces they're going to knock down. All the houses are condemned and boarded up. Nobody goes there.'

'Right.'

'But I know how to get in the one just past the broken playground. Number thirty-six. Mimsy and me used to hang out there when we wanted to get away from them for a while. We'd just smoke and talk and share a bottle. Have a laugh, you know. One of the boards over the front door is loose, the one in the middle. You just swing it to the left, like a sliding door.'

'I've got that,' Gerry said. 'What's the broken playground?'

'You'll know it when you see it. It's Leinster Street, right opposite that abandoned factory. You can't miss it. But don't park outside. Someone might notice a car parked right out front. Park around the corner, OK? There's usually plenty of space.'

'OK, Jade. When?'

'Soon as you can get here. And can you bring me a sarnie or something?'

'What sort?'

'Anything. I'm fucking starving.'

'It'll take me about three-quarters of an hour to get there.'

'I'll be here. Be careful. Keep your eyes open. Things might seem quiet, but I'm sure they're still watching.'

'Who is?'

'I'll tell you all about it. Promise me you won't tell anyone.'

'Jade, I can't do that. It's not—'

'If you don't promise me you won't tell anyone, I won't be here. And come by yourself. I can tell you what you want to know, but not on the phone.'

'Jade, I—'

'Will you promise me?'

Now it was Gerry's turn to pause as the thoughts whizzed through her mind. Without fully considering any of the options, she said, 'Yes. I promise,' and the line went dead.

After, as she stood there holding the mobile in her hand, she felt a chill run up her spine despite the warm night air. What had she done? What had she agreed to? What if it was a trap? But why should Jade try to trap her? She'd said she was going away, and this was no doubt her parting shot against the men who had shamed and humiliated her and Mimsy. Gerry understood the need for secrecy well enough, but she also knew that if she went under Jade's rules, there was a strong likelihood that nothing she got would be of any use in court. Even if that were the case, at least she would have names and the full story, so they would know where to focus their investigation. The only things she could rely on happening were another bollocking and a possible suspension, or worse. And even if Jade had no reason to set a trap for her, she could be the bait. The gang that had groomed Jade and Mimsy, or the men who had raped Mimsy, could be behind it, even the killer. Maybe Jade was being held against her will, forced to do this. But that made no sense, Gerry told herself; she was just being paranoid.

She knew that she should call DI Cabbot immediately and go in with a team, but when it came down to it Jade was still just a kid, whatever her experiences. Gerry couldn't bring herself to break a promise or to leave her out there alone. No doubt too many people had broken promises to Jade in her young life already, and Gerry didn't want to be just another person who let her down. It was a miracle she trusted anyone to start with. She tried to think what DI Cabbot or Detective Superintendent Banks would do in her situation, and she thought they would go. She would try to bring Jade in, she determined, try to persuade her to come and make an official statement, offer to protect her from the men.

But she had to go, and she had to go on Jade's terms. Before she left, she had a look in her fridge to see what she'd got for a sandwich.

Burgess had chosen the Indian restaurant on Market Street, not far from where Banks and Sandra used to live in Eastvale, partly because it stayed open late. Banks had only eaten take-away from there before, and it had always been good. The meal that evening, with accompanying canned sitar music, dim lighting and cold lager, was also good.

Burgess licked his fingers after shoving a vindaloo-loaded piece of naan in his mouth and reached for his glass. 'Bloody hot,' he said, when he could speak.

Banks was sticking to the chicken tikka masala, which was spicy enough, but not so hot it burned his taste buds to a crisp. He found that the older he got, the lower his tolerance for curries.

'By the way, how's your Annie's case going? I heard there's been a few shenanigans there.'

'Nothing much,' said Banks. 'A superintendent's nose out of joint.'

'Grooming, isn't it?'

'We think so.'

Burgess shovelled in another mouthful of vindaloo. 'Thought so. Nasty business. What is it with that lot? You'd think the only bloody career choices they had was paedo pimp or terrorist.'

'I see you haven't changed.'

'Well, I ask you. I thought we should touch base on Caxton, as it seems we've both been busy.'

'Well, I know I have.'

'It's coming together. The Met's working on active complaints from Brighton to Carlisle, about twenty-five in all between the mid-sixties and mid-eighties. He's no Jimmy

Savile or Cyril Smith, unless we're only getting the tip of the iceberg, but he's no Boy Scout, either.'

'What's the age range?'

'Youngest is thirteen, oldest seventeen. And he's not fussy about venue. One audience member from *Do Your Own Thing!* in the dressing room. You remember they used to invite a load of screaming teenage girls in the studio if they had a wannabe Cliff Richard or Elvis on?'

Banks nodded. He'd seen the programme.

'Another in his dressing room at a panto. *Puss in Boots.* I wonder if he has a sense of irony. Several girls at a home for disturbed teens he supported for a while in the early seventies.'

'You think they'll stand up? I mean, everyone's kept it quiet for so long.'

'By sheer number alone, I'd say. But we've got a lot more than that. We've got names, dates, places and a hell of a pile of missing crime reports.'

'Snap,' said Banks. 'He had quite a talent for disappearing things, it seems. Should've been a stage magician.'

'That's what happens when you take the time and effort to lose at golf to every chief constable in the country.' Burgess called the waiter over and ordered two more lagers. 'We've also been getting some interesting calls from retired police officers. Mostly junior at the time. They don't want to be seen as turning a blind eye. They say they knew about Caxton, and others like him, and they wanted to stop it, but any attempts were blocked from higher up. You know as well as I do that the police force is a hierarchical institution, almost military in its fastidiousness about chain of command. Now you and I might be a bit . . . unorthodox . . . shall we say. But most coppers do what they're told. The smooth running of the force depends on it. But that doesn't mean they don't grind their teeth in frustration when they see something like this going unchecked and unpunished. We've got allies, Banksy. People who remember stuff. People who will come forward. People who aren't afraid to stand up and be counted, now they've got their pensions.'

'I'm sure that Linda's case will make a convincing one.'

'Convincing? You're our flagship case. I've read your reports. Think she'll be able to convince a jury?'

Banks sipped some lager and thought for a moment. 'If anything goes against Linda,' he said, 'it'll be her calmness. The only emotion she showed was when she saw the photos of Monaghan and Caxton in the old newspaper file. And that passed quickly. People won't see a victim with a life blighted by Caxton's abuse. They won't see a broken woman, a junkie, a loser. She's got herself together, she's succeeded in making something of herself. But the scars are there, nonetheless, the damage was done. I think her emotional honesty, intelligence and directness will have to carry the day for her.'

'In a court of law? Blimey, that could be a first. But don't worry. From what I can see, you've got the goods. Besides, we don't want every victim blubbering in the witness box about how her life's been ruined by what Caxton did. That might sound a bit callous, but there it is. Too much emotion can sometimes cheapen a solid case.'

'Maybe. I've asked her to write things down, to see if she can come up with more detail.'

'The more, the better. I see you also tracked down the second man quickly enough. Nice bit of detective work.'

'Tony Monaghan. Yes, Linda Palmer recognised him from a photo in the *Yorkshire Evening Post* archives. A picture that appeared after his body was found in a public toilet in Leeds, unfortunately, so it doesn't really get us anywhere.'

'Why not?'

'I was hoping we'd have a live witness.'

'True enough, that would probably clinch it.' Burgess took another sip of lager. 'Look, we've got three other complainants so far telling us that they were raped by another man after Caxton. This was in the late seventies, so it certainly wasn't your Tony Monaghan, but there seems to be a pattern of sorts.'

'Any leads as to their identities?'

'Unfortunately, no. The accusers remember nothing about them, and there were no handy photos in newspapers, either. It's my guess they were employees of Caxton's performing a similar role to Monaghan, from gofer to fixer. He obviously let his minions have sloppy seconds from time to time. We're working on a list of all the man's employees through the ages, so we'll have a lot of names to check out. Your DS Jackman's doing a grand job on background, by the way. Some of them have to be still alive. We should have a few more people to interview eventually.'

'Good. It's a pity about Monaghan.'

'Yes. But you must have your suspicions about the murder?'

'Naturally. And we'll be investigating it. But that's all they are. Suspicions.'

Their pints arrived, and they clinked glasses. 'Cheers,' said Burgess. He pushed his plate away. 'That's enough of that.' Banks noticed it was almost empty. He worked on the remainder of his tikka masala and naan.

'I found out today that the Tony Monaghan murder investigation was shut down, too,' said Banks, 'according to DI Chadwick's old oppo Simon Bradley. And the case files mysteriously disappeared. I'd say from all I've heard that Chief Constable Edward Crammond is in the frame for it.'

'Which makes it even more suspicious and more likely to be linked with Caxton,' said Burgess. 'He had the clout to close down investigations, he knew chief constables, and it seems to have become a habit with him from what I've seen.'

'Good point,' Banks agreed. 'But I don't think you can convict a man for murder by trying to argue that he'd influenced several other investigations so he must have influenced that one, too.'

'No, but you can argue that he *could* have influenced that one, and once you get that pattern in a jury's mind, it's as good as done. But what are we speculating about this for? Caxton's going down for the girls. Monaghan's murder is icing on the cake if we can make it stick.'

'A separate charge?'

'It'll have to be. They all will, or all we've got is similar fact evidence, and you know what judges think about that. And you'll have to get a bit more than you've got already.'

'A confession would be nice,' Banks said. 'Otherwise, it'll never be more than speculation.'

Burgess rubbed his forehead. 'I went to see Caxton yesterday. And that slimy lawyer of his. Confronted them with one or two things. I don't think we'll ever get a confession out of him. Bastard doesn't think he's done anything wrong.'

'That was the impression I got, too.'

'Thing is, I'd like you to have another word with him.'

'I don't have much new to question him about.'

'You've got Tony Monaghan. The murder. Throw that in his face. See how he reacts. Suggest you know he had something to do with it. Play the gay card. He seemed to be faltering a bit yesterday. He's old and he tires easily. Hit him while he's on the ropes. That's what I say.'

Banks felt a bit queasy about attacking a tired and weak old man, but he thought back on Linda Palmer's ordeal, not to mention all the other victims, and reminded himself who he was dealing with. 'Right you are,' he said. 'I'll talk to him tomorrow, while he's still recovering from your visit.'

Burgess punched Banks's arm. 'I was nice as pie. Like a conversation between two old mates.'

'I'll bet. What do you think, do we pester him at home or bring him in?'

Burgess frowned for a moment, then said. 'Go see him at home once more. Gives 'em a feeling of intrusion, contamination. Next time, we'll have him down the nick.'

'That'll be fun.' Banks sipped some lager.

'Come on, Banksy, why don't we finish our drinks and pay up? Then we can go and see how that buxom blond Australian barmaid's doing at the Queen's Arms.'

11

It was dark when Gerry turned left near the end of the Strip on to Wytherton Avenue, one of the broader streets that cut through the estate, with cars parked on both sides. There was practically no traffic as she drove deeper into the estate looking for the turn. She found it and parked her Corsa under the only functioning streetlamp on a side street facing the derelict factory, as Jade had suggested.

Before getting out, she glanced in her side and rear-view mirrors to check that there was nobody around. The street was empty and dark and many of the streetlights were out as far back as she could see. These were old houses, not the compact brick council style of the sixties. They were tall, thin terraces built of solid, darker stone, and many of them seemed as deserted as the street itself. Beyond the steep front steps and high-pitched slate roofs, the night sky glowed with the lights of an urban conglomeration that blotted out all the starlight. She could still see the half moon over to her left.

She made sure to put the Krook on the steering wheel and locked the car doors before she left it. She knew that the professional car thieves of today could get around practically any security device, but it scared off the amateurs and encouraged any thief to seek out something easier. She looked over at the abandoned factory as she turned the corner. Beyond the high wire fence with scrolls of barbed wire along its top lay broken pallets and a forklift truck on its side. Weeds were growing through the cracks in the concrete. The factory buildings themselves were dark and forbidding, lit only by pale moonlight, the smashed windows leaving shapes in the remaining glass like mountain peaks or silhouettes resembling rabbit ears, running horses and birds in flight.

Further up the street, where there was even less light, she came to the broken playground. Immediately, she saw exactly what Jade meant. The place lay in shadow, in a small gap between two terraces, but she could see that it had once been a playground for young children. The frames for the swings were still there, as was the base for the seesaw, but there no swings and there was no seesaw. The roundabout had tumbled off its hub and lay at an angle like a crashed carousel, and the monkey puzzle was all twisted out of shape.

The house next door was condemned, the front door and all the windows boarded up. Gerry did as Jade had said and slid the board aside. It was a good thing she managed to stay slim, she thought, slipping through. For a split second she felt a surge of fear rush through her and wondered again if Jade was leading her into a trap. But the fear passed as quickly as it had started, leaving her tingling and wary, but determined. Jade had told her who Mimsy was; Jade was scared and needed help.

Gerry entered the house and called Jade's name quietly. 'I'm up here,' came the familiar voice from the top of the stairs.

The house was pitch dark inside, and Gerry used her mobile phone to light her way. She remembered once as a child playing in some empty houses on the edge of the field across from where she lived, but that was usually in daylight. You had to be careful, she remembered, because the stairs were often rotten, the plaster crumbling and laths weakened. In the dark it was so much more difficult to avoid making a misstep.

'Turn the light out,' Jade called down.

Gerry put her mobile in her bag, but not before she had turned on the RECORD function. She knew that she wouldn't be able to remember everything Jade told her, and there was no way she could make notes in the dark. 'Jade?' she whispered. 'Jade? Where are you?'

'I'm up here. The stairs are safe. They creak a lot, but they're safe.'

Gerry made her way carefully up the stairs, her night vision improving as she climbed. Jade was waiting for her at the top. 'Someone might notice a light,' she said. 'There's not supposed to be anybody here. You parked round the corner like I said, didn't you?'

'Yes.'

She led Gerry into what had most likely been one of the bedrooms. 'We'll have to sit on the floor unless you want to stand. It's a bit dirty.'

Gerry sat cross-legged beside her, wondering not for the first time why the hell she had let herself be talked into doing this. But she soon had her answer.

'I'm sorry about all this cloak-and-dagger stuff,' Jade said, 'but I'm really shit scared. They might be watching me. They know I was Mimsy's best friend. I'm sure they don't know about this place, though. And it's not as much of a trap as it looks. There's passages through the attics. You can get to nearly any house in the block and out the back if you hear anyone coming. Mimsy and me used to go exploring.'

'Who are "they"?'

'Did you bring that sarnie?'

Gerry felt around in her bag and brought out the package wrapped in foil. 'Here,' she said, handing it over.

Jade ripped off the foil and took a bite, then spoke with her mouth full. 'What the fuck is this?'

'It's Brie and cucumber,' Gerry said, feeling herself blush. 'On sourdough bread. Sorry, it was all I had. There's an apple, too.'

'Thank heaven for small mercies. Brie and fucking cucumber? *Sour*dough?' She continued to munch away on the sandwich despite the disgust and horror in her tone.

'Who's "they"?' Gerry repeated, determined to regain control of the conversation.

'You must know. Don't you know?'

Gerry couldn't see Jade's expression but gathered from her reply that she was a little surprised by the question. 'We have our suspicions,' she said, 'but as yet we haven't had any confirmation that we're right.'

'Sunny and his mates,' Jade went on. 'There's four of them: Sunny, Faisal, Ismail and Hassan. At least, they're the ringleaders. There's lots of others, all over the place, but those are the main ones here, the ones we knew. They've stopped now, though, now Mimsy's dead. When she disappeared they told us to stay away, lie low and say nothing. Everyone's gone to ground. I think they're still keeping an eye on us, like I said, or they have people to do it for them. Tariq and his pals. That's why I asked you to meet me here. I still have to be careful.'

'Who's "us"? How many of you are there?'

'Seven.' Jade sniffed.

Gerry could hear the sounds of an old empty house, sighs and creaks from tired woodwork. It smelled of urine, dust, crumbled plaster and rotten wood. 'Why didn't you talk to us before?' she said. 'Then Mimsy wouldn't have had to die.'

'I couldn't. None of us could. After a while you just get to thinking there's no way out. You give up. It's easier to do what they say. But then Mimsy got killed and that changed things. She was my best friend,' Jade said in a hushed and trembling voice. 'And they killed her. We didn't know they were going to do that. When it's your best friend, you have to do something, don't you?'

'Who killed her, Jade?'

'They did. The ones I just mentioned. Or their cousins.'

'Why? You'd better explain it all.'

'I don't know why. Mimsy must have got upset about something they did or wanted to do. She had a temper. And there were . . . like certain things . . . things she just wouldn't do. Sometimes you couldn't reason with her. Mostly she was fine, but if something set her off she could be a real pain in the arse. Maybe she even threatened to talk or something. I don't know.'

'Someone gave her ketamine, Jade. That might have had something to do with it.'

'Maybe. K can be nasty stuff. I don't know. All I know is they did it.'

'How did you get into all this?'

'You wouldn't understand,' Jade said, with an edge of contempt in her tone. 'You probably had a normal life – nice parents in a nice house who sent you to a nice school and gave you nice meals and nice clothes. It's not like that for everyone, you know. They were kind, they gave us things, they made us feel like we belonged, told us we were pretty. We chilled with them. It was only later, when we'd gone too far, that things changed. Then there was no way out.'

'How did it all start?'

'Me and Mimsy met Sunny and Faisal down at the takeaway on a school lunchtime. Sunny's the oldest. The ringleader, I suppose. He was friendly. He gave us a free pop and a slice of pizza each and we just, like, chatted. He seemed to understand. He fancied Mimsy, you could tell. No pressure. Not then. Just nice.'

'What did he seem to understand?'

'Us. How we felt about things. What a fuck-up our lives were. How nobody cared about us. How bored and alone we felt. All that stuff.'

'How old were you then?'

'Fourteen.'

'And Sunny?'

'He's old, more than thirty.'

'This happened when?'

'Last summer. I can't remember exactly when.'

So it had been going on for a year, Gerry thought. 'What happened next?'

'Nothing happened, not for a few weeks. We just hung out and talked. Faisal – he's Sunny's best friend, the cook – he was there most of the time, and sometimes Ismail from the minicabs or Hassan from the balti would drop by. We thought they were all our friends, like we'd found somewhere we belonged. We'd have a laugh and chill, get wasted and party.'

'Didn't you think it was a bit strange, these older men spending their time with you?'

'I didn't think about it that way at all. Not at first. It was just somewhere to go, someone we could talk to. Better than those fucking plonkers at school. I think Mimsy was the same. She was a bit nervous at first, but that changed as time went on. Look, I'm not stupid, really I'm not. I thought Faisal really liked me. He was nice. Sometimes we'd go up to Sunny's flat and watch TV. They didn't like to be seen too much with us out in the open. Sunny said it was because people wouldn't understand with them being older and Pakis, like, even though they talk just like us. Sunny's got one of those big flat-screen TVs with surround sound. It was fantastic. I never got to watch anything like that at home. I loved *Strictly* and he'd let me come down and watch it. *X Factor* and *Britain's Got Talent*. I love those programmes. Movies, too. With popcorn. We'd have real drinks, too. Vodka and cider or something. That was when it happened.'

'When you were drunk?'

'I suppose so. I'd had a bit too much, and the next thing I knew Sunny and Mimsy disappeared in one of the bedrooms and Faisal was . . . we were . . . well, it was OK because it was

Faisal and he seemed sweet. I know he was older and all that, but I suppose I thought of him as my boyfriend then. And he was a change from those spotty school kids who were always trying to grope me in the corridors. I mean, he really seemed to *listen* to me. And he made me laugh.'

'Were you attending school at this time?'

'Mostly. Yeah. I mean, I think Mimsy was excluded at the time, but even when she wasn't we wagged it as often as not. But that's where we found them.'

'Who?'

'The other girls. Me and Mimsy would just tell them what a fantastic time we were having and about all the treats and stuff. She could pick out the ones who'd be interested. The ones like me. The ones who were looking for something different. I don't know how, but it was just like she had a nose for it. She wasn't ever wrong. The men called her the Honey Monster because she lured other girls in for them. I think they paid her, and maybe it meant she didn't have to . . . you know . . . do it so much. But it didn't mean she was working for them, like, and happy with it. She didn't have no choice by then. None of us did.'

'It's OK, Jade. I understand.'

'It's just that it sounds bad. I don't want you blaming her or anything, even though she is dead.'

'Don't worry about that.'

'So she brought new girls in. I'd help sometimes. It's not as if there's anything else to do around here except hang out at the shopping mall and get chatted up by schoolboys, or by older married blokes who ought to know better. One night Sunny said they were going to chill at his, and we could bring some of our friends if we wanted. Well, they weren't close friends, or anything like that, just girls we knew at school or from the mall, girls like us, girls who didn't really feel like they fitted in, that didn't belong to any gang or clique. Mostly they were bullied and friendless and grateful to us just for talking to them.'

Lonely, vulnerable, Gerry thought. 'I'll need their names,' she said.

'There was Kirsty, Becca, Mel, Sue and Kath.'

'Their real names?'

'Yes. Only Becca's short for Rebecca, and so on.'

'Surnames?'

'No idea. You can find out from school, though. Or the social. They're all in care, or in foster homes. Will you take care of them? Will you make sure they're all right? They're all scared, too.'

'We'll do our best, Jade.' Gerry was grateful for the recorder app on her mobile. Even thinking about what she was doing made her realise what an idiot she was. She could be jeopardising her career. They should be in an interview room at Eastvale, with DI Cabbot and Detective Superintendent Banks present. But would Jade say what she was saying now, here in the dark, in a brightly lit room with two intimidating adults throwing questions at her? Gerry doubted it. Sometimes you had to bend the rules a little to get a result. 'What happened?'

'Nothing. Nothing at all. We went up to the flat. They played music – our kind of music, you know, not that Middle Eastern shit – and we had lots to eat – Hassan runs the balti restaurant down the Strip, so he'd brought a whole bunch of food, too, so we had curries and stuff as well as pizza and kebabs and burgers, and lots to drink. Vodka, gin, whisky, cider. We danced. We talked. We laughed. We got kaylied. We got silly. Mel puked. That's all. And nobody told us to shut up or fuck off or hit us or told us we were too fat or stupid. Faisal and me had already got together, like Mimsy and Sunny. Ismail hooked up with Becca that night. The girls enjoyed themselves so much they started hanging out with us, mostly at Sunny's.

He's got the nicest flat. The biggest TV and the best music. The guys weren't like creepy or anything, not like the lads at school. I mean, have you seen the lads around here? Most you could hope for from them was lager from a can down by the canal before they put their hand up your skirt. Sunny and his friends are older. Dead mature.'

'And generous?'

'Yeah, I suppose so. At first.'

'But now you're scared of them?'

'Things change.'

'Didn't you think they were a bit old for you?'

'Did you go out with kids your own age when you were young?'

It was the first time anyone had indicated that they felt that Gerry wasn't young, and it was a strange feeling. Of course she would seem old to Jade. 'No, she said. 'I suppose not.' She could have added that there wasn't much choice at her boarding school, and that the choice wasn't only limited in age but also in gender, unless you were foolhardy enough to go for a teacher. But she didn't. Her first real boyfriend, when she was eighteen and at university, had been in his thirties. He had also been a junior lecturer, though at no time was he ever *her* teacher.

'So how did things progress?'

'They treated us good at first, like real ladies. They weren't always groping and fumbling and grabbing your tits.'

'But you did have sex?'

'Oh, yeah. But it wasn't, like, all the time.'

'You enjoyed it?'

'It was OK.'

Gerry thought she heard a sound from the next room and stiffened.

'Rats,' said Jade.

Gerry didn't think she had ever seen a rat, not in the wild, so to speak. She certainly didn't want to start now. 'Was there any conflict between the men you were with and the local boys?' she asked. 'Albert Moffat, Paul Warner and the others? Weren't they jealous?'

'They didn't know. I certainly never told any of them and I'm pretty sure Mimsy didn't. They might have guessed, but I doubt it. We kept a low profile. And we didn't really hang out with lads like Albert and Paul. They were older and they didn't want anything to do with us. I mean, Albert's Mimsy's big brother and Paul's even older than him, so we did see them sometimes in the mall or wherever. They never came down to the Strip. Not their sort of people. They don't like foreigners. Maybe they were too thick to figure out what was happening. I certainly was.'

'In what way?'

'Do I have to spell it out?

'Try, Jade. For me.'

Jade turned silent for a moment, then began hesitantly. 'Well, it was all right at first, like, being Faisal's girlfriend and all that. I thought he really liked me. He'd tell me I was pretty and stuff. Me! I mean, Mimsy was really sexy and all, but me?'

Gerry realised she had no idea what Jade looked like. All she knew was a husky whisper on the telephone and a silhouette in the dark sitting beside her now. She said nothing.

'Sometimes I'd stay at his flat all night,' Jade went on. 'He had a smaller place, like, next door to Sunny's. It was a bit cramped and the wallpaper was peeling, but it was OK. It didn't smell too bad. He even got me a mobile just so he could text me when I was at school and stuff. It was cool. Ismail owned the minicab office next door and we'd go everywhere in taxis, like real ladies. We even went as far as Newcastle once, for a party with some of their mates. Like they'd do anything for us.'

'When did things start to change?'

'Not long. Maybe a month or two since we'd known them. One night I went down and there was just Faisal. It was late, like, after the takeaway had closed. We went up to the flat and there were two other guys there. Faisal said they were cousins of his visiting from Dewsbury. They seemed nice enough. We had a few drinks, like, and I was getting pretty wasted, then Faisal sort of leaned over and said that Namal, that was one of his cousins, liked me. And I could see Namal looking at me and smiling and stuff. And Faisal said it would be nice if I could show him a good time.'

'How did you react to that?'

'I nearly fell off my fucking chair laughing, didn't I?'

'And what did Faisal say?'

'He said it was OK, it was like a family thing. It was the way families did things where he was from and there was nothing wrong with it. They shared. It was a mark of respect. Everyone did it.'

'Did you believe him?'

'How could I know any different? Besides, I was well wasted. I'd been drinking vodka and taking phets. Then Faisal reminded me of all the stuff he'd given us and said it was just a little thing I could do for him, like returning a favour.'

'So what happened?'

'Namal and I went in the bedroom and . . . well . . . you know' She paused for a few moments, being remarkably coy, Gerry thought, given her experiences. Gerry could hear her breathing. 'It was all right at first. It didn't hurt all that much.'

'Then what, Jade?'

'Then the other one, Kerim, he came in . . .'

'You had sex with both of them?'

'Yes.' It was a small voice.

'How did you feel about that?'

'Feel? I don't know what you mean. I didn't *feel* anything. It's life, in'it? You don't get anything for nothing. The day after, Faisal took me shopping in town and bought me some cool trainers. Nikes. Mimsy, too. And Becca, I think. She got a new dress. She must've done something well special.'

'Does that mean they'd performed the same service as you?'

'Maybe. Yeah. I don't know. Maybe he just wanted to include them.'

'Did you tell the other girls what you'd done with Faisal's cousins?'

'Mimsy and I talked about it. That's when she said it had been the same with her. Different blokes, of course. They seem to have a lot of cousins. With her it was some garage owner who'd serviced Ismail's taxis, she said. A service for a service. We just thought it was the way they were, you know. A different sort of culture. Sunny said it wasn't unusual or weird to share where they came from.'

'But they came from Wytherton.'

'You know what I mean. Besides, not all of them did. Faisal wasn't born here. He came over later. Both his parents got killed by suicide bombers. And there were others.'

'Others?'

'It was like some kind of network. I think some of them might have been illegal.'

'Were they all Pakistani, the men?'

'Most of them, but there were one or two white blokes.'

'Here?'

'No. Just all over the north-east and down in West Yorkshire. Mostly Dewsbury. Some in Bradford. Like I said, they were linked up with other blokes and other girls like us.'

'Every night?'

'Most nights.'

'OK. What happened after that time with the two men?'

'After that it got easier. More often. Sometimes Sunny or Faisal needed to pay back a debt or keep someone happy. They'd drive us all over the place. Stockton, Gateshead,

Sunderland, Carlisle. Sometimes we had to stay for days and there were lots of blokes, one after the other.'

'How many men?'

'I dunno. Some nights, you know, like ... you'd stop counting.'

'That must have been unbearable, Jade.'

'I dunno. Maybe it hurts a bit at first, but usually you're so off your face with vodka and weed, or whatever, you don't feel anything.'

'All the girls did this?'

'Eventually. Had to. Yeah.'

'To be with lots of men for sex?'

'Yeah.'

'Always older men?'

'Yeah. Like businessmen and whatever, but some of them were like, you know, more rough, like they worked in factories or garages and stuff.'

'Did Faisal take money from the men you went with?'

'I didn't ever see him do it, but I'm sure he did.'

'So they were pimping you, renting you out as prostitutes?'

'It didn't seem like that.' Jade's voice was a plaintive wail for acceptance. 'It really didn't. They always said how we were welcome to everything they'd given us, and kept on giving us – drinks, food, free taxi rides, jewellery sometimes, mobiles, top-ups, and later some coke and phets and weed. Even money. None of us had, like, jobs, or parents that had any money to give us. Maybe we felt what we did, you know, was like a way of paying for it, doing a favour for a friend. I mean, men wanting sex with me was no big deal. They've been doing it since I was twelve, including my first foster-father and my stepbrother. I didn't get a chance to say no to them, either, and they didn't even *pay* me for it. Didn't even offer me a fucking drink. It was the same with Becca and Kath. And

Mimsy always had older blokes around her wanting a feel or a quick wank. Even her psychological counsellor from the social fucked her and he was supposed to take care of her.'

'Was that your present foster-father who raped you?'

'No. This was in Sunderland. It's better here. They don't touch me at all, not even a pat on the shoulder or a hug.' She snorted. 'They hardly even talk to me.'

'So you were just returning a favour for Faisal?' Gerry said.

'That's right. Favours.'

'Is that why you didn't go to the authorities? The social services or the police?'

'Partly. None of us had had an easy time whenever the polis or the social came on the scene. They were bastards. It was like everyone had just given up on us. We knew they'd just blame us, say we're thick, like retards or something, and we're sluts and whores and we were doing it for the drinks and drugs and free meals. What did they call it? A "lifestyle choice". Some fucking lifestyle.'

'Weren't you doing it for the drugs and drink?'

'You don't know what it was like. At first they just told us not to tell anyone we were hanging out with them because people wouldn't understand. People didn't like them because they were Pakis. But later they could be nasty if you didn't do what they wanted. They'd push you about a bit. Besides, we couldn't tell anyone by then. We'd done stuff. You couldn't get away because they knew everything you'd done, like the drugs and the drinking, and they told us we were just slags and that's all anyone would think if we tried to tell them about what was happening.' Jade sniffed. The silence felt heavy is the dark musty house. 'They'd taken pictures of us, too. You know, videos on their mobiles. With other men and stuff. They said they'd put them on the Internet so everyone would see what kind of sluts we are. They knew how to find out your weaknesses and exploit them. I think Mimsy was terrified of her mother finding out. In the end, like I said, you're in so deep you just get to thinking there's no way out. You give up. It's easier to do what they say. Besides, the presents keep coming. But then Mimsy got killed.'

It seemed odd to Gerry that most of the parents didn't seem to know or care where their daughters were most of the time, or what they were doing, yet Mimsy was terrified of her mother finding out. Things must have been really bad after Sinead found her daughter with that psychological counsellor. 'What were you most afraid of?' she asked.

She could hear Jade breathing fast. 'I don't mind the dark,' she said finally, 'but I can't stand being locked up in a small dark place. They had somewhere like that in the back of Hassan's restaurant, an old larder or something. It smelled of bad meat and rancid grease. I'd get panicky there, like I couldn't breathe, and I'd just want to die. It was like when I was little and they locked me up under the stairs if I misbehaved. My stepmother called it the "Harry Potter Room". It always made her laugh, that.'

Gerry let a few seconds pass in silence. 'But you're talking to me now,' she said.

'Yeah. Well, I mean, they went too far, didn't they? I'd been wanting out for a while, and I thought this is my chance, with Mimsy getting killed and everything falling apart, and I'd better take it. I thought if you knew who they were you could arrest them and put them in jail. And make sure you get their mobiles. And their computers. Smash them all. Then we'll be safe.'

She showed a remarkable amount of faith in what the police could do, Gerry thought, given her obvious intelligence, and the fact that the police hadn't done much for her so far. 'We'll do our best,' she said. 'What about ketamine? Mimsy had been given ketamine.'

'K? Sunny and Faisal didn't like that. It was strictly weed and coke for the most part. They wouldn't have given her it.'

'So who do you think gave it to Mimsy?'

'I don't know. One of the cousins, maybe. They always had different drugs, like E and downers.'

'The same cousins who slept with you?'

'No. Like they all had family in Dewsbury or Bradford or Huddersfield. They called them cousins. I don't know if they were real cousins or not. That's just what we'd call them. It was that network I told you about. They'd visit and we'd chill. Sometimes they'd bring friends.'

'Just you and Mimsy or the other girls, too?'

'The other girls, too. All of us. And the cousins brought girls sometimes. Girls like us from Dewsbury or wherever. They passed us around, drove us all over the place. Then . . . then Mimsy got killed.' Gerry could tell Jade was crying now, rubbing her eyes and nose with the back of her hand. She sniffled.

'Who killed Mimsy, Jade?'

'I don't know. I've told you I don't know. I wasn't there. All I know is that she told me three of Sunny's cousins were coming down from a job in Newcastle on their way back to Dewsbury that evening and they were all going to stop off for something to eat and have a few drinks and chill. They'd made some sort of deal, and Sunny was getting a cut out of it, something to do with bringing booze and fags and migrants over from Calais. I saw him earlier in the day, and he was all excited about it. He wanted Mimsy and me to come over that night and help entertain them. I couldn't go. It was my period, and I got pains something cruel, so I stopped at home in my room. Mimsy went, though. Sunny must have said they could take her to Dewsbury with them in the van to see her mates. Mimsy would have gone for that. She'd made friends with some of the girls who came up with them sometimes, see. They were a laugh. However it happened, Mimsy wouldn't have gone against Sunny. She wouldn't have dared, temper or not. We'd all learned to do what he said by then. His mood could change, like, quicker than anyone's.'

'How do you know it happened that way?'

'I don't. Not for sure. I only . . . I mean, I went in the van once with the some blokes when Faisal asked me to. It was probably the same as with Mimsy.'

Gerry's heart seemed to shrivel in her chest. She almost didn't want to ask any more questions, but she had to push herself on. 'What happened?'

'Not a lot, really. I didn't want to go, but Faisal got really nasty about it. He grabbed my shirt by the neck and shook me and said after all they'd done for us. He didn't hit me, but he said things would get nasty if I didn't do what I was told. Said it was very important. So I went in the van. There was a mattress in the back. A bit old and dirty, but it did the trick.'

'So you had sex with the three men?'

'I don't know if it was the same three Mimsy was with. I stopped in Dewsbury that night and the next day one of them gave me the money to get a train home.'

'So what went wrong with Mimsy's trip?'

'One of them must have given her the K, like you said. It can make you crazy, that stuff. I only tried it once and I'd never touch it again. Maybe she did something to piss them off. She was beautiful and all, but she could be really gobby, could Mimsy, and they didn't like that. She was getting worse and all. She was struggling. She said she wouldn't bring in any more girls. We used to talk about leaving, me and Mimsy. She wanted out, like me, wanted to move on, but she was trapped, just like the rest of us. It was almost like she'd found something else, somewhere else to go, something to do . . . I don't know, but she was different.'

'Did she say anything about this to Sunny?'

'Maybe. Like I said, she had a mouth on her, did Mimsy. She might have told him she wanted out.'

'Could he have told the men in the van to punish her? Teach her a lesson?'

'Maybe. It'd be just like him to get someone else to do it.'

'Jade, what might the men in the van have done that set Mimsy off?'

'They've might've . . . they liked it, you know, from behind.'

Gerry remembered from the post-mortem that Dr Glendenning had found semen in all Mimsy's orifices. 'You mean anal sex?'

'Mimsy didn't like that. I mean, nobody likes it, do they, but she *really* didn't. Even worse than blow jobs. She told me. She said Sunny tried it once and it hurt like hell. It was one thing she'd never do again.'

'And these men liked to do that?'

'The ones I was with did. But like I said, I don't know if it was the same ones.'

'Do you know their names?'

'No. I can't remember. And I mean I *really* can't remember. I don't even remember if I ever knew.'

Gerry paused. She didn't want to give away too much information but felt that if she gave a little she might get more out of Jade. 'As far as we can gather,' she said, 'Mimsy was alive when they threw her out of the van on Bradham Lane. Now, maybe it's as you say and she started acting up, causing trouble when they wanted to do something she didn't like, and they got angry with her and chucked her out naked on the roadside. But she was still alive after that. She walked back up the road. Not very far, but she walked for about ten or fifteen minutes. She was hurt, but she was alive. Then someone else came from the same direction and . . . Well, that was where we found her body. Not where they chucked her out of the van, but where the second vehicle stopped. Who do you think was in that vehicle, Jade?'

'I don't know!' said Jade. 'It could've been Sunny, I suppose, if she'd told him she was leaving. Or one of the others. Faisal. Hassan. Ismail. One of the young lads, even. I mean, Ismail's got all those minicabs. Maybe Sunny told the cousins just to kick her out of the van on a quiet lane when they'd done with her.'

That was a point, Gerry realised. The minicabs. Go over the CCTV footage again – limited as it was to major roads some distance from Bradham Lane – and see if one of Ismail's minicabs had been cruising there at the right time. They hadn't spotted one yet, but it was worth another look. 'But why?' she asked. 'Why kill Mimsy? After all, Sunny was the one who sent her in the van to start with.' Which also meant, Gerry realised, that Sunny knew where she was, who she was with and where she was going.

'If they thought she was going to talk, maybe,' Jade said. 'Like I said, she'd been bitchy a lot lately, mouthy, rebellious, talking back, like she didn't have to do what they said and they should give her a bit more respect. Sunny didn't like that. He was always clocking her one.'

'But you said they didn't care if you talked, that they thought nobody would believe you, that the police or the social would just think you asked for it.'

'They cared if we talked because it would put an end to what they had going. That's all. They weren't worried about getting arrested or going to jail or anything. They told us all that just so we'd know it wouldn't do *us* any good. But it would do *them* some harm. Spoil their nice little party. And it has.'

'Did the police know what was going on? Do you think they helped Sunny and the others, or turned a blind eye?'

'The polis? No way. They hate the Pakis. They're just scared of being called racists.'

'So you never had anything to do with policemen on the Strip?'

'No way.'

'Nobody ever asked you to have sex with them, or anything?'

'Like, yuk, no.'

'OK. So you think Sunny or his mates followed their cousins towards Dewsbury and when Mimsy got kicked out, they killed her?'

'It must've been like that.'

'Maybe,' said Gerry. 'But how did they know the men were going to throw Mimsy out of the van? How did they know she was going to give them so much aggro they'd want to do that?'

'I don't know,' said Jade. 'Maybe they'd arranged it all in advance with Sunny? The route, throwing Mimsy out. I don't know. I've told you what I know. You're the copper, you work it out.'

'Jade, will you come back to Eastvale with me and tell my boss what you've just told me?'

But Gerry could sense Jade stiffening and withdrawing into herself. 'No way,' she said. 'No. It's not safe.'

'But surely it's safer than staying around here? We can help you.'

'As long as they don't know about this I'll be fine. Like I said, they've shut down shop for now, and I know how to keep my head down. I told you, I'm leaving Wytherton for good. Don't worry. It might not seem like it, but I can take care of myself.'

'Where will you go?'

'I've been thinking. I've got a brother fostered out down in Leicester. I don't hardly know him, but it's flesh and blood, isn't it?'

'Yes,' Gerry said. 'You're right about that. It's flesh and blood.'

'Look,' said Jade, 'I'm sorry to ask and all, but I'm in a jam and I don't have any money. Do you think you could let us have a few quid, like for food and the train and stuff?'

Gerry didn't have much, but she examined the contents of her purse with the light from her phone and pulled out three twenty-pound notes. 'Will that do? Is that OK?' She turned off the light again.

'Thanks,' said Jade, and shoved the notes in her jeans pocket. 'You've got to go now.'

'Aren't you coming out with me?'

'I can't risk being seen with you. I'll wait here till you're gone and leave through one of the other houses. I'll be fine. Now go.'

'You've got my number?'

Gerry's eyes had adjusted enough to see Jade nod in the dark, her eyes big and shining in the pale child's face. She hated to leave her like this, but what Jade had said made sense. Jade was too scared to go public with what she knew, but with what she had told Gerry tonight, what Gerry had recorded on her mobile, they could start to take Sunny and his grooming network down first thing in the morning, or perhaps as soon as she got to her car and phoned DI Cabbot. She knew she had broken protocol and the recording might be useless in court, if it ever came to that, but it was enough to get them started, to show them where to look and who to question. Someone would break. It had to be better than nothing. They could have a go at Sunny and Faisal and the others, for a start. Find the other victims, Becca and the rest. Then they could bring the Dewsbury police in on the action. She gave Jade a friendly pat on the shoulder, then got to her feet and made her way down the creaking stairs.

Gerry felt uneasy about leaving Jade alone in the condemned house, even though the girl had far more street smarts than she did. She moved the board aside and slipped through into the deserted road. Somewhere in the distance a dog barked, and she could hear the sound of a television set a bit closer to hand, no doubt blaring through an open window. Not far away, glass smashed, and Gerry realised it was most likely kids playing around in the derelict factory. Fences and barbed wire wouldn't stop them finding a way in for very long. Her car was about a hundred yards away, around the corner past the broken playground. She found herself walking fast, head down, holding on to the strap of her shoulder bag tightly, even though there seemed to be nobody around. It was that kind of street. If she'd been wearing high heels, her footsteps would have clicked on the pavement and echoed, but she was wearing trainers, so she moved silently.

When she turned into the street where her car was parked, she didn't see them at first, but as she approached her little Corsa, four figures – or so she thought – seemed to detach themselves from the shadows into the light and move towards her. Her first thought was to stand and face them down. Surely her warrant card would be protection enough? Then she remembered what had happened to Mimosa, and the things Jade had just told her. Gerry wasn't much of a fighter, but she was a hell of a runner.

So she turned and ran.

She became immediately aware that they were coming after her, and heard one of them yell out, 'Hey, Ginger! Stop, bitch. Tariq, you get the car.' Then she felt a sudden sharp blow high on her shoulder. It almost felled her, and she stumbled and cried out in agony as the pain spread throughout her upper body. She had not thought they were close enough to get her, but one of them had hit her with an iron bar or a baseball bat or some such thing. For a moment, she lost her footing and staggered this way and that, like a newborn lamb, trying desperately to remain on her feet, to keep moving, her centre of balance wavering. If they caught her now she knew she'd be dead.

Somehow, she managed to keep going, get upright and find her footing, her rhythm, again. Now all she had to do was speed up and keep running through the pain that was clouding her vision.

She crossed a main road and still heard them behind her, though she thought they were receding into the distance. She had no idea how many of them were following her. She put on speed again and narrowly dodged a car, felt the draught of it whizzing by. She wasn't sure if it was them or not. Then she zig-zagged through back alleys and narrow streets of grim terraces until she couldn't hear anyone behind her any more. Her shoulder throbbed like hell and her breath came in rasping gasps, but she kept going, round a corner, through a ginnel, even jumping a fence at one point. Her old hurdles coach would have been proud of her, she thought. She was almost certain there was no one behind her now, that she'd lost them, but she wouldn't slow down just yet. She had an idea of where she was, could see another main road ahead at the end of the narrow street she was running on, some shops, cars rushing by. She knew where she wanted to be.

Finally, Gerry crashed through the front doors of Wytherton Police Station and immediately saw three or four officers come to the counter to see what the hell was going on. There was no way she could go any further without the inner door code, but the chase was over. Her pursuers had long since given up. She rested her palms on the counter and took a deep breath. She was aware of the door opening beside her, and just before she fell to the floor, of strong hands grasping her, voices shouting out, and a pain sharp as a knife cutting through her shoulder.

Superintendent Carver arrived about an hour after Gerry, who was wrapped in a blanket drinking her second cup of tea by then. The painkillers from the station's first aid kit had already kicked in. The police doctor had examined her and said her shoulder blade was most likely cracked, but he didn't think it was seriously fractured. He improvised a brace and sling, as Gerry insisted she needed to stay and talk to her boss, then made her promise to go to A & E and get X-rayed as soon as she had done so. She knew he was bending the rules by allowing her a little time, and she was grateful. The police bureaucracy could be touchy about insurance and work injury issues. She had also convinced the duty sergeant to send a patrol car to the old house to try to find Jade, though Gerry felt certain she would be long gone by now.

Superintendent Carver was followed after another half hour or so by Banks and DI Cabbot. Gerry had never been so glad to see anyone before. Friendly faces at last. Well, almost. Carver looked as if he'd just swallowed a dog turd, and even Annie's face seemed hard and unsmiling, but the first thing Banks did was bend over her and ask if she was all right. Gerry could have kissed him. Not that that she fancied him, or anything, but she was just so relieved that someone cared. Whatever kind of idiot he thought she'd behaved like – and she was fast coming to believe that she had been foolish – he was first of all concerned about her welfare.

Carver ushered them into his office, which was a lot messier than Banks's, piled high with reports and bulging file folders, coffee cup rings all over, an array of framed family photographs on the shelf above the filing cabinets. Gerry was amazed to see that the two children pictured, about six and seven, were almost identical to their father. 'So what the bloody hell have you lot been up to on my patch now?' Carver began. He spoke with the pent-up wrath of a man who's been reining himself in for too long already, not to mention dragged out of his bed, and he was clearly upset that Gerry had refused to talk to him until her SIO arrived.

Gerry first played them the recording, then told her story, avoiding Carver's eyes and aiming most of her answers towards Banks, who had assumed an impassive expression.

Annie appeared to be softening, too, asking for a little clarification here and there, as if Gerry were confirming what she had already suspected.

When Gerry had finished her account of the meeting with Jade and subsequent attack by Tariq's crew, everyone remained silent for what seemed like a long time, but was probably only about fifteen seconds. Both Carver and Annie had been taking notes. Gerry had already written out the salient features with her good hand while she had been waiting, while it stayed fresh in her memory. Banks had just listened and absorbed. He hadn't really worked on the case the way Gerry and Annie had – he had his own one to worry about – but he was technically the SIO, and the boss, so she knew that Annie had kept him up to date with developments. She wondered if AC Gervaise knew. If she didn't by now, she would soon. And ACC McLaughlin. Maybe even the chief constable and police commissioner. Christ, she was in trouble. The only thing that could ameliorate her errors at all were a lot of luck and her actions bringing about a quick solution to the case.

'Why did you leave her?' Carver asked. 'For Christ's sake, why didn't you bring her in?'

Just as these words were out of his mouth, the door opened and AC Gervaise and ACC McLaughlin entered. Carver stood to attention and both Banks and Annie got up to greet them. Gerry scanned their expressions for any clue as to her fate but could find nothing.

Well, Gerry thought, she hadn't expected a medal.

'I take it you know who the personnel involved in tonight's fracas are?' Annie asked Carver.

'Some of the players. Sunny, Faisal, Ismail and Hassan are part of the Town Street business association, so we've met once or twice over local issues. Not that I'd say I know them or anything.'

'Course not,' said Annie softly. 'Or anything about their other activities.'

Carver glared at her. 'No.'

'What about the girl, Jade?' Banks asked. He noticed AC Gervaise put her hand on Annie's shoulder and give her a look he assumed to say, 'Cool it.' Protocol had to be followed, Banks realised. Annie couldn't be allowed to blow off her feelings at a senior officer in the presence of the assistant chief constable, however forgiving he might be.

'Could be anyone.' Carver gave Gerry a glance of rebuke. 'It's not as if we have her in custody to check her story.'

'What was I supposed to do?' Gerry said. 'She was scared. She's told me all she knew. She hadn't done anything. She was the victim here, or don't you remember that?'

'That will do, DC Masterson,' said Gervaise.

'Sorry, ma'am,' said Gerry, wrapping herself deeper in the blanket, despite the heat. It was more a matter of comfort than anything else, like the old nightshirt she liked to cling to when she was a child. 'She told me on the phone earlier that Jade's not her real name.'

'Some of them like nicknames, or soap opera names,' said Carver. 'Sadly, not all their parents named them Schuyler, Apple or Chrystal. You say she was involved with Sunny and Faisal and that lot?'

'She said,' Banks corrected him. 'You heard the recording. She was Faisal's girlfriend, and Mimsy was Sunny's. At first. They groomed them and the others and pimped them. They were all underage.'

'That's what she says,' Carver snorted.

'Why?' said Banks. 'Do you think she was lying?'

'All I'm saying is that sometimes these girls know exactly what they're getting into, though they might not want it to appear that way to others.'

'She was fourteen years old when it started, for crying out loud.'

'That doesn't mean a lot round here.'

'It means she's underage and needs to be protected from people like Sunny and his mates.'

'They're troublemakers, all of them. If they were going around having sex with older men for money, it was probably because they wanted to. Nobody forced them.'

'That's a lie,' said Gerry. 'And your men have been protecting the very people who groomed and abused them. Maybe they've been getting a nice bonus out of it all? What were Reg and Bill doing last Tuesday night?'

'That's enough, DC Masterson,' said ACC McLaughlin. 'One more remark like that and I'll have you off the case. Is that clear?'

'Yes, sir,' said Gerry.

'Anyway,' McLaughlin said. 'How do you know the girl didn't set you up? Lead you into a trap?'

'I've thought about that, sir. It just doesn't make sense. If Jade was setting me up, why make them wait until *after* she's spilled the beans before beating me up or whatever they had in mind? She chose the meeting place. Why not tip them off I'd be arriving there so they could intercept me?'

McLaughlin inclined his head. 'Good point,' he said.

'And if you heard the recording, sir, I think you'd realise she's genuine. And she's scared.'

McLaughlin turned to Carver. 'This is a fruitless line of enquiry. There's no point in further questioning the moral character of the girl. Leave that for the courts. Detective Superintendent Banks was right. No matter what her motive, she's underage.'

'And she's been abused,' Annie added.

'Well, what do you expect me to do about it?' Carver asked.

'I wouldn't have expected anything from you,' Annie said, 'but it surprises me you have the gall to ask the question.'

'Don't you dare speak that way to a superior officer!'

'Superior?' Annie sneered. 'That's a laugh. Pull the other one.'

'Enough, I said,' McLaughlin snapped, glaring at both Annie and Gerry. 'I've already told you two. Button it before you find yourselves in even more serious trouble than you are already.'

This time Banks gave Annie the 'calm down' look. She frowned at him, then subsided in her chair and glowered silently at Carver.

'Can we get back to the matter in hand, sir?' Banks said to McLaughlin. 'I apologise for DI Cabbot's behaviour. She's under a lot of strain with this case, as you can imagine. And DC Masterson has just been injured. She has a cracked clavicle.'

'She shouldn't be out following up dangerous leads on her own,' said Carver. 'Without informing me.'

'Oh, shut up, Wilf,' said McLaughlin. 'Save it for later. Right now we've got more important things to do than worrying about covering your arse.'

Carver turned beet red but fell silent.

'Clearly, I need to listen to the complete recording myself,' McLaughlin went on, 'but from what I can gather, we have some serious crimes to deal with here and now and decisive action is required. Given the information and forensics we have so far, I'd say this Sunny and his pals have to be first in line as suspects. Perhaps this Mimsy was going to blow the whistle, and they followed the van with some vague plan in mind. Perhaps it was prearranged that the men in the van would throw her out. We'll need DNA samples to check against the ones Ms Singh took from the victim. As I see it, from what I've heard, there are four actions we should be pursuing immediately. We should be trying to find this girl Jade, we should be bringing Sunny and the rest of his friends in for a serious chat, we should contact West Yorkshire police to locate and bring in the cousins from Dewsbury, and we should be trying to find out who Tariq and the lads who hurt and chased DC Masterson are. In addition, we should also be trying to identify the girls Jade mentioned to DC Masterson and bring them in, too. Bring the school head teacher back from holidays if need be. Or try the social again. But that can wait until tomorrow. And it should be done carefully. They're victims. They're to be treated with respect and gentleness.' He shot Carver a glance. 'It's no good banging their doors down in the middle of the night and dragging them off. Now, seeing as I am of senior rank here and Detective Superintendent Banks is SIO, all that's down to us. As you'll all be busy building cases for the next while, I'll talk to the CPS about charges. I don't know to what extent you want to help, or intend to help, Superintendent Carver. From what I can gather you haven't done a hell of a lot so far except stand in the way of our investigation. I can have men sent in from elsewhere if you're short of personnel—'

'I've already got a patrol car out looking for this Jade,' Carver grunted. 'And I'll see what we can do about Tariq and his mates. I think I know who they are. I suggest your team visit Sunny and the others and take them away with you to Eastvale for questioning. If you can do it discreetly, so much the better. I'm already getting the sense that people here know there's something going on around the estate tonight, and the mood could quickly get nasty. There's also been stories in the press, hints, as I'm sure you know. Links between your victim and the Asian community. Albert Moffat had a few things to say after his interview, it appears. None of this helps. I wouldn't want you to be here when the riots start.'

McLaughlin gave him a hard glance. 'Riots are nothing new to me, Wilf,' he said, 'but I take your point.' He looked towards Banks, Annie and AC Gervaise. 'Are we all agreed?'

They nodded.

'Right, AC Gervaise,' McLaughlin said, 'will you inform Eastvale HQ to make sure the interview rooms are clear and ready as we're expecting some VIP guests in the near future, while I get on to County HQ and request a few reinforcements.'

'I'll get right on it,' said Gervaise.

'And Detective Superintendent Banks and DI Cabbot here can go and wake up this Sunny character. We'll send patrol cars to pick up his mates, just so they don't get a whiff of what's happening and try to scarper.'

'What about me?' said Carver.

'Perhaps you could find out what Reg and Bill *were* doing on Tuesday night?' said McLaughlin. 'And until you do, I'd suggest you keep them off active duty.'

In a way, it wasn't too difficult to be discreet at three o'clock in the morning when Banks and Annie knocked on the door to Sunny's flat beside the kebab and pizza takeaway. At the same time, other teams of two officers were taking in Ismail, Faisal and Hassan. It would have been a lot worse if they had had to use the big red knocker, which lay in the boot of their car. But the door was opened by a dishevelled and curious Sunny, wearing black silk pyjamas, who immediately tried to shut the door again when he saw who was there. It didn't work. Banks already had his foot in and a simple push with his shoulder was all it took.

'What's up, Sunny?' Annie said. 'Expecting someone else? At this time of night? Tariq not reported back yet?'

'I don't know what you're talking about. You can't do this.'

'We're trying to find a girl called Jade,' Banks said. 'And we have reason to believe she might be here.'

'There's nobody else here.'

'Mind if we have a look?' Annie shouldered her way past him and climbed the stairs.

Sunny turned. 'Wait! You can't just—'

But Banks prodded him and started walking up behind him, and he had no choice but to follow Annie or turn and fight. 'It's a missing girl,' Banks explained, 'and we fear she may be in danger. There's also been a serious assault on a police officer. That gives us every right to search for her wherever we see fit.'

'I have rights, too, you know. I want my lawyer.'

'We'll sort that out later. First we need to find out whether she's here and if she's been hurt.'

Annie had switched on all the lights and flooded the place. It was so bright that Sunny shielded his eyes.

'I'll keep our friend company while you have a look around,' Banks said, and gently shoved Sunny down into an armchair. The living room was sparsely decorated, just a few framed prints on the yellow walls, mostly charcoal or watercolour drawings, a large flat-screen TV set and a state-of-the-art stereo system. The smells of the takeaway shop below hung about the place: garlic, stale, cooking oil, old meat. There were stains on the wallpaper, which was coming away from the wall at the ceiling, and on the beige carpet.

'Nice,' said Banks. 'Music fan, are you?'

Sunny didn't reply. Banks flipped through the CDs and found an assortment of eighties to noughties dance compilations – the kind of monotonous machine-generated rhythm tracks you usually find in double jewel-cases on the wall at HMV for £1.99 or thereabouts. There were also a fair number of country and western compilations and CDs, which surprised him. Among the DVDs were several porn titles and a lot of action films, mostly Asian martial arts stuff. Banks had never heard of any of them, but it was easy enough to see what they were from their covers. No Bollywood.

'I'd say your technology exceeds your taste,' he said. 'I'll bet your neighbours love you.'

Sunny just snorted.

Banks picked up one of the dance party CDs. 'This is the sort of music young girls like,' he said. 'Girls who take a bit of E and dance for hours. Girls who don't like Justin Bieber and One Direction.'

Annie came out of the final room, the bathroom. 'Nothing.'

'I told you,' said Sunny, jumping to his feet. 'Now you can go and leave me in peace.'

'Where is she?' Annie asked. 'Where's Jade? What have you done with her?'

'I don't know anything about any Jade.'

'And Mimosa,' Annie said, pushing her face closer to his. 'I don't suppose you know anything about her either, do you?'

'Stop it,' said Sunny, backing away. 'You can't do this to me. This is intimidation, it's—'

'Get dressed, Sunny,' said Banks.

'What?'

'I said get dressed. You're coming with us.'

Sunny sat down and folded his arms. 'You can't make me.'

Banks took Sunny by the arm and cautioned him: '"You do not have to say anything, but it may harm your defence if you do not mention, when questioned, something you later rely on in court. Anything you do say may be given in evidence." Do you understand, Sunny?'

Sunny grunted.

'I take it that's a yes?'

'Yes.'

'Excellent. Now we know where we stand.' Banks led Sunny slowly into the bedroom, which was dominated by a queen-sized bed covered with black silk sheets and black sateen duvet. Even the pillowcases were black. Sunny didn't resist, but he complained all the way, mostly about everything being due to the colour of his skin.

'Just get dressed and stop bellyaching, Sunny.'

Sunny changed into a pair of jeans and a T-shirt. As he did so, Banks poked around the drawers in a desultory way, but found nothing of interest, just a box of condoms and some lubricating jelly in the bedside table. In the wardrobe, however, he found a rack of women's clothing – dresses, tops, skirts. Mimsy's, he guessed. The stuff she wouldn't dare take home. Some of them bore expensive designer labels. On a shoe rack at the bottom were Nike trainers and high heels beside a box of expensive tights and sleek sexy underwear. Agent Provocateur stuff. The search team could do a more thorough job later, when they had a warrant and when Sunny was in custody.

'What's all this, Sunny?' Banks asked. 'Either you get off on wearing women's clothing or this belongs to someone else.'

Sunny said nothing.

'Expecting Mimsy back, are you? Or are they for the next one?'

Sunny fastened the belt on his jeans, still silent.

'They look expensive. I suppose that's why you couldn't bear to part with them, is it? If it had been me, I'd have got rid of them right after I killed the girl.'

'I didn't kill anyone! I want a solicitor,' Sunny said. 'I'm entitled to a solicitor.'

They went back into the living room.

'A solicitor will be assigned to you when we get to the station. Don't worry, Sunny. We'll be doing everything by the book. We don't want you slipping out of our grasp on a technicality over all this, do we? In the meantime, I've already told you that you don't have to say anything. Your solicitor will probably advise you to cooperate with us.'

'How long is this going to take? I have a business to run.'

'We can't guarantee you'll be back in time to open up, especially if you want the lunchtime trade. I'd put a note on the door, if I were you. And make sure you lock up behind you and take your keys and wallet.' He held his hand out. 'We'll be taking the mobile for forensic examination. We'll take good care of all your stuff for you while you're in the cell.'

'Cell?' said Sunny, handing over his mobile.

'That's what usually happens when we take people into custody. Annie?' Banks had noticed that Annie was standing by the wall studying the drawings. He knew her father was an artist and that she had grown up in an artists' colony in Cornwall – she even painted, herself – but this was hardly the time. 'Come on. We have to go.'

'Just a minute,' she said, pointing to a drawing of two elderly Asian men standing on a street corner talking. 'What do you think of this?'

'Very nice. Now, come on.'

'It's one of Mimsy's.'

'What?'

'Mimosa Moffat. She happened to be a very accomplished artist – at drawings and sketches, anyway. I had a good look at her work in her room on Southam Terrace, and I'm telling you, this is hers.'

Banks turned to Sunny, who just shrugged. Annie took out her mobile and took photographs of all the artwork. 'I'll let the search team know we'd like them all bagged,' she said. 'They'll probably have her prints on them somewhere. I'm not an expert, I admit, but anyone who'd seen her work before would recognise it immediately.'

'I'll take your word for it,' said Banks. 'Now, come on, Sunny, hurry up, your car's waiting.'

Sunny hurriedly wrote out a notice to stick on the door of the takeaway, then picked up his jacket and checked the pockets for his essentials. Annie put the handcuffs on him, and she and Banks sandwiched him on the way down the stairs. Out in the street, the neons and sodium lights looked fuzzy in the heat haze. Next door, Banks saw two uniformed officers putting

Ismail and Faisal in a patrol car to deliver them to Eastvale. A small crowd had gathered across the street, even at such a late hour. The police had been as discreet as they could, but there was no doubt word was getting around. The feeling of tension in the air was as palpable as the heat and Banks was glad to get in the back of the car with Sunny and let Annie drive to Eastvale.

12

One by one, the team straggled into the boardroom on Thursday morning. It had been a long night for all concerned, and Annie had only managed about two hours' sleep between leaving Wytherton with Banks and Sunny and coming in to Eastvale HQ for the meeting. Gerry was still in the infirmary, resting. The police doctor had been right: a nasty crack but not an outright break. They'd probably let her out later today, the doctor had told Annie when she phoned earlier, but she would have to remain on light duties for a while until her clavicle healed.

The Wytherton police had done their job and swooped on all the other suspects while Banks and Annie were bringing in Sunny. Now Sunny, Faisal, Ismail and Hassan were all in custody, waiting to be interviewed. DNA samples had been taken and Jazz Singh had promised as quick a result as possible. The scientific process of extracting DNA didn't take long, and any wait was usually due to long queues at the labs. With Jazz on the job already they wouldn't have to worry in this case. Samples had also been taken from the cousins in Dewsbury to match against those removed from Mimosa's body. Annie was raring to have a go at Sunny, who was already in an interview room under guard, stewing until the team meeting was over. Things had been moving very fast that morning. Two of the other girls groomed by Sunny and his gang – Kirsty McVie and Rebecca Bramley – had already been identified by the school secretary, whom the locals had roused from her bed, and briefly questioned. They were scared, but they knew what had happened to Mimsy, and when they were told that Jade had told her story to the police and disappeared, it didn't take them long to talk. They all named the same crew and said Sunny had told them to lie low until things calmed down.

Today, search teams would go through all the flats and houses concerned, and plain-clothes officers from both Wytherton and Eastvale would try to find the other girls and persuade them to talk. They were dealing with victims, Banks had reminded the assembled officers, and the girls may have been convinced to see themselves as society's rejects, but they were to be treated with the utmost respect and sensitivity. If at all possible, he had added, each should be assigned a personal female liaison officer.

Superintendent Carver had grudgingly looked into Reg and Bill's alibi for the Tuesday of Mimsy's murder and found that Reg was at home with his family and Bill was moonlighting on a film set in Stockton, along with plenty of witnesses. It seemed to let them off the hook, though Annie had let it be known that she thought they were involved in some way, if only for wilful ignorance.

The three cousins of Sunny from Dewsbury had been quickly identified and taken into custody by the West Yorkshire Police, to whom they were already well known. A white van belonging to one of them was being sent up to the police forensics garage in Eastvale for testing. According to the local police, there was a dirty, stained mattress in the back, and several of Mimosa's personal items, including her mobile and her shoulder bag, were soon found hidden in the house of one of the suspects.

The search was still going on for Jade who, according to the school secretary, was really called Carol Fisher, but nothing had been seen of her so far. At least they had now managed to get a photograph from her foster parents. Gerry had tipped them off about the brother in Leicester, and the police down there said they'd keep an eye on his place.

Already, according to a phone call from Superintendent Carver in Wytherton, mobs were gathering on the estate, the shopping centre and the Strip. Bricks had been thrown, shop windows smashed, a few scuffles had taken place. One young white youth had already been taken off to hospital with blood streaming down his face after he and several cronies had mounted an assault on the mosque. The riot police were trying to keep a lid on it rather than exacerbate things, but it was getting more and more out of control as more people joined the various mobs, and he wanted reinforcements. The tabloid headlines showed a grieving Moffat family on the doorstep of their Southam Terrace house under the bold headline: THEY MURDERED OUR LITTLE ANGEL MIMOSA. Beside the story were three small head-and-shoulders photographs of Middle Eastern men, looking like police mugshots, but connected with a different story entirely. It was just a clever juxtaposition, a journalistic ploy. Adrian Moss would be over the moon, Annie thought.

Winsome and Doug Wilson were about the only ones who appeared well rested, and even Wilson had probably been up half the night going through CCTV footage with the rest of his team. Though they shouldn't call it footage, Annie thought, as it was mostly digital. *Byteage,* perhaps? Jazz Singh and Stefan Nowak were fresh, too, though they had also been working unusually long hours and had started early that morning. AC Gervaise had managed to go home for a quick shower and change, but Annie could see the dark shadows under her eyes, and her lipstick was smeared a little unevenly over her Cupid's bow lips. ACC McLaughlin, having authorised the whole business and set things in motion, had gone home to bed. Banks had also gone home to get some sleep, but he had promised to partner Annie on the interview with Sunny later that morning.

Everyone took their seats. Before they could even get started, Annie's mobile buzzed. She apologised and went outside and answered the call. It was DC Masterson in the hospital.

'What is it, Gerry?' she said. 'You should be resting.'

'I am,' Gerry said. 'They gave me some more pills for the pain along with a sedative to help me sleep. It's really quite pleasant. Now I know why junkies do what they do.'

'What's so important?'

'It might not be important, but I've remembered something. From last night.'

'Hurry up. We're just about to get started with the meeting.'

'Can you put me on speakerphone so I can participate?'

'Gerry, you're trying my patience.'

'Yes, guv. Well, as I said, it may not be important, but just before they hit me and started chasing me, one of the gang, the one who called out to Tariq, called me "Ginger", among other things.'

'Without meaning anything negative, Gerry, that's a perfectly natural thing to call you, under the circumstances.'

'I'm not denying the colour of my hair, guv, but I am wondering how he knew. It was dark out there on the street, where we were, and as far as I know he'd never seen me before. It was like a derelict edge of the estate, opposite an abandoned factory, and most of the streetlights were broken. You'd have to have superhuman vision to see the colour of a person's hair.'

'We didn't imagine it was a random attack on a lone female,' Annie said. 'But if he couldn't see your hair in the dark, how did he know to call you Ginger?'

'I think Sunny must have told him about us, our visit to the takeaway, maybe told them to keep an eye out for us. Jade mentioned that Sunny and the others had some young lads on the estate who'd do legwork for them. Maybe they do a bit of enforcing, too.'

'That still doesn't explain how they knew it was you.'

'I would imagine Sunny described us both, told them I was the tall skinny one with long ginger hair.'

'And what does that make me?' asked Annie. 'The short dumpy one with curly brown hair?'

'No, ma'am . . . I . . . I didn't . . .'

'Sorry, Gerry. It's OK. Go on. How did they know where you were?'

'I don't think they did, or they'd have probably come into the house after Jade. They could see my hair was long and that I was tall and thin. They were waiting by the car. It was the only one on the street. Maybe they were planning on boosting it when I came along, or maybe Sunny had seen it and described it to them. I suppose it's pretty conspicuous. I don't know. But don't you see? If Sunny had them on the lookout for us, that makes it even less likely that Jade set me up. She'd never even seen me, as far as I know – we'd only talked on the phone – and it was pitch black in the house, even when my eyes adjusted to the dark. All I could see was outlines, silhouettes. It's my theory that they were on patrol, maybe looking for Jade under Sunny's instructions, looking for anything out of the ordinary.'

'Excellent,' said Annie. 'If that's true, it gives us a stronger possible connection between Sunny and Tariq and the rest. I'll bring it up in the interview. Now get some rest Gerry.'

'But, guv, can't I be in on inter—'

'No. Rest, DC Masterson. It's an order.' Annie ended the call and returned to the meeting. 'Another link in the chain,' she said. 'This one possibly connecting Sunny to the attack on DC Masterson.'

Jazz and Stefan had nothing new to report yet, so Annie stood by the whiteboard, making the occasional notation, and

went on to fill everyone in about the events of the previous
night, making it as succinct as possible, but trying not to omit
any of the essential points. 'That means there'll be plenty of
TIES and actions flying around after this meeting, so catch
what you can. It's going to be another long day. Doug, have
you got anything for us on the second car on Bradham Lane
that night?'

'Nothing we can confirm, guv,' said DC Doug Wilson,
rubbing his hand over his unruly hair. 'Mostly it's been a
process of elimination. As I said before, I think we've got the
first van, but we can't get a licence plate number from it, and
there are no markings. It's a dirty white van, that's all, and we
think it could be the one that the girl was thrown from.'

'Mimosa,' said Annie. 'And the van's been found. It's on its
way. Is that all?'

'Not quite. We did find a VW Transporter that more or less
matched the time parameters and the directions we were looking at.'

'And?'

'It belongs to a bloke called Jim Nuttall. Lives out Stockton
way.'

'And what has Mr Nuttall been up to?'

'Nothing, it seems. Honest businessman. No form.'

'So what is it about Jim Nuttall that gives you pause for
thought?'

'It seems he lied, guv.'

'Lied about what?'

'What he was doing. When I talked to him a couple of days
ago, he admitted he'd been out in the van that night. He runs
a spare parts service. Specialist bits and pieces for old bang-
ers, antiques and so on, and he makes the deliveries himself to
save on overheads. Admits it's nothing that'll ever make him
rich, but he enjoys his work. He said he had a delivery to make
to a regular customer in Southampton, and he was used to

night-driving, actually liked it, so whenever he went down there he drove by night. Less traffic.'

'And?'

'Only I remembered to check with the customer in Southampton, and it was actually two days earlier that Mr Nuttall made the delivery. He'd got the dates wrong.'

'So, on the night in question, a week last Tuesday, his van was captured on CCTV travelling the route we're interested in, but he had no reason to be there?'

'That's about the long and the short of it, guv.'

'Then either he's lying or he got muddled up and made a mistake. Well done, Doug. Good catch.'

Wilson adjusted his glasses. 'Thanks, guv.'

'We'll pay him a visit later this morning.'

There was nothing else new, so Annie started issuing actions and TIES, and when the room emptied, leaving her alone with the gilt-framed photos of the wool barons who made Eastvale, she allowed herself to slump in her chair, close her eyes for a moment and cover them with her hands. But her mind was still humming with the adrenalin of the night. There was no way it was going to allow her a nap. Instead, she headed for the canteen to get a large mug of coffee before heading for the squad room to prepare the interview and wait for Banks.

Excerpt from Linda Palmer's Memoir

Let me tell you about my best friend Melanie. Her full name was Melanie Vernon, and she died of breast cancer two years ago. I know I'm jumping way ahead now, and maybe it's nothing to do with what you want to know, but her early death hit me hard and brought back a lot of memories from that Blackpool holiday, the only holiday we ever shared. And it tells you something of the cost to me of what happened. We hadn't been in touch often over the years, but we had met up on a few occasions for drinks and dinner and we always had a good laugh. She was flabbergasted that I had become a 'poet' and confessed that poetry was like a foreign language to her. In turn, I was surprised to find that she had married a local electrician's apprentice while I was at university and had two children in quick succession, then two more, never pursuing a career of her own. Secretly, I had always expected Melanie to become a model or an actress. She was attractive, no doubt about it. People said we both were, and we made quite a contrast. Back then she had wavy dark hair and looked a bit Italian, with almond brown eyes and the smoothest olive complexion I had ever seen. Chemo took care of the hair, eventually, her skin turned into cracked parchment and her beautiful eyes became red-rimmed, hollowed and frightened, underlined with shadows like bruises. The last time I got seriously drunk and cried was at her funeral. Her husband read Christina Rossetti's 'Remember' and that just did me in like a gut punch. Do you know it? You probably haven't got to the late nineteenth century yet unless you've cheated. It ends:

> For if the darkness and corruption leave
> A vestige of the thoughts that once I had,
> Better by far you should forget and smile
> Than that you should remember and be sad.

But we do remember, and we are sad. As another poet said, 'Every man's death diminishes me.' Sorry about that flight of fancy, but it's what I do.

After Melanie died, I wished so much that I had told her what happened to me on that holiday right then and there. Not telling her meant the end of something. The secret stood between us from then on like a wall. After that holiday, we were never as close as we used to be, and we drifted apart. I regret that. It was only later, when we were grown-ups, that we could tentatively breach the wall, but we were never as close as we had been that summer. We were never so innocent again, either.

Melanie's father worked in a bookie's office, and her mother was a housewife, like mine. I think my mother always looked down on Mr Vernon a bit because of his job. She wasn't a gambler, and if pushed she would probably say she thought gambling was a sin. Or at least a particularly low form of vice. But Mr Vernon and my father had something in common. Both were white-collar workers, and therefore scoffed at by some of the rougher factory workers who lived on our estate, who thought of themselves as real men doing real men's work. They were the true working class, while we were the soft underbelly of the middle class. Back then most people actually had jobs, and it wasn't being on benefits that defined your class, but the sort of work you did. My father worked in an office as a shipping clerk. It was a menial job, as was Mr Vernon's – all he did was fill in forms all day, and was paid a pittance for it – but they had to wear a suit and tie to work instead of dirty overalls, so lots of the locals thought them posh and stuck-up without even knowing them.

In some ways, Melanie seemed so much more mature than me. Her breasts were bigger, for a start, and had started to develop by that holiday. Mine had hardly grown much at all, and it had been like squeezing the water out of a lump of granite trying to get my mother to buy me my first bra. Finally, she relented, but only because I put on a tight, slightly damp T-shirt and pinched my nipples to go out one day, making sure I went into the kitchen to say goodbye, though I didn't usually. It worked. Breasts or no breasts, there was no going out without wearing a bra for me after that.

But Melanie had real breasts. You would have liked Melanie's breasts. Most men did. I saw them that week in Blackpool because we had to dress and undress together in the same room. They weren't huge or anything, but hillocks compared to my pathetic little drumlins. Firm little hillocks. Don't get me wrong. We weren't lesbians or anything like that; you just notice things like breasts and pubic hair when you're reaching puberty. I should imagine boys were the same comparing penis size. When I think of what happened, the cancer eating away at them and spreading to her lymph nodes, her liver, I still can't help but cry. One of her children, Carolyn, is an English teacher. We met at the funeral, and she visits me sometimes to chat about poetry and drink wine. Sometimes when I look at her, I think she's the spitting image of Melanie.

So in Blackpool that summer, it was going to be the terrible two. The whole town was at our feet, and we were set to grab what we could. Including boys. Melanie was more sophisticated about the opposite sex than I was. She had told me about her last boyfriend, who had tried to tit her up when she was babysitting for Mr and Mrs Delaware down the street. She said she moved his hand away gently, but she remembered that it felt nice and sent a shiver right through her. Perhaps next time, she had thought, she would let him touch her there, but he lost patience and moved on to Sally Hargreaves, who had a reputation for doing it with anyone, even though she wasn't as beautiful as Melanie. People like Sally Hargreaves excepted, it was an age when good girls mostly didn't. And we were good girls. We knew some girls who did. Sally had to leave school and we all knew why. We also knew you shouldn't give in to boys, or they'd look down on you and tell their friends what you let them do to you. Then you became a slut. Or worse, you'd get pregnant and have to get married. You had to save yourself, we believed, preferably till marriage, of course, but failing that, at least until you were genuinely in love.

I wasn't sure whether I was willing to go as far as letting a boy touch my breasts as I had only done a bit of French kissing so far and wasn't even sure I liked the feel of a tongue in my mouth, but I was keen for new experiences and we certainly intended to team up with some likely lads and get them to take us on rides at the Pleasure Beach. It wasn't as expensive then, and you didn't have to pay to get in. A kiss on the Big Dipper, perhaps, or the Ghost Train. Now that might be fun, especially when the spider webs brush across your cheek in the dark and a phosphorus skeleton jumps out of nowhere right beside you. Or in the funhouse, where all the paths are constantly changing angles and direction and you see yourself in distorting mirrors.

I remember we did meet two boys from Doncaster in the Coffee Cellar one morning and they wanted to walk on the beach with us after dark. The first night we went to the Pleasure Beach with them and went on a few rides and ate some candyfloss but we wouldn't walk on the beach with them. We arranged to meet them the next day. After we'd been to the funfair we walked with them across the prom. It was a lovely evening, I remember, and the sun was setting out on the Irish Sea, the waves rolling in, but there was still a broad enough swathe of beach to walk on.

I took my sandals off and felt the warm, moist sand under my feet, digging my toes in as we walked. He – I can't remember his name – took hold of my hand at some point and I let him. It felt nice. Melanie's boy already had his arm around her. We just walked like that and soon we came to one of the piers – I can't remember which one – and I remember it surprised me to see two or three courting couples under there leaning against the pillars or the base of the sea wall and kissing or perhaps even more. We sat on some rocks under the pier and he kissed me. It was a gentle kiss, I remember, not a thrusting probing one. He never tried to touch my breasts or anything. A real gentleman. Melanie told me she felt her boy's penis pressing hard against her tummy as they kissed but I don't remember anything like that. It was a sweet kiss, a soft kiss, and the last good kiss I remember having for a very long time. We arranged to meet in two days at the same spot, by the Laughing Policeman, but it was too late by then.

Sunny was still sulking in the interview room when Banks and Annie joined him, along with his legal aid solicitor, Haroon Malik, later that morning. Sunny had been allowed to consult with the lawyer earlier, but it remained to be seen what his position would be when they started to question him. There was going to be no good cop, bad cop, Banks and Annie had decided. Just two cops.

They arranged their papers on the table, went through the formalities of setting the recorder going, and informed Sunny that the interview would also be filmed. He didn't seem to care. He was hunched down in his chair, a slight figure, hardly the sort of man you'd expect to play such a cruel and despotic role over a number of young girls in his thrall. But appearances could be deceptive.

The room was hot and stuffy, and Haroon Malik requested fresh air. There were no windows to open, and no air conditioning, so Banks sent for a fan, which slowly swivelled back and forth on a shelf throughout the interview, making an irritating clicking sound every time it reached the end of its arc and started to swing back. But at least it stirred up the warm air a bit. Sunny asked if he could smoke, but Banks said no, and pointed to the sign on the back of the door. He loosened his tie before starting.

'OK, Sunny,' he said. 'You know why you're here.'

Sunny folded his arms. 'No, I don't. I've done nothing wrong. This is racial persecution.'

'Did you know a girl called Mimosa Moffat?'

'No comment.'

'Jade? Carol Fisher?'

'No comment.'

'Kirsty McVie, Rebecca Bramley, Melissa Sandbrook, Susan Williams and Kathleen Nielson?'

'No comment.'

'They are all girls between the ages of thirteen and fifteen, and we have information that you used them for sex and for purposes of prostitution. Do you have anything to say to that?'

'No comment.'

'Is this going to be a no-comment interview?' Annie asked.

'No comment.'

Haroon Malik had a brief word in his client's ear.

'Did Mimosa Moffat leave your flat on the night of Tuesday, the twenty-first of July with three men, cousins of yours from Dewsbury, in a white van?' Banks asked.

'No.'

Banks cupped his hand to his ear. 'Sorry. Was that "no", or the beginning of another "no comment"?'

'The answer's no. I don't know no Mimosa whatshername, and she didn't leave my flat in a van.'

'I think you're lying,' said Annie. 'What were Mimosa's drawings doing on your wall?'

'I bought them down the market. I don't know who drew them, did I?'

'Do you know a young man named Tariq Jinnah?'

'No.'

'We think he and some of his mates attacked one of our female officers near the corner of Leinster and Mill Street last night. She's suffering from a cracked clavicle.'

'Tough for her,' said Sunny. 'I don't know him.'

'Again,' said Annie. 'We think you do. We think you'd told him and his mates to keep an eye out for both her and me after we visited your takeaway. She's "Ginger". Rattled you, did it, that comment about the DNA? Stop lying, Sunny. It won't do you any good in the long run.'

'No comment.'

Banks shuffled his papers. 'We have statements from three of the girls already who claim that you seduced them first with presents – cigarettes, drink and drugs, mobile phones and top-ups, food and free taxi rides specifically – had sex with them, then threatened them with violence and used them for the purposes of prostitution, telling them it was payback time, actually using violence against them if they dared to refuse. What do you say to that?'

'No comment.'

'There'll be evidence of their presence in your flat, you know. It's being thoroughly searched right now. It'll be a lot worse for you if it turns out you've been lying to us about knowing them.'

Sunny half rose from his chair and grabbed the edges of the table. 'What's that you say? They're in my flat? Now? But I gave no permission.'

'You don't have to, Sunny. We have a judge's warrant. It's perfectly legal. Your solicitor will tell you.'

Haroon Malik asked for a moment alone with his client, and Banks and Annie paused the recording equipment and left the room. When they came back and resumed, Sunny seemed more relaxed. Sometimes interviews went this way, Annie reflected. The suspect lied and denied everything up to a point, then decided that a slightly sanitised version of the truth might be more acceptable. Next thing, maybe Sunny would be wanting to make a deal.

'The girls whose statements we have are all under the age of consent,' said Banks. 'What do you say to that?'

'How would I know what age they arc? They all look the same to me.'

'I take it by that you've decided to admit you *do* know the girls, but you're claiming you didn't know how young they were. Am I right?'

'That's right. Can I help it if girls like me? Think I'm hand-some. And there was no prostitution. These girls like to party. You don't have to pay them.'

'Now we're getting somewhere. But I thought it was you who got paid?'

'There's no call for that. And I want to make it perfectly clear that I had nothing – nothing at all – to do with Mimsy's death.'

'But you did know her, and the details of her death?'

'Yes. Of course. I read the papers.' He gave Annie a scathing glance. 'And that one came round the takeaway along with her friend and tried to fool us into believing they could tie our food to her stomach contents. No way.'

'No way she's had your food, or no way we could tie it to your takeaway?'

'I googled it. It's not possible. Scientifically. So you've got nothing on me.'

'Why did you google it?' Annie asked.

'What?'

'About the stomach contents. Why did you google it?'

'I was curious.'

'Sure you weren't worried?'

'I have nothing to be worried about.'

'But you admit you were lying a few minutes ago when you denied all knowledge of these girls?'

Sunny looked down at his hands on the desk. 'Yes. All right. I thought you were going to blame me for something I didn't do just because of the colour of my skin.'

'And now?'

Sunny turned to Haroon Malik. 'I know I didn't do anything wrong, so I've nothing to fear. I have no reason to lie.'

'Good decision, Sunny,' said Banks. 'Maybe we don't have any forensic evidence. Yet. But we do have plenty of witnesses and victims who are willing to testify against you and your friends. Your girls are starting to talk, Sunny. What you did to Mimosa has got them really upset with you. Some of them claim you beat them up if they refused to go with men you brought to the flat. They want us to put you and your friends in jail so they can get on with their lives.'

'I didn't kill Mimsy. Why would I do that? And our girl-friends were all well treated. Better than they deserved. Do you think I don't know what's going on?'

'Enlighten me, Sunny,' said Annie.

'They're trying to paint a different picture. Nobody got raped or beaten. And we didn't know anything about the girls being underage. Far as we knew, they were all willing to do everything they did. More than willing. They liked to party. We partied with them.'

'Did you supply them with drink and drugs?'

'You have a drink at a party, don't you? It's only natural.'

'So you're not a practising Muslim, then?'

'I never said I was, did I? What's that got to do with anything? That stuff's got nothing to do with me. I'm British, I am. I was born here. My father was born here.'

'No one's saying you're not British, Sunny, just that you tend to be a bit less so when it suits you. Like earlier.'

'What do you mean?'

'What Americans call the race card.'

'I don't expect no special treatment because I'm brown.'

'But that's just it, Sunny. You do. When you think you can get it. You seem to think being of Pakistani origin exempts you from the rules the rest of us have to play by. And it works the other way. Whenever we call you on anything, you'll call foul and say it's because you're of Pakistani origin, saying we're out to get you because of the colour of your skin.'

'Well, that's what it feels like. You've no idea what it's like. You'd have to be me to understand.' He tapped the centre of his chest. 'My dad told me that when he was a kid, people used to say we lived ten in a room and ate Kit-e-Kat by choice. Like we were animals or something. But we had a culture. We had a religion. We had morals. You see these young white girls today in their short skirts and torn stockings, looking like prostitutes, talking and swearing like they do, the language they use, drinking in the street, having sex whenever they feel like it, taking drugs. They're just rubbish. If any of our daughters behaved like that, we'd kill them.'

'Well, that's another issue, and not one that concerns us here. All we're interested in is whether you killed Mimsy.'

'I didn't.'

'So you say. There must have been something about the girls you liked, no matter that you say they were rubbish, seeing as you spent so much time with them. Let's get back to the parties, Sunny. Especially the young girls.'

'They were all up for it. We didn't make nobody do anything they didn't want.'

'That's a matter of opinion.'

'It's you lot who let them run wild in the first place. Where are their parents when they're out drinking and taking drugs and having sex till all hours? When they come to us, they're already fully trained sluts. We don't have to force them to do anything. And there were no drugs involved.'

'Two of the girls are cocaine addicts,' Annie said. 'Susan and Kathleen. And Mimosa was on ketamine the night she was raped and killed.'

'I don't know anything about no ketamine.'

'Isn't it true that Mimosa wanted to leave your little group? Isn't it true she wanted her own life back? Maybe she had somewhere to go, had found someone else? She wanted her freedom.'

'She was free to go whenever and wherever she wanted.'

'Where's Jade, Sunny? Where's Carol Fisher?'

'How should I know? And it's not my fault if they make a bad lifestyle choice and take drugs.'

'It is if you supplied them, got them hooked in the first place.'

'I told you. No drugs.'

'So our men won't find anything incriminating in your flat?'

'They will find nothing.'

'Very well,' said Annie. 'Now you've decided to tell the truth, Sunny, what about Tariq Jinnah?'

'What about him?'

'Was he one of your drug connections?'

'I don't know what you're talking about. I knew Tariq slightly, yes, from the community centre. He bought food from my restaurant sometimes. That's all.'

'Come on, Sunny. We think he was one of the people responsible for the attack on one of my officers. A female, alone, four men.'

Sunny spread his hands. 'What can I say. They're hotheads, Tariq and his friends. Young people today. That's why I have little to do with them. They do odd jobs for me, that's all. They have their own businesses going on, and I suppose they wanted to scare the police away.'

'Well, they went the right way about it, didn't they?'

'As I said. They are hotheads. Young and foolhardy.'

'They not only knew that she was a police officer, but they also knew what she looked like, even down to the colour of her hair in the pitch dark,' Annie said. 'As far as I know, you, Faisal and Ismail were the only ones we talked to on the Strip. Not Tariq or his friends. Did you describe us to them?'

'I might have mentioned something,' Sunny mumbled.

'Now we're getting somewhere.'

'But I didn't tell them to do anything. Just, you know, keep an eye out, scare you off if you came around asking questions.'

'Why did you want us scared off? What were you afraid we'd find out?'

'Nothing. We just like to be left alone. Most cops aren't interested in what goes on around here, anyway. They don't bother us.'

'Bother you doing what?'

'Just living our lives, you know.'

'So you admit you set Tariq and his mates the task of keeping an eye open for me and "Ginger"?'

Sunny nodded.

'How did it work?'

'They were driving around the estate and Tariq saw a green Corsa.'

'You knew that DC Masterson drove such a car?'

'I saw you and her drive away in it the other night.'

'So what did Tariq do?'

'He rang me, and I told him to wait there until you came back. Just to stand around the car, you know, but not to do anything.'

'A warning?'

'Sort of.'

'And that's all?'

'That's all. Nothing more. They have their own interests to protect. I'm not responsible for them or their actions. I suggest you talk to them about it.'

'We will,' said Banks. 'No worry. We'll have them in custody, too, soon. Anyway, we'll get back to that later. For the moment, perhaps you can tell us what happened that Tuesday night, when Mimsy got into the van?'

'It was no different from usual. I had some cousins dropping by, and they offered to give Mimsy a lift. She wanted to see her girlfriends in Dewsbury. That's all.'

'Are you sure that's the only reason she went with them in the van?'

'Yes, of course.'

'The three men had sex with her, Sunny.'

'So? That's her business. I wasn't there.'

'I think it's yours. I think you asked the men to punish her for being disobedient, for wanting to leave.'

'No way.'

Banks rifled through his papers. 'Zahid Bhatti, Younis Qazi and Masood Chaudhri. Do those names mean anything to you?'

Sunny's jaw dropped, and his eyes opened wide. 'How did you . . .?'

'Police work, Sunny. Good old police work. Well, do you know them?'

Sunny swallowed and nodded.

'That's good,' said Banks. 'They'll be here soon, when West Yorkshire are through with them, and they seem willing to help us with our enquiries. I have to say, they leave a lot to be desired when it comes to getting rid of the evidence.'

'Look,' said Sunny, a pleading tone coming into his voice. 'You have to understand how it is with us. Our culture. Things are different.'

'You're doing it again, aren't you?' said Annie.

'What?'

'That race card thing. Go on. Tell us how you're different, then.'

'We owed them one, right? The cousins. And she was it. Mimsy. They took a fancy to her. Girls are a kind of currency. There's an exchange rate, and it keeps changing. Some days it's in your favour, and some days it's not. We were repaying a debt, that's all it was. There was no punishment.'

'That's an interesting cultural difference,' said Annie. Glancing at Banks. 'We'll have to remember to take it up with PC Jawanda back at the police station, but I think I know what he'll tell me.'

'What?'

'That it's a load of bollocks. That every culture, every ethnic group, has its bad elements, its rotten apples, its psychos and sexual predators. I know mine does. I suspect that yours is no different.'

Sunny scowled. 'Nobody assaulted her. She was up for it, right enough.'

'How do you know that? You said you weren't there.'

'Zahid told me.'

'You've talked with your cousins since the incident?'

'Sure. They're family. We talk on the telephone often.'

'Of course she was "up for it",' Annie cut in. 'She had enough ketamine in her to fell a horse.'

'If she did, I don't know where she got that. It's nothing to do with me.'

'Maybe your cousins supplied it?' Banks suggested.

'I don't know.'

'What did Zahid tell you happened?'

'She got a bit frisky, like. My cousins are only human. It was like pass the parcel, that's all. They didn't kill anyone. They just fucked her. Then all they did was throw her out of the van. It was just a bit of fun.'

'So your cousins admitted to throwing Mimsy out of the van?'

'Yeah. But it was just for a laugh. She was just a silly little white slut. It was a bit of fun.'

'Fun?' Annie said. 'Fun? Throwing a young girl out of a moving van naked and stoned in the middle of the night in the middle of nowhere. That's your idea of fun?'

'They slowed down. They told me they slowed down. She wasn't hurt when she left the van. And it was a warm night.'

'How did you feel about that?'

'I don't know. I wasn't there. It was nothing to do with me.'

'But she was one of your girls. Your girlfriend, in fact. Weren't you angry to hear that she had been treated so disrespectfully?' Annie asked.

'I'm not possessive. It's not—'

'I know,' Banks cut in. 'It's a cultural thing. But are you sure you weren't just a little bit jealous? Are you sure you didn't head out after them, and when you saw Mimsy walking back up that lane, you got out and gave her a good thrashing?'

'No! You can't say that!'

'Just asking, Sunny. What did you do after the van left Wytherton?'

'Nothing. I went to bed. I watched TV.'

'Which is it?'

'I watched TV in bed.'

'Alone? Well, I suppose you would be, with your girlfriend gone to have sex with three of your cousins, wouldn't you? Unless you had Jade or Kirsty or Mel to keep you company. Did you, Sunny?'

'No. I was alone.'

'That's not much of an alibi.'

'I didn't know I'd need one. How could I know they'd throw her out of the van and she'd be on the road?'

'Why did they throw her out of the van? Did they tell you?'

'She was weirding out on them. The K, I suppose. They couldn't deal with her no more, she was like a wild animal, so they chucked her out. They didn't mean to hurt her.'

'Was it because she wouldn't consent to commit certain sex acts?'

'Come again?'

'She wouldn't let them do what they wanted to her.'

'She'd let anybody do anything to her when she was off her face like that.'

'How do you know, Sunny? You said you had nothing to do with ketamine, with drugs.'

'You're twisting my words.'

'How am I twisting your words?'

'What about the other girls?' Annie asked.

'They're all the same.'

Banks glanced at Annie. The disgust was clear to see on her face. 'Well, DI Cabbot,' he said, 'I think that's all the questions for the moment. Why don't we put Sunny here in a nice comfortable cell while we gather the rest of the statements and see what the teams have stumbled across in their searches?'

'Wait a minute. What do you mean, cell? I've told you what I know, haven't I? I've cooperated. We're done. You've got to let me go now.' He looked despairingly at Haroon Malik. 'Tell them they can't do this.' The lawyer remained impassive.

'But we haven't finished with you yet,' said Annie. 'Not by a long chalk.'

13

A sea fret shrouded Xanadu the second time Banks and Winsome paid a visit to Danny Caxton. This time they were ushered by the young servant into a large white room with a white grand piano at its centre. The mist nuzzled up against the French windows. Three navy blue leather armchairs were arranged around a huge open fireplace, though there was no fire burning. Caxton wore a white shirt and a yellow herringbone sweater fastened by its sleeves around his neck. They sat down, and there was no offer of refreshments.

'It's good of you to see us, Mr Caxton,' Banks said.

'Goodness has nothing to do with it. If I thought I had a choice, do you think you'd have got through the gates?' Caxton sipped an amber-coloured drink from a crystal glass. Banks thought he caught a whiff of expensive and old single malt whisky.

'Where's Mr Feldman?'

'Don't worry, he's within hailing distance. I think I can handle you, but if I need him, I'll give him a shout.'

'Fine,' said Banks. He gave Winsome the nod, and she took out her notebook. 'I just wanted to follow up on the little chat we had last time.'

'It wasn't a little chat. You were damned insulting. Not as bad as that mate of yours I had over here yesterday. At least I assume he's a mate. Fellow called Burgess. Nasty piece of work.'

'Mr Burgess is coordinating the investigation through the NCA,' Banks said. 'As I'm sure he told you, we're exploring many avenues.'

'Fishing expedition is more like it. Seeing what muck you can rake up from publicity-hungry bitches who think they can sell their stories to the *News of the World* for a few thousand quid.'

'Sorry to disappoint you, Mr Caxton, but the *News of the World* no longer exists.'

'Well, let's be thankful for small mercies. Still, it's no matter. One goes, another one springs up to take its place. Like weeds. Like coppers. What do you want now?'

'Some new information's come up.'

Caxton cocked his head to one side. 'New information? Like what?'

'Tony Monaghan.'

'Who? Are you trying to insinuate that I assaulted men as well as women?'

'Come off it, Mr Caxton. Don't play the innocent with me. You should remember Tony Monaghan. He worked for you from 1966 to 1967, until he was found stabbed to death in a public convenience in Leeds.'

'Ah, *that* Tony Monaghan. Well, yes, I do vaguely remember him, I suppose mostly because of the terrible thing that happened to him.' He put his index finger to his cheek. 'As I remember he was a homosexual, wasn't he? Found dead in a place known to be frequented by that sort of character.'

'How did you know that?'

'Oh, come, come, you don't think you can trip me up like that, do you? It was in the papers at the time.'

'Did the police talk to you?'

'There may have been a brief conversation. After all, Monaghan worked for me on contract. I knew nothing that could help them.'

'Of course not. But then you knew the chief constable well, didn't you?'

'Ted Crammond and I were friends, yes.'

'So you remember him all right?'

'I remember my friends. I did a bit of fund-raising for the local police. You'll find it all on record.'

'Oh, we have,' said Banks. 'But that was about all we found on record. Do you know that the investigation into Mr Monaghan's murder was abandoned just over two weeks after his death?'

'I didn't keep track of it. You can't blame me for the police's inability to catch the killer.'

'Oh, but I think we can. I don't think there was much of an attempt made. I think it would have led police far too close to you, so you had a word in your friend's ear.'

Caxton narrowed his eyes. 'Mr Banks, that sounds to me very close to a slanderous attack on my character.'

'Then call in Mr Feldman. Did you have any idea that Mr Monaghan was homosexual?'

'None at all. I never asked him, and he never said. I must say there were no obvious signs in the way he dressed or talked or walked.'

'And you already knew he was interested in girls, didn't you?'

'I what?'

'Well, you see, Mr Caxton, the important thing here is that our complainant remembers Mr Monaghan as being the other man who raped her in your suite at the Majestic Hotel in Blackpool on the nineteenth of August 1967. She picked his photograph out of the newspaper.'

'How extraordinary.'

'You think so? Why?'

'She certainly has an active imagination, I'll say that for her, whoever she is. Is one rapist not enough for her that she has to pick another one out of an old newspaper?'

Winsome looked up from her notebook at him, a mixture of puzzlement and disgust on her face. Caxton grinned. 'Oh-oh, I can see your sergeant here doesn't approve of my flippancy.'

'It's hardly a time to be flippant, sir,' said Winsome.

Caxton leaned forward. Banks tensed, feeling a sense of threat and aggression in the gesture. Caxton's mouth was twisted almost into a snarl. 'Oh, I disagree, young lady. It's a perfect time to be flippant. When you have such absurd, ludicrous accusations being thrown at you. Have you considered for a moment what your victim here has to gain by telling such outrageous stories about me?'

'She has nothing to gain,' said Banks. 'None of them do. Except maybe a bit of peace of mind, a sense of justice.'

'Justice? Well, how public-spirited.'

'And don't you think it's odd that she picked Tony Monaghan, of all the people who had their pictures in the paper around that time? And that Monaghan was an employee of yours? Quite a coincidence.'

Caxton shrugged. 'That's all it is. Coincidences happen. I'm sorry Mr Monaghan was killed, but it was nothing to do with me.'

'Were you and Tony Monaghan on good terms?'

Caxton frowned. 'As far as I can remember. As I said, I barely even remember him. It was a long time ago, and we didn't live in one another's pockets. After all, he was my employee. I like to think of myself as a generous and amiable employer, but one can't let the staff get too close and personal, can one.'

'I wouldn't know,' said Banks. 'What was his role?'

'This and that. Everything to do with public relations, media, fans, events and promotion. Charity drives. The lot.'

'Invaluable?'

'Replaceable. Obviously, as I had to replace him.'

'Who with?'

Caxton waved his hand in irritation at the question. 'I can't remember. Chris or Vinny or some such oik.'

'From the same advertising agency?'

'I wouldn't know. I didn't handle that side of the business. I was busy enough just keeping people entertained. Making them laugh, smile, cry. You should try it. It's harder than you think.'

'Oh, I try my best,' said Banks. 'I've managed to get a few laughs out of you, at any rate. But I should think you've made far more people cry.'

'Laughs at the ridiculous things you've been accusing me of. I'll grant you that.'

'Did you murder Tony Monaghan?'

'What? First I'm a rapist, now I'm a murderer. Should I be shouting for Benny?'

'I don't mean personally, with your own hands. You wouldn't do that. I doubt you'd have the guts. But did you order it done?'

'Why would I do something like that? This is beyond a joke, even to me. And I've got a sense of humour.'

Banks leaned back in his chair. 'I don't know why it should seem so ridiculous,' he said. 'A man in your employ is murdered just two months after you raped a fourteen-year-old girl in a Blackpool hotel. And he was with you there. He raped her after you did. I can see all sorts of possibilities in that little scenario. Blackmail, for example? Or a sudden attack of conscience, no money involved, but a desperate need to get things off his chest? Can't you see the possibilities, DS Jackman?'

Winsome looked Caxton in the eye. 'I certainly can, guv. Get that sort of thing all the time.'

'Do you know who the two men who carried his body across the park to the toilets were?' Banks asked.

'Now you've lost me.'

'Two men were seen carrying another between them. They looked like boxers or wrestlers, maybe bouncers. No necks. Who were they? You might as well tell us. We'll find out, you know, then we'll prove a connection.'

'Now I *really* don't know what you're talking about.' Caxton looked from one to the other, and there was nothing pleasant about his fixed smile. The Man with the Big Smile was not happy, and if Banks wasn't mistaken, he was even a trifle worried. He put his hands on the arms of the chair and pushed himself to his feet. In that gesture, it was possible to see him as an old man, struggling with stiffening joints and frail bones. 'Well, interesting as all this has been,' Caxton said, slightly out of breath, 'I have only two words to say to you. *Prove it.* And now, if you don't mind, it's time for my nap. If there's anything else, I'll call Mr Feldman in and you can talk to him about it.'

Banks and Winsome stood. 'No, that'll be fine,' said Banks. 'We're finished anyway.'

'I very much think you are. I'd like to say I'm sorry you had such a wasted journey, but I can't really mouth the words with any degree of honesty.'

'I wouldn't say it's been wasted,' Banks said, as he and Winsome started heading for the door, past the classical rape scenes. 'In fact, it's been most informative.'

'Make sure you don't lose your way home in the fog,' Caxton called out after them.

'Don't worry,' Banks called back. 'We won't.'

Annie knew that Doug Wilson must be as tired as the rest of the team. He may have felt at times like a spare part in the events of the last week or so, but he had spent a great deal of time in a darkened room with a couple of DCs from County HQ watching hours of boring CCTV footage of the roads around Bradham Lane and the Strip in Wytherton. They had got nothing from the latter. Either the cameras weren't working, there weren't any, or the drives had been reused since Mimosa Moffat's departure. And they had got too much from the former, wasting hours tracking down cars and their owners, checking movements, alibis, police records. Apart from the stolen car, finally found burned out in a quarry outside Ripon, and the white van possibly used to carry Mimosa Moffat, they had found nothing of interest. They were still trying to find the car thief, with the help of the Ripon police, but to no avail. And the car was such a mess that there was unlikely to be much useful evidence in the remains.

So they were left with Jim Nuttall, rare auto parts supplier of Stockton-on-Tees, who had lied about being on the road at the time of Mimosa's ordeal, delivering a shipment to a dealer in Southampton. And that was why Annie was sitting in the passenger seat of a police Skoda with Wilson driving, on the busy A66 east of the A1, shortly after her interview with Sunny. She thought Doug needed to get out of the darkened room for a while, and he seemed more than willing to accompany her.

There was nothing else she could be doing at the moment. Everything was in hand. The preliminary search of Sunny's flat had uncovered small quantities of heroin, cocaine, marijuana and ecstasy, but no ketamine. Sunny's accomplices – Faisal Sabzwari, Ismail Hossaini and Hassan Azizi – along with the three cousins from Dewsbury – were busy telling their stories to detective constables and sergeants who probably had far better interviewing techniques than either Annie or Banks. Three of the Wytherton girls were in Eastvale now, in the 'rape suite' especially designed for victims of sexual assault, with dim lighting and soothing music playing softly in the background. Their stories were slowly being coaxed out of them under promises of anonymity. There was really nothing to do but let the procedures follow their course and find out why Jim Nuttall had lied to Doug Wilson about the day he had made his deliveries.

Two things still worried Annie. Nobody seemed able to find Jade, and despite the successes and revelations of the past few hours, she still had no idea who had killed Mimosa Moffat. Sunny, or one of his colleagues, might have done it, but no cars caught on the CCTV had been identified with any of them – not even one of Ismail's taxis – and motive still remained a problem. Still, Sunny had no alibi, had the use of Ismail's minicabs, and as he was the leader, he might have had his own reasons to dish out punishment to Mimosa. Perhaps a punishment that had gone too far. They would keep at him, and if he had done it, Annie was sure that he would crack and confess eventually. For the moment, he was stewing in his cell. One of the Moffats may have done it, though Albert had an alibi, and Annie ruled out Lenny and Johnny. Which left Sinead. Junkie or not, she had kicked up a fuss, quite rightly, about the counsellor who had messed with her daughter, so if she had found out about Sunny, she might have gone after him, too. The problem was that it was Mimosa who had been killed, not Sunny or any of his friends. Annie thought maybe Sinead had lost it with her daughter, but the idea was beginning to seem far-fetched.

They found Jim Nuttall working in his garage on an old Morris Minor shooting-brake, the kind with the wooden frame around the back and sides that Annie's father used to drive when she was a child. It had been an antique even then. The garage was a lot tidier and cleaner than most garages Annie had seen. You didn't feel you'd end up with a grease or oil stain no matter what surface you touched, and the racks of parts were clearly labelled and, she noticed, ran in alphabetical order by make of car and name of part. It smelled of rubber, oil and sheared metal, a mix Annie really didn't mind at all. There was something comforting about it.

The door at the back led through to an office, and that was where Nuttall took them, for a brew. The office, which smelled the same as the garage, was cramped and looked out on a backyard piled with rusted car parts, mostly tyres, bumpers, radiator fronts and doors. There were two hard-backed chairs opposite Nuttall's, which sat behind the desk, and they eased themselves in. The office was a bit less tidy than the garage, but not much. Nuttall himself was a middle-aged man in a dark blue overall, a little overweight, thinning on top.

'It's a one-man business,' he said, 'so I apologise for the mess. I have to do my own books and orders and everything. Even make the tea.'

'Must be a full-time job with all the deliveries, too,' said Annie.

'More than full-time.'

'Why not take on some help?'

'Can't afford it. The profit margin's slim in this line of work. Besides, I can manage. When I can't, I know it'll be time for me to retire.'

'Anywhere in mind?'

'I've been saving. I had the Costa del Sol in mind at one time but Spain's gone bust these days, like my savings. I'll probably end up in a caravan park in Scunthorpe.'

Annie laughed. 'You could at least try Redcar. It's a bit closer to home.'

'Aye, maybe I will, at that.' The kettle boiled, and Nuttall busied himself filling the teapot and making sure the mugs he picked from the shelf were clean. He brought milk and sugar out of one of the filing cabinets and set them on the table. When he'd finished he glanced at Wilson. 'Brought the boss this time, have you, lad? It must be serious.'

'We hope not,' said Wilson. 'We just need to go over one or two points with you.' He took out his notebook and Annie picked up the questioning, starting by identifying the VW Transporter by its number, colour and logo.

'Is that the only transport you have?' she asked.

'It is. It's big enough for my deliveries and it doubles as a decent enough car for any personal trips I might wish to make.'

'Now, the last time DC Wilson was here, you told him you had a delivery in Southampton on the morning of Wednesday, the twenty-second of July, and that you drove down there from here during the night of the twenty-first. Is that correct?'

'It is.'

'Do you often drive at night?'

'Long distances, yes. It saves time, and I enjoy it. Gives me time to think. I'm not married. I live alone, so it doesn't matter whether I'm in or out. Sometimes I listen to books on tape or on the radio. LBC. I like Darren Adam and Steve Allen.'

Annie shifted in her seat and leaned back as much as she could. 'Well, it's a serious case,' she said, 'so we did a routine check with the dealer in Southampton, a Mr Rodney Pomfret – is that correct?'

'Rodney. Yes.'

'His records seem to indicate that you made the delivery two days earlier, on the Monday morning. Which means you must have driven to Southampton on Sunday night.'

'I'm not being charged with breaking the Sabbath, am I?'

'Not this time. We'll let that one slip by. But it's a bit of a discrepancy, isn't it? Two days.'

Nuttall scratched his head. 'I was sure it was Tuesday,' he said. 'I must have got the days mixed up. Old age catching up with me. My memory's not been that good lately. Maybe I drove back on Tuesday night.'

'Afraid not,' Annie said. 'Your car was definitely travelling in the other direction. It appeared on CCTV footage in the area we're interested in at the relevant time in the early hours of Tuesday morning. That's the big roundabout at the south-ern end of Market Street in Eastvale. Do you know it?'

'I know it.'

'Why didn't you stick to the A1 and M1?'

'I prefer to take the country roads. They're more interest-ing. Quieter. Contemplative.'

'Even at night, when you can't really see anything?'

'There's not as much traffic. The motorways are still busy at night. Everyone drives too fast. It's more peaceful than speeding along in three or four lanes with some bugger always on your tail and people overtaking without signalling. Not to mention the drunks driving home late from clubbing.'

'I know what you mean. But can you see our problem? If you weren't driving the van to Southampton when you said you were, what were you doing at the Eastvale roundabout that night? You must have brought the van back Monday, maybe also overnight, or even during the day Monday or Tuesday. Don't you remember?'

'Not for the life of me. It must have been another delivery. Tuesday night. I go all over the country.'

'Where did you go that time? Exeter? Birmingham? Shrewsbury? When do you sleep?'

'I can't remember. I do seem to be getting a bit muddled. Maybe it's lack of sleep.'

DC Wilson looked at Annie for the OK, then said, 'We'd really like you to help us out a bit here, Mr Nuttall. It's a muddle we need to get sorted. You must have records, surely? For tax purposes, at least. Receipts from petrol stations and so on.'

Nuttall gave Wilson a sharp glance. 'I keep my taxes in order, young lad, don't you be fretting about that.'

'Where were you going in the van at two o'clock on Tuesday night?' Annie asked. 'It's not meant to be a difficult question.'

'Let me see . . .' Nuttall examined a large desk diary, running his finger down the page. 'Bristol. That's it. It must have been Bristol.'

'May I?' Annie gestured for the diary. Reluctantly, Nuttall turned it round to face her. 'That was the previous week, Mr Nuttall,' she said. 'The fourteenth of July. It's the twenty-first I'm talking about. More accurately, the early hours of the twenty-second.'

Nuttall said nothing, just picked at imaginary threads on his overalls.

'Mr Nuttall,' Annie went on, 'something's not right here, is it? We need to know what it is. What you're not telling us. If you haven't done anything wrong, then you've nothing to worry about. Were you driving your car in the vicinity of Bradham Lane on the night of Tuesday, the twenty-first of July, around two in the morning?'

'No,' said Nuttall, looking at her with frightened eyes. 'I didn't go out at all that night. I didn't feel well. I remember now.'

'Then who was driving your van?'

'I don't know. Someone must have borrowed it.'

'Do people often borrow it without your permission?'

'No.'

'Well, then . . .'

'It must have been stolen.'

'But you didn't report it stolen.'

'They must have brought it back before I noticed. That's what happened. It was there the next morning, so I never real-ised it had been gone.'

'Don't you check the fuel gauge? The mileage. For tax purposes.'

'I must have forgotten that time.'

'Have you been out in it since, Mr Nuttall? Since the night it was "stolen" and returned?'

'No. Just for a couple of local deliveries, like. No overnights.'

That meant there could still be forensic traces, if the VW Transporter had been involved in Mimosa Moffat's murder. 'OK,' said Annie. 'I'm losing my patience just a little bit here, Mr Nuttall. No matter what, we're going to take your van in for forensic examination immediately. Now you can cooper-ate with us here and now, or you can come in to the station in Eastvale with us and we can talk further there while we wait for the results. Either way, I simply want you to tell the truth. I don't think you've done anything terribly wrong. I don't know what you're afraid of, but believe me, whatever it is, it won't be worse than getting charged with murder, which is what will happen if you don't come clean.'

Nuttall swallowed. 'Murder?'

'That's right.'

'I haven't murdered anyone.'

'Then tell us the truth.'

'But he wouldn't, not . . .'

'Not who, Mr Nuttall? Do you know who "borrowed" your car that night?'

Nuttall nodded.

'Tell me.'

There was a long pause as Nuttall seemed to consider his options. Finally, he took a packet of cigarettes from his top pocket and asked if could smoke. Normally Annie would have said no right off the bat, but she nodded reluctantly. Anything that might help him talk. It was his office, after all. The acrid sulphur of the match and smoke from the cigarette irritated her nostrils. She edged back a couple of inches and sipped some tea. She watched a black cat picking its way across the pile of tyres in the yard and let the silence stretch.

'I can't do it all myself,' Nuttall said finally. 'So I have a lad to make some runs for me.'

'Why didn't you tell us this before?'

'Because it's not on the books. I don't pay him much, not as much as I'd have to if it was official, like. And there's no tax, no worries, just cash in hand. He's always been a good lad. I can't believe he'd do anything like you've been talking about.'

'Was this lad driving your van on the night in question?'

'Aye. He'd done a delivery that day in Sheffield, and he had a pickup the following day from a scrap dealer in Sunderland, some parts from an old Humber, so I told him to just park the van where he lived, save him coming all this way in the morning. He's done it before. What are you going to do to me? Are you going to report me?'

'Not if you tell me what I want to know. Who is it? What's his name?'

There was another pause as Nuttall sucked long on the cigarette and drew the smoke deep into his lungs. As he exhaled it, he looked down, as if ashamed by what he was doing, and whispered, 'Albert. Albert Moffat is his name. He lives in Wytherton.'

'What the hell are you doing here?' Annie barked at Gerry as she walked through the squad room door, her shoulder braced, arm in a sling. They were the only two in there.

'I don't want to miss anything, guv,' Gerry said. 'We've put a lot of hours into this. It's near the end, I can feel it. I don't want to be lying in some hospital bed twiddling my thumbs.'

'Did the doctor release you?'

'I'm fine. There's nothing wrong with me. My clavicle's just cracked, not broken. I didn't have any concussion or any hidden injuries, so they let me go.'

'You should have gone home. If you're still on painkillers, you're no use to us.'

'I haven't taken any more yet.' Gerry grimaced as she lowered herself into her chair, using her good hand on the desk for balance.

'OK,' said Annie, sitting on her desk. 'That was a bloody stupid thing you did last night. You could have got yourself killed.'

'Sorry, guv. I didn't see any other way. Is there any news on Jade?'

'Not yet. She isn't in Leicester yet, and the foster-brother says he hasn't seen or heard from her in months. We've got a bulletin out. Her real name's Carol Fisher, by the way. But that's not the point. What do you mean you didn't see any other way? You broke just about every rule in the book. What am I supposed to do with you?'

'I should imagine the ACC or Chief Superintendent Gervaise will have a few ideas about that, guv. As I remember they were both dragged out of bed in the middle of the night because of me.'

Annie managed a thin smile. 'That's true.'

'What would you have done, guv, given the opportunity? I didn't have a lot of time to make my mind up. It sounded like a one-time offer with a short expiry date to me.'

'That doesn't excuse what you did.'

'But I got a result. Doesn't that go some way towards exonerating me? Besides, what should I have done? Called Superintendent Carver? Have him send in the heavy squad? You know what he's like. Or Reg and Bill, maybe?'

'You could have called *me*.'

'I ... I'm sorry. I thought I had a rapport with Jade. She trusted me. I didn't want to do something that might throw her or cause her to back off.'

'You did well, Gerry,' Annie said. 'It's just ... I've been there, you know, the wrong place at the wrong time. I still have nightmares.'

'Nothing happened.'

Annie gestured towards Gerry's shoulder. 'Tell that to the officers investigating the incident. And they will, you mark my words.'

'I'll deal with that when it happens,' said Gerry. 'Let them demote me.'

Annie laughed. 'They can't demote you. You're as low as they come to start with.'

Gerry blushed. 'You know what I mean. Put me back on probation again.'

'Or traffic.'

Gerry bit her lip. 'Would they do that?'

'Who knows? You're right. Worry about it when it happens. Until then, consider yourself bollocked by your supervising officer.'

'Yes, guv. What are we going to do next?'

Annie explained about Jim Nuttall and his VW Transporter, at present in pieces in the police garage. The CSIs already thought they had identified small quantities of blood around the brake pedal and accelerator, and Jazz Singh was checking it against Mimosa's. They were also searching for anything to connect the car with Albert Moffat. At the moment, Annie said she was waiting for the CSIs to report, then she would be talking to Albert again. He may not have been as drunk as he was acting last Tuesday, and when Warner fell asleep, he might well have decided to take matters into his own hands. How that ended up with Mimsy Moffat dead on the Bradham Road was a mystery yet to be solved.

'What about Sunny?'

'Oh, yes. I think we'll have another long talk with him, don't you? And his mates. This thing clearly stretches a lot further than we thought it did. It's more than just four blokes and seven girls in Wytherton. It sounds like some sort of exclusive club. We'll have to try and worm as many names and locations as possible out of Sunny and the others, as well as the girls themselves and the cousins in Dewsbury.'

'Can I sit in on the interviews?'

Annie didn't say anything.

'Go on, boss. Please! I promise I won't say anything.'

Annie let the silence drag on a while longer, then she said, 'Well, you'd be no bloody use to me if you didn't chip in now and then, would you? But it's going to be complicated. We'll need to work out a strategy. Are you sure you're up for it?'

14

Banks was still trying to guess from Chief Superintendent Gervaise's tone on the telephone what he was likely to be walking into when he went up to her office, as requested. At least she was alone in there, he thought with some relief, after he had knocked and entered. No Adrian Moss, Superintendent Carver or ACC McLaughlin. She even offered him coffee, which he accepted, and they sat down at her circular glass conference table, not the more formal desk.

'Guess, what, Alan,' she said. 'I've had a call from the chief constable.'

'I was wondering when that would happen. I'm surprised it took so long.'

'Apparently, Danny Caxton's lawyer Bernard Feldman called and complained about police harassment. He's had two visits in the last two days, apparently, one of them from you.'

'So what do we do, pack up our tents and go home?'

'Hold your horses, o ye of little faith. If you want the short version, our lord and master told him to sod off.'

'He what? The CC told Feldman and to sod off?'

'And Caxton. Uh-huh.'

'So they never played golf together.'

'The CC had a message for you, too.'

'What?'

Gervaise leaned forward. '"Put the bastard away." So it's my brief to ask you if you're any closer to doing just that.

What's brewing, in other words? Are we going to put the bastard away?'

Banks scratched his temple. 'Well, to be honest, I've been preoccupied with Annie's case this past little while – as you might have noticed – we're very short-staffed.'

'Budget cuts, Alan, budget cuts. Make do and mend.'

'I know, I know. I was lucky to get the promotion when I did, blah-blah-blah. Even so, things have been a bit hectic, as you know.'

'So you've made no progress?'

'I'm not saying that. No need to take your coffee back. I've had my team of highly trained elves working on it night and day.'

'And what has DS Jackman come up with?'

'She's been digging deep into Caxton's past, and she's come up with plenty since we talked to him yesterday. You know we think he was involved in the murder of Tony Monaghan?'

'Yes.'

'Naturally, there's no hard evidence. It's all disappeared, if it ever existed. But we do have a little more powder to add to our arsenal.'

'Circumstantial?'

'Most of it is, yes. But there are witnesses. Linda Palmer. Simon Bradley.'

'OK. So what did your "elves" dig up?'

'Three things of immediate significance, I think. In the first place, remember Linda Palmer saw that photo on the front page of the *Yorkshire Evening Post* for the twenty-seventh of October, 1967, just two weeks after Monaghan's murder? It shows Caxton, with a big cheesy grin on his face, handing over a cheque – well one of those enormous, fake cheques, if you know what I mean – for £10,000 for the Police Widows and Orphans fund. As you can imagine, that was a lot of money in those days. We've got a bit more on it now.'

'Where did this money come from?'

'Caxton raised it through telethons and fund-raising drives, personal appearances and the like.'

'Well we can hardly fault the man for raising money for charity.'

'It's not so much that, it's who's in the picture with him. I'll have a copy sent up to you later. For a start, Caxton's handing the cheque to Chief Constable Edward Crammond, who Simon Bradley told me was behind axing the investigation into Monaghan's murder around the time the picture was taken. Also present was Detective Chief Superintendent Dennis McCullen, DI Chadwick's SIO on the case.'

'Are you saying that the charitable donation was a bribe?'

'No, not at all,' said Banks. 'You couldn't do things like that, even then. It's just one of a number of things that show how closely Caxton was linked to the local constabulary at the time. He was known to be a mate of Crammond's, same golf club and all, best seats at Headingley for the test match every year. Winsome's still digging to see if she can find more.'

'It's not much, though, is it,' said Gervaise, the tip of her pencil against her Cupid's bow lips.

'What do you mean? Not worth a refill?' Banks held out his empty cup.

'Cheeky bastard.' Gervaise grinned. 'But you can get it yourself.'

Banks did. 'So that's one investigation we've still got going on,' he said. 'Caxton's relationship with local men of influence, especially high-ranking police officers. And you can bet that'll spiral when the other counties get as deeply stuck into their investigations as we have and start looking for lost statements and the like.'

'Are you saying that Caxton was involved in Monaghan's murder and got Crammond to put a lid on the investigation?'

'Something like that, yes.'

'It had better be more than "something like" if Adrian and the press ever get hold of it, let alone if it goes to court.'

'I realise that. But there's more. Simon Bradley mentioned a witness, a student who was crossing Hyde Park the same night Monaghan was killed. From what Bradley can remember, the lad saw two men carrying a third between them. He appeared drunk, but could have been dead. It could have been Monaghan.'

'Could have been? Did he get a good look? Does Bradley remember the details? Can we locate this student?'

'No. But Bradley does remember the young lad said the men were scary enough that he made sure they didn't see him. He said he thought they were bruisers of some sort, a couple of burly blokes with no necks and shaved heads.'

'And?'

'And after a bit of digging, Winsome came up with the Stott brothers, a couple of burly blokes with shaved heads and no necks, one of whom was a boxer.'

'And they were?'

'A couple of local Leeds villains, muscle, enforcement, mercenary. Both dead now. One by violence. Winsome's trying to find out more about them, but the one link we do have is that they were bouncers at a Bradford disco Caxton part-owned around the time of Monaghan's murder. They also ran a Leeds boxing club he supported. One of his "youth" projects. Apparently the disco was a place Caxton used to like to visit, we think because he liked the young girls it attracted. But as I say, Winsome's digging deeper. There's definitely a connection. Caxton *knew* the Stotts, and he could have hired them to kill Monaghan and make it look like a gay murder. They were known to favour flick knives, as well as their fists.'

'Was Monaghan killed by a flick knife?'

'We don't know,' said Banks. 'All the files have disappeared, including the post-mortem report and forensic examinations, if there were any.'

'Pity. It's still "could have", Alan. And good luck to DS Jackman. After all this time, she'll need it. You know we'll never be able to prove that Caxton hired a couple of deceased thugs fifty years ago, don't you? You said three developments. What's the third? I hope it's a bit better than the last two.'

'Tony Monaghan's widow. You remember, Winsome said she was following up on that? Well, she discovered that Ursula Monaghan remarried in 1974 and became Ursula Pemberton. She was widowed for the second time in 2009, natural causes this time, and she now lives just up the Northumberland coast.'

'She's still alive?'

'As far as Winsome could gather. She checked the electoral rolls and DVLA in Swansea. Ursula Pemberton still votes, pays her council tax and has a valid driving licence. Think about it, if she was in her twenties in 1967 she'll be in her seventies now. That's not so old.'

'The sad thing is,' said Gervaise, 'I can remember when it was.' She fingered a paper clip. 'It's still not a lot, is it, and some of it's a bit of a stretch. There's not much you can do with any of it in court.'

'I know. It's all part of a bigger picture we're building up. We've got the CPS onside.'

'I understand that. I just hope the picture turns out to be what you think it will be, and you haven't forgotten to take the lens cap off, or just pointed the camera at your foot.'

Banks spread his hands. 'Well, that's about where we are. You asked.'

'And Linda Palmer?'

'Linda Palmer will stand up. She's working on a sort of written memoir of her time in Blackpool. I suggested it. I thought it might bring back a few more details.'

'And has it?'

'Dunno. I haven't seen it yet. We were busy identifying Monaghan from the photo and finding out who he was.'

'Well let's hope it jogs her memory.'

'We've got enough to go on, already. Especially with the other cases Non-Executive Director Burgess told me about. He wanted to be "Special Agent" so he's a bit disappointed with his rather dull title.'

Gervaise laughed.

'It's a bit of a mouthful, I know, but I don't know what else to call him.'

'From what I hear, "Dirty Dick" will still do nicely.'

Banks smiled. 'That all, ma'am?'

'For the moment. Keep at it, Alan. Putting my reservations aside, we'll be jumping for joy if we can get Caxton on a conspiracy to commit murder charge as well as rape.'

'Can we talk to Albert?' Annie asked Sinead Moffat when she opened the door.

'You two again. I didn't think you'd have the bloody nerve to show your faces around here after what you've put us through.'

'Sinead, I'm sorry about the press and the house search and all, but it's out of my hands. Surely you must understand we have to do these things when something as serious as this happens? And as for them,' she gestured towards the pack of reporters beyond the gate, 'it's their job, too, like it or not.'

A small crowd had gathered across the street, and Annie heard a shrill voice shout, 'When are you going to do something about those Pakis instead of harassing poor honest decent folk? When are you going to put a stop to those murdering bastards?' The crowd roared its approval.

'You'd better come in,' said Sinead. 'Before that lot stone you to death. Albert's in his room. Just go on up. And don't be too hard on the lad. Remember he's just lost his sister.'

Annie and Gerry climbed the stairs of 14 Southam Terrace and knocked on Albert's door. They could hear music from inside, but it was playing quietly, and Albert quickly opened the door and asked them in.

'It's not a very big room, I'm afraid,' he said, turning the radio down, 'but there's a couple of chairs. Sit down. What is it?'

Old clothes were draped over the upright chairs, and Albert quickly scooped them up and dropped them in the laundry basket. Annie felt a bit queasy about sitting where Albert's dirty underpants had been, but she swallowed her pride and her bile. The room was at the back of the house, so they couldn't hear or see the crowd of neighbours and reporters, just the slate roofs of the houses across the alley. Albert had his window partially open, which was a mercy, as he was smoking. He sat close to the window and the smoke curled in the air as it caught the draught, which whisked it outside.

'Is it true that you've got them in custody?' Albert said. 'The bastards that did our Mimsy?'

'It's true that we're talking to some people, yes, but there's no proof that any of them killed Mimosa yet.'

'I hope you deport them. They probably cut off people's heads for killing people back where they come from.'

Annie sighed. 'They come from Wytherton, Albert. Unless things have changed since this morning, I don't think there'll be any deportation or decapitation.'

'You know what I mean.' He cast a glance at Gerry's sling. 'You look as if you've been in the wars. What happened, trip over your truncheon?'

'Baton,' Gerry muttered. She leaned forward, as if to share a confidence. 'As a matter of fact, I was set on by four lads not far from here. Asians. I think one of them was called Tariq. Know anyone by that name?'

Annie had expected her to blush or offer some sort of reproof, but instead she had to congratulate her DC for knowing an opportunity when she saw one, and for seizing it.

'It figures,' said Albert. 'They're getting everywhere these days, spreading like a pestilence, like a plague of rats.'

'Tariq? Mean anything?'

'No, but I can find out for you. Want him sorting out?'

'That's all right, thanks,' said Gerry. 'We'll deal with him.'

'I'm sorry for what happened to you, but what do you expect? They're animals. They got no respect for their own women, so you can't expect them to have any for ours. I told you before, you can't trust the bastards, now maybe you'll start to see what I mean. It was them all along, wasn't it?'

Annie looked at Gerry again, worried she might show her revulsion about being thought of as one of 'ours'. But she didn't. She just said, 'I see,' and rubbed her shoulder. Annie found herself wondering whether Albert was laying it on so thick to divert them from any suspicions that *he* might have been involved.

'How can I help you this time?' Albert went on. He beamed at both of them, the picture of youthful innocence.

'The last time we talked,' Annie said, 'you told us you didn't know about Mimosa's association with Sunny and his crowd until recently.'

'That's right. Day before she went missing, if I remember right.'

'And you hadn't told your family or any of your mates about it?'

'No. I didn't want them taking the piss out of me for having a sister who hung out with Pakis. Besides, it's none of their business.'

'And you really had no idea before then that Sunny and his friends were exploiting Mimosa, along with a number of other young girls from the estate?'

'No. How could I know that?'

'Did you ever get the impression that she was frightened at all? Being made to do anything against her will?'

'No. She'd always brazen it out, would Mimsy.'

'OK,' said Annie. 'Can we go back to that Tuesday night, the twenty-first of July?'

'The night it . . . you know?'

'Yes. The night it happened. Now, you told us before you were at Paul Warner's—'

Albert stubbed out his cigarette. 'Yeah, like I told you. We had a few bevvies in the Hope and Anchor, then went back to Paul's for a few more. You can ask him.'

'We have, Albert, and he says you were there.'

'Well, then?'

'You stayed there until what time?'

'Well, I woke up there the next morning with a fuck of a headache. I can't remember what time it was, but it was late.'

'You didn't go out again after going back to Paul's from the Hope and Anchor? Neither of you?'

'No. I've told you all this. We just chatted about stuff, you know, watched DVDs, played some music.'

'Do you remember much about the evening?'

'To be honest,' said Albert, 'I'd had a few jars earlier as well, before the Hope and Anchor. I was pretty far gone by my third Special Brew.'

'So you don't remember much?'

'No. Just waking up on the couch, like, with a—'

'Yes,' said Annie. 'With a fuck of a headache.'

Albert pointed at her and giggled. 'You got it.'

'Any drugs?'

'What do you mean?'

'Was it just alcohol, or did you take any drugs?'

'Like what?'

'I don't know. Coke, amphetamines, marijuana.'

'The wacky baccy? No, I don't do that stuff. It makes you stupid. And Paul's not into drugs, either.'

'Were you fit to drive?'

'I should say not.'

'I understand you do a bit of driving on the side, though.'

Albert's eyes narrowed. 'What do you mean?'

'Driving. You know.' Annie stuck her arms out and mimed turning a steering wheel.

'I know what you mean, but what are you getting at?'

'Do you or don't you do some driving for a man called Jim Nuttall?'

'Jim?'

'Yes. He's got an auto parts business in Stockton. Specialist stuff. For collectors and the like.'

'I know Jim, yeah. So what? What did he tell you?'

'Do you make deliveries and pick-ups for him?'

'Yeah, but it's all legit stuff. It's nothing do with drugs or anything. I just help out now and then. Us unemployed people got to take what we can get, you know.'

'I'm not saying it isn't legitimate, Albert. Did you have a delivery on Tuesday, during the day?'

'Well, yeah, as a matter of fact. I was in Sheffield in the afternoon. Got back about an hour or so before the meeting, parked the car at the back of Paul's, as usual, and got a couple down me in the Hope and Anchor.'

'And Wednesday?'

'Sunderland. Afternoon. I was a bit late. I had a f—'

'Yes, you've told us, Albert. Why didn't you tell us about this before?'

'I don't know. It didn't come up, did it? And I'd just heard about Mimsy. I was gutted.'

'Are you sure it wasn't because Jim Nuttall told you not to mention it to anyone, that he could get into trouble for paying you cash under the counter and not running it through his books?'

'Whatever Jim does is up to him.'

'But he told you to keep quiet about it.'

'Well . . . yeah. There's no harm in that.'

'So between Tuesday evening, when you got back from Sheffield, and Wednesday afternoon, when you made the delivery in Sunderland, where was Mr Nuttall's van parked?'

'I told you. Lane round the back of Paul's place.'

'Do you often park it there?'

'If I know we're likely to be going back there for a few bevvies and movies. But it depends. If I'm not working for a few days I'll take it back to Jim's yard and he'll give me a ride home from Stockton.'

'But on this occasion you were driving two days in a row?'

'Yeah. And the parts were small. Just little cogs, really, so I'd no need to go all the way back to Stockton between deliveries. What's all this about? It wasn't a big deal. Jim's a nice bloke, he's hardly a major criminal.'

'And you're sure you didn't drive it again that night?'

'Are you joking! I told you. I was pissed as a newt. You might think I'm a dangerous criminal or something, but one thing I don't do is drink and drive.'

'Doesn't stop some people.'

'No way.'

'Well, I'm puzzled,' Annie said. 'Perhaps you can help me out.'

'Uh-huh?'

'You say Mr Nuttall's van was parked in the lane behind Paul's flat all Tuesday night, so why do you think it showed up on CCTV footage heading for Bradham Lane close to two o'clock in the morning?'

'I don't know. There must be some sort of mistake. Those cameras aren't always reliable, you know. I had a mate once who—'

'Are you sure about this, Albert?' said Annie. 'Because we think you're lying, and that's a very serious business. We think you brooded about Mimosa and her Asian friends. You either already knew she was going for a ride to Dewsbury that night, or you just took it into your mind to go down to Sunny's and break a window or two to vent your anger, and you saw her leaving in a van with three men. You were curious. You followed. You held back a while before Bradham Lane because you thought your lights would be spotted following them down there, and you knew you could catch up with them later, somewhere there was likely to be a bit more traffic. It must have given you the shock of your life when you saw Mimosa walking up that lane towards you. Dirty, naked, bleeding. So you came to a stop just past her, and she turned and walked as best she could to the van. She must have thought it was a lifesaver, whoever it was. Did something snap? Was that it? Did she say something to you? Put you down? Did she laugh at you? Was that it? Or did she shame the family? Was it your version of an honour killing?'

'That's rubbish, that is. I told you I was at Paul's. He said so.'

'Paul's your mate, Albert. Either you waited until he passed out, or he's lying to protect you. Either way, we've got you for it. We're just waiting for the forensics on the van. It's my bet that neither you nor Mr Nuttall have done a good-enough cleaning job on it to get rid of all the traces of Mimosa's blood. In the meantime, we'll be wanting your clothes and shoes for forensic examination. I'm arresting you on suspicion of the murder of Mimosa Moffat. Do you understand me, Albert? We're taking you into custody. Is that clear?'

Albert turned pale. 'You're what?'

'We're arresting you, Albert, and we're taking you back to Eastvale. If you fail to say something now you later rely on in court it may go against you. Anything you do say may be used

in court. You'll be hearing that again before we start the official interview at the station. You're entitled to a lawyer, and if
you don't have one we'll provide one for you.'

Albert was shaking his head as Annie spoke, and when she'd
finished, he slumped in his chair and folded his arms. 'I think
I will have that lawyer you mentioned,' he said.

A fresh breeze skidded off the North Sea and bent the long fat
blades of lush green grass through which the trodden path
meandered along the clifftop. Across the sparkling blue water
stood the tidal island of Lindisfarne, Holy Island, consisting
of a village, a small castle on a hill and a ruined priory where
St Aidan and St Cuthbert had lived, and where the exquisite
Lindisfarne Gospels had been painstakingly illuminated in
the eighth century. The island was connected to the mainland
by a mile-long causeway, which at the moment was covered
by the tide. Banks and Ursula Pemberton were walking on the
edge of the cliffs with her dogs, two fine Irish setters. Ursula
was a hearty, outdoorsy type, wearing loose-fitting jeans and
a thin polo-neck jumper against the slight chill off the sea. She
had a ruddy weather-beaten face, and her tight grey curls
hardly moved in the wind. Banks reckoned she must be about
ten years older than Linda Palmer.

'It's a stunning view,' said Banks.

'Yes. It never fails to send a shiver up my spine,' said Ursula,
'And I don't mean the wind. It's that sense of history being
close enough to grasp, more real than what you get on the
news every day. It invigorates me. I don't know how I lived
without it for so many years.'

That sounded something of a romantic notion to Banks,
but it made him think of *Briggflatts*, the Basil Bunting poem
he had listened to on CD since hearing Mark Knopfler's song
'Basil'. There was something about that mix of landscape,
history and lost love that struck a chord deep inside him.

Maybe it was all connected with the expulsion from the Garden of Eden. At any rate, Ursula Pemberton was right. He felt it here, too, on the Northumberland coast, just as he did in Whitby, and even in Eastvale, itself no stranger to history, with an eleventh-century castle reputed to have been one of the many temporary prisons to Mary Queen of Scots.

'There's plenty of history in London,' Banks said. 'Some would argue far more than up here.'

'Yes. It's true enough, isn't it? The Tower and St Paul's and all that. It's not a competition, I know. I suppose I just wasn't paying attention when we lived there. It was all a bit in your face. It seems more subtle and mystical here, but the connection is more direct. The pace of life gives you time to pay attention to its depths. In London there's always something else going on – the noise, the crowds. Superficial usually. Parties. Theatre. I don't think I ever really stopped to look at the past there. Not really look. But then I was a modern young sixties woman, newly wed, living for the moment, not the old and the antique, except as far as clothes were concerned. I suppose it's not so much the place as me, is it?'

'I'd guess it's a bit of both.'

'A confluence? Perhaps. But you didn't come all this way to listen to an old woman prattle on about history. What can I help you with, Superintendent? You were very circumspect on the telephone.'

'Was I? I suppose it's a delicate subject. It's about your first husband.'

'Tony?'

'Yes.'

She stared out to sea. It must have been the wind, Banks thought, that made her eyes water. 'Are you all right?'

'Yes. Yes.' She called to the dogs and they carried on walking. 'It was a long time ago. Nearly fifty years. Just an acid flashback, as we used to say.'

'You took drugs?'

'Superintendent! Tony and I were an educated, hip couple about town. This was London in the mid-sixties. Tony was in advertising, so we hung out with a lot of artists and would-be writers, film-makers, photographers and models: Jean Shrimpton, Terence Stamp, David Bailey. What do you think? Not that I'd ever admit to having said so.'

Banks smiled. 'I think the statute of limitations on that ran out a long time ago.'

'Good. I know I certainly put it behind me. So what is it you want to know about Tony?'

'What sort of man was he?'

'My goodness, that's a hard one. I mean, I wouldn't know where to begin. He was a good man, certainly, quick to laugh, but serious when need be. He had gravitas. He was also considerate, attentive, loving. He *listened*. So many people I find these days just like to talk endlessly about themselves. You know the kind. While you're talking you can tell they're just thinking about what they're going to say next. But Tony was a genuine listener. He was funny, too, he could make me laugh. He liked to experiment, try new things, but I think at heart he was a traditionalist, a family man. It was as much the times we were living in as anything. We were thinking of starting a family, you know, when . . . when it happened.'

'Would you say Tony was a weak man?'

'No, I wouldn't say weak. He was certainly impressionable, suggestible, perhaps easily led. But he knew where to draw the lines. He had a moral compass, fibre, whatever you call it. He was honest, even if it was at his own cost. He was certainly capable of standing up for what he believed was right.'

Something had clearly gone askew with Tony Monaghan's moral compass, Banks thought, if what Linda Palmer had told him was true. And he believed her. Why would she lie? The thing was that perhaps a man like Monaghan, the way his widow described him, might in a mad moment lose his direction in order to try a new experience, perhaps be led astray by someone else's charisma, as she had said. And if Tony Monaghan was half the man she said he was, if he did lose his way, it would torment him. And if that torment made itself known to, say, Caxton, and appeared to threaten him in any way . . . Caxton was a powerful and charismatic man.

'How long did you live in London?' Banks asked.

'I was born there. Cricklewood. I left in my early thirties. That was five years after Tony died. He was twenty-seven when he was killed.'

'How long had you been married?'

'Five years. I know it seems very young, but people did things like that back then. He'd just come out of university and was starting in the advertising business, and I'd graduated from secretarial college. I mostly temped until Tony started making enough to live on. We were so happy. It's hard to believe in all the optimism of youth these days. Everything seems so bleak and futureless. But despite the bomb and Kennedy's assassination and all the rest of the terrible things that went on, there was hope. It was somehow more palpable then. Or am I looking back through rose-coloured glasses the way I'm looking at Lindisfarne now? Life must have been tough there back in the eighth century.' A gust of wind ruffled her curls.

Banks remembered his early days with Sandra and the kids in Kennington. They were good times, certainly, and often full of joy, even though he was doing a job that constantly brought him into contact with the worst elements of society. 'We all romanticise the past to some extent,' he said. 'You know, every childhood summer was glorious, every spring a new birth. And every winter there was enough snow for sledging and building snowmen and having snowball fights and the occasional day off school, but never so much that it made life miserable. I suppose there must be at least a grain of truth in it.'

'Yes. A grain, perhaps. Oh, Tony and I argued from time to time, but nothing serious, just little things.'

'So you'd say on the whole it was a happy marriage?'

'For as long as it lasted. Yes. Except . . .'

'What?'

'Towards the end.'

'What happened then?'

'Shall we sit down for a few moments?' She patted her chest. 'I do get a little out of breath sometimes these days.'

They came to a bench. There was a brass plaque screwed to the backrest that said: 'This bench is erected in honour of Private Charles Waters, 1920–1944, by his widow Judith Waters. Let all who sit here contemplate the beauty and the brevity of life.' Private Charles Waters hadn't lived as long as Tony Monaghan, Banks thought, and both had met violent deaths.

'I always like to sit here when I bring the dogs for a walk,' Ursula said. 'I don't know why.' They faced the sea, Lindisfarne off to their right amid the other Farne Islands, mostly nature reserves for seabirds. Gulls swooped and squawked above them. The dogs sat at Ursula's feet, panting hard after their exertions on the cliffs. Banks let the silence stretch for a few moments while Ursula got her breath back.

'When did things start going wrong?' he asked after a while.

'Nothing really went wrong, at least not at first. It was just that Tony started changing. He became more moody, more preoccupied, spent more time away from home. It was part of his job, of course, but I do think the long separations took their toll on us.'

'Did you worry about him being unfaithful?'

She shot him a sideways glance. 'It wasn't so much that. I'm not saying it never entered my mind. He was a very good-looking man. But no . . . it was more . . . we were just used to being together. Silly, really. Almost like an old couple. Comfortable.'

'When did that start to change?'

'When he started working for Danny Caxton. I presume that's why you're talking to me about all this? I do still read the newspapers.'

'I'm handling the case,' Banks said. 'At least part of it. So anything you can tell me might be of use.'

'Anything that could be of use in putting away that evil bastard would be all right with me.'

Banks stared at her, shocked by the outburst. 'You met him?'

She gave a harsh laugh. 'When the agency found that Tony seemed to have a penchant for rubbing shoulders with the stars of the entertainment world, the little wife always got to meet the big names. Kept her happy, didn't it? Gave her something to tell her dull, boring suburban housewife friends about at coffee mornings. Except we didn't have any dull, boring suburban housewife friends, and I never attended coffee mornings. I'd be talking about Ginsberg and Burroughs or the latest Godard or Antonioni film with a bunch of unemployed artists smoking Gauloises in the pub, more likely. And they didn't give a damn about the Danny Caxtons of this world. Meeting Danny Caxton was supposed to be one of the perks.'

'I gather you didn't exactly like him?'

'That was my personal feeling, yes. Right from the start. Have you ever met someone who repulsed you at first sight? I don't mean because of looks, ugliness, or anything like that – Danny Caxton was as handsome as they come – but for want of a better word, because of something you sense inside, something wrong. Something evil.'

'Once or twice,' said Banks. 'It's an occupational hazard.'

'Yes. I suppose it must be in your job. That's what I felt about Danny Caxton, right from the start. After that, I did my best to avoid him.'

'Have you any idea what it was about him that repulsed you so?'

'No. That's the problem. I can't really put it into words. There's nothing concrete at all. Nothing he said or did I can put my finger on. He was always pleasant and charming to me. There was just something reptilian about him. He gave me the impression of a man who took what he wanted without qualms. I know he was an actor, and it probably came naturally, but I felt that every word, every gesture, every expressed feeling was fake, was something deliberate, to get an effect or produce one on the listener, to misdirect or to convince people he was just like one of us, when he wasn't at all. As if he was wearing a mask.'

Banks had heard people talk like that about psychopaths: the learned, simulated responses, knowing when it would be normal to laugh, when to pretend to shed a tear. 'And your husband?' he asked. 'What did Tony think?'

'I think Tony was rather dazzled by him. Certainly the first time they worked together – 1966, I think it was – life went on much as normal. It was only later that he started to change.'

'In 1967?'

'Yes. During the summer season at Blackpool. I didn't see a lot of him over those few months, but I've never seen him so glad as when it was over and he could come home to stay. Or so he thought. He would have stayed at home, too, but Danny Caxton wanted him back, and Tony's boss wanted to keep the client happy. So off he went to Leeds for Christmas panto season.'

'What exactly did he do?'

'He handled the press, of course, interviews, TV appearances and the like, he arranged visits to open supermarkets and so on, booked hotels, arranged transportation if it was necessary, decided who should and who shouldn't be admitted to The Presence.'

'Quite a responsibility. Didn't Caxton have others to do all that for him?'

'Nothing was too much for Danny Caxton. He said that Tony was his right-hand man and he'd be lost without him, so back Tony went. He was uneasy about it, but he was doing well in the firm, and he didn't believe his contract with Caxton would last for ever, so he just thought he'd grit his teeth and see it through, do his job, then maybe the promotion he'd been after would materialise.'

'He'd been promised a promotion for working with Caxton?'

'Not in so many words, but his boss certainly gave the impression that it wouldn't do his future career prospects any harm.'

'Is he still alive, this boss?'

'Walter Philby? I've no idea. Given that he was about fifty in 1967, I doubt it.'

'Did Tony confide in you about what was bothering him?'

'Not at first, no. He just didn't seem himself. There was something on his mind. On his conscience. He wasn't himself. When he came home from the summer season, he was very pale and withdrawn. Listless. I actually thought he was ill, depression or something, and I made him go to the doctor's. The doctor said he was just jittery and edgy from pressure of work. He prescribed some pills.'

'Did they do any good?'

'Not much. Oh, there were moments when the old Tony shone through and made me laugh again. It wasn't all doom and gloom. But he wasn't home for long. The call for the Christmas season came in pretty soon after he'd returned from Blackpool.'

'And?'

'That upset him. He didn't want to go. He even argued with Walter about it, which he *never* usually did. But Walter was adamant. Danny Caxton wanted Tony, and Danny Caxton got what he wanted. At least from Philby, Leyland and Associates.'

'What was the problem? Was Caxton difficult, demanding?'

'I'm sure he was, but there was more to it than that. We never considered such things at the time, of course, so I'm speaking with the benefit of hindsight, but after Savile, Cosby, Rolf Harris, Cyril Smith and the rest, Danny Caxton was up to the same sort of thing. What you're looking into now. Something terrible happened, and Tony knew about it.'

'Did he say anything?'

Ursula stared out to sea. The dogs were busy sniffing gorse. 'The day before he left,' she said. 'He told me all about it, and I wished to God he hadn't.'

15

'What am I doing here?' Paul Warner asked Annie and Gerry. 'I already told you everything I know the last time we met.'

He seemed more nervous this time, Annie thought, eyes all over the place. Perhaps it was because he was out of his home environment and in a police interview room. They were not places designed to put people at ease. He was dressed in clean jeans and a crisp white shirt. It looked as if it had been pressed, too, she thought, and almost asked him if he did his own ironing.

'Just a few minor points we need to go over, Paul,' said Annie. 'As you might have gathered, there's been developments.'

'Developments. I'd say there are. The whole estate's going up.'

'That's a bit of an exaggeration, don't you think? The local police have it under control. But that's not what I wanted to talk to you about.'

'No?'

Annie opened a folder on her desk and lifted a sheet of paper, as if to read from it. 'First of all, something's been puzzling me about you ever since we last talked. Maybe you can help. You seem to be a fairly intelligent lad. What is it with these racist views you seem to be espousing and encouraging? Are you involved with the English Defence League or the British National Party?'

Warner leaned back in his chair and stretched. 'No matter what you or the *Guardian* might think, intelligence isn't the private property of the left wing. And no,' he went on, with a smile, 'I'm not affiliated with either of those organisations. I suppose at first glance they may seem to offer swift and positive solutions to a number of problems, but if you look a bit closer you can see they'll never progress beyond basic thuggery. There are other, more reasoned and less violent routes likely to lead to success.'

'UKIP?'

'One possibility, if they truly had the courage of their convictions.'

'And what are the problems you see?'

Warner clasped his hands on his lap. 'It's as I told you before. Unhindered immigration is bleeding our country dry, membership in Europe is a millstone around our necks and kowtowing to the bloody Scots and Welsh and Irish is sapping our national identity. Sometimes it seems almost a crime to stand up and say you're English.'

'Well, that just about covers it,' said Annie. 'Though some would say immigrants contribute more to the economy than they take from it.'

'That's what they'd have you believe. You've all been brainwashed.'

'By whom?'

'The lefties. And before you get on to it, I've got nothing against the NHS or the benefits system, or the welfare state in general. As long as they're for the benefit of our own.'

'By that you mean white people?'

'It's not really an issue of colour, but I wouldn't expect you to understand that. I mean *English* people.'

'I take it these views didn't go over too well when you were studying politics in Warwick?'

'The universities are run by lefties, just like the BBC. You wouldn't get any of them to listen to a reasonable, balanced argument from the right.'

'These men we've brought in,' Annie went on. 'The British Pakistanis. Their grandparents came here after Partition, mostly to work in the cotton and woollen mills up north. Their parents were born here, they grew up here. Doesn't that make them British?'

'It takes a bit more than that.'

'So they need to behave a bit more like us?'

'Basically.'

'Binge-drinking, football hooliganism, casual racism, and the rest?'

'That's a fringe element. Why am I here? Obviously not to talk politics.'

'Right,' said Annie. 'When we talked before, I asked you about last Tuesday, and you said that you and Albert went back to your place after you'd been in the Hope and Anchor. About ten wasn't it?'

'That's right.'

'And after you'd had a few drinks and watched some DVDs, Albert crashed on your sofa for the night?'

'That's right. Yes. You already know all this.'

'Bear with us, Paul. You went to sleep, or passed out, in your own bed, at about three in the morning, right?'

'Yes.'

'Both at the same time?'

'What?'

'Did you both fall asleep at the same time?'

'Probably not. I mean, not precisely. Why?'

'Who fell asleep first?'

'I don't know.'

'Don't you remember letting down the sofa bed?'

'Not really.'

'And why would you stay up after he fell asleep?'

'I'm not saying I did. What's this all about?'

'Do you remember hearing Albert snoring or anything?'

'No. I can't say I do.'

'But you're certain he was there the whole time? He didn't go out or anything?'

'No.'

'Would you have noticed it? If you were asleep and he was awake, say?'

'Well, of course not, if I was asleep. I'm a sound sleeper. The sign of an untroubled conscience.'

'I hear that most serial killers have no problems falling asleep. Or maybe it's just the booze.'

Warner just smirked.

'So he could have stayed awake until you passed out, then gone out?' Annie pressed on.

'He could have, I suppose. But why would he?'

'Did you know that he had the use of a van that night?'

'He did some delivery driving on the side. His boss lived in Stockton. It was a casual arrangement. He parked round the back when he kept the van overnight.'

'You say that Albert could have gone out, if you were the one who bit the dust first, so to speak?'

'I said it's possible. Yes. But he was pissed. He wouldn't have been able to drive.'

'What if he wasn't as pissed as you thought he was?'

'You mean he might have been putting it on?'

'Possibly.'

Paul shrugged. 'Then I don't know. I didn't think so. I mean, we both had a fair bit to drink, and I certainly wouldn't have thought of driving.'

'We'd like to examine your van, Paul. Is that OK?'

'But why? It can't have been on your CCTV, or whatever you've got.'

'How do you know that?' Annie asked.

'Well, I . . . I mean . . .'

'How do you know that Albert didn't drive it after you passed out? He wouldn't use Jim Nuttall's van, would he, surely? I mean he'd know we'd connect him to that eventually. But why not use your Citroën?'

'Albert's not that bright. Besides, if you could connect him to this Nuttall character, you could certainly connect him to me.'

'Maybe so. But one way or another that van you've both told us was parked in the lane at the back of your flat *did* show up on CCTV near Bradham Lane that night. A bit of a coincidence, don't you think?'

'Maybe Nuttall did it?'

'Not very plausible, Paul. He'd have to take a taxi all the way from Stockton, which he didn't. We checked.'

'Maybe he got a mate to drop him off. I don't know. There must be some mistake.'

'I agree. Let's move on. Last time we talked, you told us you said you had only a passing acquaintance with Mimosa. Is that right?'

'Yes.'

'Did you like her?'

'Well enough, I suppose. I mean, I didn't know her well enough to really say that. She was so much younger than me.'

'Not that much. You're what, twenty-three? Mimsy was fifteen? Very attractive, too, from what I hear. Sexy.'

'She was still too young for me. I prefer women my own age.'

'Got a girlfriend at the moment, Paul?'

'Not that it's any of your business, but no.'

'Did you know that Mimosa and her best friend Carol were among a group of local underage girls who'd been groomed by a gang of Asians from the Strip? That they'd been coerced, persuaded or forced into prostitution?'

'God, no! How . . . I mean . . .'

'Nobody told you?'

'Well, obviously not. I mean, you asked me about grooming last time you talked to me, said it was something you suspected, but I never thought . . . Mimsy . . . no.'

'Some people behave recklessly, especially if they get fired up with an idea. Was Albert fired up with an idea that night?'

'What do you mean?'

'Let's say you'd been talking about Mimosa and her Pakistani groomers, for example. Might Albert have got riled up? Got a bee in his bonnet? She was his sister, after all. And they were Pakistanis.'

'But that didn't happen. We never talked about that.'

'So you say.'

'Are you saying you don't believe me?'

'We know that Albert most certainly did know. And he mentioned it in conversation with Mimosa the day before she disappeared. They ended up on bad terms.'

'Well that proves it, doesn't it,' said Paul, leaning forward. 'Don't you see. They must be involved. The Pakis. They must have done it. Have you brought them in yet?'

'We're just looking for some answers here,' said Annie. 'There's no need to get your underpants in a knot.'

'I'm not. I just don't like being called a liar. Maybe Albert did know, like you say, but he didn't tell me. I can't tell you anything. This is all a shock to me. Like I said, I thought she was on our side. They must have made her do it. Is this something to do with why Mimsy got killed?'

'We think so. We're just not sure exactly how everything ties together yet.'

'And you think Albert might have killed her?'

'We're just checking his alibi, that's all.'

'I've told you time and time again. He was at my place. We got a bit drunk, watched some DVDs between about half ten and two or three in the morning, then we fell asleep. Albert slept on the couch and he didn't wake up until eleven the next morning.'

'But you weren't in the same room as Albert all night?'

'Hell no. We didn't sleep in the same room, but we were together there watching movies.' Paul folded his arms. 'I've had enough of these insinuations and innuendos. You're simply playing tricks on me, using semantics to try to get me to admit something.'

'Admit to what?'

'Christ. I mean, you surely can't think that Albert killed his own sister.'

'Why not?'

'But she was his little sister. This is unbelievable.' He pointed towards the door. 'You've got all those bloody Pakis out there guilty as hell of grooming and raping and doing God knows what else to poor Mimsy, and you're trying to pin the blame on Albert. Shame on you.'

Annie stood up and Gerry followed suit more slowly, again using her good hand to push herself up from the chair. 'Thanks, Paul. You've been very helpful,' Annie said.

Warner just shook his head in disbelief and exasperation, then he got to his feet and walked towards the door. As he left the interview room, he gave them a backwards glance and muttered, 'Unbelievable.'

'Like they say in the movies,' Annie called after him. 'Don't leave town, we might want to talk to you again.' And when he had left, she took out her mobile.

'What did he say?' Banks asked Ursula Pemberton.

'He told me it happened at a party in the hotel suite in Blackpool. They were celebrating something or other. It was a large suite and there were several rooms. At one point, Tony told me, Caxton asked him to accompany him, and they went to a darkened bedroom. There was a woman already in there, on the bed. She seemed surprised to see them and made to leave, but Caxton wouldn't let her.'

'You mean he physically stopped her?'

'I don't know. I don't remember it exactly. Just that Caxton wouldn't let her leave. Persuaded her to stay. One thing led to another and they ended up having sex, first Caxton and the woman, then . . .' She swallowed. 'Then Tony.'

'He told you this?'

'I told you he was honest, even at his own cost.'

'Let me get this straight. Tony told you that he and Caxton raped a woman in a hotel room in Blackpool.'

'Yes. I suppose that's what it amounted to. Though he never mentioned rape. I assumed I was supposed to think the woman succumbed to Caxton's charm and Tony just happened to be a beneficiary of his largesse. None of that helped.'

'But if she wasn't willing, it was rape.'

'I'm aware of that. Tony told me Caxton said she was the kind of girl who liked it rough, but Tony thought maybe her fear was genuine.'

'Yet he raped her anyway?'

'They'd been drinking. Perhaps drugs. I don't know. All three of them. Look, Superintendent, this isn't easy for me. It wasn't easy for him, either. He wasn't proud of it. He was disgusted with himself. He was in tears when he told me.'

'What did you do?'

'I held him and told him it would be all right. That was when he told me he was going to do something about it.'

'What?'

'He was going to confront Caxton. Apparently there were some Polaroids – another of Tony's jobs – and not just the official ones. Tony had taken pictures of Caxton with girls. Some while they were having sex, he hinted.'

'Did Caxton know about these?'

'I don't know. If he did, they obviously hadn't bothered him. Men like Caxton think they're above the law.'

'Why would the Polaroids be a problem for him?'

'Tony said he was certain some of the girls were too young.'

'Did he tell you why he joined in the fun that time?'

'He just said it was the atmosphere, the moment, the sense of excitement.' She sighed. 'Something new. You know, there's a thin line between experiment and sin.'

Well, Tony had certainly found out about it the hard way, Banks thought, and so had Linda Palmer. It wasn't his place to tell Ursula Pemberton that the girl had been a fourteen-year-old virgin, that there had been no party, no drugs and very little to drink. It had no doubt cost Monaghan a great deal to tell his wife what he had told her, and his state when he got back from the Blackpool job spoke volumes about the internal struggles he'd been going through. He thought he'd come to the right decision. Confront Danny Caxton, even though he'd be damning himself at the same time. That took guts, Banks thought. But none of it expunged the thought of what they had done to Linda Palmer.

'How did you react?'

'We argued. I'm afraid I told him not to do anything,' she said. 'I was afraid.'

'Of Caxton?'

'Partly. But more of the police. He talked about going to the police.'

'Even though he'd been involved in the rape.'

'Must you call it that? Yes. I was frightened he would go to jail.'

'You didn't think he deserved to?'

She gave Banks a sharp glance. 'He was my husband,' she said.

Banks decided to let it go. No sense in making an enemy of Ursula Pemberton. 'What happened next?'

'We parted on bad terms. The next thing I knew he was dead.'

Christ, thought Banks. Monaghan had gone to Leeds and confronted Caxton with his decision, perhaps evidence in the form of the Polaroids, and threatened him with the police. But it had to be more than that. Caxton knew he had the police in his pocket, that they wouldn't listen to Monaghan. They must have turned a blind eye to Caxton's transgressions before then, as they certainly had later. It was more likely than not Tony's betrayal that angered him more than fear of exposure. Caxton was a man used to having his own way, demanding loyalty, and here was his loyal servant, his chosen one, come to threaten him with exposure. Caxton no doubt knew enough people capable of doing the job. Banks had even heard of a few ex-coppers hiring themselves out for strong-arm work, even the occasional murder. It wouldn't have been difficult to arrange. And along came the Stott brothers, bouncers in his disco, old mates from the boxing club.

Ursula remained silent for so long that Banks felt she was looking to him for exoneration, both for her and her husband. Banks didn't feel that was something he had the right to give. As if she were reading his thoughts, she said, 'I'm sorry. I know your main concern is the poor victim. I didn't know her. Tony never mentioned any names. I don't even think he knew.'

Banks was about to tell her: Linda Palmer. But he didn't.

'After Tony had been killed,' he went on, 'did you say anything about this? Did you talk to the police?'

'Yes. When I had to go up to Leeds to identify Tony's body.'

'Who did you talk to?'

'Now, I know I remember,' she said. 'He was high up. A chief superintendent, I think. I remember being impressed at the time.'

'It wasn't an inspector, then? Detective Inspector Chadwick?'

'No. I'd remember that. It was a Scottish name. Smoked a pipe. McCullen. That's who it was. Detective Chief Superintendent McCullen.'

Chadwick's boss, Banks thought. 'Did anyone takes notes?'

'No. There were just the two of us, after the identification. He had a big office. I never met with anyone else on the case, if there was anyone.'

'Oh, there was,' said Banks. 'Was the interview recorded?'

'Not that I know of.'

'Were you asked to turn in a written statement?'

'No.'

So there was nothing at all, Banks realised. No record whatsoever of Ursula Monaghan's chat with McCullen, or her fears for what had happened to her husband. McCullen himself, perhaps under instructions from the chief constable, had headed her off at the pass. 'What did you do after that?'

'I'd phone him often and ask how things were progressing, but I'd get put off and put off until all he could say was that there was no more progress. In the end, I'm sorry to say, I gave up. Moved on. I was just exhausted with it all, and it seemed to be blighting my life.'

Banks was in two minds whether to tell her that the police had been told to lay off Caxton from above, but he decided not to. 'We don't solve all our cases,' he said. 'Sadly. Sometimes they slip through the cracks.'

'I know that,' Ursula said. 'You're only human. But I was a bit cross at the time. Shall we move on?' She got unsteadily to her feet and called the dogs, who had wandered off to explore a hillock several yards away. They came running.

'I'm sorry to be bringing all these bad memories back to you,' Banks said as they started walking towards the cottage. The sea sparkled around Lindisfarne and the old ruined stone seemed to shimmer in the light. 'Especially as there's nothing to be done about it after so long.'

'It wouldn't have brought Tony back. Even if they had found out who did it.'

'It's just the case I'm pursuing. I can't really talk about it, but you'll find out when it comes to trial. The thing is, we do at least have a chance of putting Caxton away, admittedly after a lifetime of getting away with sexual abuse. I'm also hoping with what I've found out about Tony's murder, from you and other sources, I can make a convincing case for murder, or conspiracy at least. I have no concrete evidence, but I think if I can construct a plausible enough scenario a jury might believe it, given everything else.'

She hung her head. 'I'm really sorry if my actions resulted in more girls getting abused.'

'You're not responsible for any of that,' said Banks. Her husband had raped Linda Palmer, he knew, but he had confessed – made up a more palatable story, perhaps – and she had gone to the police with it. 'I don't think anything you could have done at the time would have stopped it. Stopped Caxton.'

'Can you tell me if it was girls, or boys?' Ursula asked out of the blue.

'Girls. What difference does it make?'

'The way Tony was found. You know, the place he was found in. It was obvious that everyone thought it was a gay murder. I just wondered if, you know, Caxton had been fond of young boys, that sort of thing. I mean, Tony had been involved in what happened at that party with a girl, but I just wonder if he was supposed to help find rough trade for Caxton, along with all his other duties.'

'Not that we know of. Do you think your husband could have been gay, or bi?'

'Absolutely not. I never believed it. I realise that's what most wives would say, but it's true. I'm not saying that Tony was some tough sort of macho man – he was artsy, for God's sake, he dressed a bit differently, he liked ballet and opera and he wouldn't harm a fly – but that doesn't make a person gay. And in all our time together I never once got the remotest inkling that Tony had any interest, other than friendship, in his own sex. And I've known couples who *were* in that position. Gay men married to women for years. I think my gaydar, or whatever you call it, has been consistent.'

'Why did you think he was in that public toilet, then?'

'I could only assume he was put there to make it seem that way, or taken there and killed. I don't know. I'm just sure that Caxton's men did it. I don't imagine for a moment he would have done it himself, but he probably knew people who would.'

How right you are, Banks thought. 'And you mentioned this suspicion to Detective Chief Superintendent McCullen?'

'Yes.'

They were approaching Ursula's cottage over the rise. Banks could see his Porsche gleaming in the sunlight. 'I don't think there's anything else,' he said, 'but if you remember any more details, however insignificant they might seem, let me know. And I apologise again for opening up old wounds. These cold cases have a tendency to do that.'

'It's all right,' said Ursula. 'I just hope you manage to find enough evidence to convict Caxton this time around. Will the judge put such an old man away for life?'

'I've no idea,' said Banks. 'I've known cases where a judge has determined the accused too old and infirm to serve his sentence. But this is a high-profile case – Savile and Cyril Smith were dead by the time the world found out about them, but Rolf Harris is an old man, and they sent him to prison. The way things are going, there will be a wealth of evidence against Caxton. It'll be hard not to be seen to do something.'

'Have you talked to him?'

'Yes,' said Banks.

'And?'

'And he's a pathetic old man. But it's as you said. Repulsion at first sight. Perhaps the only difference between then and now is that the mask has slipped.'

After talking to Paul Warner and Albert Moffat it was late, and both Annie and Gerry felt the need to get out of the station. It was another fine evening, and they crossed the cobbled market square where tourists browsed in the gift-shop windows or sat in the little tea rooms and coffee houses looking out of the windows. They took a shortcut to the terraced river garden down a steep winding lane with high walls and came out by the falls. There had been so little rain lately that the Swain was not much more than a trickle of water the colour of pale ale, with hardly a touch of froth. Some days, after heavy rains, the water that had drained into the Swain from deeper in the dale flowed over in a noisy cataract, drowning out all other sounds and soaking anyone nearby in spray. Today, they could hear the birds, and they decided to sit in the open-air pub by the river. It was Friday, after all, and things were more or less under control. They found a table that afforded them a little distance and privacy from the rest of the customers and Annie went inside to get the drinks.

'Christ, what a day,' she said, plonking a pint of Black Sheep bitter in front of her and a Campari and soda in front of Gerry, who was a Campari and soda kind of girl. She then sat down and put her feet up on one of the other chairs, hoping none of the bar staff would see and tell her off.

Gerry held up her glass to clink. 'Worth it, though. Cheers.'

'Cheers. I don't know about that. There's not a lot we can do right now except leave Stefan and the rest to do their work. I don't know about you, but after this pint, I'm off home for some shut-eye. Maybe when I wake up Jazz will have the DNA organised and we'll know where we are.'

'I doubt I'll sleep much,' said Gerry, 'but home sounds nice.'

'So what do you reckon?'

'There are a few things that interest me,' said Gerry, tucking a strand of hair behind her ears and leaning forward. 'First off, ever since I talked to Jade I've been trying to imagine what Mimosa was like. It's not easy to put a picture together.'

'Nothing I've heard convinces me she had any more brains than a feral cat. I'm not trying to make any excuses for what happened, but she was out for what she could get, she sounds manipulative, and she was a druggie.'

'But she was vulnerable, open to being manipulated by Sunny and his gang.'

'True enough. But remember what Jade told you on the recording. Mimosa was queen bee, or whatever they called her. She got paid for luring girls in.'

'But they made her do it.'

'Maybe so. I'm just saying she was no saint, that's all. If it hadn't been this, she'd have got herself into trouble some other way.'

'So you'd have written her off, like the social workers and the Wytherton police? You think she was just some estate slut looking for an easy ride?'

'Gerry, where's this coming from? I mean nothing of the sort. All I'm saying is that, on my reading, Mimosa was a troubled personality, and headstrong, gobby, as everyone said. Some people are just destined for trouble of one sort or another. I'm not saying it was her fault she had a fucked-up life.'

'She might have made something of herself,' Gerry said, 'if she'd had some more cultured influence in her life, like Paul Warner, for example, she could have broken out.'

'Paul Warner? Come off it, Gerry, you don't fancy him, do you?'

Gerry blushed. 'No. But you can't deny he speaks well and he's educated. He seemed to like her. I know she was too young for him, but I'm just using him as an example.'

'So all she needed was the right man in her life? Paul Warner? He dropped out of university after his first year and he's a racist. Would you want that sort of influence on your daughter?'

'Well, not the racism, no, but . . . . Oh, never mind.'

'It's part of the package.'

Gerry remained silent a moment sipping on her drink, then she said, 'Well, she could draw. She had artistic talent. She could have developed that, gone to college.'

'True enough. But just because you can draw doesn't mean you've got ability in any other department. Believe me, I've known a few artists in my time, and I could tell you a story or two. There's absolutely no connection whatsoever between art and personal morality. Or art and emotional intelligence. Quite the opposite, mostly. You just have to study the lives of the great artists to see that.' Annie took a sip of her beer. 'We'll have another go at Albert tomorrow, see if we can break him.'

'Albert's not that bright,' said Gerry. 'Can you really see him *pretending* to get drunk, then slipping out while Paul Warner's genuinely passed out in his flat, then driving the car, following the van and killing Mimosa?'

'I can see him losing it with her,' said Annie, 'but you're right, I can't see the rest. Still, we shouldn't mistake cunning for intelligence.'

'Nobody noticed anything suspicious in his room when we searched the Moffat house.'

'We didn't know what we were looking for then. Now we've got his clothes and shoes in for forensic analysis.'

'Albert knows we're bound to find his prints in the car.'

'He can explain that,' said Annie. 'But he wouldn't be able to explain blood on his shoes as easily. And there's another thing.'

'What?'

'That phone call I made after the interview, when you left to go to the loo?'

'Yes?'

'I called Superintendent Carver. Gave him a chance to redeem himself. I asked him nicely to put a watch on Paul Warner. If he dashes back home and starts acting strangely, then we'll have an idea he might be covering for his mate. And we'll have Mimosa's personal belongings in our hands tomorrow, don't forget.'

'And what if we're wrong? What's the alternative to Albert? Lenny Thornton? Sinead Moffat?'

'You've forgotten Johnny,' she said. 'Maybe his inertia is just as fake as Albert's alibi?'

Gerry laughed. 'I don't think so. Sunny or one of his mates could have done it, remember, no matter what they say. They've got no real alibis. The only problem there is that we can't find any vehicle on the CCTV associated with them.'

'We can check the footage again,' said Gerry. 'Doug did a good job checking up on Jim Nuttall. What about him?'

'Don't think so,' said Annie. 'He's not connected with any of the players here, as far as we know, except with Albert Moffat. Besides, Albert's admitted he was driving on Tuesday and Wednesday and that the car was parked behind Warner's flat all night Tuesday. Somebody else could have taken it, I suppose, and left it back there later. But I think Nuttall was just working the black-market economy, that's all, avoiding paying taxes, not to mention a proper wage. We can let the girls have a look at him when they're OK to do it, see if they recognise him from any of their assignments. Jade did say some of the men involved were white, didn't she?'

'Yes.'

'Then it wouldn't be a bad idea to dig a bit deeper, just for the sake of thoroughness, but I don't see Jim Nuttall as our killer.'

'So we're looking at Albert or Paul for it?'

'I think so,' said Annie. 'And right now I'm leaning more towards Paul. He's smart. Don't forget, he's the one who alibied Albert, but in doing so, perhaps more importantly, he alibied himself. He must have known that. Probably thought we wouldn't see it, that he put one over on us. He's arrogant enough. If you ask me, Albert genuinely doesn't have a clue what happened. He was pissed out of his mind and, whatever else he is, he loved his sister. If Paul Warner was the one who was faking it, there's no reason he couldn't have slipped out in the van. He'd have more sense than to use his own car, even if he was only planning on beating up Sunny. And he knew Nuttall's van was there.'

'But why? What's his motive? And how did he know about Mimosa? How did he know she was going to Dewsbury, or that she would come walking back up the lane?'

'He didn't. He can't have. Only somebody in with Sunny and his cousins could have known that, if it was arranged in advance. But the CCTV seems to have ruled that out. It's true we don't have a motive yet, but that doesn't mean there isn't one, just that we haven't thought of it. And maybe the Dewsbury trip is the wrong thing to be worrying about.'

'What do you mean?'

'Paul Warner's not going to admit that he knew about Mimsy and Sunny, is he, or about what was going on with the girls, the grooming. But we know that Albert knew, and what if Albert, in his cups, told Warner earlier that Tuesday night and was so pissed he doesn't remember?'

'Doesn't help us much, does it? There was still no motive. And Albert can't have known about the Dewsbury trip, surely?'

'Not that we know of, though maybe he did. Again, we don't have the full picture. But as I said, maybe we've been worrying too much about the Dewsbury trip. What if Paul Warner really did have a thing for Mimsy?'

'We've no evidence of that. Look at the age diff—'

'Despite that. What difference does age make? Sunny's in his forties. We know she was drawn to older men, even abused by them. We're forgetting that although Mimsy was a child in some ways, she was a fully grown woman in others, attractive, with a nice figure, available, or so it might have seemed. Apparently, she oozed sex. Warner said he thought she was mature for her age the first time we talked to him. She also liked to hang out helping him and Albert on jobs. Maybe something happened. Maybe he got an eyeful when she went up the ladder one day and he liked what he saw? They had to be left alone together at some point. Maybe she flirted a bit with Warner, or more – again, no excuse or motive for what happened, but maybe it's part of the cause, and it wouldn't be against what we know of her nature. And there was something you said earlier, about maybe if Mimosa had a cultured person to help her break out, someone like Paul Warner.'

'Possibly. But I still think you're pushing it a bit, guv. How did Warner know where she was, or where she was going that night?'

'Well, if Albert told him about Sunny, he'd have a good idea where she might be. The rest, I admit I don't know. But if Vic Manson finds any prints other than Albert's and Jim Nuttall's in the VW, then we'll be looking at Paul Warner's for comparison first. And remember, yonks back, Dr Glendenning said there might be a chance of matching the pattern of the shoes used to kick Mimosa? If Warner hasn't got rid of them already – and why would he chuck away a perfectly good pair of Doc Martens or whatever if he thought he'd pulled off a clever one and wasn't likely to be in the frame? If we keep pushing, the most he'd admit to is giving his mate a false alibi, and Albert doesn't have the brains to wriggle out of a trap like that. Look how arrogant Warner is. He thinks we're all thick plods.'

They sipped their drinks and watched the swans swimming under the overhanging willows on the quiet part of the river beyond the falls. Clouds of midges and the occasional wasp buzzed around them.

'I could just fall asleep right now,' Gerry said.

Then Annie's mobile buzzed. She answered, listened for a few moments, then frowned and put it back in her handbag. 'There goes your early evening kip,' she said.

'What? Who was it?'

'My new best friend Superintendent Carver. He says the men he put on Paul Warner report that minutes after our lad got home, he was out again with a black bin bag, which he proceeds to put in the back of his van. They followed him into the Wytherton Household Waste Recycling Centre and apprehended him before he could dispose of anything. He made a fuss about his rights and lawyers and blah-blah. And the long and short of it is, he's on his way to the station and we'd better get back there to welcome him.' She paused and glanced at her watch. 'On second thoughts, it'll take a while, so let's have another drink, or more, it's a nice evening. A Friday, too. And things are starting to go our way. We can invite Alan and Winsome down here, too, if they're free.'

'What do we do about Warner?'

'Don't worry, I'm not inviting him. If we charge him we can't talk to him again. I'll call Doug at the station and we'll have him arrested on arrival. Then we'll have twenty-four hours. Let him cool his heels overnight. We'll see if we can put a rush on the Nuttall van forensics and get a couple of lab people to put in a bit of overtime and get started on the contents of that bin bag. Apparently, in addition to a pair of Doc Martens, some jeans and a polo shirt, there are some drugs. All that should give us enough ammunition to take on Warner again.'

'But what do we do with Albert Moffat in the meantime? We've already got him arrested under suspicion.'

'We keep him where he is. We arrest Warner for conspiracy to commit murder.'

'Do you think they were in it together?'

'It's an interesting possibility, isn't it? Your shout, I think.'

Linda Palmer was sitting in her garden that evening working on her memoir, girding herself to approach the main event. It was the dusk of another beautiful day, and she kept looking up from the page to watch the kingfisher scanning the water for fish. She had got herself as far as the Blackpool hotel, through the preamble of autographs, promises of help with her career, the ride in the plush car, the champagne. She was in the hotel suite now, on her second glass . . .

He asked me to sing him something. That's how it all started. I asked what. He said anything I wanted. It felt strange just to stand there and sing while he sat on the edge of the bed watching and listening. But I did it. I sang 'You Don't Have to Say You Love Me' because I loved Dusty Springfield and that was my favourite song of hers. I just couldn't believe it. I felt like pinching myself. There I was, little Linda Palmer from Leeds, singing for Danny Caxton! We had some more champagne and he said I was very good and with a bit of coaching I could go a long way. I would also have to pass more tests if I wanted to be on *Do Your Own Thing!* I asked him what sort of tests he meant and he smiled and patted the bedspread beside him and told me to sit down. My head was beginning to spin and I felt a bit dizzy, so I sat. It was a pink candlewick bedspread, I remember that. I can remember the texture of it to this day and I've hated candlewick ever since. I was starting to feel nervous, as well as light-headed, with butterflies fluttering in my tummy, but I sat. 'It's more than just singing ability, you see,' he said. 'You also have to project yourself, be sexy. Can you be sexy?' I muttered something like 'I'm only fourteen,' and started to get up. He grabbed my wrist. He was strong and it hurt. He pulled me back down. 'You know what I mean by sexy, don't you? Of course you do, you little tease.' He squeezed my breast and a strange expression came over his face, a kind of serenity. He sighed. I tried to get up again. My heart was beating fast and hard. My face was burning and my breast ached. I just wanted to run out of there. But he was too strong. I cried, 'No, no, no,' but he—

Linda stopped and leaned back in her chair, reached for a cigarette. Her breath caught in her throat, and the sheen of sweat on her forehead wasn't entirely due to the heat of the sun. Even now the memory had the power to move her, to disturb her. She looked across the river to the tree, but it was getting late and the kingfisher had gone. With a shaking hand, she picked up her pen again . . .

I was tall for my age, and everyone said I had the most beautiful blond hair. It tumbled down to my shoulders and the fringe at the front touched my eyebrows. I was wearing my yellow sundress, I remember, which came to just below my knees. I loved that dress, the bright colour of sunshine, the touch of cool cotton against my skin on a warm day. He pushed me on my back. Holding my wrists together and pinning me down with one hand while his other hand went up my dress, over my thighs, pushing between my legs, roughly. He was very excited now, making little grunting noises. I told him again to stop, that he was hurting me, but he just laughed and pulled at my underwear. I struggled and he turned me over so I was on my stomach, and he was holding my hands tight behind my back, like handcuffs. I was crying now and begging him to stop. I knew there was no use struggling. I suppose I abandoned myself to the inevitable. I had entered that place where there was no hope.

Then I felt him inside me, hard and rough, pushing. I cried out because it hurt so much and I think I struggled again. He kept my hands pinioned behind my back and covered my mouth with his other hand, so it was hard to breathe then his arm went around my throat squeezing hard enough to make me quiet. His shirtsleeve buttons must have been undone because I could feel the hairs of his forearm on my throat. He pushed my face into the bedspread and it smelled of the warm fabric and soap. I could hardly breathe. It was hot in the room. He was all sweaty and he tasted of something. It was like make-up, but then I didn't know what it was. Later I realised it must have been the greasepaint that he'd worn onstage. The window was open but I don't remember any breeze, just the sounds of the Big Dipper rattling on its tracks and the screams of excited riders.

I don't know if all that is true or not. Some of it is. I know he raped me, but I don't remember the details very clearly. The dialogue may be reinvented. Perhaps my imagination is working overtime. It was mostly just a blur of pain, struggle and the room spinning. Perhaps they will ask me in court, though I can't imagine why, and if they do, I suppose I will have to tell them the truth as best I can. But I do remember something I had forgotten. It may mean nothing, but when I caught a glimpse of his forearm, I noticed some numbers tattooed on his skin. I had no idea what they could have been. A telephone number written in blue ballpoint? But I've since seen enough films and read enough books to know that it was something like the concentration camp numbers the Nazis used to tattoo on people's arms. Which is odd, because I don't think he was Jewish and I thought he grew up over here. But it might mean something to you. At least it's something that might help to verify my identification, if that's required. It seemed to me that these numbers were something he wanted to keep secret, but I saw them. I'm just sorry I can't remember them the way you remember Elvis's Teen and Twenty Disc Club membership number.

When he had finished, he left me like a rag doll, sprawled there. I hurt all over. I even thought my arm might have been broken. I could hear him talking to someone. I couldn't make out the words through the fog of pain but I thought I heard him say, 'You know you want to. Go on, do your own thing!' Then he laughed. I had forgotten about the other man, the one who'd taken photographs earlier. Maybe I assumed he'd left the room. I don't know. Most likely I didn't think about him at all. I had been vaguely aware of occasional sounds in the background I suppose I must have thought they were coming through the open window. Someone must have put a coin in the machine, because the Laughing Policeman started up from the Pleasure Beach and sounded like he would never stop. I hate that sound to this day.

As I slowly turned myself over and tried to get up, I saw him again, the other man. He was very close to me and he was fumbling with the front of his trousers. I probably screamed or cried out again. I don't remember. Again I was forced down and again a man forced himself on me, in me, and again I don't remember much about it.

Maybe after Caxton I was even more passive. I'd stopped struggling completely. There was no point. They were too strong. I was frightened they'd hurt me if I fought back. I just lay there and closed my eyes, trying to imagine being in another place but failing. I didn't fight. I've always felt guilty about that. Like it was my fault for not fighting.

Maybe I blacked out with the pain and fear. All I knew was the weight was suddenly gone from me and I could move freely, if painfully. I had a bag with me, I remember, a shoulder bag I always carried, where I kept keys and money and *Lorna Doone* and my autograph book, and for some reason it was in my mind. I had to have my bag. I was leaving and I had to have my bag. It

was on a little polished wooden table with bowed legs by the
door and I must have picked it up as I stumbled out. Nobody
tried to stop me. I heard Caxton say behind me that I wasn't to
tell anyone. Something like that. Nobody would believe me.
People would just think I was a lying little whore. He said I ought
to be grateful that he'd had sex with me. That I'd lost my virginity
to the great Danny Caxton. They were talking again as I went out
but I don't know what they were saying. I was in a daze and God
knows what I looked like but I walked down the corridor, found a
lift and pressed the button for the ground floor. I don't know if
anybody noticed me in the lobby but I felt as if everyone was
looking at me and they knew I'd done a bad thing.

I must have walked around Blackpool for hours, but all I
remember is being sick in the street, people skirting around me,
looking at me, thinking I was just a drunken whore. I wanted to
scream out and tell them what had happened to me, but the
shame was too great. Was it my fault for singing that song? Did
he think it was some sort of an invitation?

I was so late back that I missed dinner. I must have looked a
sight. I just remember my father telling me off for being late and
my mother saying I didn't look well. I said I didn't feel well,
either, and I wasn't hungry. My mother was worried. She felt my
forehead, said it was a bit hot and she hoped I wasn't coming
down with something. I thought she could smell the sick on my
breath and maybe thought I'd been drinking. All I wanted was a
bath to wash off the filth of what had happened to me, but we
weren't allowed to run the hot water at that time of evening, so I
just went to our room, undressed, brushed my teeth for ages and
tried to wash myself as best I could with cold water from the
basin. Then I curled up in bed and cried and cried and cried.

I don't remember when Melanie came to bed. Perhaps I was
already asleep. She told me the next day she saw some spots of
blood on my knickers, which I had just dropped by the bedside.
She asked me what happened. I said my period must have come

early. That was also why I could get away with not feeling well and being a bit off all the following week. It was common knowledge between Mum and me that I had 'difficult' periods, that sometimes the cramps were painful and I became moody and withdrawn. It was the perfect excuse even though I wasn't due for another week and a half. I wasn't always as regular as some people—

Linda put down her pen and refilled her wine glass. She had let her cigarette burn down on the ashtray while she wrote, so she lit another. She noticed that her hand was shaking as she did so, perhaps because it had been so tense gripping the pen to write. Dusk was gathering quickly, and the shadows lengthened on the garden, the river itself already dark under the shade of the sheltering trees. A blackbird sang somewhere, louder than the other birds. She knew she was almost finished now and already felt spent, the way she did when she knew she'd got to the end of a particularly difficult poem after weeks of drafts and revisions. She put the cigarette down again and set off on the final words . . .

The rest of the week went by like a bad dream. I don't think Melanie knew what to make of me but she never said anything directly. I tried to do the things we enjoyed doing, but my heart wasn't in it and I'm sure Melanie knew. It was hard to believe at first that life just went on as normal when we got back home, that people just went about their business as usual as if nothing had happened, like in Auden's poem, while Icarus' wax wings melt, the horse scratches its behind and the dog goes on with its doggy life, when all I really wanted was to stop all the clocks. No, that's not true. That's a different poem. And I didn't want a big fuss. I didn't want anyone to know, especially after that abortive visit to the police. I wanted everyone to go on like the horse and the dog and not notice me, my imaginary wax wings melting as I approached the sun, falling, falling into the darkness of the sea. Icarus died. I pulled myself out of the darkness, shook myself off and went on with my life. I squeezed it all into a ball and hid it away in the deepest darkest place I could find, where it remains to this day, a dark star inside me.

In a very odd way, I feel that I've been feeding off it ever since, the poetry has been feeding off it, though never about it, this dark star I made of the thing that happened to me when I was on the cusp of adulthood. This dark star that I haven't told anyone about. I think even now talking about it worries me not so much because it upsets me, though that is certainly the case, but because I'm afraid I might lose something by letting out the darkness that feeds me. Lose my muse, my creativity, my poetry. I wrote earlier that sometimes I need the darkness, and I believe this is true. But it doesn't mean I wanted what happened.

It's odd the way memory works on the sense of time. When it happened, it all seemed to happen so fast. Though the pain seemed never-ending, details flashed by, hardly noticed. The texture of candlewick, smell of greasepaint, the Laughing Policeman, the numbers on Caxton's arm. When you think about it afterwards, it runs in slow motion. You remember the details. But when you recall it so many years later it has settled, then shifted and altered in your memory and become something else. Not that it didn't happen, and not that it didn't happen more or less the way I remember it happened, but I have perhaps forgotten some things and even added some. I couldn't swear to the Laughing Policeman or the click of the camera. It may have been longer between my arrival in the suite and the rape. But I do remember that two men raped me that day. Surely that is the important thing? One was Danny Caxton, the other is the man I saw in the photograph. I did sing 'You Don't Have to Say You Love Me', and I do remember the numbers. Maybe Caxton said something else when I was leaving. Maybe more was said, but if

it was it has gone now. This is the best I can do. It's as true as I
can make it.

When I first started out, my poetry was free, fanciful, shocking,
with outrageous imagery and flights of jazzy rhythmic cadences. I
couldn't get it out quickly enough, tripping over my own feet to
find out what the next metaphor would be. I hardly ever revised
anything. Now, though, my verse seems crabbed, constipated,
metaphysical, slow and hard to squeeze out. The critics like it.
They tell me it has a certain stately grace. Is that what's
happened to me? Strange that it should flow so easily in my
youth, after what happened, then seem to harden, to crystallise
and insist on taking certain rigid forms and structures in my
middle age. Stately grace is all very well, but sometimes I long
for that free loping rhythm and ringing cadence of my youth, like
I long for that carefree innocent young girl that was.

Linda closed the notebook and put down the pen. She could
hardly see any more for tears. Darkness had fallen, and the
last of the swallows were swooping and diving over the woods.
The bats would be out soon. She rubbed her eyes, filled her
wine glass to the brim and lit another cigarette.

16

'Well, Paul, it looks like the end of the road for you, doesn't it?'

'No comment,' said Warner. He was sitting nervously in the interview room beside his legal aid solicitor, who didn't seem too happy at being woken up early on a Saturday morning. Warner had balked at Jessie Malton, perhaps because she was a woman and she was black, but he was quickly put in his place and told it wasn't as easy as that to change legal aid representation, and you certainly couldn't do it simply because you objected to the lawyer's colour and gender.

'I think your attitude might soon change,' said Annie, opening the thick folder in front of her. While Annie and Gerry had been enjoying themselves at the Riverside Inn, they had managed to persuade Jazz Singh to work a late shift and Vic Manson to stay on an extra hour. Vic was married, so all he had to do was phone and say he'd be home a bit late, but Jazz had had a hot date that she wasn't too pleased about cancelling. On the other hand, she knew what had been done to Mimsy Moffat, and she wanted to contribute her best efforts to putting her killer away, and if her girlfriend couldn't understand that about her by now, she told Annie, there was no point going on with the relationship. Perhaps Annie and Gerry could have gone at him that evening, too, but they wouldn't have had anywhere near as much ammunition as they had now – including Mimosa's sketchbook and mobile – and he wouldn't have had a night in the cell to probe his conscience, if he had one, or anticipate the worst, if he didn't.

'First off, we managed to recover Mimosa's belongings from the van she was in on the night she died,' Annie said, 'and we found a couple of interesting things among them.'

'What's that got to do with me?'

'There's a little sketchbook, for a start. They were sketches of mostly people she knew – Albert, her mother, Jade, the other girls, Sunny and his pals. And you.'

'I've seen that. So what? She always had a pencil and a sketchbook in her hands, even when you wanted her to do a bit of work.'

'Then there was her mobile,' Annie went on. 'Calls to and from Albert, Jade, Sunny, home. And again, you. Mostly from.'

'I told you she helped me and Albert out sometimes.'

'So these phone calls were all work-connected?'

'What else would they be?'

'Most went unanswered. About fifteen over the past month. Couldn't you get through to her?'

'Obviously not. No doubt she was busy with her Paki friends.'

'They weren't friends, Paul. At least not towards the end. What was so important that you couldn't pass on a message to her through Albert? You saw him often enough.'

'What do you mean?'

'Fifteen unanswered calls. Your friend's little sister. It's odd, that's all.'

'I don't see why.'

'Did she tell you anything about her association with the Pakistanis?' Gerry asked.

'No. For Christ's sake, I've told you, she agreed with us!'

'Us?'

'Me and Albert. I don't understand this. Mimsy was always making disparaging remarks about Pakis. She even got in trouble for it at school.'

'But you didn't talk about her odd behaviour with Albert last Tuesday night, didn't get him all het up?'

'No. I told you. We watched DVDs and fell asleep.'

'What about the fingerprint?' Annie said.

'What fingerprint?'

'We found Albert's fingerprints in Jim Nuttall's van, as you'd expect. But why did we also find yours? The same van that Albert Moffat drove on a casual basis, the one that was parked in the lane at the back of your building on the night in question.'

'No comment.'

'You've already been told you don't have to say anything,' Annie reminded him, 'so it's well within your rights to say "no comment", but as I'm sure Ms Malton will tell you, that bit about later relying on something in court is a deal-breaker. Should this case go to court, and I have to tell you the CPS think we have a good case, then you will almost certainly be asked this question, among others, and your "no comment" from today's interview will be noted at the time. But we do have the fingerprint. Think about it, Paul.'

Warner looked disconcerted and turned to Jessie Malton, who whispered a few words in his ear. He clearly didn't like what he had heard. 'All right,' he said. 'It's a simple enough explanation. I've been with Albert a few times on road trips.'

'Including Sheffield, the day of Mimosa Moffat's murder?'

'That's right.'

'And the person who took delivery there will vouch for you?'

'Well, I don't know about that. I mean, I got Albert to drop me off in the city centre so I could do a bit of shopping, so he wouldn't have seen me.'

'What did you buy?'

'This and that.'

'Got the receipts?'

'I threw them away.'

'Pity,' said Annie. 'Did you use a credit or debit card?'

'I paid cash.'

'Right,' said Annie. 'Why did you head to the local recycling plant with a bin bag full of clothes and a pair of shoes as soon as you got home from your last interview here?'

'I'd been meaning to take them for ages. I don't know why I did it then, particularly. I just wanted something to do.'

'Why not take them to a charity shop? They were in perfectly good condition.'

'Never thought.'

'Are you sure you weren't feeling anxious about what they might reveal?'

'I wouldn't say I was anxious. I just felt like it. OK?'

He had raised his voice for the first time, and Jessie Malton tapped him on the arm and whispered in his ear.

'Sorry,' he said. 'This is putting a lot of stress on me.'

'Why is it stressful, Paul, if you've got nothing to hide?' Gerry asked. 'You were helpful enough before. Remember? You told us that Albert Moffat was with you the whole time after you got back home from the pub on Tuesday until eleven the following morning.'

'Well, I thought he was. I mean, I suppose he could have slipped out if I dozed off or something.'

'If?' said Gerry. 'Did you doze off?'

'I might have done. I don't remember. Like I said, we were drinking.'

'Are you trying to tell us that Albert nipped out and murdered his sister?'

'No. I'm not saying that. Just that I could have been mistaken. He might have gone out, if I was asleep.'

'Were you asleep?'

'I don't remember.'

'How about if *you* went out when *he* dozed off?' Annie said. 'Is that a viable scenario?'

'That's not how it happened.'

Annie paused. 'There is one other thing.'

'Oh. Yes?'

'Yes, Paul. You see, we found one of your fingerprints under the outside door handle, on the driver's side.'

'Sure. I spelled Albert for a while. He was a bit hungover. We changed places. I drove.'

'Very considerate of you. But the fingerprint, *your* fingerprint, was a bloody fingerprint. And the blood was Mimosa Moffat's. What do you have to say about that?'

'No comment.'

'I thought so.'

Jessie Malton looked as impassive as ever.

Annie went on. 'Well, I'm sure you know what that means. I'm just trying to clear up the events of that Tuesday night. We have your bloody fingerprint under the door handle of the van, not Albert's. Now, Albert has used the van since then, we know, but he didn't mention you being with him. Luckily for us, your bloody fingerprint was in an out-of-the-way spot. Easy to miss when you gave it a quick wipe down. It seems as if you might have been a bit shaken or agitated when you first tried to open the door after beating Mimsy Moffat to death.'

'Detective,' said Jessie Malton. 'Can we have no more of that?'

'Sorry. Slip of the tongue. But I'm sure both you and Ms Malton will realise that this needs a bit of explanation.'

'I must have cut myself before I spelled Albert on Wednesday, that's all.'

Annie sighed. 'Paul. Paul. I've already told you it was Mimosa Moffat's blood. Believe me, we've checked. It's hers. No doubt about it. How did you come to have Mimosa's blood on your hands on Wednesday in Sunderland, if indeed you were there at all?'

'You must have made a mistake. Lots of people probably used that van since . . .'

'Since when, Paul? Since you used it?'

'I was going to say since it was parked at the back of the flat.'

'But they haven't, Paul. Yes, Albert Moffat drove it back to Jim Nuttall's after his delivery to Sunderland the following day, and you say you were with him, but since then nobody but Mr Nuttall has used it. We checked. Albert's and Nuttall's fingerprints were close to yours, but they didn't overlap, they didn't obliterate yours, and there was no blood on them. He's so used to opening that van door, he probably grasps the same spot every time by habit. You, on the other hand, being shaken up, as I said, reached too far the wrong way and left a clear and well-protected print. There's no way around it, Paul.'

'This is all just circumstantial. You can't go to court with a case as flimsy as this.'

'Can't we, Paul?' Annie turned over a sheet. 'What about the pills?'

'What pills?'

'The ones in the bin bag you were trying to get rid of. We'll be doing further analysis, but for the moment we have it on good authority that they're Flunitrazepam, more commonly known as Rohypnol, or roofies. Inadequate men give them to unsuspecting females to put them to sleep before sex. When the girls wake up, their memories are vague. Sometimes they don't even remember they've been raped. Is that what happened to you, Paul? Did women forget they'd had sex with you? Was it that forgettable? Did you give one of those pills to Mimosa and rape her? Did she forget? Or did she remember and taunt you with it?'

'Again, Detective, I shouldn't have to tell you to give up the fishing expedition,' said Jessie Malton.

'Sorry.' Annie took a deep breath and released it slowly. 'Sometimes when you go fishing you catch something. That's not what you used them for the other night, though, is it? Sex. That time you slipped one to Albert and he went out like a light after all he'd had to drink. You'd been carefully pacing yourself, pretending to keep up with his drinking, but you hadn't had all that much, had you?'

Warner looked at Jessie Malton. 'This is preposterous,' he said. 'Can't you stop them?'

'If you don't wish to comment, then say so,' said Jessie Malton. Annie could hear her distancing herself from Warner.

'No comment,' he said.

'Let's talk about the shoes, then,' Annie went on. 'The Doc Martens you were about to get rid of at the recycling plant.'

Paul squirmed.

'They look as if they've been cleaned thoroughly, but we found traces of blood on those, too,' Annie said. 'And do you know what? It was Mimosa Moffat's blood. You tried to get rid of it, didn't you, scrubbing and polishing, but it's hard, Paul. It gets in the seams, and it's hard to get out.' Paul seemed to be shrinking deeper into his chair. Annie pressed her advantage. 'And do you know what's worst of all,' she went on. 'What's probably the most appalling thing anyone can do to another human being.' She let the silence stretch. 'You jumped on her, Paul. I don't know whether you did it while she was still alive or after you'd killed her, but you stamped on her, and that stamp made an imprint. And that imprint – from Mimosa Moffat's skin, Paul – matches the right shoe you were about to get rid of when Superintendent Carver's men apprehended you. There are several scuffs and scratches on the sole that act as unique identifying features. What do you have to say to that?' Annie let the silence stretch again. 'Nothing?' she said after a while. 'Well, that shouldn't surprise me. I mean, what is there to say after you've punched and kicked a defenceless young girl to death and stamped on her when she was down?'

'I didn't . . . I didn't . . .'

Annie leaned forward. 'You didn't what, Paul? Come on, I'd like to know. Because right now I'm just thinking you were such an arrogant bastard that you didn't even bother getting rid of the shoes you kicked her to death with after until you were worried we were getting close. Don't you think it's time to come clean with us? I told you it was the end of the road.'

Paul looked at her. His eyes were red-rimmed, his face drained of colour. 'I didn't mean to.'

'Didn't mean to what, Paul?'

Jessie Malton leaned over to whisper something, but Paul brushed her off and said, 'Kill her. I didn't mean to kill her,' before she could stop him. Jessie Malton dropped her pencil on her legal pad and looked up at the ceiling, muttering something under her breath.

Annie felt the tension leave her body like air from a tyre, but there was still more work to be done. 'You're admitting you killed her, are you, Paul?'

'Yes. I killed her. But I didn't mean to. The silly bitch.'

'Why did you kill her?'

'Can't you guess?'

'You loved her?'

'Loved? I don't know. Maybe. I *wanted* her. Or I thought I did.'

'Did you sleep with her?'

Warner stared down at the bare desk for a few seconds before answering. 'Once. Yes.'

'How did that happen? Did you give her a roofie and rape her?'

'No. She came around looking for Albert, but he was off somewhere. You know . . . one thing led to another.'

'Are you sure you didn't give her a roofie?'

'No way. She was a bit drunk.'

'She was very young, Paul. Underage, in fact.'

'But she could seem so mature. I could see something in her. I don't know. I thought if I could get through to her, you know, I could change her. I could save her.'

'Save her from what?'

'From being just like all those stupid empty-headed young sluts she spent her time with. She was really talented. An artist. We talked about her going to art college. She could study design, and with my practical skills we could make beautiful stuff, maybe get rich. She just had a bit of growing up to do first, that's all.'

It was certainly what plenty of women tried to do with men, Annie thought, change them, improve them, and more often than not to no avail. 'It was a nice dream,' Annie said. 'So what went wrong?'

'You're right about what Albert said. He'd known for a week or so that Mimsy was seeing the Paki, though I don't think he knew the full story of what was going on. You've probably figured it out for yourselves that Albert isn't exactly the brightest bulb in the chandelier. It didn't take me long to figure it out from his drunken ramblings that night. Sure, he was the one who fell asleep. Passed out would be a better word. And yes, he had a bit of help from me.'

'Go on, Paul,' said Annie. 'You were jealous?'

'Not just that. You can't psychoanalyse my feelings that simply. It was far more complicated than mere jealousy.'

'Tell us, then.'

'You wouldn't understand. The impurity. The defilement.'

'Mimosa was hardly a paragon of virtue, Paul.'

'I know that. But I . . . I mean, with the right person . . . She didn't have to be a write-off. She wasn't stupid, she just liked a good time. She was young. She would have grown out of it,

all that silliness. I could have helped shape her, make something of her. I could have changed her.'

'Proper *My Fair Lady* business again,' said Gerry. 'Teach
her to talk properly and all that?'

Warner scowled at her. 'You can talk like that if you want,'
he said. 'Cheapen it. It's just what I'd expect. I told you you
couldn't understand how complex my feelings are.'

'Well, let's not worry ourselves too much about your
complex feelings, then,' said Annie, 'and you can just tell us
what happened. The facts. Pretend we don't care why.'

'I'd had a few drinks, too, so maybe I was a bit drunk, I
don't know. You know how you get these ideas fixed in your
mind and you can't get rid of them. The idea of her with them
just wouldn't go away.'

'Was this the first time you knew anything about what she
was doing, her connection with the grooming gang?'

'Yes. She never said anything to me.'

'I don't suppose she would,' Annie said. But hadn't you
noticed any change in her over the past few months?'

'She was a bit more sophisticated, but I put that down to . . .
well . . .'

'You? The Henry Higgins effect?'

Warner looked away. 'I suppose so.'

'Anything else?'

'She was more moody. I didn't really see a lot of her, so it's
hard to say.'

'Was she avoiding you?'

'I think so.'

'So what did you do on Tuesday night?'

'I slipped Albert a roofie, like you said. It was easy enough.
He was out in no time.'

'Why did you do that?'

'So I could take the van without him knowing.'

'Why did it matter whether he knew or not?'

'I . . . I . . .'

'Were you planning to do something to Mimosa at this time?'

'No. No way. I just couldn't get the image out of my head. Her with them. I thought I might get into it with the Pakis, break a few bones, but there was no way I was going to hurt Mimsy.'

'Why didn't you take your own van?'

'Because it's got my name splashed all over the fucking side. I know about CCTV on the roads and all that. They can even get your number plate.'

'You didn't want to be seen, didn't want to be on record?'

'Well, no.'

'Why not? Unless you were planning to do something illegal.'

'I told you. All I wanted to do was see if Mimsy was there, reason with her, but I thought I might get into a rumble with the Pakis. If I hurt one of them really bad, maybe the police would try to find me. Why make it easy? The Pakis could beat seven shades of shit out of me and that would be fine. I'd deserve it. But if I do it to them it's not only GBH, it's a fucking hate crime, too. Racism.'

'But you are a racist, Paul.'

'I'm entitled to my opinions. I'm not the only one.'

'That's a spurious argument. Never mind. So Albert Moffat had nothing to do with Mimsy's murder at all? You didn't take his car in order to implicate him?'

'No. But I told you, it wasn't murder. I didn't mean to kill her.'

'I forgot. It was an accident, right? Kicking her to death. How did you know Mimosa was going to get in a van with three Asian men that night?'

'I didn't. But Albert had said he'd seen her getting in a taxi next to the takeaway the week before, that she was hanging out with them. It had been preying on my mind all evening, that she was with them. I knew about the grooming business going on around the country. She hadn't answered any of my phone messages. I wasn't really thinking clearly but I just had to go down there and see for myself. I thought maybe she'd be there, at the flat.'

'And then what?'

'I've no idea. I didn't have a plan.'

'Maybe you'd beat up Sunny and carry Mimsy off?'

'Something like that. But not Mimsy. I'd never . . . I never expected that. I would never . . . if she hadn't. It was her own fault.'

'Oh, spare us that, at least, Paul. What time was this when you set off for the Strip?'

'I don't know. Eleven. Half eleven. Something like that. I took the keys and drove the van down the Strip, parked on the other side down the road. Like I said, I was just going to watch for a while, you know, see if she came in or out. I suppose I must have been a bit pissed but I felt like I was sobering up fast. The takeaway was still open. There was only the cook bloke working there, but it wasn't busy so he mostly sat reading the paper. I thought of just going to the flat and walking up, just like that, and confronting them, but I stayed put. Then, when I'd been there about twenty minutes, half an hour, the door opened and out they came. There was the owner of the takeaway and Mimsy, along with three other Pakis. Mimsy and the three men got in a dirty white van that had been parked just down the street, then the owner bloke waved goodbye and went into the takeaway and started chatting and laughing with the cook bloke. I gave them a few minutes, then I followed the van.'

'Why did you do that?' Annie asked.

'For crying out loud! Mimsy was in that van with three Pakis. I wanted to know where they were going, what they were going to do. Maybe I could intervene at the other end, persuade her to come back, beat the shit out of them, get her away from them. I'd no idea what they were planning, but I mean she obviously needed help. She was going in a totally wrong direction here.'

'So you were going to rescue her? Play the knight in shining armour?'

'Something like that.'

'What went wrong?'

'I waited about ten minutes or so at the top of Bradham Lane. I knew they'd see me if I set off down there straight away, and there was really only one way to go at the end unless you're heading for the high dales or the local villages, and that's the main road into West Yorkshire. I figured they were probably from Bradford or somewhere like that where there's a lot of Pakis, and that's the road they'd take. I knew I could catch up with them and the other roads would be a bit busier, so they wouldn't notice me.'

'But something unexpected happened, didn't it?'

'I was driving down Bradham Lane and I saw her – Mimsy – staggering towards me. She had no clothes on and she was filthy, half covered in mud. I stopped to give her a lift and when she saw it was me, she stopped in her tracks. She was stoned on something, but she was hurt, too, I could tell. Them Pakis, they'd done stuff to her. I told her to come with me, I'd take care of her. She just stood there, so I grabbed her wrist. Then she started struggling, calling me names, saying she'd rather walk home or go back with them than with someone like me. I couldn't believe it. There she was, all dirty and bloody and I was offering to help her, to get away from all that and take care of her, and she just said of all the people she had to bump into it had to be me.'

'Why do you think she reacted like that, Paul?'

'I don't know. I mean, we hadn't parted on good terms.'

'After you slept with her?'

'Yes. It wasn't . . . I mean, she was drunk at the time, when she came round, like. When she sobered up a bit afterwards she laid into me for taking advantage of her.'

'Did you force her?'

'No way. It just, you know, it happened.'

'But Mimosa wasn't quite the slut everyone thought she was?'

'She said she didn't want to be around me again. That I was like all the other men who just took from her. But I wanted to give. I tried to tell her but she wouldn't listen. I tried to talk to her the next time I saw her with Albert, but she just cut me, as if I wasn't there. I wanted to help her. I thought we could really get somewhere together. It didn't matter how old she was.'

'Is that what all the phone calls were about?'

'Yes. I wanted to tell her that she meant something to me.'

'So why didn't you help her when she needed it most?'

Warner hung his head. 'I don't know. She was on drugs, strange drugs, not like she usually was if she was high or pissed. I couldn't get her to calm down. I couldn't make sense of her. And I couldn't help myself. I snapped. Simple as that. I slapped her, just to try to snap her out of it, like, and she tried to slap me back. There was a bit of a scuffle. She called me some names. I saw red. Called me a perv and a paedo. I mean, *me*, when she was with them Pakis. Next thing I knew she was on the ground, not moving. I didn't mean it. I didn't. Really.' He put his head in his hands.

'So this was the girl you loved. Maybe? Someone you wanted to help, wanted to be with. And when you saw her naked and dirty and hurt, instead of lust you felt rage, and instead of pity you felt anger. Is that right?'

Warner nodded, his head in his hands, crying now. 'It came out all wrong, all fucked up.'

'She was coming down off ketamine, Paul,' said Annie. 'It's a bit different from roofies. Much harder to control people on K. And she'd been gang-raped by three men. Did you know she was dead when you drove away?'

Warner sniffed and looked up, wide-eyed. 'No. I didn't know anything. Only that I'd lost it.'

'So you just left her there, to die naked in the road,' said Annie. 'Good one, Paul. I'm sure Albert and his family will be proud of you.'

'They're a waste of space. They didn't care about her. At least I tried.'

'To do what, Paul? Do what everyone else did to her except her family? Take advantage of her? Use and abuse her?'

'No. To give her a better life. The life she deserved.'

'What route did you take back to Wytherton? You didn't go the same way you came.'

'I took a longer route, back up the lane then left and over the tops.'

'Why?'

'No CCTV.'

'So by then you were thinking clearly enough save your own skin?'

'Of course I was. I knew what I'd done. I'm not an idiot.'

'No, of course not.' Annie put the papers back in the file folder and closed it. She and Gerry both shook their heads. Jessie Malton looked as if she'd rather be anywhere else. Then, while Paul Warner sobbed into his cupped hands, Annie and Gerry left to consult Banks and the CPS about the specifics of the charges. On their way out, Annie asked the PC outside the door to take Warner back to his cell. It was Monday before he'd come in front of a magistrate, so they had plenty of time to get things right.

★   ★   ★

There was no way Banks or Adrian Moss could keep the media at bay when Danny Caxton was brought into Eastvale Police Headquarters by two plain-clothes officers, shortly after the Paul Warner interview. There wasn't even any point going around the back or in at the side. Adrian Moss threw up his hands in despair when he saw the mob. Caxton himself seemed to take it as a publicity stunt and smiled for the cameras, waving his handcuffed hands in the air triumphantly for his public. Anybody who didn't know him better would guess that he was mad, thought Banks, staring down at the crowd in the market square from his window.

On the Strip in Wytherton Heights, or so he had been told, angry mobs were throwing bricks and Molotov cocktails through shop windows, and the terrified members of the Asian community hid in cellars and attics if they couldn't leave town quickly enough to stay safely with relatives far away. Banks wondered if the tide would turn when it came out later in the day that the person responsible for Mimosa Moffat's murder was white.

Banks and Winsome let Caxton wait in the interview room with Bernie Feldman. Banks had read Linda Palmer's memoir of the holiday in Blackpool, and while it hadn't furnished many hard facts, it had given him a couple of points to pursue and a lot of insight into the way her mind worked.

When they finally entered the room, Caxton rubbed his wrists theatrically. 'Bit tight, those cuffs,' he said. 'I know a lass or two who'd appreciate that.' He winked at Winsome.

Winsome ignored him, went through the formalities and set the voice recorder and video going.

'So what is it this time?' Feldman asked.

'We've got some new evidence, if you'll bear with me,' said Banks.

'Evidence? I doubt that very much.'

Banks ignored the lawyer and looked directly at Caxton. 'And I'd be remiss if I didn't tell you now, Mr Caxton, that the other investigations are coming together. We have strong rape and sexual assault cases for you to face from Brighton in 1965, Leicester in 1968, Bristol in 1971 and Newcastle in 1973. There are plenty more in the works, too.'

'Get to the point, will you,' Caxton said. 'I want to go home. I don't feel well. I'm an old man. You can't keep me cooped up here.'

'Then we'll move right ahead. First of all, I want to talk to you about Tony Monaghan.'

'What about him? I told you he worked for me. He was a homosexual. He got killed in a public toilet.'

'As a matter of fact, Mr Caxton, he wasn't actually killed *in* the toilet, and there's no evidence that he was gay.'

Caxton glanced at Feldman. 'What do you mean? That's what I was told.'

'Mistakes were made.'

'Not my fault.'

'Going on evidence of the position of the body and blood loss, we have determined that Mr Monaghan couldn't have been killed in the Hyde Park public toilets but that his body was placed there after his murder.'

'So what?'

'It wasn't a gay killing,' said Banks.

'I don't really see what any of this has to do with my client,' said Feldman. He turned to Caxton. 'Danny, this was going on for fifty years ago. There's no way this is solid evidence.'

'I think it will become clear soon enough,' Banks said.

'And what is this evidence you're talking about?' Feldman went on. 'Where is it? I assume you have some crime-scene photographs, forensic reports, a post-mortem perhaps?'

This was where Banks knew he was stumped. He didn't have any of those things, only Simon Bradley's slightly unreliable memories and the things Ursula Pemberton had told him. That might be declared hearsay, though a good prosecuting barrister might successfully argue for its admittance on the grounds that Tony Monaghan was unable to testify himself. Even so, it was a long stretch from getting Ursula Pemberton's evidence admitted to proving that Danny Caxton had anything to do with her husband's murder. 'You know we don't,' said Banks. 'But we do have witnesses, one of whom was involved in the investigation at the time.'

'A boffin, is he?' said Feldman. 'Home Office pathologist, perhaps?'

'He was a serving police officer, now retired.'

'Long memory, then? And honest with it?'

'We also have another witness.' Banks moved on quickly. 'A witness who saw two burly men half-carrying and half-dragging someone towards the toilets the night Tony Monaghan died.'

'This gets better,' Feldman said. 'Two someones carrying a third someone in the dark.' He folded his arms. 'Please go on. I'm intrigued. I assume you can produce this witness?'

Caxton wasn't saying anything, but Banks had noticed him getting progressively paler, an anxious look in his eyes. He pressed the advantage. 'We think those two men were the Stott brothers, well-known criminal enforcers at the time and, we understand, acquaintances of Mr Caxton.'

'They worked at a club I had an interest in,' said Caxton. 'I—'

'Danny, be quiet,' said Feldman, raising a hand. 'Don't say another word. Leave this to me.'

'We know where they worked,' said Banks. 'They were bouncers at the Discothique nightclub in Bradford. You first met them at a boxing club you had also had an interest in, and we have it on good authority that they were employed from time to time as your minders, Mr Caxton, and that on at least one occasion they faced criminal charges for GBH.'

'That was nothing to do with me,' said Caxton.

'Are you saying you have a positive identification on these two gentlemen?' Feldman asked.

'Maybe not,' Banks went on. 'But their victim in the GBH case was the boyfriend of a waitress who claimed to have been sexually assaulted by Mr Caxton at the Discothique nightclub shortly after closing time one night.'

'Rubbish,' said Caxton, though he was looking paler. Banks noticed a tic developing under his left eye. He seemed worried by the direction the interview was taking.

'There's nothing to worry about, Danny, they've got nothing,' Feldman assured his client. 'And even if what they're saying about these Stott characters is true, there's no positive identification, no way they could be linked to the body found in the public toilets.'

'You think I don't know that, Bernie?' snapped Caxton.

Banks leaned back and turned to Winsome. 'DS Jackman.'

'Let me tell you what we think happened,' said Winsome. 'Tony Monaghan was with Mr Caxton in the Majestic Hotel, Blackpool, when the assault on our complainant occurred. In fact, she was raped first by Mr Caxton and then by Mr Monaghan.'

'So you take the word of a rapist—'

'Danny, be quiet,' said Feldman. 'Let's hear the lady out.'

Winsome inclined her head. 'Thank you, Mr Feldman. I've done a lot of hard digging on this case, so I think I can spell things out clearly for you. One thing Mr Caxton might not have realised was that Mr Monaghan was a man of conscience. He'd done a foolish thing, a serious thing, committed a crime, but he couldn't live with it as easily as . . . well, as easily as some people seem able to do. He felt the need to unburden himself, so after a great deal of soul-searching, he told his wife all about what happened and what he intended to do about it. Monaghan's widow is still very much alive and was able to fill in a few blanks for us.'

Caxton shot Feldman a frightened glance. 'What is this, Bernie? What are they saying?'

'Let the lady talk, Danny. They tell a good tale, but they still have no evidence. Witness to the crime, was she, this wife?'

'Though she wasn't present when the crime was committed, we do have a strong witness in Mrs Monaghan,' said Winsome. 'Her husband told her what happened that afternoon in the hotel. She was horrified, of course, that someone she loved could commit such an act, but she also saw that he was genuinely repentant and wanted to atone. His atonement was to confront Mr Caxton with his decision to go to the police. Apparently, he also had in his possession a number of compromising Polaroid photographs of Mr Caxton with young girls, some of whom are also in the process of telling us their stories. Needless to say, these photographs disappeared long ago.'

'Pity,' said Feldman. 'It's a touching tale, but no evidence there, either. Hearsay. And from the man's wife. In fact, it seems that stories are all you have.'

'Perhaps so,' Banks cut in. 'But juries love a good story, as I'm sure you're aware, and we think we can put together a good narrative of events. Carry on, DS Jackman.'

Winsome turned over a page in her file. 'So Mr Monaghan crossed Mr Caxton in a serious way. It wasn't so much the threat to tell the police that worried him, or even the photographs. He could easily have squared all that through his establishment contacts. It was his right-hand man's betrayal. He couldn't stand that. Either he lost his temper and killed Mr Monaghan himself, then got the Stott brothers to get rid of the body in a place where it would be assumed to be a gay killing, or he had the Stott brothers do the lot. Either way, Monaghan was killed and his body placed in the toilet. Sad to say, police at the time didn't exactly pull out all the stops on homosexual victims. After a cursory initial investigation

– which we do know revealed that Tony Monaghan most likely *hadn't* been killed in the toilet and that two men had been seen half-dragging a third towards that very place on the night in question – orders came from above that there was no case, nothing more to be done. A short while later, the few case files that had been kept – including medical and forensic reports and witness statements – simply disappeared.' Winsome took the enlargement of the newspaper photograph from her file and slid it across the table so that Feldman and Caxton could look at it. 'As you can see,' she went on, 'here Mr Caxton is handing over a large cheque to Chief Constable Edward Crammond. Also in the photo are a number of other high-ranking police officers of the time, including Detective Chief Superintendent Dennis McCullen, who was immediately in charge of the Monaghan case. Both Chief Constable Crammond and Chief Superintendent McCullen were dismissed from the force in a corruption scandal over accepting bribes some years later.'

'I take it this scandal has nothing to do with my client?'

'It was a separate incident, drug-related, but it indicates the characters of the men concerned. Mr Caxton and the chief constable were known to be good friends. They dined together, played golf together and even, on one occasion, went on a holiday in Majorca together. All paid for by Mr Caxton.'

'I did a lot of charity work for the police,' said Caxton. 'You can't accuse me of bribing Ted Crammond with—'

'But isn't that exactly what you were doing, Mr Caxton?' said Winsome. 'This photograph was taken on the twenty-seventh of October, around the time the Monaghan investigation came to a full stop.'

'You can't possibly think that such a senior police officer would cover up a murder,' said Feldman.

'Perhaps not,' said Banks. 'Though stranger things have happened. It's possible that, despite his later troubles, Chief

Superintendent McCullen had no idea that Mr Caxton had killed Mr Monaghan, or arranged to have him killed. What he was covering up was his friend's involvement with a man who, it appeared, had turned out to have homosexual inclinations. The fact that Mr Monaghan worked for Mr Caxton was never mentioned in any of the media reports at the time. That, I think, would have been a far easier thing to do, and easier for Chief Constable Crammond to settle with his conscience than murder.' Banks glanced at Caxton, who seemed to be slipping further and further away from the conversation, looking puzzled and confused, as if he couldn't understand what he was being accused of any more. It was either arrogance, Banks guessed, or another act, an attempt to put the faltering mask of innocence back in place.

'All you're really telling me,' said Feldman, 'is that Mr Caxton's press officer did a good job. I don't see anything criminal in that.'

'Let's get back to the allegations of rape, then,' said Winsome. 'When we asked our complainant if she would immerse herself in the difficult and painful process of trying to remember as much detail as she could about the assault, there was some-thing specific that she remembered, and we think it will link her most effectively with Mr Caxton. Would you roll up your left sleeve, please, Mr Caxton?'

'What . . .?'

'Your left sleeve.'

Caxton looked at Feldman, who nodded like a man who knew it would have to happen inevitably at some point, even if they objected now. Slowly, Caxton pushed up the sleeve of his jacket, then unfastened the button at the cuff of his shirt and pushed that up, too. The inked numbers were plain to see. Banks noticed that Caxton's hand was shaking, and his skin had turned even paler, looking dry, like parchment. He began to worry there was something more serious going on than nerves.

'What are those numbers?' Winsome asked. 'What do they mean? We know that you were in England during the war, not in Auschwitz. Can you—'

Banks tapped Winsome gently on the arm to indicate that she should stop. 'Mr Caxton,' he said. 'Are you all right? Do you need me to call a doctor?'

'Ggggah bbrrridddd ahh.'

Caxton couldn't get the words out. His face looked oddly lopsided, Banks noticed, as if the right half had fallen away from the cheekbones, and spittle drooled from his lower lip. His right arm hung limp, and that whole side of his body seemed to sag. Banks knew what was happening. He dashed to the door to tell the officer outside to call the paramedics immediately.

Danny Caxton was having a stroke.

By Saturday night, when Banks again knocked on Linda Palmer's door in Minton-on-Swain, a great deal had happened. Paul Warner was in custody for the murder of Mimosa Moffat, and the forensic evidence was fast building up against him. They also had his confession. Sunny and his colleagues were all under arrest and facing a number of serious charges, though DNA tests showed that none of them had any connection with Mimosa's murder. The DNA of the three cousins from Dewsbury, however, was a clear match for the semen samples found inside Mimosa, and they faced a whole lot of charges, though they continued to deny rape and insist that the sex had been consensual. Mimosa had been under the age of consent, so it didn't matter too much, but their sentences would certainly be a lot longer if a jury believed they had also physically assaulted her and forced her to perform sex acts against her will. The problem was that there was no one to say Mimosa wasn't willing, though the three men who said she was had every reason to lie. The five other victims of Sunny's grooming gang were being cared for and were all giving detailed statements of their own experiences, though the whereabouts of Jade, aka Carol Fisher, were still unknown. The Strip had quietened down a lot, but there were still isolated incidents and rumblings of unrest around the Wytherton Heights estate. Two more women had come out with complaints against Danny Caxton since he had made his grand entrance and exit to and from Eastvale Police HQ, one in Great Yarmouth and the other in Weymouth. Caxton was still in hospital, still hanging on by the thinnest of threads.

Linda Palmer opened the front door and led Banks through to the garden. It was another fine summer evening early in August, but Banks sensed a slight autumn chill already in the air. It wasn't enough to drive them indoors, though, and Banks took the same chair as he had on his previous visit. Music played through the open French windows, swirling strings rising and falling, and there was a bottle of wine open on the table. Linda asked Banks if he would like some.

'Just a glass, please,' he said. It was a crisp Pinot Grigio, nicely chilled, and it went down well. The river was in the shadow of the trees, but Banks could hear it, and was constantly aware of its presence beyond the music, which he didn't recognise. Persy was lying on the lawn near a flower bed.

'Who's this?' Banks asked, referring to the music.

'Mahler's Ninth. The last movement, the adagio. I'll put something else on if it's not to your liking. Some people have a hard time with Mahler.'

'No,' said Banks, 'don't change it for me. It's someone I've been meaning to get into for a while. All I know of Mahler is the soundtrack from *Death in Venice*.'

'Ah, yes. Magnificent.' Linda paused. 'I heard about Danny Caxton on the news,' she said. 'Are you in trouble?'

'Famous TV personality has stroke in police custody? I should think so. There's bound to be repercussions. There'll be an inquest, maybe even an investigation. They take anything unusual that happens in police custody seriously these days. On the plus side, his lawyer was there. He saw everything that happened, and he said we couldn't have responded faster. It was so quick. And Caxton had never told us before that he had any problem with his heart. I probably shouldn't tell you this, but there's not much chance of a trial now, so what the hell. According to a disgruntled employee on the staff at Caxton's home, Xanadu, his doctor had warned him to be careful with his health, prescribed various drugs to combat hypertension and elevated heart rate. But Caxton didn't take them. He said they interfered with his sex life, which, according to our source, was mostly catered to by high-class call girls shipped into Xanadu on a fairly regular basis. He didn't change his lifestyle either, kept on smoking cigars, drinking cognac. Too arrogant to listen to the doctors, I suppose. The only indication he'd given was that he said he wasn't feeling well, but nobody feels well when they know they've been caught.'

Linda smiled. 'There's an irony in that, isn't there,' she said. 'The great man brought down by his own perverse desires. But surely the lawyers will argue that the stress of being interrogated must have had something to do with it?'

'No doubt that's what they'll say. But we played it by the book and it's all on record, audio recording and video. There was no use of restraint, not that we'd be likely to need it with an eighty-five-year-old man. Caxton arrived under his own steam, with his lawyer, and he was well treated at all times. He behaved quite normally at first. Nevertheless, there'll be trouble, you can be sure of it. They'll want their pound of flesh.'

'Will you lose your job?'

'Maybe. If they need a sacrificial lamb. Or perhaps I'll just be demoted, or promoted to chief constable, where I can do no harm. It was, after all, my first major investigation as superintendent. I enjoyed being detective chief inspector, though, so demotion wouldn't bother me too much. Chief constable I'm not so sure about.'

'You're being very flippant about it, but I feel terrible.'

'Why? It's not your fault. We can't let people who do the things Caxton did to you and others go free just because they're old and frail. I hope you understand that. It's simply that the politics of the job demands sacrifices.'

'What do the doctors say?'

'They don't hold out a lot of hope. Apparently he had a second stroke on the way to hospital and a third when he got there. He's in his mid-eighties. Even if he does survive, he'll be bedridden and incapacitated for the rest of his days.'

'I wish I could feel something,' said Linda with a shiver. 'Pity. Compassion. I can't.'

Banks just looked at her. 'Save it for someone who deserves it.'

She caught his gaze. 'Silly of me, I suppose.'

'Not at all. Most of us try to be good people.'

'What about the other case? The girl who was groomed and raped.'

'A friend of her brother's has confessed to the murder,' said Banks. 'That's about all I can say right now.'

'You believe him?'

'No reason not to.'

'Why?'

'I wish I could say I understood, but I don't, really. He was infatuated with her, even though she was a few years younger than he is, and he's somewhat of a racist. The idea of her going with people of a different ethnic origin set his teeth on edge. He'd just heard, or so he says, and he couldn't get the images out of his mind. He followed their van. When she came walking towards him, it didn't go as he expected. The things she said, the way she reacted. Partly because she'd been on ketamine and partly because . . . well . . . he just lost it. Saw red. I suppose that's believable enough. It'll have to be, at any rate. It's all we're likely to get from him.'

'"An old black ram is tupping your white ewe."'

'*Othello*,' said Banks.

'My, my, you *are* a literate copper. Not only Wordsworth, but Shakespeare, too. I suppose you did it at school?'

'Yes. Amazing how you remember quotes like that when you're a dirty-minded teenager.'

'Iago uses sexual images like that to drive Othello over the edge.'

'Maybe the girl's brother did that to our suspect,' Banks said. 'But it probably wasn't intentional. He's not that bright.'

'What about the men who raped her?'

'They'll go away for a long time. Rape, conspiracy to rape, sexual activity with a child, sexual assault. A range of charges. The CPS will throw the book at them. Something's sure to stick.'

'Good Lord. It's all so sad. This is the sort of thing you deal with day after day, isn't it?'

Banks sipped some wine. The strings held a long note, then the brass came in and another melody began. 'Not every day, no.'

'But it must get to you, seeing so much of the dark side, the cruel side of human nature.'

'You've been there. You know what it's like. Besides, it's not all doom and gloom. I see plenty of good, too. Plenty of decent people trying to help others. They're just not always who or where you expect them to be.'

'I don't think I could do your job.'

'That's just as well. The world will be a far better place if you stick at what you do already.'

'You've read my poetry?'

'Some. It's really good. Of course, I know nothing about such—'

'Oh, tosh. Do you think I write for reviewers and literary critics? Half the time I don't even get reviewed. How many poetry reviews do you see in your weekend papers?'

'The *Observer* does a few.'

'Beyond the *Observer*.'

'Dunno. That's the only one I read, except for the *Mail on Sunday*. It's true they don't review much poetry.'

'The *Observer* and the *Mail*? Are you schizophrenic or something?'

Banks laughed. 'No. It's just that I find if I read both, the truth usually comes somewhere in between. And the *Mail* has a better TV guide.'

'Well, that's a novel way of looking at it. Are you still reading your poetry anthology in chronological order?'

'I'm afraid I haven't had much time for it lately, but I think I'll take your advice and jump around more. After I've finished your poems, that is.'

Linda offered a top-up of wine. Banks hesitated for a moment. 'I'm sorry,' she said. 'Am I keeping you from something? It's Saturday night, after all. Do you have plans for the evening? Maybe celebrating with your colleagues?'

'No, not at all. We'll do that next week when we know we have something to celebrate. I was just thinking of the drive home. But why not? A drop more won't put me over the limit. As a matter of fact, I was going to drop my car at home and walk down to the Dog and Gun in Gratly. It's folk night. I think Penny Cartwright's back home. But there's plenty of time for that.'

'She is,' said Linda. 'I had coffee with her this afternoon.'

'You know Penny?'

'Known her for years. We're old friends.'

'She never said.'

Linda smiled. 'She talked plenty about you.'

Banks felt himself blush. 'Don't tell me. She's never forgiven me for suspecting her of murder thirty years ago.'

Linda laughed. 'Something like that. I mean, really. It's not something one gets over that easily, I shouldn't imagine. How could you? But I think she likes you.'

'That's a surprise.'

The wind rustled through the leaves and birds called from the trees by the riverside. 'Kingfisher not around?' he asked.

'Not today. But he'll be back.'

They listened to the wind and the birds and the river for a while, Mahler's notes and chords drifting between sound and silence through the evening air as if they belonged there, then Linda said, 'Those numbers on Caxton's arm. Did you find out what they were? Were they what I thought?'

'Yes,' said Banks.

'Can you tell me?'

'I don't see why not. I knew from talking to Caxton's ex-wife a while ago that he'd been sent to England as a young lad, when he was about three, I think.'

'So he can't have been in a concentration camp.'

'No. He never went back. He was in England throughout the war.'

'So what, then?'

'She told me that his mother was in a camp and that his father fought with the Germans. This was in Poland.'

'People did that?'

'Apparently so. Places like Poland, Estonia and the other Baltic States were torn apart by the Russians and Germans. Some families fought against their own kin. Some found themselves in one side's army one day and the enemy's the next. Stalin or Hitler? Who would you choose?'

'So where did the numbers come from?'

'It was his mother's camp number. He found out only years later, from someone who was with her then and survived. They have records.'

'He has his mother's concentration camp number tattooed on his arm?'

'Yes.'

'I don't know whether that's sick or sentimental.'

'A bit of both, really,' said Banks. 'He can't have had it done until after he was divorced, as his ex-wife had never seen it. Others must have, even though he always wore long sleeves, and he tried to keep it concealed. You saw it.' Banks didn't tell her that it was when he asked to look at Caxton's arm that he had his stroke. No point making her feel guilty. She'd done the right thing in noting it down, and he'd done the right thing in asking to see it. The rest was just bad timing. He didn't really know what was going to happen to his career because of what happened in that interview room. Neither he nor Winsome had behaved in any way offensively or aggressively during the interview, but Danny Caxton had keeled over and would most likely die. Adrian Moss had a hell of a job on his hands with this one, and for once Banks appreciated that he might prove a useful ally. Not that ACC McLaughlin and AC Gervaise weren't a hundred per cent behind him. The chief constable and crime commissioner were waffling and waving this way and that in the prevailing winds, but that was only to be expected. The best Banks could do was tell the truth and try to protect Winsome from the shit storm as best he could. Even if there were no professional consequences, there would be a big fuss in the media for a few days.

The music was so quiet now that Banks could hardly hear it above the birds and the wind in the leaves. Occasionally he would catch a slow, soft phrase, then silence came again. Linda swallowed and turned towards the river. He couldn't see her expression or the look in her eyes. 'It always makes me cry, the end,' she said. 'You really have to hear it inside to get the full impact, but the quiet strings and silence alternate like a dying man's breath for a while, and finally it just disappears into silence. More Shakespeare. "The rest is silence."'

'Was it Mahler's last work?' Banks asked.

'Not technically, no. He'd sketched out a tenth symphony before he died. But he was ill. He'd lost his favourite daughter and been diagnosed with heart problems. The ninth is often regarded as his farewell to the world, especially that adagio.' She paused a moment then asked him, 'So Caxton won't be going to trial?'

'The CPS will declare him unfit to stand,' said Banks. 'Even if he lives that long.'

'So there'll be no real closure?'

'I always thought closure was overrated,' said Banks. 'What's so special about an old man sitting in a prison cell for the rest of his natural life?'

'Well, if you put it that way . . .'

'I don't mean to belittle anything you've been through,' said Banks, 'but everyone's going to know what he did, and he's not going anywhere. He's too old to recover from what happened to him, even if he survives for a while longer. That'll have to be enough.'

'Do you think it has all been worthwhile?' Linda asked. 'Has justice been served?'

'I think that's a question you should be answering. Has it?'

Linda seemed lost in thought for a moment, her brow furrowed, then she said. 'I don't know. Not yet. Maybe it's too soon. I just feel numb.'

'Well, perhaps his stroke is justice of a kind,' said Banks.

'But it isn't, really, is it?' Linda replied. 'I mean, it's the sort of thing that happens to all of us in one way or another, at some time – strokes, heart attack, Alzheimer's, cancer. There's no justice in that. Just arbitrary endings. We all die, some of us in great agony, so how can Caxton's stroke be anything like a judgement, or justice?'

'Do you want more?' Banks asked. 'Do you want him to suffer more? If he'd gone to jail before he had his stroke, he'd be spending his time on the hospital wing. Would that really make a scrap of difference to you?'

'No. I'm not saying I want him to suffer more. I don't know what I'm saying. I'm confused. It doesn't feel like I thought it would. I'm not jumping up and down for joy because the man who raped me has had a stroke. Maybe I should be. I'm not one of those people who thinks criminals should be hanged, drawn and quartered. I don't know. It just feels sort of meaningless.'

'Perhaps it is, then,' said Banks. 'But it might mean more to some of his other victims.'

Linda lit a cigarette and regarded him through lowered eyes. 'Are you saying I don't make a good victim?'

Banks smiled. 'Victim isn't the word that comes to mind when I talk to you,' he said. The sun was at such an angle that the river looked like a burning oil slick and the undersides of the overhanging trees were lit by its fiery light. Banks finished his wine and put his glass down. 'I should be going.'

Linda didn't react for a moment, then she leaned forward and said, 'Do you mind if I come with you to the Dog and Gun? I really don't feel like being here on my own tonight. I want people and music and dancing.'

'Not at all,' said Banks, standing and offering her his arm.

'Are you sure it's OK, me being a witness, a *victim*? You won't get into trouble?'

'I'm already in trouble. A bit more won't make much difference.'

Linda smiled and took his arm and together they walked out of the garden.

EPILOGUE

It was a bitterly cold night but the nature of Jade's work didn't allow her to dress for the weather. She was shivering in her tube top and micro skirt as she paced her corner near the city centre. Streetlights and neons reflected in the puddles, and the noise of revellers from nearby pubs and clubs filled the air – a laugh, a glass smashing, a sudden cheer or whoop, loud music from a cover band imitating the Rolling Stones' 'Satisfaction'. There was plenty of traffic, and the cars occasionally slowed down for a closer look at her, sometimes stopped to pick her up. But she still had hours of work ahead of her before she could get back to the flat and experience the rush and the euphoria that followed. That anticipation of blissful oblivion had quickly become all that kept her going in the cold city night.

The girls were spaced well apart, and Radnor came by every once in a while to make sure everything was all right, and to pick up the earnings. He was OK, she supposed. Better than some. And she wouldn't be doing this for ever, she thought as she paced. She was still young. There was a man she'd been talking to, a pal of Radnor's, who said he thought she'd be perfect for some films he was going to make. The work paid well. About a thousand euros a scene, he said, with extra for unprotected sex, gangbangs and fake rape. A few months of that, and she'd have a nice little nest egg to do with what she wanted. She didn't know what that was yet, but she wanted to move somewhere far away from here, perhaps a village in the country. She'd kick her habit and live somewhere people were nice and there were trees and birds and sweet-smelling flowers and maybe a river at the bottom of her garden.

The wind seemed to rake against her exposed flesh and she felt the first drops of rain on her cheek. A car pulled up by the kerb about ten yards ahead of her and a hand beckoned out of the window. The engine purred and the red brake lights glowed like a demon's eyes. She felt that same tightening in her stomach she always felt when a car stopped. You never knew what was going to happen next. Then she pulled herself together, thrust her chest out and remembered to swing her hips as she walked towards it.

ACKNOWLEDGEMENTS

Many thanks to Carolyn Mays my editor at Hodder & Stoughton. Also thanks to Abby Parsons for all her assistance and to Justine Taylor for clear and clean copy-editing. At McClelland & Stewart, I would like to thank Ellen Seligman, and at William Morrow, my editor Daniel Mallory and assistant editor Marguerite Weisman. I would also like to thank my wife Sheila Halliday, who read the manuscript when I thought it was ready to submit and found even more room for improvement.

Thanks to my agents Domnick Abel and David Grossman for their continuing encouragement and support. Also thanks to the publicists – Kerry Hood at Hodder, Ashley Dunn at McClelland & Stewart and Megan Schumann at Morrow.

Thanks to Nicholas Reckert for the interesting walks that somehow always seem to suggest a possible crime scene. In this book, he is by no means responsible for Wytherton Heights, which is entirely of my own imagining.

As far as research is concerned, I want to give special thanks to Jenny Brierley, ICT Archivist at the West Yorkshire Archive Service, for her invaluable help in tracking down old police records.

I feel it might also be useful to mention three books I found particularly useful when researching the themes of my novel: *In Plain Sight: The Life and Lies of Jimmy Savile* by Dan Davies; *Smile for the Camera: The Double Life of Cyril Smith* by Simon Danczuk and Matthew Baker; and *Violated* by Sarah Wilson.

Last but not least, thanks to the sales teams who make the deals and set up the speical promotions, to the reps who get out on the road and sell the book to the shops, and to the booksellers themselves, without whom you wouldn't be holding this volume in your hand. And thanks, of course, to you, the reader.

Do you wish this wasn't the end?

Join us at www.hodder.co.uk, or follow us on Twitter @hodderbooks to be a part of our community of people who love the very best in books and reading.

Whether you want to discover more about a book or an author, watch trailers and interviews, have the chance to win early limited editions, or simply browse our expert readers' selection of the very best books, we think you'll find what you're looking for.

And if you don't,
that's the place to tell us what's missing.

We love what we do, and we'd love you to be part of it.

www.hodder.co.uk

@hodderbooks

HodderBooks

HodderBooks